The Inside City

The Inside City

Anita Mir

Unbound Digital

This edition first published in 2019

Unbound
6th Floor Mutual House, 70 Conduit Street, London W1S 2GF
www.unbound.com
All rights reserved

ISBN (eBook): 978-1-78965-009-9
ISBN (Paperback): 978-1-78965-008-2

Cover design by Mecob

Printed and bound in Great Britain by Clays Ltd, Elcograf S.p.A.

This book is dedicated to my family:
Nachi Butt, Arshed Mir, Khalid Mir
and Dara Taufiq Mir.

With grateful thanks to Talat Mahmood for
helping to make this book happen.

Dear Reader,

The book you are holding came about in a rather different way to most others. It was funded directly by readers through a new website: Unbound.

Unbound is the creation of three writers. We started the company because we believed there had to be a better deal for both writers and readers. On the Unbound website, authors share the ideas for the books they want to write directly with readers. If enough of you support the book by pledging for it in advance, we produce a beautifully bound special subscribers' edition and distribute a regular edition and e-book wherever books are sold, in shops and online.

This new way of publishing is actually a very old idea (Samuel Johnson funded his dictionary this way). We're just using the internet to build each writer a network of patrons. Here, at the back of this book, you'll find the names of all the people who made it happen.

Publishing in this way means readers are no longer just passive consumers of the books they buy, and authors are free to write the books they really want. They get a much fairer return too – half the profits their books generate, rather than a tiny percentage of the cover price.

If you're not yet a subscriber, we hope that you'll want to join our publishing revolution and have your name listed in one of our books in the future. To get you started, here is a £5 discount on your first pledge. Just visit unbound.com, make your pledge and type MIR19 in the promo code box when you check out.

Thank you for your support,

Dan, Justin and John
Founders, Unbound

Super Patrons

Aayla Aftab
Naz Aftab
Amana Ahmad
Asad Ali
Mian Shehraz Amir
Afshan Butt
Kanita Butt
Kasim Butt
Khurram Butt
Mohammad Waleed Butt
Mohammad Waseem Butt
Nachi Butt
Naeem Butt
Waleed Butt
Robert Cox
Esther Das
Mohammed Feroz
Jane Grant
Vincent Guiry
Riaz–ul Haque
Jalees Hazir
Tabish Hazir
Aayesha Ikram
Zeerak Ikram
Mohammad Javaid

Omar Javaid
Shahida Javaid
Syed Moneeb Javed
Efthalia Kalegoropolou
Tabassum Kashmiri
Aftab Khan
Furrukh Khan
Mohammed Ahsan Khan
Ahmad Khwaja
Imrana Khwaja
Maha Khwaja
Dan Kieran
Patrick Kincaid
Rauf Klasra
Eva Lewin
Nargis Mahmood
Asad Malik
Sidra Malik
Amir Mateen
Bushra Mateen
Sanjila Mayor
Amer Mian
Arshed Mir
Asad Mir
Hajirah Mir
Khalid Mir
Maimoona Mir
Mustahsan Mir
Mustansir Mir
John Mitchinson
Alexandra Murrell
Kevin Offer
Vishal Panjwani
Farrukh Parvez
Justin Pollard
Tej Purewal

A Q
Mozaffar Qizalbash
Naveena Selim
Sikander Ahmed Shah
Amna Shariff
Naseer Sheikh
Sandy & Marie Sneddon
Jatinder Verma
Rae Williams
Aasima Yawar

Jine Lahore Nai Vekhya O Jamya-e-Ni
Who hasn't seen Lahore hasn't lived

Deep within a city within a city a crow and a pigeon conversed. No, that's not true. The crow talked and talked and the pigeon pretended from time to time to listen.

'Secrets,' said the crow, finally clocking onto the fact that the pigeon's attention was lax. 'Great secrets. The least you could do…'

The pigeon yawned. He'd seen people do it all the time and had been at great pains to learn this newest of skills, wondering what reaction it'd kindle.

The crow whispered, 'So rude, so rude,' but because, above everything else, it was an audience he yearned for, he ignored the pigeon's effrontery and went on. 'I can tell you…' said the crow.

'Can you tell me,' said the pigeon, 'where to get some bread?'

The crow sadly shook his head.

The pigeon, his pity growing, said, 'Tell me what you were going to say.'

'You don't want to hear.'

'But,' said the pigeon, 'I do.'

The crow rustled in slow-burning pride and said, 'I can tell you how secrets are broken and how they are made.' The crow waited. In his head he could already hear the applause.

'Is that all?' laughed the pigeon.

The crow didn't reply. He shed a feather, black-ink-dry because crows have learnt not to cry – what's the point? Even ugly-looking animals are loved by someone but crows are too strong a reminder of what no one wants to be reminded of, and so are spurned. Down down the feather swirled – into the depths of the walled city, the inside city of Lahore…

1

MARCH 1928, THE INSIDE CITY, LAHORE, INDIA

Despite the fact that their three-storeyed house had so many rooms, as a family the Dars lived, like almost everyone else they knew, in the rooftop courtyard, summer and winter, day and night. Adjoining the courtyard was the narrow kitchen with its mesh door, in its top left-hand corner a gaping hole through which flies and mosquitoes smothered in and out all summer long, and the corridor that led to the family bedrooms and to the stairs down to the other rooms: the round room – the best room; the guest room; and rooms which had become a dumping ground and which no one ever really entered now. The stairs also led to the front door. Early on this Sunday morning the whole family except Dar Sahib was at home.

At his mother's bidding, Awais moved the *charpoy* into the sun. She sat down again. Pulling her feet up, she sighed, content. His sisters Batool and Tanveer flitted in and out of the courtyard, their heads together, as close as twins. Batool picked up little Maryam, who'd been lying beside him. Just him and his mother now.

Tanveer called to their mother. Slowly, she got up. Awais bent his head, waited. When he was sure she was gone he skidded down the worn brick stairs, stood on his toes to open the latch of the front door. There he was, away from her eyes, outside on the streets. He looked back up at the house. His father had told him the story, of how when he'd got married he'd had the brick front painted white, which many people had quietly said was showy and not so quietly said was a waste of money and time. What paint there was left was now yellow, like paper which tea had spoilt.

Raj, his neighbour, poking his head through an open shutter, called down. Awais grinned. They talked using their hands.

The Dars' was one of three houses ringed together. Many years ago Awais's father had had a quarrel with Raj's father, and though the families' courtyards were only separated by a two-inch wall and each family saw and heard exactly what the other family did, they weren't on speaking terms. The women and children played along, the men not suspecting a thing.

'Raj!' called his mother and he ducked back inside.

Brighter now. As the corner house, the Dars' house had, as his father proudly and repeatedly said, the best of the light.

The street vendors began to emerge, shouting their trade. A short man, his eyes sour, carrying sticks of green and yellow candyfloss shaped into hookahs, birds; a boy pushing forward his cart, stopping to spin his wheel – 'Sharpen your knives!'; a man with near-blue lips selling coloured ice drinks.

Awais put a hand in his pocket, fingering his two coins.

Click, click. He looked up, smiling, expecting Raj to have reappeared. Awais's gaze ran across all the shutters of Raj's house then turned to his own. The kitchen shutter was open. His mother? He stood there adamant, growing surly. The kitchen shutter rattled to the slow-rising breeze. He peered harder but couldn't see her. He began to run. Run through the narrow streets, swerving past the vegetable and fruit carts, the languorous movement of people for whom time was indefinite.

He began to cough – the sound of metal scraping on stone. He couldn't stop. No, he thought, not again. He bent double and waited till it was over, his body harrowed and hurting. He straightened. Awais was tall; he looked more eleven than eight.

Ahead of him the road was blocked. Two Englishmen, dressed in civilian clothes, so not officials, were surrounded by an array of strange devices – a rod holding up what looked like a giant protractor, a measuring tape, and, most interestingly for Awais, a tripod on which was fixed some kind of telescope. The men were taking it in turns to look through the telescope contraption and observe something. Awais so wished he could see through their machine. Maybe if he asked? He felt his face flush. He knew he never would. They were English and he'd never spoken to an Englishman in his life.

The younger of the two men, as tall, thought Awais, as two men put together, picked up the measuring tape and, bending down, began measuring the road. After a little while, he returned to the man who was clearly in charge and said something. Awais caught only a stray word or two. The older man, with his thick ginger moustache and short beard that had gone awry, opened his notebook and began to write. The other man respectfully stepped back, waited. Looking up, he spied Awais; through pointy teeth, the sound of a whistle. The older man looked up, frowned.

'That boy's watching us,' said the younger. The older man turned to Awais, stared. 'What if…?' continued the younger.

The older man cut him off. 'To them it's all gobbledegook. Indians don't have a scientific bone in their bodies. Now be quiet while I finish this.' And with that, his head bent again to his notebook.

The younger man turned his back petulantly on Awais.

Leaning against a closed shop-shutter, not too far away, someone else was watching the English officials – Awais was now convinced that's what they were. In his hand the man clasped a long stick of sugarcane, which he bit into when he remembered, hardly chewing, spitting the debris out like a small mat of hay. When Awais approached, the man looked at him with blood–veined sleepy eyes.

'*Bhai* Sahib,' said Awais. The man tugged at his *lunghi,* tucking a loosened end of the cloth back at his waist. He then pulled himself up to honour the address. 'Do you know what they're doing?'

'Mapping,' said the man. He held out his hand, offering Awais a bite of his sugarcane. Awais shook his head. He turned again to look at the two Englishmen. The younger was crouching, searching in his bag for something. His face full of confusion, Awais turned to the sugarcane man.

'Why?' he asked.

The man bit his sugarcane, chewed, then spat to his other side.

'Why?' asked Awais again, thinking he hadn't been heard.

The man laughed, a braying sound. 'They're English,' he said.

The two Englishmen picked up their equipment and moved on.

What are they mapping? Awais thought. And why?

2

APRIL 1928, LAHORE

Desperate as he was after a two-week absence to return to Amrau, Awais's father, Dar, didn't rush back home. If I do, he thought, then she'll know.

A fierce wind sped in and shook up the British flags which had been raised on the sprawling red-brick Mughal–Gothic buildings which lined one side of the city's main road, the cold road – the Mall.

Two weeks travelling from one small town to the next. Trying to sell things to people who listened with great respect – as they did to all city dwellers – though they had nothing to spare and couldn't buy or even pledge money for something from his box of wonders. How could it be, he thought, that there were so many realities in one small world? The tenderness he felt for these people would, he knew, soon wane. He couldn't sustain the feeling and live. He entered the inside city. He made his way to the *hammam*. The *chowkidar* was asleep. Dar pushed open the gate. The guard awoke with a jolt. 'Oh,' he said, 'Dar Sahib, it's you.'

'Yes,' Dar said, grinning, 'it's me.' As he walked across the ashen ground a few people called his name. He raised a hand here, nodded there, walked on. Rare as it was for him, he didn't want to talk to anyone today. Shivering, he undressed in the darkness of the *hammam*'s first hall. He handed over his clothes to an attendant and walked to the second hall, where the springs were warm. Neck-high in water, he nodded at the few other bathers and then closed his eyes.

Amrau intruded on his thoughts – again.

He'd got into it because he'd wanted a family – a big robust family; children's voices laughing, crying; things breaking, even. His marriage would be like all the rest, only he'd do knowingly what people did without thought. It'd be an arrangement, in which each party would receive the thing they most desired. He knew what he wanted and wouldn't question what his wife set her hopes on. And then on the very first night with Amrau his marriage became irrevocably something else. It deepened in that one instant, and he felt a new shyness emerge, as if she'd bored a hole into a place he'd never shown the world. He wanted to know her, but the more curious he became the more closed she grew. The first intimacy hadn't frightened her; this slower one, he saw, did. He learnt a new temperance and with it, gentleness. The rewards were, in the beginning, small: the way her forefinger circled her thumb in an endless game of halo-making when she was faced with people or situations which were new; the way a few curls of her hair skitted at her temples, escaping the tight rigidity of her plait.

His sisters, with their unthought smiles and laughs, were an altogether different species. It was not, he'd come to realise, that Amrau didn't see the current to which everyone else flowed; she was simply incapable of fitting herself to its shape. Its force touched her skin – how could it not? – but it couldn't reach beneath the surface. To be a creature of a culture and yet have parts of you – the most important parts – that stand alone? How on earth, he thought, does she do it, and why?

His fingers stroked his lush moustache. He'd seen some men now going without. He'd considered it, for a moment, then dismissed the idea as decadent somehow. A bare face? What – pretending to be a boy? He closed his eyes, splashed his face with water, his hands caressing, as he wanted her hands to caress, the chickenpox scars spread across his face.

One hour later, he was refreshed. His clothes had been washed and pressed. He put them on, grateful to the *hammam*'s hidden hands. He put a few coins in a bowl.

As Dar neared home – he was but two streets away – he had a strong impulse to see his oldest friend, Shams. Male company, buffoonery, news of the city and no one to watch him while he ate. He pulled in his stomach.

He hadn't expected to love his wife – but he did. That first year they'd had together had been perfect. But now the house was full of children. Awais, and then eighteen months after him, Batool. Between Batool and Tanveer there were another two years. Their last child, Maryam, had been born when Awais was seven.

He looked up. Without meaning to, not really, he'd arrived at Shams's house. He knocked and Shams opened the door. Shams brushed a hand self-consciously through his rough-grown hair. The henna had turned it bright orangey-red. He tried to get Dar to come inside.

'Let's go and get something to eat,' said Dar.

'We've got food here, you know.'

But Dar, for once, stood his ground, and Shams yielded. He called to his wife that he was going out with Dar. He waited. Pans rattled in response. He closed the door behind him, and together, the men left.

'Alim's shop?' said Dar, and Shams agreed.

As they entered the roadside café, with its rows of tables at which sat throngs of men, all engaged in the serious act of eating, Dar felt a buoyancy he hadn't felt for some time. It's not escape, he thought. I've got nothing I want to escape from.

Shams was in a quiet mood, which suited Dar. Politics was, he'd realised, gossip for men. And he had some tales to tell. He placed their order and sat back, relaxed. Dar talked and Shams listened. Dar felt how strange it was.

Shams and Dar had shared a passion for the history of the inside city and its stories, though for many years now, Dar accepted, Shams's knowledge had far outstripped his own. Dar had tried to keep pace but it was pointless; he didn't know how Shams learnt half the things he did. As Shams's knowledge grew stronger and Dar's fainter, Dar had expected the balance of their relationship to change, but it remained what it had always been – a field not of battles but of play. *A comedian – that's how he sees me.* Sometimes it felt too little and sometimes, most times, it felt enough.

'But then, Gandhi,' said Shams, as if he could hold himself back no longer, 'is an idiot. Equal status for all classes and castes, too? And women?' Shams laughed. 'That'll make him popular with the educated whisky-drinking class. And anyhow, what does he know about the poor? He's as privileged as Jinnah. What leaders we've got!'

Other men stopped to listen. Shams sounded like a man who knew things. Opinion wasn't, they saw, enough. It needed to be bolstered.

'Let Gandhi go and live in the villages,' continued Shams, 'not just set up camp there for a day or two. It's just a rich man looking at the poor and thinking how vital and stoic they seem. The poor may be physically resilient, but inside they've been beaten to death. And now he comes to them as the new Prophet, as clueless as to what he's leading them to as all the rest. Gandhi's seeing it only now: the civil disobedience movement is out of control. And as for non-violence? What a joke.'

Dar listened, but, for the first time, he left Shams bristling. 'I still like him,' he muttered on his way home.

As he turned into Bhatti Gate he saw a man wearing a Gandhi hat, laughing at the police who were about to thrash him. 'You can't hurt me!' the man cried. 'Gandhi's hat will protect me.' The policemen turned to each other and smiled before raising their batons.

Nothing, thought Dar, angrily moving on, can break the hold of superstition on our people. He was nearly home.

Shams is wrong. The thought made him stumble. Shams was, had always been, the clever one, but Dar knew that this time it was his own instinct that was right. Our love for the past is tricking us, he thought. In 1919, like thousands of Muslims across India, Dar had been roused by the Khilafat movement to restore the *khalifate* leadership of Islam in Turkey. When Mustafa Kemal Atatürk turned the Indian Muslims away, many were furious. Not Dar. He saw that Atatürk, with his dreams of modernising, was a man after his own heart. From that moment on, Dar gave up on history. Everything was to come from the future now.

If he'd talked to his wife he would have discovered how much her thinking, in its broadest strokes, tallied with his own. Amrau too

7

was future-bound, but her future was not linked to men with angry urgent voices, but to what the pir had promised for her son.

Dar pushed open the door and began climbing the stairs. He was smiling. I covet my wife, he thought.

Later that night, as they lay on their *charpoy*, Dar thought how the city that had roared up against them was, in their stillness, still. Its wonders held back. Its tyranny too. A tyranny so subtle he only sometimes felt it, like the passing of a cold, steady-pulsed wind. It called surrender. He touched her unbraced hair. Its curled resilience amazed him even now.

'Amrau,' he said. Khurshid softly sighed. She'd never told him how happy it made her that he continued to call her Amrau. He lay down on his side, his head below hers, and listened. Her heart began to slow.

The *dai* visited, as she did from time to time, in the hope of a gift. Khurshid's gaze swept across the courtyard. Awais and Batool, both tall and slim. So clearly her children, if you ignored how black Awais was – though, she thought with a pang, that's hard to do.

'Tanveer!' she called. Tanveer looked up from her plate of *channay*, dazed. The girl only had stealth when it came to hiding food. And Maryam, short, dark and pudgy, unremarkable in every way. Maryam was laughing up into Awais's face. Khurshid sent the girls to make tea.

'Not talking?" asked the *dai*, her gaze levelled at Maryam.

'She's still young,' said Khurshid.

'Nearly two?'

Khurshid nodded.

'How many words?'

Reluctantly, Khurshid said, 'None.'

The *dai* made her way towards Maryam, who, fearing the threat, huddled behind Awais. Awais, at a signal from his mother, gave Maryam into the *dai*'s arms. The *dai* slapped her; Maryam screamed. The *dai* blinked, surprised. She prised open Maryam's mouth, then checked her ears.

The girls returned with the tea tray.

'Speak,' said the *dai*, looking the child in the eyes. Maryam just stared back.

'Something's wrong,' said the *dai* and handed Maryam back to Awais. She returned to her place; lifting her saucer, she blew on her tea and sucked it up like a cat.

'She's a brainless idiot,' Dar said when Khurshid later told him what the *dai* had said.

'That's what you say about everyone.'

He shrugged.

'Take her to see a doctor? What do you think?' she said.

He ignored the comment and picked up his paper, the *Akhbar-e-aam*. Khurshid went to the kitchen.

After a while, Dar, who hardly ever talked to Awais, came over and said, 'I bet they all know your name at school.'

'Yes,' said Awais. They called him 'Awais the black' or just *kalu*, blackie. He'd never wanted to be liked. Not that he wanted to be disliked. But he didn't seek being liked as some of the other boys did – with their small gifts, their smiles, their adulation and their willingness to be nothing more than the tip of someone else's shoe. He knew he had to endure. That had been drummed into him since he was very young. But endure what exactly, he sometimes wondered. His father stood over him, saying nothing, and the floor on which Awais sat, though covered by a small rug, began to feel cold. His eyelashes, thick, like a girl's, swooped down. Awais was waiting for his father to give up, leave him alone. He couldn't read while his father was there, so he just stared at his book till his father moved away. Awais, with Maryam still at his side, began to read again.

'Ais!' said Maryam.

Startled, he picked her up and stared into her face.

'Say it again!' he said and she did.

Proudly, he carried Maryam over to his parents and said, 'She spoke.' They turned to look at him. 'Maryam,' he said, 'say it again.' She looked around the courtyard, oblivious, it seemed, to what he'd requested and to the tension her silence was creating.

His mother believed him straight away. His father didn't call him a liar to his face, Awais noticed. Just as his father was turning away, Maryam said it again.

Once Maryam began talking, she wouldn't stop. She was a strange one; that's what they all thought. While everyone else understood how to behave around Khurshid, Maryam seemed to understand absolutely nothing. The other children watched in amazement when, in response to their commands, Maryam asked her whys. It was funny – in the beginning. Even Khurshid thought so. No one remembered when it took a serious turn.

'Is she slow?' asked Tanveer.

Batool didn't tell her sister off. She weighed the question and finally said, 'I don't know.'

In 1928, the year Maryam spoke her first word, there was talk all over India, and alliances were broken and made. Dar had just bought his first radio, a mahogany cabinet, thirty inches by fifteen inches, with two immense dials that no one but he was allowed to touch. When the family were at dinner, where they couldn't move, he told them the news. Khurshid and the girls hardly attended to what he said; Awais listened, or tried to listen, because politics was men's business. When his father spoke about politics he sounded like another person – but who? It was only years later that Awais discovered whose voice and even whose ideas his father had sometimes dressed himself him in, like a naughty boy spinning in his sister's sparkly new dress.

'There've been endless negotiations,' said Dar, 'but now the eight-sided faces of diplomacy have become haggard. The politicians are trying to hide their growing sense of fear and despair. One wrong word, one sign of an inability to stay strong when the wind whistles, one indication, however slight, that one can't stand one's ground, and everything will be lost.' He told them how in Delhi at the All Parties Conference and later, in Lahore, questions had been raised about rights, justice and how the federation would work.

'One man, one vote or something else? Congress wants joint electorates,' he said. 'Jinnah too.' Awais looked perplexed. Dar said, 'Awais, if you don't even know who the main players are...' He sounded disappointed. Awais pulled himself up. Dar continued, 'Jinnah's head of one branch of the Muslim League. The head of the other branch, Shafi, says joint electorates won't work. Shafi's for separate electorates. Separate electorates? Which idiot thought of that? Well, says Shafi, Muslims can't be represented by Hindus. Hindus are numerically more than us – four to one. They'd have their own interests at heart.' Dar stroked the outer ridges of his nose, cupped the tip then let it go. 'The world's turned upside down. Aren't we all Indians? It's as simple as that. But Shafi's dug in his heels. No wonder negotiations broke down.'

3

MAY 1928, LAHORE

On the second day of Eid, Dar said, 'I'm going to take the children out for a while.' And he did, even little Maryam. With the house to herself, Khurshid didn't know what to do. The silence disturbed her. She wished she'd listened to Dar's plea that she accompany them. They'd all be racing about in Company Bagh soon, and here she was, stuck. She picked up one of Awais's books, staring at the rectangle of dust it left. Though she'd cleared away immediately after the last of the guests had gone, to her pernickety eye, order hadn't been fully restored. She began cleaning.

The gossip, she missed. Bilquees had been a fiend for collecting all the news, and generous in sharing it. 'How do you know all these things?' Khurshid had asked her friend.

'People just tell me,' Bilquees had said, grinning. 'I must have that kind of face.'

Just those few months of friendship, and still Khurshid felt that there was no one who knew her like Bilquees had. She put down her cloth, sat down. But Bilquees hadn't come, all those years ago, when she'd needed her the most. Yes, Awais had got better, but that wasn't the point... She willed up a picture of Awais and the buzzing inside her eased, though it didn't stop, not completely. She hadn't exactly instigated the falling out with Bilquees, but had she wanted something to pull them apart? Abruptly, she sat up, picked up the cloth and began cleaning again. Awais so ill she'd thought he'd... If I can get through that she thought, I can get through the rest.

The family came back in time for lunch and Awais began to cough.

That fever that had caught him at the start of his life had made him weak. He was often, as a consequence, too ill for school. He hated it anyhow, Khurshid knew. For the first two years she'd ask, 'Made any friends?' and he'd say, 'No.' When he began to speak of 'my friends this' and 'my friends that', she listened, unconvinced. The knowledge that he was lonely ripped at her heart, but she didn't know what to do. So today, as she listened to his spasms of coughing, she didn't say anything, knowing how he detested attention of that kind.

The next day he cried off school and she let him stay back, happy that Dar had left early for work and she didn't have to face his long-drawn-out reprimands.

She popped out of the kitchen from time to time to see how Awais was. Oblivious to the world, he lay on a *charpoy* in the courtyard, reading. How he could be so ordinary – or was that too undamning a word for how awful his grades were? – when he loved books so much, she didn't understand. Neither she nor Dar were bookish people and in this, at least, they agreed. They found his fascination for books strange, extremely strange.

It was only last year, during one of his more serious bouts of illness, that this fascination began. Looking out into the street when she'd been hanging clothes to dry, she'd seen the *Anna* library van stationed outside. She'd waited till she spotted the library assistant emerge, then had shouted down.

'What book do you want?' he'd shouted back.

'A good one,' she'd replied. It must have been very good indeed, thought Khurshid, for Awais had been hooked, and these days, if a while had passed and he hadn't been able to exchange his old book for a new one, he read anything that was to hand: his father's paper – afterwards neatly folded again – or even the half-stories covering the newspaper bags in which tea and sugar and other provisions were brought into the house. Nothing, she thought. He's happy, but empty. It was a cruel wind that brought in these thoughts. *All these years, unmarked. I could take okay, average, even.* And then she felt as if she were being pelted by stones. Liar, sang the stones. Liar, liar. Okay is never enough. Greatness – the pir had promised it. Where was it? If it were going to manifest itself, wouldn't it have done so by now? Had she missed something? Forgotten something? She rummaged for a clue. This was a game she'd played a hundred times and more. She always came up blank. What if the future he'd been promised never emerged? An ordinary life? One more in the multitude, all shallow breaths. The cruelty that now lined her skin and made her body more angular was borne of fear. But repression was control, and control was good, wasn't it?

It was when he began to slouch that she first had an inkling that something was wrong: he'd locked her out. 'Stand up straight!' she'd shout. He did what he was told but she saw, as she knew she was supposed to see, that as soon as he left the room he returned to what had become his normal gait. He didn't even make a pretence of listening to her any more. She thought back to all the times people had told her what an obedient boy she had. If she could just fix this one thing; if only he'd listen, she was sure everything would fall into place. He was a bright boy; that's what she believed – most of the time. And he was lucky. Later, when she was back in her room, distress impaled her, yet she knew they – he and she – were bound together in a circle from which neither could escape. Remorse shifted to anger again. One question was driving her mad. Why was he laughing at her? For she was certain that he was.

The next morning Khurshid was standing at the balcony, pulling a comb through the tangle of her wet hair. She'd begun to fasten the shutter when she saw a boy passing through the crowds. 'Boy!' she shouted. He looked up in her direction. 'Boy!' she said again. 'Go to the milkman and ask him why he hasn't come.' He looked puzzled and she said, 'Three shops away. Come back and I'll give you some money.'

She was just about to go back in when he said, 'Will you listen to my song?'

'What? What did you say?'

'Will you listen to my song?' the boy asked again.

'Is your head okay?' she asked.

'Will you?' he asked.

'Yes, yes. Now—' she began but he was off, running and whistling.

A few minutes later, the boy knocked on the heavy wooden door.

Khurshid opened it and then began to ascend the stairs. The pot of milk in his hands, the boy followed. She walked steadily, like one used to the lie of the land; he stumbled on the uneven brick steps and then put his free hand against the wall as a stay.

Once upstairs, Khurshid took the pot; the boy looked around. 'Well?' she said. She wanted this over with.

He breathed in, then on the fall, he began to sing. The beauty of his voice was not a flourish; it was a whip. She glared at him, angry at the attentiveness his voice demanded. The song was Ghalib's '*Ye na thi hamiri kismet*' – 'It wasn't in our fate'. He couldn't possibly know what such things meant, she thought.

When he'd finished she rushed in: 'Who taught you? Is your family musical? Why this song?'

He seemed surprised at the questions and tried to answer them. She nodded in reply, though hardly taking anything in. She asked him to wait and returned a few minutes later with two coins and some sweetmeats wrapped in a clean green cloth. Only when the door closed behind him did she realise she hadn't asked his name. She forced a laugh. What did it matter what he was called? He'd looked as if he were fourteen or fifteen, just six or seven years older than Awais.

One year later Dar told them that Ruttie Jinnah, Mrs Jinnah – whose beauty was as famed as her husband's aura – had died. 'Remember this year: 1929. The year Jinnah and Shafi met and the two Muslim Leagues became one. The Congress are in shock. Wonder what Jinnah's playing at, off in London. The new British prime minister, Ramsay McDonald, is sympathetic to the Congress cause. That's got to be a good thing. Can you sense it? The British know it's a losing game. Egypt and Ireland – gone. Their days are numbered. Bet they've already started working out an exit plan. Wouldn't put it past them to have come here with one already tucked away in their back pockets. Just in case. Why don't they scrawl *that* on their flag? Know what they did in Calcutta…?'

Even Tanveer knew the answer to that.

'Cut the—' she began.

'Cut the fingers off,' he interjected, 'the local weavers because their cloth was so fine. Who'd want English cotton when you could have the purest Indian cloth?'

While Khurshid and the girls were tolerant, Awais was embarrassed. The English were the future. Didn't his father see that? Dar continued to talk and when he was done he looked at his unwilling audience, a huge smile branched across his face.

On the last day of 1929, Dar called them to his alcove, his voice as firm as a claw. 'Amrau! Awais! Everyone – come.' He told them that the civil disobedience movement had been launched. 'Now,' he said, looking smug, as if he'd been first across the finishing line, 'politics is on every tongue. The call for independence has been unequivocally made. Politicians have set up their tables, their papers and pens and are ready, once more, to talk. All we have to do now is wait.'

I could teach them a thing or two about waiting, she thought. She looked at Awais. The force of certainty that was in her was not, she saw, in her son. She thought, did I miss something? Was there something the pir told me to do, and I forgot? She was exhausted from trying to work it out. What would Bilquees have said? And then she remembered what Bilquees *had* said.

She rushed to her room and began searching. No paper anywhere. She opened Dar's bag, burning with guilt. All the paper he had was in tiny sheets and anyhow, none were blank. Neatly as she could she put everything back. Awais, she thought. She went to his room and entered. He was lying on the bed, reading. With a sudden ferocity, she wanted to burn his book, all his books.

'Paper?' he said, repeating what she'd said as if the idea were the most complex he'd heard. He made a steeple of his book and got off the bed. He lay down and reached for something under his bed: a copybook. He stood up and opened it. She noticed the pages were mostly empty. He ripped out a page.

'Give me two more,' she said. Back in her room, Khurshid wrote to the pir. She wasn't happy with what she'd written, and started again. The third attempt would have to do. She folded the letter so she wouldn't have to think about it any more, put it in an envelope and returned to Awais's room.

'Post it for me,' she said, putting it on his table. He nodded and then bent his head again to his book.

A month later a letter arrived to say the pir had died several years ago. She wrote back to say she prayed his death had been a peaceful one. There was no further reply. Even in that one visit he'd made to her years ago, she'd seen how old he'd become, the blue veins of his feet rising to a tempest, as if they'd carry his blood away.

How do I right what's gone wrong? she thought. The future she'd been promised was running away, and she was scared.

4

At ten, Awais still didn't have a single friend. Then a week into middle school he came home and said to his mother, 'My friend's coming home tomorrow, after school.' Khurshid was careful not to say anything.

The next day Awais was listening for the knock on the door and, when it came, he rushed downstairs. When Awais saw Mitoo he understood why Mitoo hadn't wanted to come straight after school. He was wearing a newly pressed white half-sleeved shirt and tan short trousers held up with braces. Awais saw more than one person turn to stare at Mitoo. He took his friend's hand and led him upstairs. His mother was waiting.

Awais said, 'My friend, Mitoo.' Khurshid frowned. Then quick as a flash, she smiled. Awais's gaze turned back to his friend. With his cat-like green eyes he should have been a Billo or a Billa, thought Awais, not for the first time.

'*Beta*,' Khurshid said, 'do I know your mother? What's her name?'

'Bilquees Khanum,' Mitoo said. Khurshid approached. Awais saw that Mitoo stood very still. She curved Mitoo's face in her hand and kissed his forehead. In that one minute Khurshid had a strange gentleness to her, something Awais had never seen before. She nodded, then left for the kitchen. Maryam ran up to Awais and settled herself on the sofa between the two friends.

'Does she always follow you around?' asked Mitoo.

'Do you follow me around, Maryam?' said Awais. 'Come on. Give us an answer. Mitoo *bhai* is waiting.' He began tickling her and she giggled, pulling in, then offering him her feet. Awais turned back to Mitoo, still grinning.

Mitoo was the most popular boy in school. Because Mitoo didn't need those who tailed him, their need for him grew. For some, to become Mitoo's shadow was the greatest aspiration they had. The only time Awais had seen him sit still was when he drew. Mitoo seemed embarrassed about his love for drawing and hid it from everyone, but because Awais watched him so closely, he knew. At school Mitoo lagged behind but didn't seem to care. Outside school he was superlative at whatever he did. He didn't have an athletic build. He had a long torso and shortish legs; you wouldn't have thought him a good runner till you saw him run. And so it was with every sport.

The day Mitoo approached Awais – during the break – and asked a few questions, Awais felt the jealous eyes of those others watching him; with raised hands they silenced the noise, the better to hear. The questions Mitoo asked him were everyday and Awais's replies were – how could they be anything else? – without meaning. From then on, Mitoo tagged Awais as if he were a stray in want of an owner.

Awais was dazzled by Mitoo, like you're dazzled by a too-bright sun. Even the very colour of him was golden: his milky-tea skin and his hair the lightest shade of yellow-brown. His hair was like that of the street children – but where theirs was stiff with wind and sand and deposits unimaginable, Mitoo's was clean and smooth. Each month his mother dragged him to the local barber, a man on the roadside with a chair and a few chosen implements laid out on a rickety table, one of whose legs was supported by a half brick. Several coloured towels hung on an electricity wire from two trees. Their formation never changed: red, blue and blue again. 'Give my son an English cut,' Bilquees said and then watched the process as if the barber were an underling she'd trained. The barber tolerated her comments for one reason and one reason alone: he never worked so well as when Bilquees stood barking orders at his side.

And like anything that is touched by gold, Awais's shares went up. The other boys looked at him now with a charged look of respect; and even if they were in the middle of saying something when he spoke, they closed their mouths quick-quick as if it were they, not he, who'd been rude.

Why me? he thought. He didn't want to know, not really.

Tanveer entered. She laid out some plates, and was followed by Batool, who brought the drinks and food. Awais saw that Mitoo was taken aback – as everyone was – by Batool's beauty. At just nine, she was already marked. People found it strange that though the features of the sisters were so alike, one of them was merely good–looking, which, by itself, should have been enough, while the other's features had a mobility, a fire almost, that raised the stakes of what beauty was. Khurshid knew she'd have to rein her in. Not yet though, she thought, fascinated, like everyone else, to see where Batool's beauty would take her. She called the girls to her side. They went happily.

By the time Khurshid returned to the courtyard, it was getting dark. Mitoo said he had to go. 'Go halfway with him, Awais,' said Khurshid. The boys were now eager to escape. Once outside, the anomaly of meeting within the frame of courtesy when they were already friends was forgotten. A cool breeze had begun to blow. Mitoo raised his face and started to run – his answer for everything, and Awais followed.

'Come on, Awais!' he cried. 'Keep up.'

Awais stopped; his breath came hard and slow. Mitoo ran back for him and shouted, 'Come on,' and again, they were off.

A stray ball began its descent. Mitoo caught it, not even thinking to catch it, then threw it back the way it had come. It would only have been an effort, Awais knew, for Mitoo to not catch the ball.

Awais watched Mitoo from out of the corner of his eye and was glad Mitoo had chosen him as his friend. And then Mitoo raised his hand. It hovered above his cheek: the spot where Awais's mother had held his face. The wind now felt cold, like metal kept in the shade. Mitoo rocketed off. Laughing, he turned his head and called to Awais. Deliberately, Awais slowed his steps. Mitoo stopped and waited for him, a curious look on his face. All around them the city hummed.

Late that night, after the city's gates had closed, a man who had once been one of the inside city's most prominent residents sat on the steps of a tailor's shop that belonged to the son he'd quarrelled with five years ago. A gaunt man with eyes that were dimming fast, his clothes old, dotted with cigarette holes, an insult to the son who didn't know he was there. On his lips, a song – badly sung. His son had offered a conciliatory hand but the father hadn't believed him; in the son's voice there'd been laughter.

The old man didn't like the city's silence. It made him afraid.

In Awais's room Mitoo asked, 'Why does *khala* go on about a pir?'

Awais pulled out his carrom board from under the bed. Mitoo sat down on the other side of the board. Awais picked up the powder, sprinkled then smoothed it down. Mitoo put the counters in place.

Mitoo leaned forward. 'Here I come!' he said and made his first flick. The counter lay a thumbnail away from one of the four pocket holes. Awais studied the board. He bent forward and took his first shot. In it went like a meteorite. He interlaced his fingers and stretched, avoiding looking at Mitoo – he didn't want to be thrown off his game – and then he bent forward again. For once, maybe because he was angry, he won.

Mitoo straightened and looked at Awais, surprised. 'Tell me now,' he said.

Awais began piling the counters together then set to cleaning the board. 'It's a mistake,' he said. He then told Mitoo what the pir had said. When he'd finished, Mitoo clicked his fingers like he'd seen gangsters in movies do. A click, followed by a sharp circle of the hand.

'And if it's true?' said Mitoo.

Awais looked at him, a sloped smile on his face. 'What kind of greatness am I ever going to do?'

'That's the way to take it,' said Mitoo. 'Lying down.'

'What do you want me to do?' Awais got up and walked to the small window that looked out at a concrete wall. On a good day he could see a scrap of blue sky. He turned to Mitoo, leaden. *He'll never come back now.* Part of him didn't care – even for this.

Mitoo was standing at Awais's desk. Awais saw him pick up half of a rubber eraser and surreptitiously pocket it. It wasn't the first time he'd seen Mitoo do something like that, he realised. *He's becoming an inveterate thief.* The things he took were always small, damaged, as if the rational part of his brain were arguing that these things would soon be thrown away or lost anyhow, so why not...?

Mitoo caught Awais watching him and laughed exuberantly. It took him a few minutes to calm down.

'Know our mothers used to be friends?' Mitoo said.

Awais's top lip curled over his teeth. Mitoo was waiting. 'What happened?' he asked.

Mitoo shook his head and said, 'Another time. Come on. I'll buy you a glass of *sharbat.*'

Awais's eyes, unblinking. Mitoo knew something. Why wouldn't he tell?

As they reached the front door, they found Khurshid there, waiting. Dar came in and accosted them all.

'You'll want to listen to this,' he said. 'Hear about the votes in the election? What they found in the voting boxes?' He looked at them, his eyes laughing. 'Voters used the boxes to slip messages to Gandhi, as if they were letterboxes that required no stamps.' Khurshid turned to him, irritated. He, of all men, should have understood that. Gandhi's name was always on Dar's lips. Only once had she seen Dar shaken: when she'd asked him what Gandhi's criticism of modern life meant. She tried to recall what he'd told her – that a poet, Muhammed Iqbal, had begun to talk of a Muslim India within India. What did that mean? Dar hadn't known either. All he'd said was, 'There's time. We don't have to decide yet.'

Awais made a signal to his mother. She nodded. He and Mitoo bolted out of the house.

Mitoo and Awais tried to draw each other into what they each loved: Mitoo wanted Awais to feel for sports what he felt, and Awais wanted Mitoo to be able to submerge himself, like he could, in the lives and places he read about in books. But neither of these other things took – not, at least, like they wanted them to. After arguments galore, and feelings of disgust at the other's stupidity, they arrived, somehow, at a middle ground. Awais played those games which didn't leave him too weak and breathless, and Mitoo, though he wouldn't read, would suffer being read to – though even in this, his patience didn't last long. He had an appetite for adventure, and so Awais, who'd just become a member of the Punjab Public Library, scoured it for books that were fast paced.

The chief librarian looked at the adventure books Awais now took out, his mouth a thin line of reprobation. Awais told himself he didn't care. His books stamped, he put the card safely back in the special wallet his mother had made for him and went home.

Mitoo and Awais didn't learn to love what the other loved but sometimes they saw a glint of what made these things so wondrous for their friend.

Then, one day, Mitoo ran away. Without any planning. Without any word.

Mitoo had an instinct, brutal and honest, which pushed him always to break free of things. It wasn't curiosity about the world that made him leap forward to test its boundaries – he didn't have anything of the scientific spirit in him; it was an abhorrence of patterns. If two steps took him forward to a goal he thought he desired, at the last minute he rushed the other way, just to see what would happen. He thought it the best trick in the world – to trick himself. And once he'd got into the habit, though each successive act required increasing discipline, he couldn't let go.

So he got on a train, no money in his pocket – the last thing he'd bought was some new marbles – with no idea where the train was headed for, whether it was a local train or one which would cross a province or two; and instead of shying away in hidden parts of the train like the other freeloaders, he took a seat opposite the carriage's most respectable, suited and booted man.

A conductor arrived. But Mitoo could tell his mind wasn't on the job. Mitoo sat back relaxed, legs spread out before him as if the world could never change him. And then after some time, another conductor arrived. Mitoo saw that this one – who was young – had a different disposition from the conductor who'd come before.

Mitoo looked for an escape. But at one end there was the conductor, making his way forward, and, at the other, a man with his young boy. And then the man opposite pressed Mitoo's arm with excessive force, smiled and said, 'Sit.' When the conductor arrived, the man showed his ticket. The conductor then turned to Mitoo. 'Ticket,' the conductor said. Mitoo didn't answer. 'You shameless son of a…' the conductor began. Mitoo's fellow passenger intervened and paid the fare. When the conductor left, Mitoo looked down at the ticket in his hand – a return. When the train stopped Mitoo didn't get off to explore the new city he'd entered. He switched platforms and returned straight back to Lahore.

Awais paused over his shot and said, 'And you didn't even think to ask me?'

They were in Awais's house, in a corner of the courtyard, crouching, playing marbles.

'As if your moth…' Mitoo began.

'Boys,' Khurshid said as she approached. 'Don't lean on the floor. You'll catch a cold.'

Mitoo got up at once as if he were a dog obedient to her voice.

'I'll bring you a drink,' she said.

When she'd gone he sat down again and, before Awais could say a word, he jumped in with, 'Are you taking that shot or not?'

Awais leaned forward and aimed. His marble, a translucent piece of glass with entrails of blue, ricocheted back, after whispering past Mitoo's green marble, which remained unmoved by the attack. Khurshid returned with two bottles. She put them on the floor and left.

Awais and Mitoo sat up, monitoring the movement of the other's hands so that their timing was exact. They pressed down on the glass beads fatly squeezed into the bottles' necks. They raised the bottles up to their faces, their gaze following the trajectory of the beads as they dropped down inside the bottles of forest green. The liquid spluttered to the top. As it hit the beads it exploded in a white fire; ready, the boys screamed, 'Tah!' Faces dripping with fizz, they laughed like madmen on a day's release.

When Mitoo left, Dar said, 'I like that boy.'

'He's a devil,' said Tanveer, who, at seven, was going through her first and only pious phase.

'He's as a boy should be,' Dar said. Khurshid said nothing.

Soon Mitoo was off on his next escapade.

Although Mitoo liked to think of himself as prince of the streets, Awais sometimes found out things before Mitoo did. It was from a poster that Awais learnt that the famous singer Raja Mohan would be coming to Lahore to sing. It was Awais's news but it was Mitoo who went.

Not having a ticket, Mitoo manoeuvred himself into the hall in Minto Park somehow, long before the event was scheduled to begin. He sat under one of the benches and when the crowds began to enter he crawled out and sat down like the paying customer he wasn't. The hall was soon packed. The performance was supposed to begin at 7pm. At 6.50 the electricity died.

The audience heard someone offstage say, 'I'm not doing it!' And then a cajoling milky voice, whose words they could only hear as sound, not sense, said something in reply. The crowd was getting restless.

Mitoo sat next to a man and a boy. The man said to the boy, 'Go on, Bablo, you do it.' Mitoo thought the boy called Bablo wouldn't do it, whatever it was. But Bablo got up and the man followed and they went straight to the back of the stage. Again the man with the milky voice: 'Master Pankaj Gopal will be entertaining us till the electricity returns.'

'I didn't pay for this!' shouted somebody. And other voices joined in and said, 'It's come to this? The audience have to entertain the star?'

Though there wasn't much light coming in from the windows, Mitoo could just about see the boy's face. He began to sing; the crowd fell silent.

Bablo sang three songs and near the end of the third, the light returned. The audience blinked and shook their heads as they searched the stage for the virtuoso. A boy? A boy with an intense-looking face and limp, thin arms poking out from his half-sleeved shirt, like carrots dug free from a warren and left exposed. The crowd broke into riotous applause. The singer Raja Mohan stepped forward onto the stage. He couldn't hide it. There was both awe and pain on his face. Bablo bent his head and when the clapping had ceased he pressed his hands to Raja Mohan's feet. Raja Mohan laid a hand on the boy's bent head. Bablo and the man returned to their seats and Mitoo, who was listening, overheard Bablo say, 'Do you think he meant it, Shashi *bhai*, about us going to see him tomorrow?'

'Of course he did,' said the man, 'or at least,' he added as he grabbed Bablo's wrist tight, 'I think he did.'

Mitoo followed Bablo and the older man home. And the next day he made his way to their house again. He didn't know why. He didn't even like music that much.

Wacho Wali bazaar, like Suha bazaar, was never at rest. The crowds moved slowly, if they moved at all, and only disappeared when late into the night the shopkeepers closed their doors and padlocked what remained inside. Mitoo discovered that Bablo and his family lived above a jewellery shop. Mitoo knew the shop owner – a friend of his father's, a man who used to travel across many states to see and to collect new designs and had, in this way, gained both riches and a name. These days the shop owner went nowhere; he sat all day in his shop talking softly to his young son whose eyes were so weak he couldn't go to school.

Mitoo turned to look at the workbench outside the shop and he saw another boy, the same age, or thereabouts, as the owner's son. The skill of the boy's hands was a great thing to watch. Finishing a job, the boy left his slippers outside as he entered the cool shop and awaited the appraisal of his master. His master inspected the filigree of silver the boy had wrought, then put it on the counter. Mitoo watched as the master smiled, and, now turning to his son, gathered up the child's hands in his own. As he left the shop, the apprentice pushed his feet back into his *chappals*. He glanced back. The boy's hand was still held in his father's palm.

A few minutes later Bablo appeared and, seeing his friend hard at work, hummed a tune. The silversmith's apprentice smiled.

Passing through one dark alleyway to the next, Mitoo came to a square, and it was here that all the light which had been robbed from the alleyways was stored. And here that the glass–bangle makers lived. They had none of the sobriety of the makers of silver and gold for theirs was an ephemeral art. As Mitoo stopped to watch the bangle makers blow patterns into glass – dots and tiny rivulets and crazy lines copied from a child's copybook – one of them laid down his rod of molten iron on his bench. His face was luminous from the heat. Grinning, he said to his apprentice son, 'Ours is the best profession in the world!' The boy looked at Mitoo and winked. Mitoo moved on.

5

NOVEMBER 1931, LAHORE

Walking to Mitoo's house one Saturday afternoon, Awais saw some children racing at the gutter's edge, following the traffic of paper and other refuse, and remembered the time his mother had taught him how to make newspaper boats, and how, once he'd made his own fleet of three, he'd taken them down to the street and set them off. 'Don't you know nothing?' a man had said and Awais, still crouching, had looked up. 'They'll sink. And if they don't sink, they'll break.' But they hadn't sunk or broken. They'd floated to the end of the gutter and then he'd had the awful task of picking them up, stink-laden. He'd then laid them on the next gutter track. He'd watched them for a moment, then given up. His hand smelled of pee. He held it in front of him as he walked home. 'Been a naughty boy?' said an old man with grizzled, chewed–up teeth. 'Come here. I'll cut it off for you. No charge.'

Now, he was nearly at Mitoo's house. When he'd first gone round – and it had been ages before Mitoo got to inviting him over – he couldn't stop staring at Mitoo's mother. Like Mitoo, she found it hard to be still. Strangely though, she deferred to Mitoo in absolutely everything, and when Awais and Mitoo spoke, she fell immediately silent, as if the rules pertaining to civility and age had been reversed. Sparring with Mitoo, he soon forgot they weren't alone. Mitoo's mother watching, listening, pleased. If Mitoo hadn't pointed to a kite overhead Awais wouldn't have looked up and caught the sweep of sadness that shaded Mitoo's mother's face, a look similar, he thought, to the way his own mother had looked at Mitoo when he'd first brought him home.

'I could cut that easily,' said Mitoo, his gaze locked on the kite. Bilquees got up. She returned a few minutes later; in her hand, a tray. Mitoo leapt up to take it from her. Awais, needing hardly any prompting, began to wolf down the *kebabs*.

'Make yourself at home,' Mitoo joked.

'Mitoo!' said Bilquees. She held out a plate of *barfi*. Awais, not looking at either of them, took just one piece.

Mitoo put another on Awais's plate. 'At least have twins,' he said.

When Mitoo's father, Ahmed Sahib, entered the house, Awais jolted up to say his *salaam*. Ahmed Sahib half smiled, his head bending to one side. Embarrassed, Awais didn't know what else to say. Ahmed Sahib loitered for a while and then staggered – which made Bilquees shake her head – out of the courtyard, laughing at one of his own jokes.

'So Awais,' Bilquees said as if there'd been no break in their conversation, 'what do you like best in school?'

'Nothing,' he replied. Though Bilquees and Mitoo laughed and Awais smiled, it was still a while before all trace of Ahmed Sahib's presence could be swept away. Awais didn't stay long. He walked home fast, planning what to tell his mother.

He shouldn't be lonely, he thought, not now that he had Mitoo.

As he walked up the stairs, he could hear his parents in the courtyard, talking. They came to a sharp halt when he entered. He made his way to his room. When he was sure they couldn't see him, he stopped in the corridor to listen.

'I thought,' Dar was saying, 'he might get touched by some of Mitoo's spark. But that's not happening.'

Awais bolted away.

Back in the courtyard, Dar leaned back and rocked. 'Did you say something?' he said tipping forward, his hands rubbing his corpulent knees. Khurshid shook her head. 'What does he even see in Awais, anyhow?'

'He sees what I see in him!' she said. Dar flicked a hand through the air, dismissive. She hadn't yet told him whose son Mitoo was, and what this made her feel: that bits of her life were now floating back to Bilquees.

'Can I get some tea?' he asked. She looked at the half grandfather clock she'd bought from her father's house.

'It's not time yet,' she said.

'I'll wait, then.'

'No, it's fine,' she replied. 'I'll get it.'

Dar was right, she knew. There was something strange about Mitoo's friendship with Awais. Now they seemed to fit – more so, at least, than when she'd first seen them together – but there were times when she felt suspicious all over again, especially when she caught Mitoo staring her way. He was so much Bilquees's boy, a boy so observant she mentally began to close doors.

Lucky, she thought. Once she'd thought her boy the luckiest in the world.

Everyone was spreading out, Awais thought. Mitoo. His own father, whose business had picked up, and who now travelled further away. It's just me who's not been anywhere.

A few days after Mitoo's train escapade, Awais, for the first time, went to see the Chauburji monument. He looked up at its arch covered with frescoes.

He'd believed it – once. He'd liked, no loved – even when he'd groaned at – the story she told him that began, 'Before you were born...' But now it hurt. *It's like I'm wearing an invisibility cloak. I could walk anywhere, go anywhere, and remain unseen.*

'Oi Awais!' called a voice behind him. Awais turned to answer.

From Chauburji, he brought home five chrysalises and put them in a jar in which he'd poked breathing holes. He watched them change from things you could squash to their juicy death to things of beauty. And when they changed, he let them go. All he'd wanted to know was, was the change hard? He prayed: when the moment comes for me, let it be as easy, like stepping from one room to the next.

That night, as they did every night, the people in the inside city, secure behind the city's twelve locked gates, fell into an easy sleep.

The next morning, a Sunday, was the festival of Basant to mark the first official day of spring. Lahoris would celebrate it with a thousand and one kites. In the nearby villages the corn had been cut, the fields were lush green and damp, each plot having received its morning share of the water course. There were those now living in the city who could remember childhoods when they'd run in mustard fields, chewing on leaves, eaten dishes of meat and spinach and *rotis* with lashings of fresh white butter which had melted and spread like ice hit by the sun, drunk cool yogurt *lassi* and stuffed their mouths with sweetmeats that were always sweet enough, even for their young rapacious taste, and waited for dusk to fall and the show by the wandering singers to begin. The city's children, those who had only heard these stories from parents and grandparents, and those who only knew that the sun would not let them sleep, all rushed out of bed. The women cooked, then changed into outfits of orange, yellow or green: a suit for the rich woman, a *dupatta* and glass bangles for the poor. From wall pegs boys carefully unfastened their kites of many colours and shapes – subtle and ferocious – where they had stood guard over sleeping bodies, waiting for this moment, waiting for this war. They took the kites to the highest points of the highest buildings and, checking the direction of the wind with outstretched wet fingers and unravelling the strings which fastened the kites to earth, they raised them to the sky and let them fly. And so the battle began. Cries of joy and pain erupted as strings were cut and kites, sad and looming, fell to the ground, to be retrieved hours later by the hands of younger children, who, with no money to buy their own, came upon these ones by good fortune. A piece of string, and their kites too could fly. Not so high as they had once flown. But fly nevertheless.

Flying kites was the one sport Awais was better at than Mitoo. They'd been on Mitoo's roof since early morning that day.

'It's getting boring,' Mitoo said. Awais ignored him, keeping his eyes steady on his kite. Once it was free, he counted up the kites he'd cut and thought of all the others he still had a chance to kill. But he knew what Mitoo meant. Reluctantly, he drew his kite back in. His hands were sore with sharp cuts even though his string had been armoured with flour paste and levigated glass by the best in Mochi Gate.

'Why did you make friends with me?' blurted out Awais.

'You've seen my mother,' Mitoo said. Awais waited. He was surprised at his own composure. 'I wanted to find out,' said Mitoo, 'what your mother had done to mine.'

Mitoo didn't walk Awais to the door so Awais let himself out. He knew, without a doubt, that what Mitoo had told him was true. He began the walk home.

He didn't want to be the favourite child anymore. Favourite – why? It was supposed to be the prettiest child, the fairest child, who was picked out for adoration, but his mother had chosen him. *It should have been Batool. I know why it's me, black as I am, useless as I am. Because I'm a boy. And because of that stupid prediction.* Again, he wished the pir had never come. A life lived without that weight over his head. How would that have been? Why wouldn't she just stop? The same story again and again. The urgency with which she watched him. When he wasn't angry, he was tired.

As always, as he walked through the city, he read the public notices plastered to the walls of buildings: a political meeting at Minto Park; the best *ghee* in town; the last of the *hammams* that were proving to be a health hazard would be closed on the fifteenth.

He began to cough.

By the next morning the cough had become so severe he told his mother he couldn't go to school. Khurshid and the girls had been invited to a neighbour's house. 'I'll stay?' she said to Awais but he shook his head. After making sure he was as comfortable as could be, Khurshid and the girls left. Awais had the house to himself. He was on the last few pages of his book. Finished, he languorously walked to the courtyard wall and looked out. On the branch of a prickle-back tree, two crows looking his way. He stared back, matching hard stare for hard stare. And then, from nowhere, he heard the beat of a *dhol*. Awais's gaze swooped to the street. To the side, the drummer, a goofy smile splashed across his face; around his neck, a tatty red scarf. The drummer pushed it back with a flourish, as if it were an expensive shawl. In the middle of the street two bicycles, stuck together like conjoined twins, one on top of the other. The drummer began his beat and the cyclist, who was perched on the lower of the two bicycles, pedalled hard then climbed up, pedalled some more then climbed down. The drummer moved on and the cyclist followed. Awais couldn't not look. Tacked onto the bike's tail was a cloth. As the biker pedalled, the cloth unfurled. Awais saw a painted picture of an elephant, a man on a trapeze and a midget clown. The circus had come to town for the first time in his life.

He laughed and ran to the door. The clap-clap alerted him. He looked down at his *chappals,* and then at his clothes. He was still dressed in last night's *shalwar kameez* and his house slippers. He couldn't go out like this. He changed with lightning speed, the sound of the drum playing in his head, but faster, faster than it had played in the street. Where was the front door key? He'd never had to lock the door himself. Where did she keep it? He rummaged about in her room – nothing. Back in the courtyard, just when he was near to giving up, he spied the keys lying on top of the radio. 'Stupid place to keep them,' he said. He ran downstairs. On the second but last step he stopped. What if his mother came home? She wouldn't be able to get in. Did she have a spare key? And if she did, what would she think if she found him gone? He was supposed to be ill. He coughed to remind himself why he was home. 'Rubbish,' he thought and tried another cough. He locked the door.

He turned round to face the street. Of course the troupe – if that's what they were – were gone. What had he expected? But he still felt the cut of disappointment. He looked around. Which way to go? Then he heard the drum again, and began to run.

'Seen a man with a *dhol,* and a bicycle – no – two?' he asked when he stopped for breath. The man he asked shook his head no and walked away. Awais saw another man a few feet away, his face slate-grey. He approached and asked, 'Where are we?'

'Khizri Gate,' the man said.

Awais nodded. The gate built in memory of the green saint who lives in a river boat and who had three times tested the Prophet

Moses, who had three times failed. He listened. All he could hear were the other sounds, of people, of movement, sounds that were always there: the sound beneath the sound he'd been listening for. And then, as if Khizr himself had set the test to show that time is not an arrow that flies and cannot be recalled, but a river that can be stepped into again and again, he heard the sound of the *dhol*. Swiping his hair back from his forehead, he turned and smiled at the man he'd spoken to; the man seemed to grow paler the more intensely Awais looked. Awais raised his hand in *salaam* and began, again, to run. But the *dhol* player was always several steps ahead. Exhausted now, Awais walked on, not ready – not yet – to turn back. His knees buckled. And then he saw the edge of a red scarf tethered in the wind. As if it was being pulled, it disappeared round a street corner. The *dhol* player had worn a red scarf; Awais was sure he had. He began to run again, dodging vegetable and fruit cart *wallahs* as he went, all of whom rained on him a swarm of curses big and small.

A cat came running out of an alleyway, screeching. Awais swerved and smashed into a big clump of thistles and thorn bushes. He pulled himself free; there was a huge rip in his *kameez*. His hand went automatically to his neck to touch the talisman his mother always made him wear and which was now as close to him as skin. It wasn't there. The tear in the *kameez* she'd forget, but the *taweez*... With a sigh, he returned to the thicket and began to grope. Nothing. Just a wall. He pulled his hand back and looked at it; it was covered in scratches and dirt. He wiped his hand on his *kameez* and reached out again. But this time he touched, among the bricks, metal – solid metal, smooth. As his hands spread out, he felt grooves. A spasm ran through his body. He stepped closer, his hands moving urgently now. He knew what this was. But it couldn't be! It wasn't possible. Slowly, methodically, he concealed the gap in the thicket with the thorny stems he had ripped off the bushes. It was getting dark; no one would notice this place now, he thought, he hoped. He raced back home.

He kept his head low; he didn't want to see anyone or be seen. This quivering in his belly – unsettling and, at the same time, settling every single thing. His body softened; his mind, always tense with waiting and wanting, eased. He'd never felt so alert. Joy, and knocking against the joy, the first throb of fear.

Of course she spotted it straight away. 'Where's your *taweez*?' she said.

'I lost it,' he said. He ran to his room. Looking around for something. He pushed a chair against the closed door. From his table, he plucked a copybook and took it to his bed; kneeling on the floor he began to draw, excitedly, pausing, clasping the pencil, relaxing his hand, beginning again.

When there was nothing else to note, he looked at his map. He laughed nervously, thinking of the English map-makers with all their machines. He slipped the map under his mattress. And then straight away pulled it out again, looked at it, then put it back once more. He couldn't be right. Could he have found it? Found something that shouldn't exist? He closed his eyes. The sky, as it had looked in that one moment when he'd stepped away from his discovery into the light of the street, still shone before his eyes: its blue a different blue from the blue of skies he knew. The wood and the metal of what he'd felt was one key; the canvas of blue, another. He'd never been more sure of anything in his life. The stretch of blue made him feel a longing for distance, a distance he wouldn't have to run to like he'd run today, but that he could walk to, taking his time. This picture produced neither a thought nor a question, but a sensation, as if he'd touched something that was unlike anything he knew. Time passed as he dwelt on what had happened. What if he were wrong? It could be something else. Only one person would know for sure.

He went in search of his father. When Awais approached the alcove, Dar looked up, surprised. 'What is it?' he said.

'Emperor Akbar. Did he live in Lahore?' Awais asked.

'How many times have I told you? If you ever bothered to listen, you'd know. Akbar made the city what it was. From 1584 to 1598, Lahore was the seat of his court. His palace is what we now call the *killa*, the fort. Till then, Lahore was just another city. Under Akbar, Lahore, along with Delhi and Agra, became an alternative seat of the imperial court.' He laughed. 'Emperor Akbar who challenged God himself and lost.'

'How many gates are there?' Awais said.

'What's wrong with you? Every child knows that. Twelve. Bhatti, Delhi…' Awais, distracted, walked away before his father was done.

'Amrau!' shouted Dar. 'Did you see that? See what your son just did?'

Awais kept his find secret because he couldn't let it go. And then two days later he saw some boys near the path, getting close. Emboldened, he ran towards them; flapping his hands and clucking his tongue he scatted them away as if they were birds who'd settled on a crop he'd cultivated over long hard months.

'Idiot!' one boy said, turning to look back. Awais sat on the pavement, guarding the place. It was a sullen dusk, the light hard–drawn. The next day Awais went back. The boys didn't return. But the day after that, there they were again, showing off an older boy at their side who walked almost lazily, as if he'd been pulled straight out of bed. And the slowness of the boy's movements made Awais think him dangerous. Awais watched and waited. What he'd found remained undiscovered. And then the idea struck him, and he felt sick: what if, like him, the boys found it by chance? And if not them, someone else? When it was dark he ran home. Standing before his father he again asked, 'How many gates are there?' Dar turned from his radio to face his son. He was angry like Awais had never known him to be before.

'How many what?' Dar said.

'Gates,' Awais said.

'What kind of joke is this?' Dar said.

'No, *abba*,' Awais said. 'I'm serious.'

'I told you just the other day,' Dar said looking at Awais as if he wanted to slap him. 'Twelve!' he said.

'*Abba*,' said Awais. 'I've got something to show you.'

'Show your mother.'

Awais rushed on. 'I've found something and only you can tell me what it is.'

'Where?'

'Near Mochi.'

'What is it?'

'I think it's… Only you can tell me for sure.'

Dar looked at Awais's earnest face; he didn't need any more per-suading than that. 'Come on, then,' he said, and they moved towards the stairs.

Khurshid, who had been standing in the corridor watching, listen-ing, cried, 'Where are you going?'

'Out,' said Dar.

'At this time?" she said, looking up at the darkening sky.

'She's right,' said Dar. Khurshid made a clucking noise with her tongue. 'Awais,' said Dar, 'get a torch.'

When Awais returned his mother said, 'Awais, at least wear a jumper. It's getting cold.'

'Amrau…' said Dar. They left.

When they got closer to the spot, Dar let Awais take the lead. At one point Awais halted, looking to his father for reassurance. Dar nodded and on Awais went. They stopped.

'Behind the clump of thistles?' said Dar. Awais stepped forward and came back a few minutes later, his head bent.

'Never mind,' said Dar. 'Look again.' And Awais did, but he couldn't find it. 'You didn't leave a mark?' asked Dar, his voice sharp. Awais shook his head *no*. 'You're sure it's here?' asked Dar. Awais didn't reply. He started searching once more. He bumped his head hard on the wall but didn't howl, didn't even whimper. Fear was pulling at him, dragging him, just when he needed to be calm. He stretched out his hand, then snatched it back; there were scratches and blood pricks all across his palm, his wrist. He turned to see his father watching him, disappointed. He rolled down his sleeve and reached forward once more. *A mark*. Why hadn't he thought of that? He'd never find it again now. And then the boys who'd been hang-ing around here would discover it and… His hand touched metal. He turned and waved to his father with his free hand. Dar rushed for-ward.

'Hold this,' Dar said, giving him the torch as he stepped forward. Awais stepped back. He turned the torch off but his hand kept rub-bing against the button as if any minute he'd change his mind and set the street ablaze with light. After a few minutes, Dar returned.

'*Abba*?' said Awais. Dar looked up, then. He walked over to his son. Awais knew somehow that the one thing he had to now do was keep very, very still.

Dar grabbed Awais's face in his colossal hands and said, 'You've found it! Loha – the thirteenth – the lost gate!' He let go of Awais and stood staring at him. On Dar's face, an incipient pride. 'Hurry up,' he said. 'There are people I've got to tell.'

On the way home Dar talked to Awais like he'd never talked to him before – about the inside city he loved and knew so well; even about some of the escapades he'd got up to as a young boy and, as always with Dar, about politics.

Halfway back, Dar said, 'Go home. Go on. You'll be all right.' He leaned down to look at Awais face to face. 'Tell your mother. Just like you told me.' When Awais turned back to look, his father had vanished. It was all forgotten: what Mitoo had said; the reason Mitoo had given for wanting him as his friend. He ran to Mitoo's house.

'Open the door, Mitoo. Hurry up!' Awais shouted. A desultory Ahmed Sahib opened the door. He didn't bark at Awais for disturbing them this late in the day. Awais said his *salaam*. Then he shouted to his friend: '*Aray bhai* Mitoo, come out!' Bilquees came running into the courtyard where Awais stood.

'Awais,' she said, 'what is it? Is everything okay?'

Awais was embarrassed now. He'd only thought of telling Mitoo, not realising he'd have to confront the whole household as well.

'*Khala*,' said Awais, 'all's well. It's just…'

Mitoo was grinning as he said, 'This better be good.'

'You haven't had dinner, have you, *beta*?' said Bilquees. Awais shook his head. She went off to bring dinner for them all.

'Well,' said Mitoo, sitting down cross-legged on a *charpoy*. 'Tell me.'

'I've found it! Found Loha!'

'Loha what?'

'Didn't your father ever tell you…?' began Awais. Mitoo brushed the question away. Awais tried to go on. 'The thirteenth gate.'

'What're you talking about? There are only twelve gates. Everyone knows that.'

'No. Thirteen. One went missing, oh, I don't know… *Abu* says it was hundreds of years ago.'

'And you found it?' asked Mitoo.

'Yes!'

'Sit down. Now tell me. From the beginning.' By the time Bilquees arrived with their food, Awais had finished his tale. They ate and then Mitoo made Awais repeat it all for his mother.

'*Beta,*' she said when he was done, 'do you know how great a thing this is? Your mother must be very proud.' Awais frowned, remembering. He hadn't told her yet.

Mitoo leapt up. 'Come on then,' he said. 'Let's go.'

'But,' said Bilquees, 'you can't go out dressed like that.'

'Be back soon,' said Mitoo.

Awais was still nervous; Mitoo was sure. Outside, Mitoo linked his arm to Awais's and whispered, 'Listen, this is what we're going to do…'

6

It was Dar who told Khurshid. She listened to Dar but looked at Awais with a craving so deep he couldn't return her gaze. When Khurshid had Awais alone she said, 'Come here.' When he approached she made him bend his head. 'This one,' she said, 'don't lose.' Another *taweez*. He stepped back. 'It's coming true,' she softly said, 'what the pir said.' Awais turned away.

Once he was in his own room he pulled shut the curtains, leaving a small sliver of a gap. He sat down on the bed and looked at the chest which stood with its back to a wall. It was a shiny aluminium trunk with brass locks.

Awais had asked his mother for the trunk. When the delivery men brought it to the house he'd surprised her by asking for it to be put in his room. The household's other trunks were all stored together in a separate room; they contained sheets and quilts and presents received and presents yet to be given. There was also a special chest in which Khurshid stored what would one day form the girls' dowries.

When the delivery men left, she'd handed him the key.

He knew each object that lay in its cavernous interior: a selection of clothes, a few toys, books. He fingered the key as he sat on the edge of the bed. He stood up, and before he could change his mind – the temptation to look always being so great – he walked towards it. He struggled for several minutes to work the key. Finally, he pulled back the lid and stared into the trunk's depths. Everything was just as he'd left it. It was more empty than full. That was how he liked it, so he could see, with one glance, what it contained. Under the books was the map of the world his uncle Jamshed had sent him. He unrolled it and lay it flat on the bed, weighing each corner down with whatever came to hand. He was still gazing at it when his sister called him for dinner.

Awais spent the next three days either at school or holed away in his room. He wondered where Mitoo was and what he was up to, but mostly he was just glad to be left alone. On the fourth day, a Thursday, Dar woke Awais at five in the morning.

'It's too early for school,' said Awais, turning his back towards his father.

Dar laughed. 'No school today.'

Awais rolled over. 'Is it a holiday?'

'Get up and get dressed. It's starting any minute soon.'

Despite his mother's glare, he left the house with his father.

As they approached the site of the lost gate, Awais saw that there was a battalion of workers armed and ready with shovels, hammers and an assortment of other tools. Some passers-by, curious, had stopped. Some stood, some sat on their haunches.

One man asked, 'Will they start soon? I've got work to get to.'

'Start what?' said the second man. A car rolled up and the first man's response was lost to the engine's sound.

Only Dar and the municipal officer, who now walked onto the scene, knew what was about to happen. Dar walked over to his friend, with Awais tagging behind.

The municipal officer said, 'How you got me to agree to this, I don't know. It better be there – that's all I'm telling you. I don't get the workforce out for nothing.'

'*Acha langra* – all right, cripple,' said Dar. 'You're not sitting in the sky, you know.'

'Is that black boy yours?' said the municipal officer, lighting up a cigarette.

'He is,' said Dar. 'He's the one who found it. Awais, come and say your *salaam*.' He opened his arm and welcomed Awais into its fold.

First the thorn bushes and thistles were cleared. Behind them, a wall. The foreman stepped forward to inspect it. 'Five inches,' he said.

'We're going to be here all night,' said one worker to another.

'What're you complaining about? Think of the pay.'

'The wall is constructed according to a method that's completely different from the way we build walls today,' said the foreman to the municipal officer. He went into a long explanation of materials and methods used. The municipal officer nodded and the foreman smiled. He turned his back on the municipal officer and under his breath said, 'Duffer.'

Sensing the public wanted a show, the workmen took their time. A lot of drama: the flaunting of hammers and pickaxes, and much wiping away of sweat, went into the knocking down of the wall. Someone in the audience began to sing. The workmen stopped; falling onto their haunches, they listened, along with everyone else. Someone brought the workmen a cigarette which they lit and passed around. No one was in a rush today. Slowly, the wall came down, brick by brick, to reveal a gate exactly like all the other twelve – over thirty feet tall. A lull of disappointment hovered in the air. Two workmen, at orders from the foreman, picked up a cloth each and began to clean the mud away from the gate. Where the others were a solid brown, this gate was tinged with sea shades of metal oxide in blue and green.

The municipal officer turned to Dar and said, 'Happy?' then limped back to his car.

'Loha,' whispered Dar. He stepped back to look at Awais. Awais couldn't hold his father's gaze, so lowered his head. Dar saw his friend Shams standing at the back of the crowds and went to say hello.

'My boy did that,' he said. 'Found Loha. Awais, Shams Sahib, is...'

But already someone was calling Shams away.

Late that night Dar and Awais brought the family out to see the gate. Other families were there, too.

'Lost for hundreds of years,' said a man to his wife, 'only to be found by a boy.' Dar smiled. Others, who'd heard it was Dar's son who'd found the gate, came over to hear how the discovery had been made.

Secure behind her *burqah*, where no one could see how hard she was trying not to blink for fear that, if she did, she'd blink red–hot tears, Khurshid looked at the gate and the faces of the people who'd come to see it. They were transformed. Their jubilance wasn't a party-induced merriment that would peter out as soon as they left the site: it went deeper than that, and each man, each woman knew this, she thought, whether they had the words to articulate it or not. Her son had done that. 'So,' she said softly, 'it's finally beginning.' Dar, who'd heard her say something – though what, he didn't know – turned towards her.

By early the next day Awais was big news. All morning, Khurshid answered callers, and at school the other boys couldn't hear Awais's story enough times. Escaping the hordes, Awais found Mitoo crouched in a corner of the playground with three other boys. When Awais appeared, Mitoo put something in his pocket, made a signal to the boys and up they got and wandered off.

'It was you who put the word out?' asked Awais.

'Like it?' said Mitoo.

'No!'

'Then it wasn't me,' said Mitoo and grinned. Mitoo stretched out his hand and Awais who, like everyone else, was helpless against Mitoo, helped him up.

In the days after Loha's discovery, some of the inhabitants of the city began to see that the orderly lines they'd followed all their lives were now not enough. Abandonedness, they'd been taught, led to madness. One touch, one sniff; you were caught. Those gentle on their idiots had chained them in back rooms; others, harsher, had sent them beyond the edge of the city to exile. But now, some people saw that madness was not just a break in reality; it could make reality more keenly felt. They were now scared by how much they wanted to let go. There was digging and searching all over the city. People had thought the inside city complete. At the discovery of the thirteenth gate there was both sadness and joy: sadness for what they had not known, and joy in the certainty they now felt – that the city was finally revealed.

If everyone was busy, no one was more so than Mitoo, who'd developed a system – though Awais couldn't badger out of him how it worked – of receiving gifts in kind, which he distributed with great magnanimity between Awais, Batool, Tanveer, Maryam and himself. 'Tokens of people's appreciation,' Mitoo said, depositing a box of sweetmeats and a box of pencils on Awais's courtyard floor.

'Do you think it's legal?' Dar asked when Mitoo left.

'Don't say such things!' said Khurshid. Dar laughed.

'What do you think?' Khurshid asked Awais once more. 'Are there more gates?' He shrugged. He didn't know. But as a week passed and no new gate was found, his assurance grew, though he kept the feeling in low ebb, just in case. At the beginning of the second week when nothing more had been discovered than the bones of a man with a cardboard tag around what would have been his neck that read 'Ghulam Sheikh', the search was called off.

'But,' said the leader of a gang who'd taken advantage of the newly dug holes to stash his loot, 'we've just begun! They can't stop now.' Other arguments were made, better formulated than this, but they all counted for nothing. It was Mitoo who told them the news. Loha was the city's thirteenth and last gate. The search was over.

Leaving Bhatti Gate, strangers called out Awais's name and asked how he was. Within Bhatti, people began to link their name to his and create stories in which he – and they – discovered something else: not something as important as a gate but something that still had the potential to change lives. It wasn't Awais who told Khurshid all this, but Mitoo.

To become someone who seeks people and whom people seek? They asked him for all kinds of advice; his opinion on everything mattered. To change like this? Khurshid thought. So quickly and so wholly? It must have been in him all along – this facility with people. No one was more pleased than Dar, who measured a man by the influence he held over others.

Awais entered the kitchen and grabbed an apple from the basket. 'Awais...' Khurshid began. He was at the door, and turned back slowly, waiting. 'Nothing,' she said.

His body, so thin for so long, was beginning to fill out.

She wanted him back. This wasn't her boy. But would she, even if she could, be willing to go that far, and tilt back the good fortune that had come so hard their way?

Until Awais found Loha, Khurshid hadn't realised how frail her belief had become, like the link of a chain that has loosened through wear. But now it was back, stronger than ever before.

Days passed and they were all glorious. The excitement she'd first felt had mellowed. It now had to it a constant humming sound.

All week she'd been trying to get Awais alone and then one day he came of his own accord. He walked into the kitchen for a drink. Dar was at work; Maryam, Batool and Tanveer, next door. Awais's class had been sent home because his teacher's father had died. They had stood in the yard as their teacher climbed into the tonga that would take him to the station to catch a train for his village. 'He's always late,' said Awais, finishing his tale. 'We think he'll be late for the funeral, too.'

Khurshid didn't like his tone and on any other day would have upbraided him. She sat on a *piri*, pulling at spinach leaves. There was a sheet of newspaper at her feet for the waste. He looked from the paper to her wrist, on which were a dozen red glass bangles. He drank some water, then sat down on the *piri* opposite. Although he was still shorter than her, his legs were long. Like her, he bent his knees till they almost touched the ground.

She continued to pull at the spinach heads although her movement was slower now. 'Tell me how you found Loha,' she said. He'd told her the story countless times but, nevertheless, told her again. She demanded a detailed description of what he'd seen, how he'd felt. Her hands stilled. 'And it's been here all this time. And no one found it,' she said when he was done.

'It could have been anyone,' he said.

She smiled. 'It's started,' she said. 'Finally, it's begun.' She felt she could look at him now. They were so alike. Only where her hands were square, his were long, the kind of hands, she'd always felt, that should have played an instrument.

'When you were born...' she began. She saw him take in a breath, as if bracing his body for a whipping. She spoke softly.

'What did you say?' he asked.

She hurried on. 'The pir said it would begin with a discovery. And that you would save someone's life.'

'You never told me that before!' he said.

'I did,' she said. 'There's great joy ahead.'

'And danger?' Laughing. And then he saw her face.

The next few weeks were heady. Khurshid's happiness infected them all. They'd never been like this before – seeking each other out.

'Hurry up!' barked Awais, 'Why are you walking so slowly?' Mitoo didn't smirk but looked as if he might. Dar's eyes sought out Khurshid's, but she turned away, robbed of the desire, for once, to watch her son.

Later, when they were alone in their room, Dar said, 'This is your doing. Happy?'

She considered replying that she didn't understand what he was talking about, but she was tired, and anyhow, he'd see through the subterfuge. Yet she couldn't bear to be mocked, not now.

'You were always saying he wasn't confident enough,' she said.

'Amrau…' The name he always called her.

Why did I give up my name? The sound of it now made her restless, skittish. *Must he always remind me of what I've done?*

'What did the pir tell you?' he asked. When her gaze flickered, nervously, towards his, he stared her out.

'Why now? You said you never wanted to know.'

'Tell me.'

Her lips, dry; with one lick grew an immeasurable thirst. Water, she thought. I need water. She contemplated going to fetch some, but she knew that, without any force, he'd got her just where he wanted and could hold her here for ever if he so chose.

'The pir said that Awais would do great things.'

Dar smiled, a good-natured smile, as if they were friends again. 'Is that all?'

It was she who was angry now. *What – doesn't he understand? Or is he being deliberately stupid?* She wanted to hurt him but didn't know how.

'Our son will be a great man,' she said.

His mouth twitched. The irony was back. 'Know what happens to great men? They get shat on – that's what.'

The vulgarity hit her like a blow. *How easily it falls from his tongue, as if I'm no longer a woman, a wife.*

'And that,' he said, his voice sharpened to a dangerous lilt, 'is what you've been telling him all these years?' He snorted. 'Is it any wonder—'

'This is not my fault!'

'It's mine then, is it?' He broke her silence. 'Any more arrogance and... Did you hear how he spoke to Mitoo today?'

'Mitoo would never leave him!'

'Then he's more stupid than I thought.' Dar turned away and began to change his clothes.

Not bothering to undress, Khurshid climbed into bed. Her eyes closed, she heard him discard his shirt, then trousers. Even though he was angry, he folded them neatly and put them on a chair. He opened the cupboard and picked out one of the *shalwar kameezes* she'd hung up for him. He got into bed, and turned his back towards her. She lay awake all night, her throat parched, too exhausted to get up and fetch a drink.

The fever of excitement lasted exactly three weeks. First, someone knocked at their door to tell Khurshid that a baby had died: a healthy baby born to a mother of eight. And then other things – all equally strange – began to occur. Khurshid tried not to panic.

Two days later the municipal officer whose men had knocked down the wall came to call on Dar. Khurshid told the children to go to their rooms.

'No, let the boy stay.' And then turning to Dar, the municipal officer added, 'If that's okay with you?' Dar nodded and invited his guest to sit down and took a seat opposite him. Awais remained standing.

'I'm sorry, Dar,' the municipal officer said. 'I've received too many complaints. Since the gate was opened, all sorts of things have gone wrong. Don't,' he said as Dar began to speak. 'It's not rational. I know it's not. But the wall goes back up tomorrow. I thought you'd want to know.'

'What time?' asked Dar.

'Nine am. Would have done it earlier but the crowd wants a spectacle. Nothing I can do.' They talked of other things, then the municipal officer left. Khurshid returned to the courtyard. She looked at Awais and he went to his room.

'He can't do this, can he?' she asked.

'You heard?' said Dar and sat down again, his head slightly bent to one side. He reached back into his *kameez* and tried to catch a scratch.

'There must be someone higher up who we can approach. It can't be right. The gate is part of the city now. People will complain,' she said. 'Won't they?'

'Amrau,' he said, 'that's just it. People have been complaining. They've been coming to you, too.'

After a brief silence she said, 'Yes.'

'And they've been saying the same things. Oh for God's sake, get this scratch, will you?' She raised his *kameez* and scratched his back. 'Higher,' he said. 'Yes. Ah. Harder.'

'Enough?' she asked. He nodded and she turned to stand before him again.

'It could just be a coincidence,' she said.

'*Now* do you understand why I hate all forms of superstition?' he cried. 'Just because some people believe the gate is bringing evil into their lives! And how ridiculous is that? It's a gate, for God's sake. I even heard one man complain that since the gate was found his hair's begun to fall out! So these people believe – and God knows what the word means for them, anyhow – that the gate is evil; they pass their beliefs on to someone else. Notice how susceptible we are to the lowest of ideas? The ideas a dog would spit at rather than entertain, we hold and wave about, proud because others believe them too. If everyone says something's right it must, of course, be true.'

She stood there, waiting. His face was red, his voice gruff. 'Anyhow, you heard what my friend said. His hands are tied. There's too much bad talk about the gate.'

He left the courtyard, looking tired. She walked over to his chair and, after hesitating a few minutes, sat down. She wanted, for once, to feel what he felt. Her own emotions had become too hard to navigate. That it was over she couldn't accept. This was just a transient phase; she'd weather it out as she'd... Her thoughts turned for the first time that evening to Awais. 'Poor boy,' she whispered. 'My poor boy.' Pity was not an emotion she wanted to associate with her son. Her head blared as if inside it someone was hammering hard pins.

Father and son stood with the others on the path facing the gate, watching it being re-sealed. The municipal officer kept his distance. As the final brick was put in place the crowd grew ecstatic; the workers turned to face them, confused. The municipal officer made a little speech about safety and the will of the people, and then his junior officer shooed everyone away. Dar turned to Awais but Awais stepped back, ready to leave.

'Where are you going?' asked Dar.

'School,' said Awais.

Dar flicked back his sleeve and looked at his watch. Saying nothing, he turned to go.

Awais waited for the workmen and the passers-by to leave, then he approached the wall. He picked up a stick from the ground and wrote the date on the still-wet patch of cement: 1932. He didn't feel sad and he was surprised at that. And then, because he couldn't resist the joke, he added 'AD: Awais–Dar'. From behind the green door of the nearby school he could hear the singing sounds of lessons being learnt by rote. He saw a yellow wagtail swerve in and rest for a moment on the wall. Awais waited but it had come alone. And then suddenly he rushed forward like a pilot with a death wish. The wagtail flew off. Beneath where the bird had sat, he saw something: a mark or a scrawl. It was on a patch of the old wall. He rubbed hard. There were four numbers: one, zero, six, six. Strange, he thought. Then his eyes widened. Just numbers? Or a year in the Islamic calendar? Had someone else done what he'd done? Had the alleyway been found and sealed before? Had someone else – he stopped – had his thoughts? He rubbed at random spots. But there were no other numbers. None, at least, that he could see. The wagtail hovered in the air, waiting for him to go. Awais walked on, and his thoughts turned once more to the *dhol* player who'd led him this way.

Khurshid stood, unnoticed, a little distance away. She watched Awais turn a corner and disappear.

An old woman straightened from her rummage of the gutters. She looked boldly into Khurshid's face, as if daring her to judge. Chin jutting out, pointing to the path Awais had taken, Khurshid asked, 'Is that where Rang Mahal School is?' The woman spat and laughed. 'Over there,' she said, her gaze pointing in the opposite direction. A red fort, but scaled to the size of children, not men. Khurshid couldn't take her eyes off the school. The woman laughed again. Her arms, scaled like a fish, lifted her hoard of salvaged goods to her chest, and she walked away, her gait as loose as a girl's.

In the sky, a beam of yellow light. *Maybe Dar Sahib was right, after all. I shouldn't have changed my name.* Khurshid didn't want to remember. Not from the beginning. Not now.

7

MARCH 1919, LAHORE

12am: the hundreds who passed through the tight gullies of the inside city, their voices always a pitch too loud, as if cultivated in an arena for the deaf, were now tucked away in bed, their dreams mellow, sad, crackling with life. *We live to eat and sleep and dream. The rest is just passing time.* Snaking the city, a wall, ancient in parts.

12.30am: no decent person who didn't belong to the inside city or wasn't visiting family or friends had any business being there beyond this hour. Click, click, the twelve giant gates were locked and twelve gatekeepers set up their *charpoys* – not to sleep but to keep guard.

In a corner house in Bhatti Gate, Amrau, who loved the city's silence, lay awake. Three consecutive nights. What surprised her was how untired she was; in fact, she was the opposite of tired, her body throbbing, alive. Only her eyes were tired. They'd sink into the depths of her skull if she didn't consciously hold them open. Her waiting was nearly over.

At her side, her husband, who, like everyone else, she'd come to think of by his last name, Dar. She didn't want to open her eyes – not yet. If I open them, she thought, I'll never get to sleep. He pulled at the sheet that covered them both. Her feet, extraordinarily flat, left exposed. She didn't pull the sheet back.

When she'd first come to this house, three months ago, they'd slept in their bedroom. But as the heat peaked, more and more people in the inside city brought their *charpoys* out onto the rooftop court-yards. As the houses were stacked together with no breathing space in between, Amrau had felt shy. 'You'll get used to it,' he'd said, but she hadn't, not really. That her neighbours might see her asleep, might see Dar's arm circle her... She shivered.

She felt him move. He hadn't said anything on the subject for the last few days but she knew he wasn't happy. She'd been surprised by just how unmovable his anger could be.

In his sleep, he laughed.

She sensed that he was, with his friends, a funny man. She'd never seen him, of course, in only male company, but she knew from the few incidents she'd witnessed between her father and his friends that men were a different species when they were with other men; with women there were always constraints. She'd seen sparks of Dar's humour once or twice but then he'd reined himself in, embarrassed, as if that wasn't how you were supposed to speak to your wife. He'd said she was funny. She'd blinked rapidly, not understanding. All she'd said was the innocuous 'Shall we eat?' He'd been unable, even when she'd scowled, to stop himself from laughing. How that was funny, she didn't know. She'd tentatively tried one of Dar's stories on a neighbour who'd called, but the woman had just stared her out and, shortly afterwards, left. And Amrau had then known, despite what Dar said, and the yearning in her that those words had fuelled, that she just wasn't funny.

He shuffled again. Her hand went out to lightly stroke his arm. His bigness still affronted her though, even in the midst of her desire.

Hoping, this time, she'd see herself in a better, softer light, she played out the scene, again, in her head.

'You have to be joking!' he'd said.

She'd stood very still, her eyes jet black, eyelashes burning like kindling.

Was *he* joking? He invariably joked and invariably she didn't get it. She'd learnt to smile and hope for the best. So now she smiled but that didn't crack it, not this time. His hands began to move in half–circles, then faster, as if he were building a fantastical animal world: huge horns, quivering tails, two heads – no, three, four.

'You think,' he said, dropping his world flat, hands falling to his sides, 'you really think the future can be mapped and read?'

This is it then, she thought, our first fight. Three months of unexpected bliss and now this. She didn't know what she was supposed to do. She'd never learnt what her sister Munni knew – how to soften a man. Until now, it was something she'd never needed to know. She looked at Dar.

'You think I'm stupid?' she said.

'Don't be a fool, Amrau,' he said.

'The pir has...' she began.

'Enough!' he cut in. Legs apart, arms inching up, he was ready for the long haul. But she didn't want to fight. He couldn't make her.

'I've written to him now, inviting him here.'

'So,' he said, 'write him another letter. And say...'

'He can't come?'

She smiled again. It was meant to be a reconciliation, an exit route if he wanted out. The obedience that had been drilled into her called her to submit. I will, she thought. As soon as this is settled, I will.

'He's told the futures of my family for as long as I can remember,' she said. The look he gave her hollowed her out, as if she were a dog, who, to his command, would keel, lie down. I can't do this, she thought. Then found herself saying, 'He...'

'Tell me, Amrau,' he said, 'what you want me to say and I'll say it.'

She pushed back a loose tendril of hair.

'Well?' he said. To her silence he said, 'Do you really believe...?' He sucked in his cheeks as if ramping up the air he needed to sail. 'Oh, for God's sake, Amrau. What do you think this is: the eighteenth century? It's 1919.' He waited a moment or two then rushed in – as if knowing before he said them that the words were wrong: 'You think your pir can tell what's written in the future? Send him to the English, then. There's trouble brewing in all,' and he scoffed, '*their* lands. They're the ones who need advice, not me.'

How it had ended she couldn't remember. He had left the room a shade prouder, thinking he'd won the argument. He'd thought it all finished. She saw it had just begun.

She hadn't wanted to be cold, not with him, but couldn't in the end help it. He looked surprised, then lost. There are darker shades to everyone, she thought, and as she fell she hoped and prayed this was her deepest realm. And then it was her turn to be surprised: he didn't try and rub her warm. They became, in those days, strangers to one another again. The friction of their first days together as husband and wife, full as they were of anticipation, was replaced with this, a friction altogether bleaker. In the end, he gave up and said the pir could come – if she wanted it so much. As she watched him stumble out of the room, she felt an overpowering sense of a defeat. But after a while, she sat down to write to the pir. And seven days after that, she began to count down the days to when she thought he might arrive.

He's punishing me, she thought, as she turned on her side.

As the first light broke through, she crept out of bed – as if all she'd been waiting for was this permission – and slipped her feet into her *chappals*. She walked to the courtyard boundary wall.

When they'd first brought her here it had been night. Inside, she'd been screaming. She'd wanted to plead with her sister Munni to stay, but Munni had countless family responsibilities to attend to, so in the end Amrau had said nothing. Munni and her brothers Jamshed and Babar left the next day, Munni for Gujranwala, which at least, she consoled herself, wasn't too far away, and Jamshed and Babar for Karachi. Her aunt, who'd brought her up, stayed, and Amrau tried to ignore her presence as she had in all the years they'd abided together. Three days later her aunt and the other guests left as well. At the door, her aunt said to Dar, 'She's a lucky girl. Remind her how lucky she is.' He'd looked at the old woman, surprised, and that had assuaged some of the hurt Amrau had felt.

Dar had taken her aunt to the bus depot and Amrau had been left alone for the first time in her new home. She'd looked out at the city, startled by how ugly it was. Buildings skewering up, wherever you looked. One mad blow, she thought, and they'll tilt, smash. In the streets, as much rubbish as there was space, kicked back to the edges of walls, into gutters, by passers–by. And the smell! She couldn't bear the smell. It was as if the city were one giant hole in the ground for whoever wanted to piss. Although her last years in her village in

Kashmir had been, in so many ways, hard, she missed the sweetness of the air, the unadulterated blue of the sky – even in the heart of winter. And there, around her, not a wall, but mountains. Her aunt had told her there could be none of her wild ways here, no walking off by herself. She was a woman now, a married woman. In her trousseau, three new and unworn *burqahs* – white; they reminded her of the shrouds the dead were draped in before being dropped underground – for ever.

On the street corner two Englishman, smoking, relaxed, as if they were in their back gardens, passing the time of day. A young man began to walk towards them, as bold as brass. He wore a beret, French style. The Englishmen looked at the Indian quizzically, as if he were a strange beast. The young man turned towards them, smiling. Khurshid wondered what he was going to say. The men's faces furious. They made short shrift of the intruder. He pulled his rather ragged army jacket around his breast and walked away. The war had ended last year and Dar had told her that the Indians who'd come back from serving abroad were either overly hopeful – their contribution had to, they felt, be acknowledged, rewarded – or angry as hell at what they'd seen of how the other half of the world lived.

In a distant tree, she spied a crow. She should have recoiled from its sadness, the sense it gave that the world was a bereavement ground, but instead, she laughed. Maybe, she thought, Dar Sahib's right, and I am funny. She smiled and the city responded as it had hundreds of thousands of times before. A city to explore. I'll look at the world from here, she thought, from the height of angels. She looked at the sky. Not morning yet. A cry rent the air, bloodying it. Craning forward, her gaze skimmed the streets – empty still. *A wolf? Something worse?* She spun around to Dar. He hadn't heard it and lay as she'd left him, face down. She leaned further forward, listening. She recalled what he'd told her one night: how, though the twelve massive gates locked them in each night, the city could still be a dangerous place. 'Animals used to roam around here,' he'd said, 'and thieves.'

'And now?' she'd asked.

He'd drawn her in and held her tight. 'Even now,' he'd whispered. Watching her face, he'd laughed.

The street was silent now; even the echo of the cry had drained away. The first knock on the door was faint and had she not been listening so closely she wouldn't have heard it; the second knock was more assured. She picked up her *dupatta* and draped it over her head. She shivered.

She walked down the dark stairwell, though she wanted, as always, to run. Downstairs, she checked her *dupatta* was in place and opened the door. The pir stepped forward and reached out to touch her bent head in blessing. His two assistants stood a little distance away, respectful, waiting.

'We woke you,' the pir said. 'You weren't expecting us so early?'

'I was already awake,' she said.

She led them to their room on the first floor. Had the pir noticed? Her skin had, she knew, begun to gleam and her voice was, she thought, but couldn't be sure, growing deeper, as if she were a boy edging closer to the brink. A boy. She knew she was having a boy. A girl would have defeated everything, so she'd dismissed the idea and spooled a bandage round its skull so it could never be revived. Dar might, she thought, come along one day with a kiss and that would ruin everything. These one or two signs aside, there was no telling, not really, not yet. Her body was still remarkably unfull. But as the *dai* who'd come to see her had said: it was early days yet. She had looked at her with the pity she reserved for all first-time mothers; anxiety always unravelled them in the end. 'The waiting,' said the midwife, with a searching look, 'will be tough, but you'll learn.' *What does she know? Six months is nothing. I've waited three years. Three years, almost.* With the pir's arrival, the first break of time had arrived; the second would come with the birth of her boy, Awais. She couldn't look at the pir yet.

She turned to the pir's assistants who were near buried away in a corner of the room. They'd already begun unpacking. One wore spectacles, and in the place where the lenses should have been were cardboard cut-out no entry signs with blue, rather than red, through–lines on white. His hands, which were fat–fingered, moved adroitly enough, so she didn't know: was he blind or was it a joke, and, if a joke, why? The other assistant was still a boy and so beautiful that to describe him, she thought, would be like chasing the wind. *Beauty is ephemeral, but God, while it lasts...* All she could think of was a man she'd once seen on the street who'd done a magic trick with upturned cups. It had all looked so easy but each time he'd set them up, hiding his stone, they'd been beguiled.

She turned from the pir's assistants to the pir and was surprised, no, taken aback, to find that he was watching her. The pir had been her father's friend and she thought, but couldn't quite remember, that they might be distantly related as well. Something about the *nani* – the maternal grandmother – of all Kashmiris being the same woman. Her second finger stroked a line between her brows. It only now struck her how ridiculous an idea that was.

'Your aunt is well,' he said. She didn't answer.

After her father had died she'd been under the care of his sister, who hadn't wanted her but had taken her in because she wasn't given a choice; the village had seen to that. Her aunt had declined all the proposals from the village and boundary villages that had come Amrau's way, and accepted the first one to come from outside Kashmir.

For the four years she was with her aunt, even right up to her wedding day, her aunt had taunted her. 'Look at your face! Who'll want to look at a face like that?' And now Amrau had, she thought, come to be seen as beautiful in someone else's eyes. She wanted the pir to see this and take the news back to her aunt. The pir smiled, welcoming her forward. She felt as if she were falling down a staircase which had just opened up. She approached him and, at his beckoning, took a seat in front of him on a cushion on the floor. She sat cross-legged and it began to feel a little like school; she tried to swill the feeling down. *Fear's just a state of mind.* She'd read that somewhere – in one of the many Urdu digests her father had devoured and insisted she read. It had seemed meaningful then.

The pir's eyes, which were blue–grey, reminded her of her father's eyes, or, at least, her father's right eye; his left had been, in its brown nearing blackness, the same as all the other eyes she'd beheld, though people told her again and again with wonder and sometimes suspicion that her own eyes were an unmitigated black. The pir looked tired and she wondered for the first time whether he was here just for her or had he, perhaps, other business in Lahore? Now that they faced each other she didn't know how to begin or even if she was the one who was supposed to start. He was her father's age, nearabouts. And she was a woman. These two things compelled silence. But now, she thought, confused, I'm also the host.

'Amrau,' he said, his voice sodden. Embarrassed, he coughed. *He's just an old man. Dar Sahib's right. What can he possibly tell me about the life I want to open up? What did I expect?* Then he spoke again. She sat quite still. He no longer saw her as a child. He told her everything: who'd taken a loan; what whisperings of marriage there were, and even the deaths. *Toba, toba* – God forbid. When he was done and had rebuilt her world, he said, 'Breakfast?' She nodded and left. Upstairs, Dar lay on the bed, much as she'd left him. She pushed open the kitchen door, trying to still her thoughts. She began to roll out the balls of dough for the *parathas*, on the top, a thin circle of butter ghee, the dough strung into a spiral and then rolled out again. As she set the water to boil she went to check on Dar. He was up. She told him the pir had arrived. He didn't say a word.

'Come down and pay your respects,' she urged.

'I don't want to meet him,' he replied. She darted past him and her hand inadvertently brushed his tailbone. She turned to him in apology. His face darkened but not in anger. Her face grew hot. She returned to the kitchen, laid out the tray. As she pushed open the door he took it from her and followed her downstairs.

In the guestroom Dar stared too hard at the pir's albino face, with its peeled and unpeeled skin, said a few words, then went quickly back upstairs. Amrau turned to the *pir*, embarrassed. But he hadn't noticed.

'Strange profession – sales,' said the pir, 'for someone as quiet as Dar Sahib to choose.' That rattled her, but she said nothing.

'Amrau,' he said, 'sit down.' He nodded to his two assistants. The beautiful boy, his head lowered, came forward, picked up the tray, took it to their side of the room. He made the sign of the cross as his companion turned his head aside and then they began to eat.

'Five days,' the pir said, 'that's what I need. Leave us alone till then.'

Five more days, she thought. Five days to break my back.

Today, she thought. I find out today. It was already two o'clock and they hadn't come for her. Whoosh. Her stomach spiked with fear.

She and Dar had come back late last night from a wedding. Dar was sleeping it off. Her shoulders were bent forward. She remembered what she'd overheard. 'She never looks you in the eye – even when you're sitting face to face.' She'd known straight away they were talking about her, so had lingered, hidden, to listen. 'What do you expect, when she's as tall as a man, almost?' The women had laughed. 'She's used to looking over people's heads.' Another woman then said, 'Maybe she's got an affliction of some kind?' At this, the women had gathered the youngest of their children up into alcoves of arms and legs.

Amrau, unobserved, had moved on.

'Amrau,' Dar said, waking up, his voice still soft from sleep. She turned towards him, not smiling, not ready to be cajoled, not yet. Strange that she should feel so weak and need him to hold her. If there were days on earth, not only in heaven, that were a reckoning, she knew this was her first.

'Whatever the pir says,' Dar said, sitting up. She smiled, relieved that he'd come around. He stretched and continued, 'I don't want to hear it.' She blanched. His voice grew colder still – and how, she wondered, had she thought it would be anything else? Looking at her with great deliberateness he said, 'Understand?' He got up, uncreased his clothes with his outspread hand and moved towards the staircase. A few minutes later the front door banged shut. *Something's lost – irretrievably.* She took the last word back and buried it. She couldn't dwell on this now. She went downstairs to the pir's room.

She knocked at the door, hesitant. 'Come in,' the pir called. The rancid smell of the room, which the men hadn't left for five days, hit her hard. In the air, dust motes collided, rebounded.

'I've been waiting for you,' the pir said. He turned to his two assistants, who approached, nodded to Amrau, then left.

She wanted to run upstairs again and never come back. But she'd chosen this, asked for it and now the pir was sitting there, waiting, a huge chart – for which she'd provided dates and names and places of birth – before him. She felt exposed, as if he could see deep into her soul and that it was she who'd given him the tools to do so. How stupid, she thought. No one more stupid than me.

'Sit down, Amrau!' he said, and only then did she realise she was still standing. His face looked stern, she thought. No, soft. She sat down on a cushion on the floor, and looked up, as if he were a teacher who could change her life.

'Is it good?' she asked. He frowned. Her colour changed. She'd pre-empted him and knew, in the moment, that that wasn't right.

'What are you calling him?' he asked.

'Awais.'

He looked down at the chart and wrote the name down. 'Yes,' he said. 'Good.' Schooled by him how to behave, she waited now. Any moment, she thought, he'll speak.

'He's made for great things, your son,' he said.

'Yes,' she said, her voice low, wary still.

'You have to change your name,' he said.

'I thought you liked his name?'

'Not his,' said the pir. 'Yours.'

Her fingers reached for the bare floor. My name? she thought. The name my father gave me? The name which nearly turned our house upside down? A poet and a prostitute's name. How many people love their names like I love my name?

'Change it to what?' she asked.

'Khurshid,' he said. Already it felt branded on her forehead. And already she felt old. Old at twenty-four.

And how would she tell Dar? Though she'd never seen him in a rage, if anything were likely to do it, it was this, what the pir was asking her, no, commanding her to do. Dar had told her late one night that her name was another mark of her beauty. She'd reached out and touched him then, the first voluntary movement towards him she'd made. And from that moment, things between them had changed. By being desired she'd learnt desire.

'Fine,' she said to the pir.

Dar wouldn't understand why'd she'd agreed; why there'd really been no choice. With hardly a sound, she tried rolling the name around her mouth; it was clangy with sharp points.

'Come closer,' he said. She found she couldn't move. *Are they so dreadful, these things he has to say, that he can't say them too loud?* She leaned in.

Dar answered her questions only when it was absolutely necessary. Questions pertaining to food always got answered; very little else. He seemed, she thought, to be enjoying the fight. She felt the onset of rebellion, the desire to do what he did – walk away without explanation and think it a right.

'What's the matter, Amrau?' he asked. 'Didn't everything turn out as you expected?' He heard the mocking tone in his voice and regretted it at once. This wasn't how he'd wanted this day to play out.

'Our son,' she began.

'Our son?' he asked.

'I told you he's going to be a boy,' she said. 'Our boy will…'

'No!' he said, cutting her off. 'You promised… I don't want to hear.'

'Later?' she said.

'No,' he said. 'Not now. Not ever.'

'My name,' she rushed in. 'He said I have to change it.'

'What?' he said.

'Pir Sahib said…'

'Your name?'

'It has to do with the chart.'

'You refused,' he said. He waited, but she didn't reply. 'Tell me. What did you say to him?' he asked.

Finally, she said, 'The name's Khurshid.'

8

APRIL 1919, LAHORE

One kiss for warmth. Two to remember me by. And with the third, possession.

He'd left yesterday after lunch. Today, she had an invitation to a neighbour's house. She didn't want to go. *It's not that I don't like people; it's that they don't like me.* 'If you don't go,' Dar had said, 'I'll know.' How? she thought. How? But she didn't say anything, the frankness between them not having transformed into words.

She went about her work but at a much slower pace than usual. *This listlessness is new.* It made her feel strangely breathless. At three o'clock she began to get ready.

Within half an hour of arriving she'd offended a woman by saying the Khilafat movement of India's Muslims in support of the Turkish caliph was a joke. Wasn't that what Dar Sahib had said? Maybe she'd misunderstood.

The woman said, 'So you think it's all right for the British to destroy the caliphate of Islam?' Not waiting for a reply, the woman walked off to join a large group at the other side of the room. Khurshid was relieved; she wouldn't have known what to say. She thought she saw some of the women look her way. Soon, it seemed, the whole room was giving her a wide berth. And then a sparrow of a woman zipped over to Khurshid and introduced herself: 'Bilquees.'

'Khurshid,' said Khurshid. The name still felt like a rash.

Bilquees took her over; that's how Khurshid later came to think of it. Someone called to Bilquees, and with a smile, she told Khurshid she'd be back. Khurshid wanted to, but didn't, believe her. She watched Bilquees glide across the room. Wherever Bilquees went, people gravitated towards her. And then she was back at Khurshid's side again. 'Jallianwala Bagh,' she said. Khurshid lowered her head, not willing to reveal how little she understood. 'Hundreds killed,' said Bilquees. 'It was just a peaceful protest.' She shook her head. She motioned for Khurshid to come closer. 'They say General Dyer thought it was the 1857 rebellion all over again.' Bilquees looked at Khurshid curiously. 'Amritsar,' she said.

Khurshid flinched. Pir Sahib had left them for Amritsar. When did Bilquees say it had happened? She was too embarrassed to ask. No, he must have got home. He wasn't a political man. Bilquees picked up Khurshid's hand and held it. Khurshid's hand was dry. Bilquees touched the sleeve of Khurshid's *kameez*. 'It's very beautiful,' she said. As Bilquees continued to talk Khurshid thought: she chose me out of pity. That hurt, but nevertheless, she listened to Bilquees with great attention; for some reason, that day, she didn't want to be left alone.

Back home, she sat on the *charpoy*, her feet pulled up, and released her veil. She could feel the breeze only if she remained ever so still; it blew in shafts of hot air but even that was a relief. *I've never had a friend, not like other women have friends.* She'd always been a quiet woman who secretly feared the revelations, big and small, that passed for women's conversation. She could listen but not tell and after a while other women found her reticence suspect and left her alone. In her household, the men had done most of the talking. Her father had been voluble and her eldest brother, always a little mad. Dar's retreats into silence had at first pleased her but then she'd begun to wonder what she'd done wrong. And the wondering led to a shadow-play of fear. She began to unplait her hair. In the growing night light, the tail ends shone in swirls of blue below the ringlets of black.

The next morning, there was a short sharp rap at the door. She opened the door to Bilquees. She wasn't, she realised, surprised.

Like Khurshid, Bilquees was expecting a baby at the end of the year. 'A miracle, this baby,' said Bilquees. Khurshid didn't like to ask. A week went by in which Bilquees, on edge, waited, then said, 'Not a man, my husband. Husband!' She cut and quartered the word. 'But one night... I don't know how...' Khurshid nodded, not at all sure what Bilquees meant. When, later that night, understanding began to dawn, Khurshid blushed. *Why did she tell me that?* Of all the strange alliances, political and economic, that were made that year, none was as strange as that between Bilquees and Khurshid.

Bilquees was interested in everything, and under her influence, Khurshid grew curious about the world, too.

From lowered lids she now watched as Dar read his paper. Was that where the world hid? There were so many questions she wanted to ask but didn't know how to begin.

Dar shook his head and said, 'You'll never believe what this man's written...'

Khurshid tried to listen. It was important, he said. It sounded important. But her thoughts soon flew elsewhere. She'd never had a friendship like this before. This was the first truly intimate relationship of her life. Dar knew – she blushed – her body. But Bilquees knew her, well, deeper than that.

At first, she'd succumbed to Bilquees from something like awe. Then it just became easier to agree. Most of the time, she told herself, she just didn't feel as strongly about things as Bilquees did, so it was hardly worth putting up a fight. By the time she'd realised what she'd done, how much ground she'd actually conceded, it was too late.

She looked again at Dar.

He brought her *phalsay* berries wrapped in a muslin cloth; cut sugarcane for her to chew and chew till all the sweetness had been drained out, barley and raw sugar that would sink to the bottom of a glass like a city of sand when she poured water in. In Kashmir, time had been marked by the seasons. In her new home, it was marked by the season of food.

Even now, when she was this ugly fleshy being, four months heavy with child, he held her, stroked her, till the disquiet that raged within her grew tired.

How do people do it – look at and read faces? Khurshid thought;

faces were tricky things. What compelled her to go on when she sensed Bilquees's reluctance to listen, she didn't know. But she found herself telling Bilquees how it had all begun.

'On my twenty-first birthday, I…' She stumbled, stopped. She had to get the words out. Looking at her lap she continued, 'You've seen those boys who leap out of tongas, their backs arched? They always laugh when they land. That's what it felt like. I knew my life couldn't pass away without meaning, just like that.' She was talking too rapidly but couldn't stop. 'When Dar Sahib lifted my veil and I saw his face, it all became clear. Our son.' She shook her head, 'When Pir Sahib came he said…'

'Said what?' asked Bilquees, raising herself up slightly in her chair.

'I can't say,' said Khurshid.

'Good things?' asked Bilquees, looking down sadly at her own swelling tummy.

But Khurshid wouldn't be drawn into any further revelations. She looked at her friend. *Does she pity me? Think I'm a fool? She's right. Who'd believe a story like that?*

Smiling, Bilquees said, 'A Genghis Khan, then?'

'You think I'd let him ride a horse?'

'Khurshid!' said Bilquees, laughing.

'What's so funny?' Khurshid asked.

When Dar returned Khurshid said, 'The pir said this would be a good year.'

'A good year?' he said, thinking of the fast-moving current of news he'd been following. Gandhi had appeared on the political scene from nowhere and had gained, among the peasants and the artisans, a following that was making the British wary and the Congress ever more watchful. Dar sensed that there was something bigger on the horizon as well.

'A good year?' he said again.

Khurshid pulled at her fingers. Crack of bone after bone. Dar looked at her, surprised. That was a Bilquees thing to do.

Outside, there was a tonga waiting, the horse's head in a sack of hay.

'Nishat Apa's house – is it that far that we need…?' Khurshid said.

Bilquees didn't reply. But I'm a grown woman, thought Khurshid, as her aunt's voice, with its tone of dark foreboding, came to mind.

Bilquees's face. What is happening to her face? 'Where are you going?' a voice called. Bilquees turned to answer, smiling. Khurshid climbed onto the tonga. When Bilquees turned back and saw that Khurshid was already seated, she looked at her strangely. She dropped her veil and climbed on board.

The driver raised his reins and they were off. They approached the River Ravi. Bilquees asked the driver to park for a while. 'This is not where we're going. I just wanted to show you this. You've never been here, have you?' She looked at Khurshid. Silence. 'Khurshid,' she said, her voice urgent now. Khurshid understood and raised her veil. Families in boats laden with baskets of food, brides and grooms, shiny and polite, all on their way to the gardens of Baradari.

At the edge of the river bank, a young boy clutching the hand of his father.

'Look!' said the man. 'The river's alligator.'

'Where? Where?' the boy asked and the man raised him up to his thin shoulders, though the boy was really too old for such hoistings.

'Do you see him? See how fat he's got on the river's fish?'

'Yes, over there,' said the boy but his voice sounded flat, as if he couldn't, in truth, see what his father saw.

Bilquees smiled, dropped her veil, as did Khurshid, and with a word to the driver, they were off.

After a while – half an hour? An hour? – Bilquees spoke to the driver; he brought the tonga to a halt. Bilquees stepped down and proffered her hand. Khurshid ignored it.

After the driver left, Khurshid asked, 'Where are we?'

'It's a theatre,' said Bilquees.

Khurshid looked around. Before them a squat, red-brick building of the kind Dar had told her the English were putting up all over India. Wherever she looked, huddles of men, their eyes boring into her.

'There aren't any women here,' said Khurshid.

'They'll come!' said Bilquees, as if she needed to believe it was true.

Khurshid stuck close to her friend as they entered the building. She looked around. 'No women,' she mumbled.

For a moment, Bilquees looked lost, as if Khurshid had pulled her back from a particularly brilliant line of thought. Then she seemed to collect herself, bought two tickets, and sailed into the hall with the quick judgement she was famous for. She found them two seats all by themselves. As the lights dimmed a man, his moustache curling out like two wings, smelling of mustard hair-oil, stomach extended before him, shirt one button too tight, waddled over to their row. He stood for a moment considering how bold he could be, then sat down two seats away from them. After a few minutes, the curtain rose. The man turned in his seat. His eyes never left them, as if they, and not the people on stage, were the show. For the whole hour of the play, Khurshid was mesmerised by how still her hands lay on her lap. When the lights went on again the man hurried away. Khurshid sat waiting for Bilquees to tell her what to do.

Outside again, as Bilquees arranged for a tonga, Khurshid watched an English woman walk by bow-legged, her eyes sad and tired. The woman whistled at her dog, who was lagging behind, then whistled at her boy, who was further back still. Both dog and boy raced towards her. Bilquees returned to Khurshid's side, then led her to where the tonga was waiting.

Khurshid didn't say anything to Bilquees on the journey home. Just once, her eyes sought out her friend. That strange look was gone, erased. Bilquees sat back, her mouth slightly open, one hand playing with the two gold bangles on her wrist. *She doesn't realise.* For Khurshid, the friendship snapped, just like that.

Her aunt had been right. The city wasn't safe. She wouldn't venture out again, not even if her life depended upon it.

That night, as she lay in bed, she tried to hold her body still. Used as he was to the shifts and shuffles that preceded her settling down to sleep, Dar turned to her and asked, 'Everything all right? Want me to get you something?'

'I'm fine,' she said, 'go to sleep.' She was surprised when, a few minutes later, she heard him snoring. But her mind and body were pulsing. If Bilquees had asked, she'd have said – she had the words all packed and ready – she'd never been in the mixed company of strangers in all her life. But that wasn't it. Not all of it. Not the most important part. Her breathing grew raw. She now knew where she'd seen that look before, the one that had so transformed Bilquees's face as they'd left the house. A man in her village, naked but for a loose cloth over his genitals, chained to a tree. It was the hair that had frightened her the most. It looked as if from birth to middle age no mother had ever brushed it. In his watery eyes, the same look: of imploding madness.

In the realm of beauty, she thought, if there were two forts, of the same dimension, though distinct in design, which would you choose? What if the choice you at that moment made laid the foundation for every single thing that subsequently occurred in your life? She smoothed a hand over her belly.

Since they'd first met, she and Bilquees had spent a few hours of every single day together. When Bilquees knocked on her door in the morning, what would she say?

She cut her loose, like you cut a kite. There was something vicious in the act. Bilquees knocked and knocked, sent letters of entreaty. Khurshid was immune to everything.

Those who came to the house spoke admiringly of the glow of her skin and nodded approval; only the forthcoming birth of a boy child made a woman's face as radiant as that. Khurshid smiled and thought how clever it was of God to have obscured the inner workings of our hearts within bodies that could, if called to, lie so adroitly, without a hint of shame. Sidling over to what she'd come to think of as her corner of the rooftop courtyard, she looked out at the still night and felt the intensity of the cold that tomorrow would bring.

9

From his look of pity, she knew he thought it was Bilquees who had broken with her. She didn't correct him.

Faster than she'd thought possible, she arrived at her due date.

A *dai* was called in to guide the birth. Within an hour, she'd taken over the house. By late afternoon, she came into the courtyard and called out to Dar.

'A boy,' she said. 'Both mother and child are fine.'

He moved towards the *dai*. Her hand opened and he fitted a one-rupee coin into it before she clinched it closed.

'Can I see them?' he asked.

'She needs to rest. I'll bring the boy to you.'

The *dai* came back within minutes, her hard feet clapping on the brick floor, the baby wrapped in a sheet in her arms.

'He's asleep now,' she said.

'Already?' he asked.

'He's a baby. That's what they do.'

'Not just lazy, then?'

She stared at him, reluctant, it seemed, to give him the baby. He opened his arms and she handed the boy over. Dar looked down at his firstborn. The baby was so dark skinned he was almost black. Black like no one in his family, or in Amrau's, he thought.

'Babies' faces change all the time,' the *dai* said, watching him.

He wanted to say, 'But their colour – that can't change.' He handed the baby back.

Two weeks later, Dar told Khurshid that Bilquees had given birth to a boy, Malik, once named and always called Mitoo. Khurshid bent her head and began to pull at her *kameez*, ready to feed Awais. Dar hurried out of the room.

A few days later, he stood at the doorway, unnoticed, watching her adoration of the child. He couldn't help but ask, 'Who do you think he looks like?'

She smiled up into his face, hardly seeing him, he thought, and said, 'You, of course.'

'He looks nothing like me!'

'Who does he look like, then – the neighbours?' He wanted to remain stern but, helpless, laughed instead. 'Come and hold him,' she said and he did. He looked down at Awais and thought he caught a glimpse of something that was him. But he'd grown mistrustful. Hadn't she planted that idea in his head? He handed Awais back.

When Awais wasn't in her arms, she lay at his side, staring at him.

'Amrau,' Dar said, 'aren't you going to get out of bed?'

It had been a whole week now. He'd got so used to the smooth intricacy with which she ran the house that he could no longer fend for himself. Didn't want to either, he thought. He wanted her to do it. But all she did was feed, change and look at the boy.

'He's perfect,' whispered Khurshid. Dar turned on her as if she were mad. She'd managed, with some monumental effort, to pull herself up onto her knees. She was playing with Awais's feet. His sisters had, Dar remembered, been practical mothers – the number of children they'd had had precluded anything else. At Awais's wriggling, she giggled. He left the room, his thoughts suddenly turning from Amrau to food.

Two weeks later, Khurshid's brother and family arrived from Karachi. Jamshed Butt had the energy of a firefly. His wife, a plump young woman with immense resources of patience, could have gathered him up and slapped him between her hands with the same dexterity that made her *rotis* so perfect had she not been permanently occupied in trying to control her four boys. Her sons ranged in age from five to one. They had rapidly grown from being indulgently naughty to completely mad. Khurshid's youngest brother, Babar, had been left in Karachi with relatives so he could study for his exams.

The Butts' youngest boy had had a fever when they'd left Karachi, but Jamshed had convinced his wife it had cleared. She'd agreed to this visit because not only did she know what was due to Amrau – or Khurshid as she now insisted she be called – but she liked her as well. A relationship unique in the annals of sister-in-law-hood, it surprised people all the time; some of the more cruel-minded thought the two women were putting on an act, each trying to out-holy the other.

But the youngest child was not, as Jamshed had claimed he was, completely recovered, and within days of their arrival, his fever transferred to Awais. As one boy grew stronger, the other began to collapse.

'He won't make it,' said the doctor to Dar.

'What kind of doctor is it,' said Dar to Jamshed after the doctor had left, 'who tells you there's no hope?'

Bilquees left a note with someone she considered a friend, asking Khurshid if it were all right to call. The letter was mislaid and the woman was too embarrassed to tell Bilquees, so when Bilquees asked, 'What did she say?' the woman, with complete honesty, replied, 'Nothing at all.'

The pir had told her the first years would be hard. *Once they are past…* She, who'd never listened, not really, to anyone else in her life, grew silent before the mass of advice that was thrown her way. She picked it all up, like a beggar, uncrumpling it and holding it close. *Just let him get better.* But the medicines weren't working. She could see that. When someone suggested she visit the city's most renowned healer, she didn't hesitate, even though she'd been told Roshanay Begum lived in Heera Mandi, the red light district of the city. Her sister-in-law she trusted, but not the men. Her brother Jamshed could never keep his counsel and Dar would say such healers were quacks. So she got her sister-in-law to help.

For one minute, just one minute, she thought of the last time she'd stepped out into the city without the company of a man. Then she put on her *burqah* and called for her sister-in-law to hurry up. She, Awais, her sister-in-law and her sister-in-law's four children were soon huddled into a tonga. As they entered Heera Mandi – she knew they were there from the music that poured out of the houses and onto the streets – she looked out boldly. *Just make him better.*

The first room they entered was packed. When her name was finally called, she pulled Awais close; he hardly moved in her arms. She stepped into Roshanay Begum's private chamber. Roshanay Begum listened to Khurshid's flurry of words. When Khurshid was finished, Roshanay Begum approached. She placed a hand on Awais's head, and looking into Khurshid's face said, 'Pray.' Khurshid lowered her head and waited, but Roshanay Begum, her hazel eyes beginning to glaze, just turned away, as if she were done. Khurshid tried to hold it at bay, the thought that was spluttering for release. No medicine. No cure. She scurried out of the room.

Her sister-in-law said, 'What did she say?'

'Let's get out of here,' said Khurshid. 'You won't tell, will you?'

Her sister-in-law slapped the hand of her eldest away from her second-born. 'Enough!' she said, snarling, then, turning to Khurshid, said, 'What do you take me for?'

Furious as Roshanay Begum's advice to pray had made her – anyone could have told her as much! – that night was the first night since Awais had become ill that she slept soundly. It only took that one instant, and she entered the fold. She'd always prayed, but now her words to God were more slowly spoken. She sent her brother out to buy something for her boy and when he returned she tied the black cord loosely around Awais's neck and pulled the silver *taweez* around till the talisman lay flat on his thin chest. Inside, folded many times, was a square of paper with the words of Surah Yasin to keep him blessed.

'Has she gone mad?' Dar asked Jamshed.

'Ssh,' said Jamshed. 'Now's not the time to say anything.'

In the beginning, as Awais improved, and in those nights when his tiny body was so wracked with pain, she held tight to God. Slowly, the shivering ceased and his stomach began to hold the small spoonfuls of milk she fed him. When the worst danger seemed over, she pushed God back to a corner where he diminished before her very eyes. Awais's fever returned. She now clasped God back to her, vowing never to let go. Awais grew steadily stronger.

The influenza pandemic of 1919 claimed millions of lives. Awais was, Khurshid knew, lucky to have survived.

10

DECEMBER 1931, LAHORE

Since they'd been told the gate was going to be closed, Khurshid had begun to avoid Awais. He shook his head and dismissed any further thoughts of his mother from his mind.

I'll go to Mitoo's, he thought, but when he reached Mitoo's house and passed by without stopping, he realised he wanted this day to himself.

Mitoo's intelligence service – the boys on the street who told Mitoo all the news – had failed. He knew Mitoo would be furious. But he'd been preoccupied with the wrestling at the *akhara*, and his attention on other things had grown lax. Awais walked on. The city was waking up properly now: the shops, the businesses opening, getting ready for a day of startling normality after the fervour of the last few weeks. Who'd have thought anyone would come to long for the everyday? And that it would make them feel a sense of belonging to each other and of ease. He was sinking. He knew he was. His feet leading him on, he turned a corner. He kept his gaze to the ground. He didn't want to stop and talk to anyone, not today, perhaps not ever. He could only imagine how furious his mother would be. She was right, of course. A chance like this came but once in a lifetime. After this, what else could there be?

He stopped and looked around. He'd come somehow all the way back to Bhatti Gate. A few feet away stood a Jain *mandir*. He stopped. The three-towered structure, with its central dome and conical roof, had been newly washed and was festooned with garlands. A young man sat on the steps, a *dandasa* root in his mouth with which he was cleaning his teeth. Awais took off his shoes, ready to go in. The man sprang up and collared Awais, twisting one of Awais's hands behind his back.

'Ow!' cried Awais.

Pocketing his root, the man said, 'What, are you a girl?'

'Let me go!' said Awais, struggling to get free.

'Easy does it, my lion,' said the man smiling. He peered close into Awais's face and said, 'You don't look like a Jain.' He sniffed Awais. 'Don't smell like one either, which means...' He pulled at Awais's arm. Awais clamped down on his lips, refusing now to cry. 'Hmm,' said the man, examining Awais as if he were a novel species he'd found. He was gearing up to something when an older man stepped out of the temple, a hurt look on his face.

'Ram,' said the man, 'what's all this noise?'

'He was trying to get inside.'

'Yes, so?' Awais turned slightly and the man spotted the clasp Ram held him in. 'Ram,' he said. With one last pull, Ram let Awais go. 'I'm the priest of this temple,' the older man said, addressing Awais. 'Can I ask what it is you want?'

'To look inside,' said Awais, 'if that's all right, *panditji*.'

'Why?' asked the pandit.

Awais didn't know what to reply.

'You just want to have a look?' Awais knew he'd been let off the hook. He nodded. The pandit opened one arm and led Awais in.

'Want to hear about the temple's history?' the pandit asked. Awais nodded again. 'Know anything about Jains?' he asked.

Awais, eager to show off, said, 'It's a branch of Hinduism.'

'No,' said the pandit, laughing. 'Come on in.' They walked into the four-column alcove and entered the central chamber.

'Is that one of your gods?' asked Awais, as they stood before the immense sitting Buddha.

'No, we don't have gods. It's the Buddha. He was a prince who left it all behind, all his palaces, his gold, his servants, to become a holy man.' He looked at Awais closely, then said, 'Before he became the Buddha he was a prince – Siddhartha – but a prince who found no pleasure in the world and had yearnings for higher things. Sitting beneath a tree one day, he heard a voice. That voice said: "I'm the world within which the world seeks the world. I am both attention and love but above all, it is compassion which awakens me." "And compassion is?" asked the Buddha. But the voice was silent. Would he ever hear that voice again, the young man thought? He rose, and though the future that now lay ahead of him was harder than any he'd conceived before, his heart was the lightest it had ever been. Smoothing down his tunic, he began his travels.' The pandit paused, then said, 'And it's his way we follow.'

'Are there many Jains in Lahore?'

'Hardly any, any more.'

When Awais came out, his countenance had changed. He looked from the pandit's face back to the temple.

The pandit smiled and said, 'You'll be back.'

'Yes,' said Awais.

Awais walked on, looking at the large Hindu houses with their outspread balconies, so unlike the homes he knew. He then began to run, and because running always made him think of Mitoo, he wondered again what his friend was up to. But still, when he spotted a few of Mitoo's spies ahead, he didn't wave to them or even acknowledge the signals they sent his way. And now he was running like a madman, not from something or to something, and with his mind a blank. His thighs began to ache. His lips turned dry. He licked them again and again. He saw a café and stopped. He asked for a glass of water. Then he began to walk, slower now.

He reached Wazir Khan mosque. He took off his shoes and marked where they were: near a pair of cobalt–blue *chappals*. He walked up the steps. As he reached the courtyard, his feet began to tingle. He looked down, then up. He hadn't noticed it till now but it was a sparkling day. He watched – as he always did – the light at play on the mosaic frescoes that adorned the archways. On the roof, a bevy of birds: pigeons and crows, ghettoed off from one another, some chattering amongst themselves, some looking sullenly away into the distance. A tabla began to play. Awais walked over to the old banyan

tree where a woman, cloaked in a shawl, her face hidden, was sounding out her voice, getting ready to sing,

Cross-legged, Awais sat somewhat removed from the other wor-
shippers. The woman began to sing. She tried to break the beauty of
her voice in order to harness it to the pain of her song, but her voice
bore up the pain and transformed it; from two things, it became one:
beauty and pain conjoined. When she was done, Awais wished he
had money to offer her like the other men did. He stood up and then
helped an old man up.

It was growing dark. He felt so tired, too tired to run any more,
too tired even to walk. He bent his head to his knees and when he
pulled himself up again, one foot slipped back. He smiled. It was sign
enough. His body was telling him what to do. With sudden energy,
he began, somehow, to run.

He reached a green, leafy hedge. It was an uncommon sight in this
city of cement and brick. In the distance he could smell his mother's
favourite plant, whose aroma only broke loose at night – Raat ki
Rani – Queen of the Night. It had a cloying, unforgiving smell. He'd
never liked it.

'All I have to do,' he thought, 'is look over the hedge and those
who called me this far will be waiting, ready to tell me any story I
want.' He sat down on the stump of a tree, smiling. Any minute now,
he thought.

Then after a while, he thought, my bum hurts. No one had come,
aside from an old man who'd stopped, looked to see what Awais was
looking at, stared at Awais, spat. Drops of purple-red juice from his
paan sprayed Awais. The man apologised, then left. Awais, wiping at
his trousers, laughed quietly.

He stood up and, head bent to the path, he walked home.

Maryam was sitting on a *charpoy* with her sisters when her body
began to shake. Her eyes glazed over, as if she were looking far,
far away. Batool put a nervous hand on Maryam's shoulders. The
tremors began to ease. From the corner of her eye Batool saw Tanveer tentatively smile. Batool began softly kneading Maraym's shoul-

ders. A convulsion ripped through Maryam's body. Batool's hand flew away. Another convulsion. Maryam fell back, collapsed.

'*Ama!*' cried Batool. Tanveer was crying.

Batool turned to her sister and said, 'Go get *ama*.' When Tanveer didn't move she poked her and said, 'Go!' Tanveer leapt off the *charpoy* and went in search of their mother. Batool bent over Maryam, words of prayer on her lips.

'Tanveer! *Ama!*' screamed Batool. She soaked up what she could of the foam with her *dupatta* and then placed the dry end under Maryam's chin.

The whole family appeared, with Awais just ahead of his mother and Tanveer and Dar following. Awais ran to Maryam's side. Batool conceded her spot and Awais clambered on to the *charpoy*, sitting behind Maryam, his hand reaching out to stroke back her hair. He looked from his sister to his parents, pleading. Khurshid and Dar knelt before Maryam's bed. Khurshid picked up one of Maryam's hands, while Batool sent Tanveer to fetch some towels. The foam had stopped spitting out of Maryam's mouth. Maryam's eyes flitted to her brother, then closed.

'What is it?' Khurshid asked Dar, terror in her eyes.

'I think it's...' Dar began. 'I'm not sure. I've never seen it... I think... epilepsy—' He looked at his prostrate daughter; the spasms had ended but her body shivered intermittently. Tanveer returned with the towels and she and Batool wiped Maryam clean.

'She's freezing,' said Awais.

'Get a blanket,' said Dar and Tanveer ran off again. 'I'll go and fetch a doctor,' Dar said.

'No,' said Khurshid, 'there's a healer...'

'Amrau!'

'She saved Awais's life,' she said. He stared at her; one more piece of the puzzle that didn't fit.

'All right. Where does she live?' he asked. She didn't answer. 'Amrau?'

Her head lowered, she said, 'In Heera Mandi.'

'You took my son to the red light district?' he said in disbelief.

'Well then, come on, Awais.' Awais kissed the back of Maryam's hand, unwound himself and stood up.

'But you can't take Awais there!' said Khurshid.

'Why not?' asked Dar. 'You already did.'

Dar and Awais left for Heera Mandi.

When they'd finished telling her what had happened, Roshanay Begum said she couldn't accompany them as she had a houseful of clients, but she gave them a small bottle of medicine and told them how to administer drops on Maryam's tongue three times a day. Dar asked whether Maryam would be cured but Roshanay Begum didn't reply. Then she said, 'You must never leave her alone.'

One of Roshanay Begum's assistants rushed to her side to whisper in her ear while another led Dar and Awais to the door.

Other epileptic attacks followed this one. But they were less violent, and Maryam's recovery time was faster. Awais volunteered to take responsibility for making sure they were always well-stocked with medicines. He didn't want to think what would happen if they ever ran out.

11

'I've found the perfect place!' Mitoo said, bursting into Awais's room.

Awais had been kneeling by the bed, using it as a table. He rolled up the sheet of paper he'd been examining and tucked it under the bed.

'What's that?' Mitoo asked.

'Nothing. What perfect place?'

Mitoo said, 'Just wait.'

When he left, Awais unrolled the sheet again. No one had noticed the new tenor of Awais's quietness and Awais didn't bother to explain how he now spent his free time. Mitoo thought Awais was doing what he always did: studying. Awais's sisters thought Mitoo was the raconteur of adventures that their brother also shared. Meanwhile, Awais's journeys were taking him deeper and deeper into the inside city. Each building that seemed to have been randomly built, to have sprouted up in a matter of days or weeks, each change in shape and colour – all fitted. The buildings were giving form to his map. It had started with the lane that had led to Loha and had grown from there. His first maps were nothing more than a few badly drawn lines. And then he learnt to see better. To map a city? A whole city?

So strong was this desire, he felt he had to control it somehow. Or else he'd be out on the streets all the time and then someone would be bound to find out. Two days a week – that's all. That's what he'd limit himself to, he said.

The inside city, now that it had opened up to him, seemed immense. I'll never find out all its secrets, never draw them up on my map, he thought. To begin with, his mapping was random. He went to a place, wrote down, sketched, tried to memorise how things were fixed, and then returned home to try to draw accurately what he'd seen. One day, about three weeks after he'd begun, out on his wanderings he heard laughter. He turned. He'd thought he was alone. A group of young boys were poking each other. One boy, a twig in his hand, was considering what Awais had been looking at. His twig swirled madly on the ground. The other boys came flying towards him and, with skids and jumps, mussed up his mud drawing. The child began to cry and then, staring at the boys, joined in, laughing; mud and gravel bursting everywhere. From that point on, Awais left his copybook at home. He looked, closed his eyes and tried to see if a picture would stick. Once he thought he had it he'd go home. But all it took was for someone to say something, and the pictures floated away and no trying could bring them back. It took him nearly a month to learn how to hold them in his head. But, once he'd learnt, he forgot why he'd thought it so hard.

'Teach me?' he said to Mitoo, pulling out some paper from under the bed.

'Why?' said Mitoo.

'Just because.'

'Go and get something,' commanded Mitoo.

'What?'

'I don't know.'

Awais left and brought back a plate of fruit. Mitoo scoffed a banana, then two, and then positioned the apple on the empty plate. They began.

'Look, it's not round. It has a flat base!' said Mitoo, looking at Awais's drawing. 'Are you sure you want to...?'

'Yes,' Awais said.

'Then look.'

'I'm trying, Mitoo.' But Awais couldn't see the way Mitoo saw.

'Anything special you want to draw?' Mitoo said after a week of their drawing fruit.

'Buildings,' Awais said.

'Buildings?'

'Yes,' Awais said, 'houses, shops…'

'I know what buildings are!'

Looking one day at a drawing Awais had made – a temple – Mitoo said, 'Not bad.' Awais grinned. He had maps now, drawings, and lots and lots of notes.

Just outside the inside city, at the top end of the Mall, he turned right into the Punjab Public Library. It had been his best ever find. He raced up the steps and into the library; he loved everything about this building: its solid mahogany doors, its tall glass windows, and the possibilities it contained. He found some new books on British Raj architecture, and some older ones on the early Mughal style, but nothing on the period that fell in between. He went to the librarian's desk.

When Awais finished his request, the librarian, a temp or a new boy who didn't know who Awais was, was at first reluctant to leave his seat, which it had taken him hours to get warm. But he couldn't, in the end, hold out against the barrage of Awais's enquiries and so went down to the cellar where the less popular books were kept. He asked Awais to wait and, though he knew exactly where the box he'd come to fetch was, he dusted a stool, put one foot on it, like a film hero he'd seen, and smoked three cigarettes in a row.

'Bastard,' he thought, 'for making me come down here. For making me…' And so on he fumed until a good half-hour had passed. He then picked up the box and went upstairs. He'd expected – no, hoped – that the boy would be angry or, better still, have left. But the bastard was, he saw, still there. Giving him a thorough look up and down the librarian thought: he's ordinary enough – thin, lanky, black.

'Well,' the librarian said, 'going to help me or what?' and Awais took the box from him. It smelt of cigarette smoke.

'Can I…?' Awais asked, looking up the stairs.

'Why do you think I nearly broke my back bringing it up here? Well, go on, then. But remember, I know how many books it contains,' he lied.

Carefully, Awais climbed the steps into the reading room. One old man sat with his head deep in a newspaper, his finger and eye reading together. And in another corner there were two boys giggling over something they'd found. On seeing Awais, one pulled at the other; they turned and showed Awais their backs.

Awais set the box on a large, polished table. Standing, he emptied it, piece by piece, of its contents. The books were dusty, some mildewed. He looked around and then went downstairs again.

'A cloth?' shouted the librarian. 'What do you think this is?' He stopped then said, 'Your home? A shop?' Awais waited.

'Here,' the librarian said, and, digging deep under his desk, he handed Awais a cloth that was even dirtier than the books. Awais took it, held it out and gave it a good shake.

'Over there!' the librarian said, pointing to a tap. 'Wait till it dries before you use it.' Awais nodded. He rinsed the cloth, wrung it and climbed back up to the reading room. He put the cloth out to dry on a chair while he began sorting the books into piles: interesting, possible, useless. Some were so old he feared to turn their pages. Under the whirr of the ceiling fan, the cloth was soon dry and Awais began to clean the books, watched by the two boys whose book had yielded, for now, all the pleasure it could. Soon, he was ready and could begin. He took out his notebook and his pen and started to read.

Lahore's inside city was the only walled city in the world with thirteen gates. All the others had twelve. Was the thirteenth gate a joke, a mistake, or did it have some meaning in the past, he thought?

As he read, his wonder grew. He'd never thought of Lahore this way, as a city of gardens as well, but yes, he realised, these writers must be right. There were gardens wherever you looked and each revealed an identity as clearly as a face: Mughal, British. He'd never considered *history* in terms of style. He thought of the buildings he was mapping. Before he'd begun to look, he'd thought of the city, if he'd thought of *the city*, as fixed in time. But now he saw it too craved change. He had started to be able to tell which buildings were ready to fall, their centres seeming to give. From weariness to the final end was but one step. He could also tell, before the land was cleared, where new shops and houses would be built. That land seemed to attract a particular quality of light, a sweet, soft light.

Silence teaches you what words can't, he thought. In the midst of the city and all its noise Awais learnt to hear silence.

He stood before a blackened building. It had burnt down the night before, though no one knew how, or whether the fire had been started deliberately or by accident. One of the younger boys who'd once tailed Awais told him the news.

The boy had been lingering outside Awais's house, his face thin and earnest. His words came fast. Finished, he stood waiting, his little body stiff with expectation, but Awais didn't know what to say. The boy's head cocked back, as if he'd heard something Awais had missed. He rushed off.

How did the boy know? Are others watching me as well? He ran to Delhi Gate. There were people there, too. Young and old, men and children alike. A boy was trying to pull out the scorched beams of wood.

'Idiot!' a man shouted. 'Leave it alone. Do you want the whole thing to collapse?'

The boy grinned, whistling as he swaggered back to his friends.

Awais was close enough to touch the building now. He walked around its dying shape. He couldn't tell what it might have been.

'A warehouse,' said a man who suddenly appeared on Awais's right. The man smiled, his hennaed hair shining bright in the light.

'A warehouse?' Awais said, again looking at the building.

'Anyone called the police?' a man asked.

'The police?' another said and laughed.

'And the owner?' Awais asked.

'He's gone.'

'So he...'

'Never make rash judgements, Awais,' the red-haired man said. 'It can cost...'

'You know my name?' Awais was alarmed.

'We met the day they revealed Loha. Remember?'

Awais remained noncommittal.

'Come and join me for tea,' the man suggested. 'It's not far.'

'I have to get back,' Awais replied.

'I hear,' the man said, as if weighing his words, 'you've been asking about the city's stories.'

'You know?'

'My name's Shams.'

'I've heard my father speak of you.' Awais looked up into the man's face with a new respect.

'Your father and I've been friends since class three. He should have brought you to see me a long time ago. But never mind that now. Hurry up, Awais.' Shams began to walk ahead and Awais, slow to understand, watched his retreating back. He shook his head and rushed to follow.

Shams stopped before a tree, its bark slanted as if made by a human hand, its leaves lean.

'The ashoka,' he said. 'The Buddha's tree.'

'I've heard of him!' said Awais.

'Yes,' said Shams, 'you went to a Jain *mandir*, I was told.' The vague sense of fear Awais had felt was returning. Had he done something he oughtn't? Would his father be angry? Would his mother find out?

'The Buddha lived here?' Awais asked.

'Years ago.'

'In the city?'

'The city, Awais,' Shams said, 'wasn't always a city, you know.'

They arrived at Shams's house. Shams pushed at the wire-meshed door and they entered and took off their shoes. The room was thick with carpets, each one overlapping the next. A stained pistachio-coloured cloth hung over the window to keep out the sun. And piled high in one corner of the room were files and files. They looked dusty as if once placed there that's where they'd remained, untouched, for years. What kind of business did Riaz-ud-din Shams run? Shams pointed to a corner and Awais sat down. Shams left the room and Awais heard voices. Shams returned and then sat down, opposite Awais.

'Do you follow the news?' asked Shams. Awais shook his head. 'You should,' said Shams. Awais looked perplexed. 'In a few years we'll have our own dominion and then, who knows? Listen to your father. That's not just me telling you to respect him – which, of course, you should.' Shams was suddenly serious as he said, 'That radio he always listens to. That's why you need to listen to your father. You understand me, Awais?' Awais nodded although he understood nothing.

'To live within a city, Awais,' Shams said, 'is to live within history.' Awais sat very still.

'History isn't only marked by events,' Shams said, 'it's marked also in bricks and stone.' Shams was watching Awais's face.

'Shall I go on?' he said.

Awais nodded.

Politics, politics everywhere. On the radio, in the papers. People recalled past hurts, petty things whose sting should have died long ago, words spoken in haste, and politics gave them an assembly of reasons to hate – all anyone had to do was pick and choose.

In the heat of midday, an untouchable walked the streets, casting his shadow and inflaming passers-by with fear. They rushed back to their homes for a great purge. Water had never been so lavishly employed. Meanwhile, a boy and a girl, aged twelve, who'd played with each other since they were two, and who were shining with the first waves of romance, broke apart because of what his father said about her family's faith. He'd reported it back to her, like he reported everything else; neither understood the words in their entirety but she knew where her greatest alliance lay – wasn't family everything, she'd been told? A cow queened the streets, fearing no man. Her eyes shot with blood as the dagger swept silkily through her throat. And buffeting all this were the voices of politicians. A man walked the streets and claimed he could discern, and for a price, reveal, whose voices were sincere, but nobody believed him.

That's all it took, for the imaginings of a people to grow rough and soiled. Cynicism spread like a disease. There were shards of hope but they felt, sometimes, a little cold.

For all Awais's own explorations, it was Mitoo who took him to what would become one of his favourite spots, a place he'd return to again and again whenever he needed to be alone. Though it was outside the inside city, it was where most Lahoris would end up: the graveyard of Mianni Sahib. At the gate, sellers of red rose petals and burnt-orange marigold necklaces sat in a respectful silence, their carts spread with cloths of holy green; worry beads and talismans engraved with the words of God, blessed and sanctified, hung from their necks; their lips were brown-red with *betel* juice, and all around was the strong smell of incense burning. Here the dead were forgotten every day of the week except Thursdays and holy days. A little token – a stone, a stick – was sometimes all there was to mark a grave, but even where there were headstones marked with names and dates, the right prayers were sometimes said by total strangers over the mounds of other strangers. The dead did not stir nor offer any reproach.

'Well…' Mitoo said, looking around.

'If this is where the dead go, burn me.'

'Like a Hindu?'

'Why've we come here?' Awais asked.

'Wanna look around?'

'No.'

'If I listen to one of your stories?'

'As it happens, I've got a book in my bag.'

'What are the chances of that, eh?' Mitoo said. 'What's it about?'

'A poor boy who's made into a prince.'

'A true story, then?'

'Want to listen or not?' Awais said, and Mitoo nodded and sat down on a mound. 'For God's sake, get up! That's someone's grave.'

'I don't hear them complaining…' Awais turned sharply away. Mitoo moved to sit elsewhere. 'All right.'

Awais began to read.

'…And it was said that all those who had died would one day rise again.' Awais closed his book.

Mitoo, who'd been waiting for Awais to finish, ran to pick up the two empty melon–skin halves he'd spied at the foot of a nearby tree. He put one on Awais's head and one on his own. Red juice trickled down their faces; Mitoo licked and Awais brushed the juice away.

Then Mitoo began leaping about. Watching him, Awais didn't feel twelve. He felt a hundred.

'Come on, Awais, run, we're in the army, hiding in this graveyard. I can hear the march of approaching feet.'

'Probably the family of the man whose grave you sat on.'

Mitoo prodded Awais with a twig he'd found and was holding like a rifle.

'Coming or not?' he said, and began to run. Awais followed, dragging his feet.

It was late when the tonga brought them home. Awais was halfway up the steps when he heard shouting. And although he knew he shouldn't, he stood on the landing leading to the courtyard and listened.

'What about the girls?' Dar said.

'What about them?' Khurshid replied.

'Amrau, you know what I mean.' Dar's voice sounded bereft. 'Awais,' he said. Awais held his breath. 'You have no time for the girls.'

'Everything's fine,' she said.

Awais thought he heard his father sigh. 'They're raising themselves, Amrau…!'

Awais waited but there was nothing else to hear.

Later that night she came to his room and stood in the doorway, thinking him asleep. Awais lay there all fired up. *Abba*'s right, he thought. What's she doing just standing there? Why doesn't she leave? Just go? He raised his lids so that his eyes were tiny slits through which he could spy her out. She was dressed all in white. And he hated her too for that. What reason did she have to be dressed as if in mourning? He closed his eyes. It was a full five minutes before she left.

12

OCTOBER 1933, LAHORE

Dar entered the courtyard and the girls rushed at him, demanding their presents. He held one high, laughing, and said, 'Whose is this?'

'Mine,' shouted Tanveer and, leaping, tried to grab her present from her father's outstretched arm. Frustrated, she said, 'Oh,' and he lowered himself slightly, smiling. She reached out again and this time got hold of her gift and ran off. He offered Batool hers in his open palm. She took it, thanking him.

'And you?' said Dar, hoisting Maryam onto his shoulders. 'What's your gift?'

'I don't know,' she said, sad and wan.

'We'll have to look, then, won't we? Coming down!' he said. He grabbed her legs, she began to giggle and upside down she went. She rolled over and righted herself. 'Could it be this?' he said, producing a pink ribbon from his jacket. She shook her head. 'No,' he said, 'what was I thinking of?' He reached in his pocket again and brought out a wad of receipts. 'Not yours?' She shook her head once more. Crouching at her side, he brought out a small jewellery box.

'Open it,' he said. Inside, a little bird as real as any likeness could be. 'You have to wind it up,' he said and showed her how.

'Music,' she said in awe. They waited till the tune had finished and then Maryam carefully closed the box and held it to her chest. 'Thank you, *abba*,' she said. Batool approached. '*Apa*,' said Maryam, 'did you see my little bird?'

'Come on,' said Batool and led her off.

Dar got up from his haunches and turned to Awais. 'So, my boy, ready for your present?'

'Yes, *abba*,' said Awais. Dar pointed to a chair. Awais sat down while Dar remained standing.

'The town was like a playground, a fair,' said Dar. 'Have we been to a fair? I can't remember.'

'Last year.'

'That's right. They say that under the town is buried a maze so fantastical that no one who goes down can ever find their way out, however long the string they pull.' Dar stopped to see if Awais was listening. On Awais's face, a glow. Dar continued, 'Did you see Maryam's music box? The little bird comes from that town. I didn't take him: he dug into a hole in one of the trees, brought out this box, and told me I should open it. Of course, he couldn't speak! This is not some children's story. He just got his message across to me somehow. I opened the box, he hopped inside and began to sing. In that town, even the trees sing. What are you smiling for? Don't you believe your old father?'

Khurshid came in then. 'Don't fill the boy's head with nonsense.'

'Nonsense, me?' said Dar, turning on her with venom. 'Couldn't you give me one minute with my boy?'

'He'll believe—'

'Just one minute. That's all.' She began to reply when he said, 'Leave it, Amrau. You don't see it, do you? Don't see when you're wrong.'

'I'm not wrong,' she said, the words barely above a whisper.

'First time in months I've…'

'*Ammi*,' said Batool, running in, 'is everything all right?' Behind her, Maryam and Tanveer.

'Awais,' said Khurshid, 'take the girls out. I want to talk to your father.'

Batool said, 'But it's night time!'

'Ssh,' said Tanveer and pulled her away to get ready. Maryam put her hand in Awais's and they waited for Batool and Tanveer to return.

'Come back quickly,' shouted Khurshid down to them as they were about to open the front door.

'What's the point of us going if we have to come back so soon?' asked Tanveer.

Batool nudged her. 'Be quiet, Tanveer. Have you got no sense?'

'No,' said Tanveer, looking out at the street and beginning to skip. 'Out in the night time!'

'Actually,' said Awais looking at his watch, 'it's just half-past six.'

'That's still two hours later than I've ever been out,' said Tanveer. 'Where are we going?' Both she and Batool looked at Awais.

'A surprise,' said Awais.

'Is there food at the end of this surprise?' asked Tanveer.

'You always think with your stomach!' said Batool.

'What else do you want me to think with?'

Awais noticed that Maryam was looking up.

'What you doing?' he asked.

She didn't answer for a while, then said, 'Counting.'

'Counting?'

'Yes,' she said, looking up again.

'What a silly baby,' he said.

'I'm not a baby!' she said solemnly.

'Sorry, sorry, little girl. Silly little girl. Is that okay?'

'Careful!' she shouted, and he smiled. But she pulled at his hand and he saw what she saw. Tanveer was about to walk into a cart.

'Tanveer!' he shouted. Just in time, Batool managed to pull Tanveer back.

'*Ya Allah*,' said Batool.

'Don't pretend to be *ammi*. You're not our mother!' said Tanveer, pulling herself free of her sister's hold.

'Think we should go back now?' asked Awais.

'But you were going to show us something, Awais *bhaia*,' said Tanveer.

'That was before you decided to collide with a cart,' said Batool.

'*Apa*,' said Tanveer, 'I was not...' Turning to Awais, she pleaded, 'Awais, *bhai*...'

'Okay, then,' he said. 'Come on.'

They were late coming home but their parents, sitting on opposite sides of the courtyard, didn't say anything.

This time it was Awais who laughed. Khurshid just didn't understand. Almost eight years between them. What could they possibly have to say to one another? She felt the old anger rise but then something about Maryam's face in that instant, in that light, put a hold on all that. I haven't done right by her, she thought. Batool and Tanveer, she'd at least given some time to, but Maryam, none.

Why she suddenly remembered the deaths she'd been witness to, she didn't know. First, when she was only eleven – her mother. Her *ama's* look of shame as she'd fallen to the ground. By the time her father grew ill, both Jamshed and Munni had left Kashmir to begin their new married lives. Jamshed had taken Babar with him and raised him as a son.

Her father's getting ill hadn't happened in one fell blow but slowly, as if his body were still deciding which way it would go. His knees and then his bones. From his mouth, the odour of flowers gone to rot. His sister came over to help when the illness began, a woman of inestimable control who'd buried a husband and five children and yet had still come out intact. The village didn't give Amrau time to mourn her father; they pushed her to her aunt's house. Amrau had never noticed it till then, when she went there to live – the pervading smell of death. She began to crave life, a life with no fixed points but with infinite possibilities. Women didn't have any real choice. She agreed with her aunt. What Amrau wanted, her son would give her. For the first time in her life she felt like any other girl and couldn't wait to get married.

Maryam laughed. Khurshid looked again towards Maryam and Awais, trying to soften her heart. Tomorrow, she thought, I'll fix it tomorrow.

'Where's Awais?' Khurshid asked as she entered the courtyard.
   'Must have gone to Mitoo *bhai*'s.'
   'And Maryam?'

'I'll go and look for her,' Tanveer said, getting up.

'No,' Khurshid said, 'I'll go.'

Khurshid checked the girls' room, Awais's room and then her own. Her temples throbbing from the headache she hadn't been able to throw off all morning, she climbed down to the guest room. No, she wasn't there. Then on to the round room, with its one curved wall. Maryam had to be there. There was nowhere else to look. As she pushed open the door, her back automatically straightened. Only formal guests were led to this room. She'd spied Awais working here from time to time, and although she didn't like it, she couldn't object: it was the quietest place in the house. She looked around: as always, on the sofa and cabinets, sheets, to keep them dust free. She spotted her in a corner, her head bent over some books.

'Maryam,' she said, 'look at your dress!' Maryam, scrunching her eyes, looked up. 'Just look,' Khurshid said.

Maryam's hands went to her Eid dress, blotting it even more with ink.

Khurshid approached and said, 'Didn't you hear Batool call? Lunch is ready.'

Maryam closed her book. Khurshid knew Maryam couldn't have heard Batool, not from this point in the house. But she wanted Maryam to say something. Her gaze dropped to the name on the book. She bent down and grabbed it.

'What're you doing with Awais's book?' Khurshid brushed her right hand down her *kameez* to clean it before opening the copy-book. The numbers were newly dry. They glistened horribly at her. She looked from the book to Maryam's rapt face. She put the book back down and softly said, 'Come up for lunch.'

Khurshid left the room, not turning to see if Maryam was following behind. She heard the hard click-click of Maryam's new Batla shoes behind her. Lunch was a silent affair. And when it was over, Khurshid went to her room to lie down – an unheard of thing for her; she was not a woman who held with indulgences.

Back and forth, the pir's words. A promise. That's what he'd said. A promise of greatness for her son. Now all the things she'd been taught came back to her in shards. The Prophet's sense of justice.

And above that – his acts of forgiveness. To forgive. She couldn't do it. Everything would sink if she were to forgive. The bitterness was leaving her out in the cold – away from everyone, even Awais and Dar. Again, that image: Maryam, her head bent over Awais's book. She fingered the glass bangles Dar always bought for her. Today their cling-cling sound brought no comfort.

The fan turned slowly, hardly slicing the air; she tried not to think. It was getting on for two in the afternoon when her eyes, so heavy, finally closed. She was running, running like mad. In her middle, a ring-shaped hole and in the hole, a child, four or five, cumbersome, squirming, trying to find the perfect spot. If she fell... *I won't fall.* She surfaced from the dream twice, her heart aflutter, and then she fell into a deep sleep. When she awoke she was surprised at how late in the day it was. It was the first time in over a decade that she'd missed the Maghrib prayer. She'd still pray. As she began her ablutions, the image in her mind's eye was not Maryam or Awais, but Dar Sahib. She'd always kept, she realised, the softest side of herself for him. He mustn't see this, she thought.

In the courtyard Tanveer asked, 'Was *ammi* angry about your dress?' Maryam shook her head, a small uncertain movement. 'She was angry about something,' Tanveer persisted.

Maryam began to gather the plates. 'Leave it,' Batool said, 'we'll do it.' The girls watched Maryam leave.

'Bet it was the dress,' Tanveer said.

Three hours later, Awais returned home. He opened his trunk and pulled out his latest rolled-up sheet. He unfurled the sheet and weighed it down on one side with his pencil box and, on the other, with two copy books. The map was filling out nicely. Calm now, he rolled it up and put it back in place. He went downstairs to the round room to gather his books.

Even from the door, he could see it: on the cover, a blot of ink. Maryam! He'd spent hours in there, trying to work. Maths was his worst subject. He laughed grimly. He wasn't much better at the rest. At least, he thought, trying to calm down, she'd have had the sense not to draw on his equations. He opened his copybook. Sure enough, his equations were intact. He was only surprised at how few of them he'd done. He turned a few pages – they were blank – and then he came to what Maryam had done. There were no one-dimensional cats or square houses with roofs like Chinamen's hats. Instead, there were pages and pages of equations. He grabbed his maths text book. Maryam had copied from it. That's all it was. He looked at the text book and from it to the copybook in his hand. No, Maryam hadn't copied. She'd solved. He picked up the books and went to his room.

An hour or more passed and then there was a knock at the door. Maryam, her head lowered, said, '*Bhaia, ammi* said dinner's ready.'

He rushed towards her and picked her up. Pointing to the books, he said, 'You'll show me?' She still wouldn't look him in the face. 'This will be our secret,' he added. He picked her up, began spinning. She laughed and couldn't stop.

He put Maryam down and bent forward, steadying his hands on his knees.

She laughed again and said, '*Bhaia*, you're weak.'

'You,' he said, 'are getting fat.'

He straightened and looked down at her. 'Go,' he said, 'I'll be along in five minutes.' She remained where he'd planted her. 'Five minutes,' he said and smiled.

It was a fluke, he thought, her skill with maths.

Winter dragged on. The thrill of waking to dark mornings had long passed. And the stillness of everything was frightening.

Four months left to go till his Matric exam. He tried to recall what his teachers had said. But as he opened one book after the next, he found only a broken knowledge. He couldn't fix it now. He pushed on.

'*Bhaia*,' Maryam stood in the doorway to his room, looking across at the spread of books with admiration. 'You're working,' she said and began to leave.

'No,' he said, dropping his book. Laughing, he raced to the court-yard with her close at his heels.

13

'What does he say?' Tanveer asked Khurshid.

Khurshid finished reading her letter, then looked up. 'He's invited us to go and stay.'

'Karachi?' whispered Tanveer. She turned not to her mother but to Batool for confirmation.

'What's all this?' said Dar, arriving home from work. 'Shouldn't you be studying?' he asked Awais.

'He's been working hard all day,' said Khurshid.

'Can we go?' asked Tanveer. 'Can we, *ammi?*'

'Jamshed has invited us to his eldest boy's birthday,' Khurshid said to Dar.

'Birthday!' huffed Dar.

'He says,' she said smiling, wanting to win him over, 'he'll pay for the tickets.'

'What do you mean?' Dar asked, his eyes blazing quietly.

'Can we go, *abba?*' interrupted Tanveer. Batool came to her side. Dar looked from the girls to Khurshid. 'You want to go?' he asked Khurshid. She thought, then nodded.

'That's decided then,' said Dar.

'We're going to Karachi!' said Tanveer.

'Tanveer,' Khurshid said, 'be quiet!' Batool squeezed her sister's hand, silencing her.

'When does he want you to go?' asked Dar.

'In two weeks.'

Dar raised his thumb and forefinger and circled the end of his nose. 'I'll be in Delhi then.'

They all looked to Khurshid. 'I'll just tell him we can't come,' she said.

'*Ammi*, no!' said Tanveer. '*Apa*?' she said, appealing to her sister, but Batool, who acquiesced with everything and everyone, couldn't be made to feel the injury Tanveer felt.

'What about going later, when I come back?' Dar said.

'But it's a birthday party,' Khurshid said.

'We could still go,' said Tanveer, her voice growing uncertain, 'couldn't we?'

'And Awais?' asked Dar. 'He has to study for his exams.' Awais stood stock still.

'Yes,' said Khurshid, thinking fast, pulling her gaze back from Awais's. 'What about Babar?'

'What about Babar?' Dar asked, his voice suddenly cold.

'I could stay here,' she said. They sensed there was more to come, so waited. 'And Babar could take them.'

'Babar?' In his voice, contempt.

'My brother...' she began, then noticed the children were listening. 'Let's talk inside,' she said. He assented and followed her to their bedroom.

'What do you think?' said Tanveer when they were gone. 'Will they let us go?' No one replied although the question preoccupied them all.

'Didn't Babar...?' began Tanveer

'You shouldn't speak about *mamun* like that!' said Batool.

'I didn't say anything. Did I say anything?' asked Tanveer.

The fifteen minutes they waited for their parents to return felt inexorably long.

Coming back into the courtyard, Khurshid said, 'Babar will take you.'

'*Apa!*' cried Tanveer, grinning at Batool.

'God help you,' said Dar softly.

'And Awais *bhai*?' said Tanveer.

'He's staying here with your mother.'

Maryam looked over at her sisters: Tanveer was dancing around Batool's stock-still form. Maryam clasped Awais's hand, scared.

The day of the journey came round. It was the first time any of them had been to the railway station. I'm not looking, Awais thought as he helped his mother and sister off the tonga. Shams Sahib had told him the British had built it almost overnight after the 1857 mutiny so they'd have an escape route if they needed one. He'd nodded as if he understood, then later asked his father. 1857. The failed rebellion by Indian sepoys who worked for the British East India Company. 'India's never been the same for the British since then,' Dar said, sounding pleased.

Tanveer was excited, Batool restrained. Awais, Khurshid and Maryam remained quiet, each in their own way. Maryam hadn't let go of Awais's hand since they'd got off the tonga and entered the courtyard, and then the station proper. The station was, felt Awais, a city in itself. And part of him thought, I'll come here again another time – when it's my turn to go somewhere.

For the first few days that the girls were away, Mitoo called on Awais as frequently as he always had, but before Awais could reach the door, Khurshid would be there, saying, 'He has to work. Shouldn't you be studying too, Mitoo?' He just grinned. The idea that books could have any meaning had long been ridiculous to Mitoo. Despite his friendship with Awais, he'd kept other boys in his coterie, as you keep supplies against a contingency you don't know the shape of yet. These hangers-on did the studying for him and then fed him with enough to get by.

Whenever Khurshid challenged him, Mitoo adopted one of his studied poses that told the world he didn't give a damn, but Khurshid saw through him. The next day he would be back. Awais, who from his room could hear the daily conversation between his mother and his best friend, thought Mitoo was enjoying himself.

Awais pulled out all his books from his cupboard and, picking up an armful at a time from the floor, threw them on the bed. In their disarray, he looked for a pattern. But no, he thought, to look for a pattern in what was random was not to *see* but to *impose* a design. That's what Shams Sahib told him the British were doing. *It's not India they're mapping but British India. They only see what they want to see.*

He thought he heard a knock on the door. He knew it was her. Who else could it be? He kept still. After a while, the knocking ceased.

His whole life was now regulated by her. One day he'd said he needed some fresh air and, instead of letting him go outside, she'd sat herself on his one chair, a hand fan pulsating in his direction. He'd begged her to stop, saying he couldn't study.

'But I'm not saying a word,' she said.

'I can't,' he said, closing his books.

He missed them both: Maryam and the inside city. What had gone on out there in his absence? What had been razed to the ground? The itch to know – by seeing for himself – propelled him to a point where he knew he was defenceless and weak. The city had overtaken his life. Once he'd begun, he'd had to go on. No building was dull enough for him to ignore. He opened a book, stared at a page, surprised how blurry the words had become.

He'd been waiting for it and at 9pm it came: a knock, short, sharp. She entered. Each evening before she went to bed, he had to give her a progress report. You can't learn like this, he thought when she was gone, under a whip. But despite all these constraints, he was learning. She knew it and he knew it. He just wondered whether it would be enough.

The next morning Khurshid entered his room and said, 'They get back today.' He nodded, and she left.

He opened his trunk, picked out a couple of books and took them to the bed. There was the Nelson Reader, and a book of poetry written by his uncle Babar, who wrote badly but who had inscribed this copy with 'To my nephew Awais – for future days'; his maps, and underneath, at the bottom of the pile, an ordinary copybook, the kind all children had. He didn't open the Nelson Reader. Instead, he opened uncle Babar's book, read the inscription, which anyhow he knew off by heart, then flicked the pages till his hands told him to stop. He read:

We do not know what we know
We do not live where we live
Angels and the devil too
Cannot teach
This voiceless heart.

He put his uncle's book back. There it was: the copybook Maryam had filled. He'd crossed out his name with a perfectly ruled line; that's how he recognised it. He opened it; his writing looked unsure, as if the numbers were not striding anywhere, merely hobbling along. Each time he began to probe a question he thought he could do, halfway through or before, he became stuck. There was a time, he thought, not long ago, when I could tackle these questions, sometimes even getting a few right, but now... He slammed the book closed. Once it was put away in the trunk, his mood lightened. His gaze swept over his maps, and then he closed the trunk.

Someone had sent the family a box of sweetmeats. His desire for something sweet was overpowering and though he knew she hid such things away, today he was convinced he'd find the box. He pushed open the kitchen door and saw her sitting on the *piri*, plucking small stones from a bowl of *dhal*. She looked up.

'The sweetmeats are in the second cupboard,' she said. He opened the cupboard and took out the box. He picked out a square of creamy white *barfi*. He was at the door when she said, 'It's nearly time.'

'I know!' he said.

'What's that in your hand?'

'*Barfi*,' he said and raised his hand for her to see.

'No, the other,' she said.

'Nothing.'

He put the *barfi* whole in his mouth as he opened the door. In his left hand, his key felt heavy and a little damp. She'd let him keep the secret, not knowing that behind it were two more.

At the courtyard wall, looking out towards the city, he finished his *barfi*. A man began singing the *azaan*, for Zuhr, the midday prayer. It was time to go to the station and pick up his sisters.

14

The year 1935 saw one of the coolest summers anyone could remember. Awais and Mitoo had taken their exams three months earlier. On the day of the results, the entire family gathered in the courtyard as Dar checked Awais's roll number in *The Tribune*. When Dar looked up from the newspaper he was smiling.

As soon as he could, Awais left for Mitoo's house. As he walked, his gaze lingered longingly and lovingly on the buildings he passed; he thought of the time he'd lost and would have to make up.

'What d'you get?' he asked Mitoo.

'You first.'

'Lower second class.'

'Me too.'

'The boys got you through,' said Awais.

'The boys!' said Mitoo, laughing. 'Sheer hard work.'

Soon afterwards, Awais left for Shams Sahib's.

'Awais,' said Shams, 'we have to talk.' Shams picked up his right arm with the left and lay it on his lap. Awais saw and glanced away, embarrassed. 'There's something I haven't told you yet.' The words bolted out. 'I'm the city's custodian, the keeper of its stories.' He paused to watch Awais's face. 'I'm telling you this now,' he said, 'because...' and he stroked his immobile arm. 'Sometimes, I have to dig them out, but mostly, people come to me. They think they're seeking advice, but what they're doing is revealing things about themselves. Embedded in what they say are important facets of the city's history. Ours has always been an oral history.' He sat back now, relaxed, remembering. 'The custodian before me had a wonderful memory. Mine has grown better with time.' The hand on his lap began to shake, calling attention to itself. Awais, shocked, averted his gaze once more. Shams waited till the trembling ceased, then said, 'Okay. Where to begin?'

'Can I ask something?' interjected Awais.

'Ask.'

'How did you become the custodian?'

'Loha.' Shams looked steadily at Awais.

'You found Loha too?'

'That's the test.'

'But,' said Awais, 'I came upon it by chance.'

'Did you, Awais? Let's go on. There's a lot I have to tell you. Twelve gates, one custodian. The British…' He stopped, watching Awais. 'No,' he said, 'I'll tell you about that another time. Want anything to eat?'

Awais shook his head *no* and said, 'My father told me Loha had been lost for hundreds of years.'

'Your father wasn't here when I found it. His family came here from Sialkot.'

Awais looked puzzled. No one had ever told him that. Hesitating, he asked, 'Shams Sahib, the English, what are they mapping?'

Shams's face hardened, the lines strongly drawn. Awais had never seen Shams Sahib angry before. He wanted to retract the question. He wanted to push on and know. His voice a soft lilt, Shams said, 'They're mapping the whole of India, every inch they can cover. Stick it on a map, put a picture of a British lion on it and suddenly, it's yours. They're doing it all across the world. They think that to govern territories you must know them and to know them you must collect specimens, data, make maps.'

'And the inside city?'

Shams laughed. 'It's too messy for them, too smelly, too unplanned.'

'They tried?'

'A long time ago, they tried. Tried and gave up.'

Awais didn't tell Shams Sahib he'd seen the English map-makers in the inside city when he was younger.

Shams raised his good hand, as if to dismiss the British for now. 'The custodian,' he continued, 'is the keeper of the inside city's stories, the history of its people. We also guard the buildings, of course.' Again, he paused. 'Yes, it's easier to start here. Shall I begin with the large buildings or the small? Are you listening to me, Awais?'

Awais frowned. *Why ask?* He hadn't moved.

As Awais listened, a growing sense of fear. *I can't tell him about my maps.* But eventually, the words spilled out.

When he'd finished, all Shams said was, 'You're making maps?' He looked at Awais, squinting. 'Just like the English.'

No! Awais wanted to scream. Not like them at all. He idled on his way home.

When Awais told his parents he'd like to take history and geography for his FA exams, he thought they'd say those weren't practical subjects and wouldn't lead anywhere, but when they made no objection at all, he wondered if they even knew about such things. His father had passed his seventh grade but hadn't gone further with his studies than that. His mother had barely finished fifth grade. But, like most Indians, they valued education above everything else. It was the portal from which, if you passed through, everything would change. Awais was, he thought to himself, fast on the way to becoming the most educated person in his family. He laughed then remembered his mother's brothers, Jamshed and Babar. Quickly, he revised the thought: the most educated person in his *immediate* family. It still sounded pretty good.

Maryam never learnt of the battle her father fought so she could go to middle school. Whether Batool and Tanveer should continue with their studies had never been a point of debate between Dar and Khurshid. No girl in either of their families had gone through the tarnished gates of middle school.

'She's nine!' said Khurshid. 'She'll be two, three years younger than everyone else.'

'Amrau, she can't keep on repeating the same year at primary school.'

She remained appalled at the idea and fought furiously in her corner. He listened, and her body relaxed.

Two days later Dar came home with three full coats: red for Batool, green for Tanveer and, for Maryam, blue.

'Maryam's joining middle school in a few weeks and I thought...'

Khurshid looked at him, startled.

'Thank you, *abba*,' said Batool.

Tanveer put on her coat, stroking its thick wool. She rushed to her room to see what it looked like in the mirror. Khurshid called Batool to the kitchen. When she was done helping her mother prepare lunch, Batool went to the room she shared with her sisters. Tanveer was lying on her bed, still in her coat.

Batool, whose mildness pleased everyone but herself, felt as if she'd stepped into an array of blazing lights. All she could think was: arms, legs, stay on. They felt as if, any minute, they'd loosen and fall. Even though she hadn't been much good at anything, she'd liked school. No one had ever asked her if she'd wanted to stay.

Tanveer rolled onto her back and began giggling. 'Poor Maryam,' she said over and over again. Batool couldn't help it; she sometimes felt, though she didn't want to, that her sister was – and there was no other word for it – silly. To compensate for the thought, she called Tanveer to her side.

Batool positioned Tanveer between her outspread legs then began brushing and plaiting her hair. One sister's body eased as the other's remained tense.

15

'We'll get some breakfast on the way,' said Awais. He took her bag and swung it up on his shoulder with his own. Her new light-blue coat hung stiffly from her shoulders. Outside, a day remarkably bright for this time of year.

'That *mandir*,' he said, pointing to a squat temple, its stone slabs greyed, 'was built in 1811. One day I'll take you inside and show you the names of all the builders scrawled on a wall. They were all Muslims except for one.' He would have continued but saw she was looking elsewhere.

'Das *kulchay*!' cried a voice. Ahead of them, a young man. Awais waved the man over and said, 'Das *bhai*, two *kulchay*.' The young man, Das, lowered the huge basket on his head and handed the two *kulchay*, wrapped in newspaper, to Maryam while Awais searched his pockets for change. Basket atop of his head again, Das walked away.

Awais had never seen Das smile or say anything but these two words. Das was a few years older than Awais and walked with a strange gait, as if he were measuring out the world to see if it fit.

'*Bhaia*,' said Maryam, 'what did he say? *Udas kulchay* – sad bread?'

'No,' said Awais, laughing. But it wasn't just Maryam's mistake, he knew; that's what other people heard, too. They'd buy them by the dozen, thinking the *kulchay*'s sadness might mitigate their own.

'That's—' he said. 'Maryam!' She was looking at a family of pigeons who'd zipped to the ground and seemed unafraid of human passers-by. 'Maryam!' he said again. She looked up.

'Awais *bhai*, I was listening. What you said about the *mandir*…'

'That was fifteen minutes ago.'

Her gaze had returned to the birds. 'Awais *bhai*, have you ever—'

'I don't care about the birds!' he said. Her eyes welled with tears. He walked on and she trudged behind.

'Don't say don't care,' she said softly.

They walked on. And suddenly they were in front of the four-tiered Victoria School. Why hadn't anyone told him how beautiful it was? He went towards the open door, was about to look in, when a baton slammed against his arm. He pulled back, cradling his burning arm to his chest, and looked angrily at the *chowkidar*. The gatekeeper, grinning, threw open his military-style coat.

'Yes?' he said. 'Where are you going?'

Awais, pointing to Maryam, said, 'My sister—'

'Yes, so?' said the *chowkidar*, his shoulders twitching, as if under that heavy coat there were mice.

'She starts here today.' Awais's head turned again to the open door. 'Can we go inside?' The *chowkidar* looked puzzled as if he'd never had a request like this before. 'Just five minutes?' Awais said.

'Uncle,' said Maryam, 'can we?' The *chowkidar* considered them, his attention focused on Awais.

'No,' he said.

The building's exterior was magnificent, with intricate mosaics. The inside will be nothing, he thought. Someone called the gatekeeper; he turned. Awais pushed Maryam in and then sneaked in behind. He looked around in wonder. Four levels with four court-yards, and pillars supporting balconies galore. He wished he could go up. He turned to look back at the *chowkidar*, who was greeting some teachers, head bent. Could he risk it? Maryam pulled at his arm.

'Look,' she said. He followed her inside. On each of the doors, the name of the class year. They walked from room to room.

The windows were small, the rooms dark to encourage the eyes of students, if they were likely to wander, to wander indoors. The students of the higher classes had desks and chairs; Maryam's class had a mat of blue, black and red stripes. There were no pictures or charts on any of the walls: everything was left blank. And yet it was beautiful, each room, each... He heard the *chowkidar* shout, and turned. Eye to eye. The *chowkidar* slowly approached. A teacher pulled him aside. Awais swiftly touched Maryam's arm then hightailed it out of the school.

And when the day was done he went to pick her up.

'Why are you walking funny?' he asked.

'I'm not,' she said, and after a false step, adjusted back to her regular stride. She gave him her tuckshop money.

'You didn't have anything to eat? Wasn't there a break?' he asked.

'I wasn't hungry,' she said.

He put the money away in the deep recess of his pocket, stuffing a handkerchief on top to stifle the click–click rattling sound. And then she began to tell him about her day.

Maryam didn't know any of her new classmates. No one in her old school had gone up to middle school. Most of the girls at this new school were Hindus. There were some Parsis too and, counting herself, only three Muslim girls. During the break, all the girls had run down the two flights of stairs, already familiar with their surroundings, to squat in front of the *channay*-seller and buy half a paisa's worth of red peppered *channay* in newspaper cones.

The two Muslim girls had approached Maryam. The elder of the two had said, 'I'm Fatima and this is Pinky. Pinky and I are going to get some *channay*. You can come too, if you want.' They'd walked on and at the head of the stairs Fatima had turned to see if Maryam was following. 'I'd just wandered to the window. I didn't mean to be rude,' Maryam now told Awais. 'Will they still like me, do you think?'

As she talked, he sensed, though she didn't come out and say it, that the school wasn't what she'd expected it to be. Awais thought he knew what lay ahead. And then she spoke of the maths teacher, Miss Alvi, and as she did, her grip on his hand loosened.

That was the last thing Khurshid had expected: this childish voice. Not only was it high-pitched, it seemed unsure, almost apologetic. What kind of teacher has a voice like that? Khurshid thought. She looked at Miss Alvi's hands, which were wide and capable. Her wrists were bare. Not even one bangle. She saw Miss Alvi look towards Maryam. Maryam though was trying to untangle her legs, as if they were not just two but many – and couldn't help her teacher. Khurshid, feeling her power surge, knew she could afford to be kind.

'Have you been teaching long?' she asked and waited for Miss Alvi to smile.

Miss Alvi looked confused. 'I came here to talk about Maryam,' she said.

Khurshid didn't know how to respond. How, she thought, to play with no rules or with rules you'd just invented and no one else knew? Her lips thinned as if she were crushing a pencil between them. Miss Alvi's skin, grey-brown, like dry clay, her almost manlike, plain *shalwar kameez* – all of these things affronted Khurshid. The girls were, she noticed, looking at Miss Alvi with curiosity, too. Of them all, Awais seemed the least concerned.

'I think you'll have seen from Maryam's reports...' began Miss Alvi.

'Is she behind?' said Khurshid. Smiling at Miss Alvi, she said, 'You know what girls are like. Not really interested in their studies.' She paused, waiting for Miss Alvi to react.

'The reports...' said Miss Alvi again.

Reports, thought Khurshid. Who reads reports?

'Batool, Tanveer,' she said, 'go and get the tea.'

'There's no—' began Miss Alvi.

'Batool, Tanveer,' said Khurshid again, in her steady public voice, 'didn't you hear me?' The girls reluctantly got up. Awais began to fidget and Maryam clutched his hand.

'Is it all right if Maryam stays?' asked Miss Alvi.

'Yes,' mumbled Khurshid, looking down at her lap. She considered her hands; the hardworking right and the plump, unmarked left which never pulled its own weight. She lay one on top of the other; pushing the ugly one out of sight. Awais coughed. Khurshid darted him a look. Maryam's gaze flitted between Awais and Miss Alvi, who was saying something. *What did she say?* 'I didn't hear...' began Khurshid.

'I'd like to give Maryam extra lessons,' said Miss Alvi again. 'At no cost to yourself, of course.'

Maryam pulled herself free from Awais and ran to her teacher. Miss Alvi looked confused. After a moment she gingerly patted Maryam's shoulder. Maryam stepped back. Her teacher's mouth smelt of *betel* juice. They all looked at Khurshid, waiting.

Because Miss Alvi never gave anyone an easy ride, her students thought her forbidding. And then there was the whole marriage thing. Why hadn't she married? Everyone got proposed to, at least once, even the ugly girls. Their parents, they knew – because they always listened carefully when their parents became unnaturally quiet – didn't like the fact that Miss Alvi was a Miss, and at her age, too.

When the girls in her class found out that Miss Alvi had offered Maryam extra lessons – even though they were free – they couldn't but help but pity her.

'Why didn't your *ammi* say no?' asked a girl with impossible hair that had to be braided really tight.

Maryam replied, 'You can't say no to a teacher.'

The girl, nodding, agreed, and ripping her banana in two as if she were lopping body from head, offered Maryam the larger share. She then skipped off, half a banana short but with a great storm of news to tell.

After the last school bell had been rung, Maryam went to the downstairs courtyard to wait for Miss Alvi, as arranged.

'What are you doing here?' asked Miss Alvi as she approached. Maryam looked puzzled and Miss Alvi smiled. 'Can't a teacher make a little joke? Come on, then,' she added, 'it's this way.' She led Maryam to the back of the school, past the servants' quarters to where some of the teachers' residences were. Miss Alvi began to climb up a wrought-iron spiral staircase, looking down from time to time to see that Maryam was still behind her.

Miss Alvi unlocked the door and entered. Maryam lingered outside.

'Come on in,' said Miss Alvi. The long lounge had a sofa positioned near the middle of it, and placed in front of the sofa, a small table. In a corner stood a dining table and chairs. You couldn't see the walls; they were covered in books.

Miss Alvi, clearly somewhat embarrassed, gave a small laugh.

'Now you know my weakness,' she said. 'Want to sit here?' she said, pointing to the sofa, 'or over there?' and she gestured to the dining table. Maryam was confused; she'd never been asked for her opinion on anything before. Miss Alvi followed Maryam's gaze and said, 'Good choice. Sit down.' Maryam pulled out one of the dining chairs. 'I'll get you a drink – *sharbat*?' Maryam nodded.

Facing the archway through which Miss Alvi had disappeared to make sure she wouldn't be seen, she spun in a slow circle.

So many books, she thought. Awais *bhai* would love this.

Miss Alvi returned and laid the tray on the table. 'Sit down, Maryam,' she said. Maryam returned to the table, sat down and picked up her drink. She took a sip. Miss Alvi looked at her satisfied. 'We've got a lot of work to do, me and you.' She paused. 'That doesn't frighten you?' Maryam shook her head.

'Good,' said Miss Alvi. 'Finish that and then we'll begin.' Maryam looked at her teacher, puzzled. The Miss Alvi of school had gone and in her place sat this woman who'd borrowed Miss Alvi's face. Maryam just hoped that this woman was as good at maths as Miss Alvi was. She bent forward and from her bag, brought out her copybook and pen.

'My mother says I have to tell you something,' Awais said to Miss Alvi. She waited but he wouldn't or couldn't go on. After a moment, she understood.

'Maryam,' she said. 'I've laid out some things next to a tray in the kitchen. Will you go and bring them here?'

Maryam turned to her brother, full of pride that Miss Alvi had trusted her with such a responsibility. She left to do her teacher's bidding.

'Oh,' Miss Alvi said when he'd finished. Maryam returned, walking slowly, her eyes never leaving the tray.

In order to hide how distraught she was, Miss Alvi went into overdrive. She laid out the snacks and drinks on the table and entreated them to eat and drink. Awais drank as quickly as he could; she pushed the plate of biscuits forward and he ate two, too nervous to brush away the crumbs on his lap.

Miss Alvi sent Maryam back to fill the jug, then leaned towards Awais and said, 'What can I do?' Awais looked at her in silence. 'Should I tell the principal?' Miss Alvi asked.

'Tell the principal what?' asked Maryam, coming back into the room.

'How bright you are, of course,' Awais said, grinning.

Two weeks later, Miss Alvi handed Awais a message to give to his mother.

'It's early days yet,' Miss Alvi had written, 'but I think your daughter is not just good at maths; I think she might have the potential to do wonderful things.' Khurshid read the letter, then handed it to Awais.

'*Ama*!' he'd cried, jubilant.

She burnt with anger. At Maryam. At him. Didn't he understand? Even when it was spelt out as clearly as that? When he'd gone, she read the letter again, then again. She folded it into one square, then another, and though it was harder this way, began to systematically rip it apart. She took the fragments to the kitchen and pulling up some rubbish from the bin, put them deep down and then covered them. She washed her hands and returned to her room to lie down.

Surprised awake by the light, she lay still, her hands empty. To speak to Awais now would be to ruin everything. He wouldn't listen. He loved Maryam too much. She had to say something though, had to let him know. To speak would be to lose him. But to not speak?

In prayer she tried for greater feats of concentration. 'Just these words, just these words,' she said, attempting to smother all other intruding thoughts. But God, who had till now been so beneficent, remained silent. Was she, she wondered, asking for too much, or was she not asking for enough? She tried to remember those moments in which she had truly loved Maryam. But there was nothing, no picture, no sentiment, nothing she could call upon. Her eyes widened in animal fear.

The recognition that it was not love she wanted nearly broke Khurshid. Not love? Startling her, it was Dar, not Awais, who first came to mind. With his many attentions over the years, he had softened her. And though she'd never regretted this, welcomed it even, she now wondered if the innocence with which he'd taught her to see hadn't blinded her to all this, all this... She pushed back her hair which had become unpinned in parts; stray tendrils lay limp on her high forehead. Like a young girl she stood confused, with the burden of too-great hopes and fears. The pir had promised her it all. What then, was this life she'd been given? But what – and she could hardly think the words, they were so awful – what if the pir was wrong? Or what... and now her heart began to squeeze, pushing... what if the pir had been right about the house but wrong about the child? What if the promise had been meant for Maryam all along? No. And then it came to her. It was so obvious, so clear. She sat on the bed, leaning back against the headboard; she reached for the covered glass of water which was always at her bedside, and slowly drank. The first thing she had to do, she decided, putting the glass back in its place, and dabbing her lips with the edge of her *dupatta*, was tell Awais.

He sensed something, so kept away.

Three days passed, and on the fourth morning she woke up in a strange mood. She tried to remember if any sad dreams had waylaid her during the hours of darkness, but for once, she couldn't remember.

She went to make breakfast. The milk boiled over. Dar came in, said something. Busy as she was making *parathas*, she wasn't quite sure what he said, but she didn't like his tone. Batool and Tanveer joined her after a while and began carrying the plates out to the new table which Dar insisted they now sat at. She missed the ease of the *dastarkhwan* on the floor, and found sitting at the table and chairs an unnatural way to eat.

Awais's hair was still wet. She was on the verge of saying something but held herself back.

'Maryam,' she said. Maryam looked up. 'Did you wash your hands?'

'Yes,' answered Maryam.

'With soap?' asked Khurshid pointedly. Dar looked at Khurshid. She'd always been a skinny woman but the skinniness of youth and of middle age were different somehow.

Maryam pushed back her chair and left for the bathroom. The older girls talked as always between themselves; Dar was telling Awais some item of news he'd just heard when Maryam returned and began to eat.

Dar was the first to leave. Batool and Tanveer cleared up and Maryam went to the bedroom she shared with her sisters. Khurshid followed Awais to his room.

'Awais,' she called. The door remained closed. She thought nervously, he won't open it. But eventually he did. His bag slung over his shoulder, he was ready to leave for college.

'Put that down for a minute,' she said, and stepping back, he let her in. His room was immaculate and she still found it strange that a young boy – she looked at his face, which was growing thinner the taller he got... no, not a young boy, veritably a young man – should be so precise and neat. Though in looks he was more her child than any of the others, he had ways about him that were so foreign to her, she didn't know how to behave, never mind what to think. It wasn't just his friendship with Mitoo or that business with Loha, the gate he'd found. The thing that was unknowable in him piqued her; she wanted to scratch at it and make it bleed.

'*Ammi*,' he said, 'I'll be late for college.'

'Doesn't matter,' she said. 'Sit down.' He sat down on the edge of the bed while she sat in the room's only chair. She saw him sigh and felt herself harden more.

'You heard what Miss Alvi said?' she asked. He nodded. 'I don't think,' she continued, 'you understand what it means.'

'It means Maryam's good at maths.'

Dumbfounded, she just stared. 'Yes,' she finally said, 'but what else? What have I been telling you all these years? The pir—'

'*Ammi*,' he cut in, 'the pir could...' and she saw him hesitate before continuing. 'He could have been wrong. What are the chances that two children in the same house are meant to do great things? It was Maryam he meant.'

She got up and stood over him. 'It was you he meant. Only you,' she cried. She realised her hand was raised and she slowly let it fall. Soft and grave, she said, 'She's stolen it – that which should have been yours.'

Later that day in his room, Awais sat on the floor, his back against the bed, for once not knowing what to do. Usually, taking out the maps and looking at them or adding to them was enough to alter his mood. But he didn't, he realised, actually want to change his mood. The sullen lack of hope, as if something were clogged deep in his heart, was strangely something he wanted to feel.

Was his mother right? There'd never been a time – even when he'd snubbed her – that he hadn't believed what she'd said would come true. Was he giftless, just like everyone else: born to this earth with limits already defined?

She was exacting. He'd tried indifference. That hadn't worked. Then he'd tried failing. But she'd pulled him through even that.

The impulse to escape was so strong all he needed was a fuse. But he knew he mustn't heed that impulse now. He must instead sit here and recall all that his mother had said. The idea was stupid, completely utterly stupid, yet…

There are dreams you have, she thought, that you faintly remember, and then there are those which recur, gaining in strength. She wondered if by latching on to one dream and playing it again and again she hadn't dispelled others of equal or greater beauty. And so that night, each time the pir's words brought up the old image – of Awais flying high on a horse, though she tried and tried so hard to erase the horse, knowing to think of him like that was a sin – she tried to drown that image; down, down it went, beginning to quake from the pressure – it spluttered then rose again. It was early morning when she gave in. And as the familiar story unfolded, a warmth spread over her. She pulled the sheet up so that it covered her face. *Is this what dying will be like? What if dying doesn't just happen? What if you have to push it out, into being?* She held a hand to her throat.

115

That's what the dying do. Are they trying to say something – share a mark of revelation? Or is it all so much more basic than that – and they're trying to hold their breath because they don't want to expend anything else on this world? Her body curled like it had when she'd been a girl and had spent hours and hours in bed, not sleeping as everyone thought, but building, in her head, piece by tiny piece, a world not of fantasy but of possibilities, real and assured. *How stupid was I?* She pulled the sheet down and uncurling till she lay like a slab of lead, she looked up at the ceiling.

The next morning Dar teased her for being a lazy so-and-so. She didn't reply so he got up, ready to shower and dress. When he returned he was taken aback to see that she was still in bed. This wasn't like Amrau. He raced to her side. Her eyes remained closed. He put a hand to her forehead. Her skin was burning.

Her delirium was so strong, her speech so strange, Dar couldn't make out half the words; they were so scrambled, and what she did say and what he understood frightened him. This couldn't be Amrau, this woman with these whiplash thoughts; she'd always been, he realised, his safety net. He drew the curtains and kept the children away. A doctor was called.

Dar couldn't afford to take much time off work and so after two days of leave, during which Khurshid's fever remained unbroken, he set off to make some sales. But his head was so busy with thoughts of his wife, he explained to his bosses, he couldn't go on for the present, and with understanding nods they agreed. He went home to nurse Khurshid, and sat and watched her restless movements.

The less she slept the more ill she grew. But she couldn't sleep. She had to keep guard. Three days became four and, soon, she'd been ill for over a week.

'Amrau,' he said, 'look at what you've done to yourself.'

He hadn't expected her to hear but she gave a bitter laugh.

'Come closer,' she said. 'What are you doing over there?'

'Don't talk,' he said.

A lock of hair fell to her forehead. She was surprised at how greasy it felt.

'Batool oiled it,' he said.

'Where is he?'

'All the children are home. Shall I call them?' he said.

When he'd gone she pushed the quilt away, arching her legs. Maryam's face, not as it was now but as it had been when she was eight or nine months old, came to mind. She'd been a good child and, like Batool and Tanveer, had never given her any trouble.

Outside, she could still hear Dar calling the children. After a few minutes, they'd all gathered at her door.

Her eyes not leaving Awais's face, Khurshid said, 'Come here.' Seeing that he was reluctant to approach, she added, 'You won't catch a disease.'

Awais went to her and she took his hand. 'Can I get you anything, *Ama*?' he asked.

'Ice,' she said. 'I want ice.' She licked her lips in anticipation.

But it was September and there was no ice being sold in the streets. He didn't move. Her grip on him relaxed.

Suddenly Maryam squealed, 'Spider!' and Awais ran to her side.

'Where?' he said, removing his *chappal*. She pointed, then shut her eyes. He pulped the spider to death with his *chappal*, put his *chappal* back on and grinned at his little sister.

'You shouldn't kill spiders,' Khurshid said, her voice grown sad. 'One saved the Prophet's life.'

Her gaze turned from Maryam to Awais, then back again. She looked as if her stomach could retch out a world, diseased and lacking, forever, in hope.

16

They'd drummed it into her so hard that the first fit she'd had had been near to catastrophic – though she remembered nothing of it except feeling exceptionally cold – that she grew fearful of a recurrence on that scale. They watched over her, none more so than Awais. Sometimes, when she caught him out, she'd smile as if to say sorry. Her mother watched her too, but her watching had a different quality to it. Maryam thought back to the time when she'd been left alone. That had been the happy part of her childhood.

What she hadn't told anyone, not Awais, not Miss Alvi – they'd think me mad, she thought – was that since that first attack, she'd been able to see numbers not as digits and abstract values but as things: a banana was a six, a gun, five. Each number also had its distinctive smell. Soon, she had a complete arsenal of colour and sound at her command, and once she understood a formula, she didn't have to even calculate anything; the answer popped up by itself. And because it was so easy, she began to grow bored and just a little bit lazy.

Coming back from Miss Alvi's one day, she saw her mother hanging around in the alcove where her father usually sat. Her *dupatta* had fallen to her shoulders and her mass of hair, unbound, made her head look huge. Maryam hastened away.

Khurshid would now wander into the alcove, wait a while – sometimes just a few minutes, sometimes close to an hour – then wander off again. When she first took to doing this, Dar hadn't asked her anything or said anything. Instead, he had turned his chair towards her, as if that were all he was willing to concede, but still she came. An orderly man, Dar minded most the idiosyncrasy of her visits, that they didn't follow any rule of time. Then one day he put out another chair, exactly like his own, but polished. And when she approached, he directed her with his eyes to the empty seat. She stood there for a moment, as if not understanding what he meant, as if he were the one who now disturbed her. Again, she stalked off without a gesture or a word. The next day when he did the same thing, she stood a while then took a seat. From then on, when she was not working, she sat with him. The news, discussion programmes and dramas washed over her; sometimes she dozed. But when the song hour began she sat up straight, ears to the speaker, eyes to the red light.

Seeing her there one day, Mitoo had stopped in his tracks. He'd looked from the radio to Khurshid and back again.

'Let's go,' said Awais, but Mitoo refused to move.

When the song ended, he approached the alcove and said, 'I've heard him sing live.'

'You've heard Pankaj Gopal?' she said.

'Yes. Some years ago.'

'Describe him to me,' she said. She listened to Mitoo, hardly seeming to breathe. 'Yes,' she said when he was done, 'that's him.'

Mitoo looked at her questioningly and was about to ask how she knew when Dar said, 'That's who?' Khurshid shook her head as if what she knew was too riddled with complexity for minds such as his to comprehend.

Maryam made her way to Miss Alvi's flat. She scuttled in as she'd learnt to do so that Miss Alvi's downstairs neighbours wouldn't spot her and trap her with their thousand and one questions. They knew she was being tutored by Miss Alvi but that wasn't enough; they wanted to know more. Up the stairs she climbed. Miss Alvi had left a message tacked to the door. She was going to be late. Maryam, warned what to do in such a contingency, unearthed the key from its pot. She turned the key one way, then the other, pulled it out and tried again. She was scared the key would drop through the stairway's grating and here she'd be, whenever Miss Alvi returned, without a key and embarrassed beyond words. She wiped the key with her *dupatta* and tried again. The door opened. Once inside, she put her bag on the sofa, got a drink of water from the kitchen, made herself a *sharbat*, took a few sips and then sat down at the dining room table, opened her books and settled down to work.

By the time she'd finished the exercises for the day, Miss Alvi still had not returned. Her gaze wandered around the room. She got up. She knew the books – many of which she'd now worked her way through. She smiled at her favourite Euclid and at Hardy's treatise on invisible numbers, and continued to scan the shelves, then stopped abruptly at a gap between two books. She reached up but it was too high. She pulled up a chair, throwing its cushions to the floor, then climbed up and stretched out a hand. Pushed to the very back, lying on its side, she felt the edge of a slim book.

She pulled it out. It was bound in red leather. She frowned. There was no title. Was it Miss Alvi who'd had the book bound? And if so, why was it so special that it had to be bound? As she opened the first page a dried orange leaf, shot with red, fell out; she caught it and held it by its stem. On the title page, she read, *Celestial Numbers* by Rajmohan Rao. And underneath, in ink, in a large scrawling hand, were some words she couldn't at first decipher. She tried again: 'To my dearest Rani. Hoping this will make you change your mind: 23:11:1911.' Putting the leaf back in place, she closed the book, climbed down off the chair and returned to the sofa. Her half-drunk glass of *sharbat* stood before her on the table like a temptation she knew she must not now touch. She began to read:

Numbers represent the perfection of this world. There are numbers representing the earth and numbers representing the heavens. Here we consider the celestial numbers, their content and their meaning.

Maryam began turning the pages more rapidly. She closed the book and stared hard at its unrevealing red cover for a long time. She then turned once more to the first page and started reading again.

It doesn't make sense, she thought as she read on. Numbers are created by man. But Rajmohan Rao says they stand for something else. What does it all mean? She was still reading, growing more and more angry with herself – why don't I understand, she thought –

when the door opened and Miss Alvi smiled at the sight of Maryam. She tugged at her sari, trying to wrap it across the back of her shoulders; the drape of the *palu*, though, was too short. Instead of a purse, she was carrying, as she always did, a wooden pencil box which held chalk, pens, keys and a few coins she said might come in useful for emergencies; this, she now dropped on a nearby chair.

'Maryam?' Miss Alvi said.

Maryam shut the book and looked up. The door was still open and she saw that the sky was blackening fast.

'I'm sorry, Maryam,' Miss Alvi said, entering the room. 'The class inspector was in today. I was hoping to get a message to you but there was no one around.'

Maryam fumbled, not sure whether to leave the book on the sofa or to return it to its place on the shelf.

'Just leave it,' said Miss Alvi. 'I'll put it back.' Maryam put the book down. Miss Alvi's body stiffened as she saw the red leather. In a voice little more than a whisper, she asked, 'Where did you find it?'

'On the shelf.'

'There was a leaf inside?'

Maryam opened the book to show Miss Alvi the leaf nestling on the front page, covering the dedication, but leaving the urgent scrawl visible.

Miss Alvi nodded slightly and stared at the book. There was a knock at the open door.

'Awais, *bhai*!' Maryam said, relieved.

Miss Alvi turned, then said, 'Awais, come in.' She tried to smile, but the effort just made her look more haggard.

Maryam gathered her books, said goodbye and left with Awais.

'Tonight's the night of destiny,' her mother said when they entered. Maryam started. *How had her mother known?* But as her mother tightened her *dupatta* around her head for prayer she realised her mother meant something else: it was one of the last few days of Ramzan – the month of fasting – and on one of these uneven-numbered days – no one knew exactly which – the Prophet had ascended to heaven where he'd been shown the construction of eternal time.

'You okay?' Batool asked as Maryam entered their bedroom.

'Yes, *apa*,' she said.

'You're not even...' began Tanveer.

'Leave her alone,' said Batool and Tanveer mumbled but said nothing else.

Maryam closed her eyes. How could she find another copy of that book? She couldn't ask Miss Alvi, that was for sure. She sensed somehow that that would hurt her teacher too much. There was only one person she could ask.

In his mind, growing darkness. *What are the chances that two children in the same house are meant to do great things?* His words, not hers. Once a shadow, now pushed into the light. He'd always thought it – even his adoration of the city couldn't diminish the idea. The thing she'd discovered – maths – was higher than what he'd found.

She asked, and he couldn't refuse. But if I hadn't told her, he thought, she'd never even have known it existed.

Everyone has a special place – a room, a spot under a tree – which is theirs alone. For Awais, that place was the Punjab Public Library. He didn't mind the other people who came there: over the years he'd got to know a few by face, though neither he nor they had ever been tempted to talk. The library imposed its own rules upon its readers, which anywhere else they might have resisted and broken, but here, they acceded to a will that had no face, no form, yet which governed how they thought and behaved within the building's four walls. He'd never taken anyone else to the library, not even Mitoo. Mitoo had asked him once, to test him he'd later thought, and laughed at the slowness and the puzzled shape of Awais's reply.

Awais picked Maryam up from school. They walked for a while until they reached the main road, where he hailed a tonga. He sat with her in the back, which he rarely did, never comfortable with not seeing where he was heading.

They moved along swiftly till they reached the Mall and then the crush from Anarkali bazaar halted their progress for a while. They turned into a side street and parked. Awais helped her down. 'That,' he said, pointing to a building nearby, shaped like a long barracks with a shiny red-brick roof, 'is Tollinton market.' People entered and bustled out of the building with great speed as if they knew what they were about. At the sight of an Englishman, Maryam snuggled up into Awais's arms, half-hiding.

'What's got into you?' he asked.

'What's it like?' she said.

'It's the coolest building I've ever been in. Even in the fiercest heat.'

He took her hand and led her onwards. 'This is it. This is the Punjab Public Library,' he said. He could see by the way she looked at its plain walls and the small plaque on which was inscribed the library's name that she was disappointed.

In the near-empty courtyard she looked around. 'Do you think we'll find it here?' she asked.

But he hadn't heard her because he was bounding up the steps, as he always did, into the library proper. More cautiously, she followed. He stood inside, waiting for her. She entered and gasped at the wooden darkness. She looked longingly at the narrow passageways which branched out from either side of the librarian's raised booth.

As Awais and Maryam began to ascend the stairs, the librarian called out, 'Does she have a card?'

They turned back. 'No,' Awais reluctantly admitted.

'And she's not sixteen, is she?'

'No.'

'So no card.' The librarian chewed at his pencil, making them wait. 'She can't go up,' he concluded.

Maryam looked up at the staircase.

'Just this once?' asked Awais. 'I've been coming here since—'

'Rules are rules,' interjected the librarian.

Awais tried to think of how to get round the librarian. He was, he knew, an implacable man. 'All right, Maryam,' he said at last. 'Wait here and I'll go and look.'

'But, *bhaia…*'

'You heard what the librarian said. He's right.' Depositing Maryam on a chair which looked as if it had been salvaged from a fire, Awais ran upstairs. Ten minutes later he was back at her side.

'Come on,' he said, pulling her to her feet, 'we don't have much time.'

'But the librarian? He said he'd be back in a few minutes.'

Awais shook his head knowingly. 'He's off to make a bet. Pigeons. He won't be back for another hour.' They raced up the stairs. He pushed open the heavy doors. She stood on tiptoe, looking across the sea of tables and cabinets of books. From the top windows, gusts of light. Grinning, she glanced at him, about to say something. Awais put out his hand and pulled her on. He'd seen the way the boys in the corner had looked at her. In the corridor he said, 'Mathematics is over there. What did you say it's called?'

'*Celestial Numbers* by Rajmohan Rao,' she said.

He glanced at her quizzically. 'Celestial numbers – what's that: the numbers of God?'

Slowly she answered. 'I don't know.'

He saw that she was seriously hurt by his quip, but how could you be hurt by a book's name? Nonplussed, he wondered: what if it were true – if there were such a thing as God's numbers? 'You'll tell me what it's about?' he said.

'Yes,' she replied, mollified. She quickly turned away. But it was too late. He'd seen her expression and understood. Even if she were to tell him, he wouldn't understand. And he realised that the things that they were each gathering to themselves were so disparate they'd never find any common ground. She opened a glass cabinet and looked inside. He stood back, waiting.

'Hurry up, Maryam,' Awais urged. She looked up from the shelves, half dazed, and walked over to him.

'I've checked all the Rs,' she said. 'Maybe I've missed it but I don't think it's there.'

He heard the quiver of panic in her voice and took her hand. 'Come on, I'll help you find it.'

She led him to the bookshelves and he looked.

'It's not here,' she said.

'No.'

'Now what do we do?'

In answer, Awais seized Maryam's hand once more and led her

downstairs, through a narrow passageway. She stood transfixed before the rows and rows of cupboards with small drawers.

'You look under C and I'll look under R,' he said, opening a drawer.

'*Bhaia*,' she said, coming closer, 'you do it.'

He nodded. The book wasn't indexed under R but Awais finally found it listed under C. It hadn't been categorised under mathematics but under astronomy. Returning upstairs, they looked for the astronomy section, with Awais keeping a close eye on his watch. 'There!' said Awais, and handed Maryam the book.

Looking at the stamp page and seeing it was blank she said, 'It's never been read!'

Awais didn't tell her that this might not be true. The unmarked stamp page might be covering a multitude beneath.

He found Maryam a spot where she could sit and read, and left to find some books of his own. He looked over at her once or twice, and saw that she never lifted her head from her book. The afternoon sun, which shone high from the window behind her, changed strands of her hair from dark brown to russet red. If Maryam is becoming more herself, he thought, do I too have to become someone else?

When he returned, her elbows were on the table; she leaned into the book as if she'd like to sink in and disappear. 'Ready?' he said. She nodded. Downstairs she returned to her seat in the foyer and he stood guard over her as they waited for the librarian to return. When he did, the librarian was whistling. He stamped Awais's books, which included hers, without a murmur.

17

DECEMBER 1935, LAHORE

Khurshid had received a telegram to say Dar was in Delhi. That was all. No date of return. All this while, Khurshid left the radio switched on, as if it were a motor that had to be kept running. She sometimes lingered in the alcove for a while, but she never sat down on what they'd all come to think of as her chair.

Khurshid had always told her children how brilliant a salesman Dar was, though how she knew – when she, like them, had never seen him sell anything, not even a button or a balloon – they didn't know. Dar never contradicted the stories she told, though sometimes he laughed when there was no apparent joke.

What did these other places his father went to look like? Awais wondered. Smell like? What kind of buildings did they have? But what seemed marvellous to Dar – the people he encountered on his travels and his sales – held no interest for Awais.

All the salesmen Awais had ever seen, in shops and on the streets, had a manner about them that his father lacked. But perhaps, he conceded, those other men didn't possess it at home either. Maybe their smiles and their belief that the world could be righted by what they had to sell only emerged when they opened their boxes, their bags.

During the two weeks Dar was away, the family were gripped by their individual obsessions. Tanveer and Batool had been given a new, stiff pack of playing cards by their neighbour's son Raj. He'd made his younger sister present the gift so it couldn't be refused. He watched from his rooftop courtyard as Batool raised the cards to her lips or spread them out on her lap while she planned her next move.

Batool especially loved the Queen of Hearts, saying she reminded her of the pictures she'd seen of Queen Victoria. She was loath to give her up, even if it meant losing a game. Dar wouldn't allow cards in the house, but in his absence Tanveer and Batool were free to play Rummy and Rung for as long as they chose. They giggled and laughed a lot. Batool stamped a bare foot on the ground every time she won a card and the tiny bells of her new anklet rang.

Khurshid turned to the girls. 'I don't like it,' she said, looking at Batool's feet. 'Girls from good families don't wear such things.' Batool was silent, waiting. 'Where did it come from?' Khurshid asked.

'It's a present,' said Batool.

'You seem to be getting a lot of presents these days. Who gave them to you?'

'Tahera, *ama*,' said Tanveer.

'Batool?' Khurshid asked.

'Tahera, *ama*,' Batool said, not looking at her sister.

'I'll ask her,' said Khurshid. Then a new song began to play on the radio and she turned away, distracted.

'If she...' whispered Batool. The world of love was not far from them now and they felt it subtly closing in. Tanveer tapped Batool on the thigh. Batool, understanding, complied and raised her feet to the *charpoy* on which they sat. Sitting cross-legged, she touched the anklet with one hand; Tanveer scowled but Batool just smiled, and with her other hand, fanned out her cards, ready to play.

Khurshid watched her girls with a mellow pride. They would soon be young women. She'd married late; she'd marry them young. She wouldn't have the troubles other people had. Tanveer's good looks and Batool's beauty would see to that.

Each day, Awais rolled out his sheets. The complexity of his maps astounded even him sometimes. Never had he felt closer to his sister. How many people feel, can feel, what we feel? he thought.

He gave her some time, then asked, 'Understand it yet?'

'No,' she said. Another two days passed before he asked again. 'No,' she replied.

'Why don't you just ask Miss Alvi?' he said.

'I can't.'

'Why?' he said.

'I can't,' she said and scurried away.

But the very next day, on the recommencement of their classes after the local government had been sworn in, she sat with Miss Alvi and wondered if she could.

'You're not concentrating,' Miss Alvi said. 'It's not like you to make mistakes. I know it's hard to come back to something after a break but... What's wrong, Maryam?' What Awais had told her about Maryam's epilepsy was never far from her mind. 'Maryam, are you all right?' She reached out a cautious hand to touch Maryam's. Maryam pulled her hand back, then bent her head. Miss Alvi rushed to the kitchen and returned with a glass of water. 'Here,' she said, 'drink this.' Maryam did as she was told. 'Now how do you feel?'

'Miss Alvi,' Maryam said, 'I'm fine.' She looked with fresh hesitation at her teacher, then said, 'There's something I wanted to ask you.'

Miss Alvi smiled in relief. 'Maryam, is that all? Tell me.'

Maryam raised a finger to stroke through the bridge of her brows. 'That day you were late – you remember?'

'Yes,' Miss Alvi said. 'When the inspector came. Was I very late?'

'When you came in I was reading a book.'

Miss Alvi took a few minutes to reply. 'Yes,' she said, watching Maryam carefully.

'Will you teach me that book?' Maryam asked.

'You want to know about celestial numbers?'

'Yes.'

'You haven't reached that level of mathematics yet,' Miss Alvi replied. 'No, I can't.'

'But if I study really hard?' asked Maryam. 'How long do you think it will take before I'll be ready?'

'I don't know.'

'But when I am, you'll tell me and we can start?'

'Maryam, I can't! Don't ask me.' Maryam looked at her teacher, eyes open wide. Miss Alvi watched her, torn. After a while she said,

'All right, Maryam. Maybe, one day.' Maryam smiled. It was enough – for now. Miss Alvi continued, 'Shall we return to the exercises? Let's see if you can concentrate this time.'

Maryam had been studying with Miss Alvi for a year. To mark the date, Miss Alvi brought out, with their usual drinks, a plate of small pastries. Then, in the middle of the lesson, she got up and went to her bookshelves. Maryam watched her return to the table, a red leather-bound book in hand. Miss Alvi sat down and opened the book before Maryam. The first thing Maryam noticed was that the leaf was no longer there. When Maryam looked up into her teacher's face, she wished she'd never asked about celestial numbers; she'd never seen Miss Alvi look so beaten. 'So...' Miss Alvi said. And so, they began.

It was around this time that Awais realised he didn't have the words to describe what he was seeing. What were these carved window screens called? This design of tile? What was the name of the wood that was stained red, and which felt light to hold? He looked at his maps. Did not knowing matter? He must ask Shams Sahib. He bent his head again over his drawings.

'*Bhaia!*' Maryam said, bursting into his room.

'Where's the fire?' he replied.

Laughing and clutching Rajmohan Rao's book, which he'd had re-issued countless times on her behalf, she said, 'Guess what happened today?' And before he could even begin to reply, she rushed on. 'We started the book. Miss Alvi thinks I'm ready...' When she'd done telling him, she smiled hopefully, but he didn't ask her anything, didn't say anything. She hesitated a moment, then ran out of the room, dropping her book. Awais leapt up, ready to follow, to make up, to explain that some strange devil had momentarily possessed him and ripped up all that had ever been good in him. He saw the fallen book. He picked it up and threw it on the bed.

He sat back down on the bed, his back to the wall, one foot perched on the other. Broad and flat, his feet looked as if they'd been hammered thin. They felt cold. He felt such an overwhelming sensation of revulsion. But at whom? Myself, he thought? But also at something, someone else.

Stillness. How hard it is, he thought, to hold myself still. He looked at his toes: they resembled rows of earthworms whose faces had been rubbed clean off.

That night Maryam dreamt that someone, she couldn't see the face, was scrawling on her tongue: a whole configuration of figures and equations. Still half asleep she got up, searched for the notebook she always kept at her side, and began writing in the dark.

The next morning Batool and Tanveer woke up to find Maryam sprawled on the floor. Slowly Batool turned Maryam over, touched her forehead. It was hot. She ran to fetch their mother.

'*Ama!*' she shouted, banging on her mother's door.

The door opened, Khurshid flew out and gripped Batool by the shoulders. 'What's happened?'

For a moment Batool didn't answer and then, all at once, the words spilled out. '*Ama*, it's Maryam. Tanveer and I keep on calling her but she won't wake up. She'll be all right, won't she?'

'Go and wake Awais,' Khurshid said, and Batool ran off.

On entering the girls' room, Khurshid saw Maryam exactly as Batool had described her, balled up on the floor, and Tanveer on her knees beside her.

Awais came rushing in. He stopped short at the sight of Maryam. He lifted her back onto the bed, then placed a hand on her forehead. He took one of Maryam's hands and, rubbing it, said, 'Maryam, Maryam. Wake up.' Maryam's eyes slowly flickered open.

'Awais, *bhai*. Is it time to go to school?' As she spoke, her tongue showed black in her mouth.

'Open your mouth!' cried Awais. Maryam did. Hesitantly, Awais put his finger on her tongue and the blackness came off. 'Ink,' he said, relieved.

Khurshid, as if shaken from her stupor, said, 'That's it. It's finished. All this study rubbish.' She lunged for the notebook. 'First, I'm going to burn this and then...'

'Awais, *bhai*!' said Maryam, struggling to sit up.

Awais laid a hand on her arm. 'Don't worry, Maryam; *ama* won't burn it.' He held his mother's gaze until she put the notebook down.

'I can look after her now,' said Khurshid. 'Aren't you going to be late for college?'

Maryam tightened her grip on Awais's hand. He smiled at her, then turned to his mother. 'I'll stay here today,' he said. He sat down by Maryam's side.

Khurshid turned in the doorway and, avoiding Awais's eyes, said, 'Tanveer, Batool, let's get breakfast ready.' Tanveer followed Khurshid out but Batool stayed back.

'Do you want anything to eat?' Awais asked Maryam.

'No,' she replied. After a pause, she said, 'I'd like *nimbu pani*, Awais *bhai*.' Batool went to get the lemon water drink.

Awais shuffled, uncomfortable whichever way he sat on the narrow bed. He'd begun to get up when Maryam tightened her grasp on his hand.

'I'm only going to get a chair, silly. I don't want to crush your head, do I?' He came back with the chair and said, 'Now try and sleep. I'll wake you when Batool brings your drink.'

Miraculously, Maryam fell asleep quickly. Batool came with the drink. It was another two hours before Maryam woke, hungry and thirsty. Batool returned and said she'd take over the watch. Maryam began to whimper but when Batool bent down and whispered in her ear how tired Awais must be, Maryam let him go.

Before he left for his own room, Awais picked up Maryam's notebook, which he'd promised to keep safe, and told Batool to call him when Maryam awoke again. He found his mother waiting for him in the corridor.

'Now, do you see?' she said, as if continuing a conversation that had only recently been interrupted.

'*Ama*,' he said, 'I'm tired,' and though he saw the pleading in her eyes, he walked away. In his bedroom, he opened Maryam's notebook. As he'd expected, the pages were riddled with mathematical equations. Having done quite well in his Matric maths exam, he'd expected to understand something of what Maryam was studying.

But he understood nothing. He put the notebook to one side, and placing the palms of his hands on his closed eyes, he pressed hard, as if to push down to the bone. He was tired, but it was a tiredness that affected no other part of his body but his eyes, which was strange, he thought, for Maryam's notebook aside, he'd done no other reading today. It was as if something had lodged there, like in that story he'd come across when he'd first begun to read English books, about the snow queen and her broken mirror, the shards of which lodged in the heart and eyes of a boy. If he slept now, or laid down to rest until sleep took him over, would he wake to see the world like that little boy had seen it: a place too impossibly harsh to bear? Half an hour and then an hour passed, and still he couldn't sleep. If the future is built on the past, he thought, then it can't be changed. He got up, opened his trunk and took out the one map he hadn't drawn himself: his much-coveted map of the world. In the top right–hand corner, in a box, the words: Political Divisions of the Indian Empire. A lion with its front paws clamped on the Himalayas. He spread the map out on the bed and named its places. Then he rolled it up again and put it away.

As everyone lay asleep that afternoon, he let himself out. Once in the streets and the alleyways his breathing eased.

The city was changing. There was both growth and decay. New storeys had been added to existing buildings, and new buildings which shone brightly for a few days had been raised with great speed to meet the demand for houses and business. The city was changing from a fortress to a commercial centre. New people were arriving and the older residents looked at them with suspicion from their small corners, gossiping about the strange ways these newcomers had: crass and impolite, with their habit of spitting as they walked, as if they were not traversing paths built for men but those made for cattle and sheep.

Old men and old women who'd seen all the change they could wish to see, and change too that they'd not asked for, listened to the voices of discontent and said, 'Either the city will change or the new-comers will change.' Bets were laid on who or what would win.

If the newcomers were frightening, so was the decay, and as building after building, deceived into old age, collapsed, so a whole generation of old-timers died within three months of each other as if – said their children and their children's children, senselessly echoing the words they'd heard – they'd signed a pact to remain in one another's company till perpetuity itself was cleaved apart. The changes in the outside world had never been of much concern to those who lived safe within the city's walls. But as the order they'd built began to break and their universe began to shift, they too looked outside those walls, questions in their eyes and strange half-formed words on their lips.

It wasn't important to Awais that people saw what he saw. He didn't require their seeing it to know it existed. It existed whether they saw it or not. And again his heart grew full. Like it had been back in the days when he'd just discovered Loha and everyone had been excited at the find and wondered if there were more gates hidden away behind other walls. He lowered his head. He didn't want anyone to know what he felt. To think so much of yourself was wrong, he knew. But he couldn't help it.

'*Abba*, why's it wrong to feel pride?' he'd asked his father once. His father had laughed.

His mother had interrupted and said, 'False pride is wrong. But pride in what is good is right.'

His father had sighed. 'Amrau, don't fill…' He'd turned away muttering, 'Oh, never mind.'

Back home, he was on his way to his room when he heard his mother say, 'Nothing's gone right. Just look at him.' He stopped in the corridor to listen, his heart hissing.

'So he's dark–skinned.'

'The pir said…' she began, then stopped.

'My God, Amrau,' his father replied, 'your whole life tied to one man's words?'

'It's not my whole life,' she said. 'It's…' She fell silent then loudly said, 'It's not… it's not my life.'

Awais heard his father get to his feet and at the approach of his footsteps, Awais scampered to his room. He stood before the mirror and looked at his reflection. He hated mirrors and thought: they tell lies, and none that are kind.

That night, as the darkness rolled in, he smiled to himself. Darkness had always meant to him what light meant to others. Awais the Black. He'd come to like the name.

The next day he stood at Masti Gate, the gate where once, said his father, you could have seen elephants and wrestlers and things which did not belong to a street, but still somehow belonged to Masti. These days, it was like all the other residential areas: full of people and their ordinary noise. He walked up to the wall on one side of it. Earlier this year, the largest earthquake the country had ever seen had hit Quetta, a city in the north. With one massive jolt on 31 May, the earth had split and close to 60,000 people were killed. Although Lahore had remained safe, some within the inside city had begun to speak of how they'd felt its tremors. For those who would not believe such a thing had occurred, they'd pointed to the wall around Masti Gate, which showed two large cracks, each eight feet long. Bringing out the small penknife he kept in his pocket, Awais carved on the wall: 1935.

18

It was Mitoo who first noticed, or at least, who first said something.

'What's wrong with *khala*?' he asked.

'With *ammi*?' said Awais. 'There's nothing wrong.' But later, when Mitoo had gone, he watched her as she'd once watched him, and was taken aback by what he saw. For a start, she was thinner, much thinner than she'd ever been. But worse than that was the way she held herself. She, who'd have run them to the ground for any kind of slovenliness, no longer seemed to care about her attire, her hair. He remembered that there'd been a precedent for this, but then she'd been ill and now she was... He looked more closely; yes, of course, she was fine. She had to be. But he watched nevertheless, to make sure. It was as Shams Sahib had once said: with time, everything becomes visible: the good, the bad, beauty and pain. Perhaps, he reconsidered, it was something less grand than that and she was simply missing their father. He felt relieved and held tight to the idea.

Awais had only been special to his father that once, the time he'd found Loha, and never again. He therefore missed him hardly at all. They'd all adjusted to their father's absences, he saw; all except their mother. But if it hurt her so much, he thought, why didn't she plead with him to stay?

He watched as she played with the radio dial then sat back, seemingly content. He smiled. He would plan a surprise for her – why not?

'You want me to what?' exclaimed Mitoo when Awais told him.

'Can you do it?' asked Awais.

Mitoo just grinned.

Three days later Khurshid was sitting in the alcove in a new outfit Batool had forced her to wear. She'd been told they were expecting guests but not who they were. Maryam was still at Miss Alvi's. Everyone else was there and knew; their ebullience was high, as if this were the one party they'd always wanted to attend. Mitoo entered. Khurshid didn't even turn, so used was she to Mitoo's comings and goings. The two men behind him approached the alcove and, together, raised their closed hands in greeting. Khurshid shrank at their proximity and turned to find Awais, with Batool and Tanveer, watching her keenly.

'*Khala*,' said one of the two men and raised his bent head, his once buoyant curls now in adulthood settled into waves.

'Do I know you?' she asked.

'I'm—'

'Pankaj Gopal,' Khurshid and the young man said together.

'Those who are close to me call me Bablo,' he said.

'Bablo,' she said softly. 'How did you—?'

'Mitoo *bhai* came to find me.'

'Do you know,' she said, and lowered her head, 'all these years…'

'It's meant that much to you?' he said.

She nodded.

'*Khala*,' he said and touched a hand to his heart. He then stood back to introduce his companion. 'Kashif,' he said, 'my friend.'

Mitoo glared at Kashif and whispered to Awais, 'I've seen him somewhere before.'

'Ssh…' said Awais.

'What can I sing for you?' Bablo asked.

'You'll sing?' she said. 'Just for me – here?'

He turned, smiling, to include the rest of the family. 'For you all. What shall it be?'

'Do you remember that song you sang that day?'

Embarrassed, he gently said, 'Remind me?'

'*Yeh na thi*,' she said.

'Ah,' he said, '*hamiri kismet* – It wasn't in our fate. Yes.'

'Some water please,' Kashif said. Tanveer hurried to fetch some.

'You started out poor, with nothing, no one to support you, and still you made it,' she said, looking not at him but at Awais. 'I've followed you all the way.'

'God has been good,' Bablo said in the steady tone he kept for answering the same questions he was always asked. He accepted the glass Tanveer offered him, took a few sips then returned it to her with thanks.

His eyes closed and he began to sing.

When he'd come to the end, after a short silence Khurshid began, 'That was…' Bablo grinned like a boy who'd escaped the dreariness of home for the open world, and with that grin she was thrown back in time, remembering how, on the day they'd met, she'd been waiting and waiting to hear what the pir had to say.

'My sister sings,' Tanveer said, stepping forward.

'Tanveer!' said Khurshid. 'She doesn't even have a singing voice.' She looked angrily at her daughter. 'Now *that*,' said Khurshid to Bablo, 'is a voice.'

'You liked it?' he said.

'You've never thought of me in all these years, whereas I…' said Khurshid.

'*Khala*, no!' he said and knelt at her side. 'You were the first one to hear my voice as I wanted it to be heard. How could I forget you?' He reached out a hand. He hesitated. She pulled it into her own and kissed it.

'What beautiful bangles,' she said.

'Yes,' he said, turning to his friend with a familiar smile. 'Kashif made them. His hands can guide any metal into any form. Here,' he said, slipping off one of the bangles and handing it to her.

'No, no,' she said. 'I couldn't. He made it for you.'

'*Khala*, take it, please,' said Kashif.

'The old don't take from the young,' she said.

'It would make us happy,' said Kashif.

'If you stay for dinner,' she said, her hand going out to touch the bangle Bablo had put in her lap.

Bablo looked at Kashif who said, 'We're late.'

'*Khala*,' said Bablo, 'another time.' Mitoo and Awais took them down to the waiting tonga. Tanveer and Batool were bent over their mother, admiring the bangle's intricate design.

'It's a fish,' said Tanveer.

'It's not,' said Khurshid.

Mitoo and Awais returned. Mitoo couldn't take his eyes off the bangle. 'That's where I saw him!' said Mitoo. 'Kashif. He's the silver-smith's apprentice. Awais, did I—'

'Mitoo,' said Khurshid, 'thank you, *beta*.'

'*Khala*,' he said, 'what difference is there between a mother and an aunt?' The old saying, heedlessly spoken, stood between them, revealing a past neither could look at without hurt.

19

Maryam was growing ever brighter. Just eleven, he thought, and she never plays or seems to have friends or appears to miss any of that. Awais had overheard enough of Miss Alvi's words to know that things followed the motion of the principle to which they were set. There was no going back – for either of them really.

As he went in search of her one day he remembered how, before, it had always been her who'd come looking for him. He pushed open her bedroom door. His mother was sitting on the floor, amidst Maryam's open books. She looked up, startled, when he entered.

'*Ammi*,' he said, 'what are you doing?'

'Tidying,' she said, closing the book on her lap and dusting it with the edge of her *dupatta*. 'Did you want something?' she asked, beginning to put the books back in their place.

'No, I just…'

She looked directly at him. And what he saw in her eyes was frightening. Her eyes brimmed with pity. And he knew the pity was for him.

The next day Awais was in his room when he heard Maryam call, 'Awais, *bhai*.' He glanced at his door; it was locked.

'Awais, *bhai*,' she said again, softly this time. He turned on his bed so his back was to the door. After a few minutes she went away.

The next day he saw Maryam looking at him, two of her fingers held between her uneven teeth. He wanted to laugh. And then he was scared. She looked like the one thing he knew she could never be: an idiot. Her eyes grew watery and unfocused, and her mouth… but he couldn't look any more. It's her, he said to himself. It's her who's changed. I'm what I've always been. Maryam smiled and reached out a hand to him. He turned away. And what was worse, he saw his mother had seen it all.

Later that evening Khurshid came to his room. She stood unsure, like someone who had no right to be where she was.

'*Ammi*, sit,' he'd sometimes say when she appeared like this and then she'd lift a corner of the bedcover and sit on the edge of the bed where he'd have to move to better see her. But today he didn't ask her to sit. He didn't want her to stay.

'You see…' she began and he knew what she wanted to say. But he couldn't listen.

'*Ammi*,' he said, 'I've got a headache.'

'I'll get you some water?' she said. This hesitancy towards him was new.

'No, it's fine,' he replied. 'I have…' and he gestured to the glass of water on his desk. Her shoulders twitched, she turned and left. Awais sat still. No. It wasn't possible. But again the question rose, like a dead man turned out to sea, bloated with gas, never to sink. No. She couldn't know what he felt.

Born to be great? he thought when she was gone. The impulse was there. He thought it through. It was there for everyone, he acknowledged, whether to a grander or smaller degree. Maybe there are, he thought, embedded in this impulse, two distinct desires: the desire to make others think we are good and the desire for it to be something we know in ourselves, which ticks away in our heart and makes life – in all its dimensions – something pleasant to contemplate. Good was, he accepted, good enough.

In the following days, when he turned her way he thought his mother's eyes cruel. And he couldn't bear that either, and so inch by inch he moved further away from her. He knew she was hurt, but what could he do? She'd started it. If I'd been good, he reasoned, this thing wouldn't have dared grow. And then her words came back to him: *Maryam's taken…* He knew then, fully and with no room for doubt, that that which was corrupt within him had been given life by her, by his mother.

Dar, hungry to be told what to think and yet despising himself a little more each time he asked, said, 'The Unionists?'

Shams's face grew hard, a ready, switched-on hardness, as if he'd been waiting for just this moment.

'Ensconced in their palaces – what do they know?'

'They're so rich, though,' said Dar, 'there's no chance of them being corrupt.'

'Is that what people are saying?' asked, Shams shaking his head.

Dar's face raged with heat. As if, he thought, I have no opinion of my own! 'Sir Sikander Hayat seems like a good man,' he persisted.

'Thought it was Gandhi you liked?' asked Shams. Dar was about to reply when Shams said, 'No premier could have suited the British more.'

Dar had more questions, plenty of questions, but knew it was time for him to leave.

It had taken two years for the 1935 Government of India Act to be transformed from a paper on provincial autonomy into a reality. In all the provinces, Indians representing Indians. This is it, Dar thought: political good has diminished all other goods. He pulled himself up a little straighter. He knew this even if Shams didn't. Maybe, he wondered tentatively, I don't need him, after all.

20

Tomorrow was an important day. That night he slept hardly at all.

Before the household awoke Mitoo came to fetch him. Looking at Mitoo's strained face it came back to him – what he'd wanted to forget. They stole out of the house.

They'd decided to do it together. They bought a copy of *The Tribune* and walked to a disused *gurdwara*, a Sikh temple, now used as a grain storehouse, and sat on its steps. They checked the date: June 1938, then scanned the newspaper for their roll numbers.

'What d'you get?' asked Mitoo, closing the paper neatly.

'Just passed. And you?'

Mitoo grinned, 'Just failed.'

'My parents will kill me.'

'I know why I got what I got – but you? You should have been in the top bracket. Not that I'm saying you're clever; you're not. But that's all you do: study.'

'The maps,' said Awais. Even though Awais had never spoken to Mitoo about Shams Sahib, he'd told him a little about his maps.

'What am I going to tell my parents?' said Awais, his head bent.

'Your mother, you mean?'

'*Khala* won't be angry?' asked Awais, still looking glum.

'Not for long,' said Mitoo, crumpling the newspaper and getting ready to throw it. Awais grabbed it off him and pocketed it.

'Oi,' said Mitoo.

'And your father?' Awais asked, knowing he was on dangerous

ground but wanting suddenly to hurt Mitoo. He felt sickened with himself. Ahmed Sahib had only ever been polite to him and here he was, using him as dynamite. Mitoo's face shut down.

He said, 'I told you before…'

'He thinks…?' Awais said.

'I said!' cried Mitoo.

'They say—' Awais began but he didn't get any further. Mitoo lunged at him and Awais fell back against the steps. He sprang up and went for Mitoo's legs, trying to pull him down. Mitoo looked at him, shocked. Though he should have known, thought Awais. He's the one who taught me all his wrestling moves.

Awais's fist was at the ready and hit the mark of Mitoo's unprotected chest, hard as lead. Mitoo walked away as if he'd forgotten something on the other side of the clearing. He bent, picked up some dirt, pocketed it then turned around, smiling at Awais. He came hurtling for him then, head first. Awais collapsed on the ground. Mitoo crouched, his legs pinning Awais down. Awais fought to be free.

'You're like a fly,' Mitoo said, grinning down.

'Get off!' Awais shouted, struggling to unbalance him. Mitoo let him squirm for a while, then finally stood aside, letting him get up.

They didn't talk for a while until Awais, still on the ground, though sitting now, said, 'Will they have seen the result yet?'

'What d'you think?'

Awais pressed his palms to his eyes. When he released them the world was blurry. 'That's it, then,' he said. 'I can't go home.'

'Never?'

'Get lost!'

'Come on. Up you get,' said Mitoo, hoisting Awais up.

'Ow,' Awais said, rubbing his armpits. 'That hurt.'

'Leave it,' said Mitoo.

Awais fell quiet. They began to walk. The city was waking up. Laughter, a vendor's song and in the air, the first real breeze in twenty days.

'Okay,' said Mitoo, coming to a halt, 'look.'

'Majid's café? That's your big plan?'

'Look at the poster.'

'Diamond jewellers: gold and silver jewellery?' he said. He turned
to read a second poster: 'Master Hanif: Delhi's most famous palmist?'

'The other one,' said Mitoo.

Awais looked. 'Are you mad?'

Mitoo was laughing. 'Let's go and find out what it's about.'

'No!' said Awais. Mitoo kicked some dust with his shoe then, without turning to look at Awais, began to run. Awais caught up with
him at a street corner. 'You didn't even wait!' he said. Didn't I?
Mitoo's shining eyes seemed to say. They walked on in pace.

They had to pass through the High Court itself, a world in mono-
chrome, with its black-and-white tiles, black-and-white-suited and
booted people rushing from and to benches covered by once-cream
awnings. It was here, they'd been told, rather than in the court,
where judgements were made over property, marriages and deaths.
Mitoo wanted to rush through, but Awais slowed him down so he
could look.

One chair and one good desk, with a locked drawer for docu-
ments, receipts, stamp paper and pens was the domain of the head
clerk; a small frail man, no more than five feet tall, with thick curly
hair and long nails encrusted with dried ink. Another chair was left
empty for petitioners, who, often too wary and too many in number to sit, remained standing, gathering around the chair as if it
were a holy object. Everything around the clerks was, Awais realised,
there for the purpose of intimidation: the busyness of the lackeys; the
surge of documentation and the language of subpoenas and affidavits
which no ordinary mortal could comprehend. The petitioners, their
backs bent from a lifetime of supplication – to God, their *chaudhry* or
their landlord – and which only bent further every time a daughter
was born into their homes, waited, hopelessly, to be addressed and
offered no defence against the abuse of the lower clerks and even of
the *chai-wallah*, the young boy who smirked at their village ways and
who flitted between the different servants of the law keeping them
and their cronies in constant supply of tea. They all knew, as did
the lawyers who slipped the clerks rupees, not for work done, but to
curry favour, that it was here where real power lay.

Awais wanted to linger but Mitoo had had enough and pushed him ever on. Avoiding the lure of the cries around them – *Ay baba, want to get married? Annul a marriage?* – Mitoo and Awais weaved their way through the throng and finally stood before the annex which the military had taken over. Around this space there was no shuffling, no recalcitrant clerks looking for business. The order of its red–brick front was imposing.

A door opened and a *sahib*, an Englishman, with rolls of flesh padded onto him like a winter coat, rushed out in a steam of anger. He said something which neither of the boys understood. Mitoo and Awais broke apart, allowing him to exit.

Mitoo touched Awais's arm. Awais turned on him and spat, 'No!'

'Why d'you follow me then if you don't want to go in?'

Awais shook his head and said, 'I'm just stupid, I guess.'

'Come on, Awais,' said Mitoo, 'Just a few more steps: one, two…'

'I'm not doing it. Know what kind of trouble I'll be in?'

'Look,' said Mitoo weighing his words, 'it's simple.'

'Who're you calling simple?'

Mitoo smiled. 'Can't distract me like that.'

'What if I stand on my head?'

Mitoo's smile grew broader. 'What're you waiting for?' he asked. He paused then said, 'Look!'

'You said that already.'

'Just checking you're listening.'

Awais kicked the gravel and said, 'I'm not.'

'You're already in trouble,' said Mitoo. 'How much deeper can you get?' He paused then said, 'Thought you wanted to leave home.'

'I never said that. I can't leave home. There's Maryam,' he said, 'and there's my—'

'Maps?' said Mitoo, and Awais nodded.

'Anyhow,' said Awais, 'I don't have a bag.'

Mitoo raised his chin to the building in front of them. 'Maybe they'll give us one.' He touched Awais's arm again and led him in.

Once inside, they were made to fill out some forms. They were then called into an anteroom. On the other side of a desk sat a middle-aged man, glum, stroking his too-small chin. He looked up from his papers.

When all the tests were complete, the sergeant said, 'You're in. Welcome to the Indian Army.'

'Abroad?' asked Mitoo.

'Abroad,' said the sergeant.

Afterwards, Mitoo treated Awais to lunch.

They agreed they wouldn't tell their families until they'd received their confirmation letters. Awais told Mitoo he had some errands to run so Mitoo travelled home alone; Awais then rode out to the grave-yard of Mianni Sahib.

The flower sellers nodded as he walked along the path to the entrance; a few called him by name and asked after his family. They should be pale, he thought, seated, as they were, near the gates of death. As they joked and laughed, he wondered how it was that death and what it meant did not touch them. Or had death robbed them of something essential and they didn't even know it yet?

It was getting dark. Awais watched a family of fireflies emerge and spread themselves out as if they were at a late-night picnic. Their lights at first looked indistinguishable from each other but the harder he looked the more clearly he saw that they all glowed differently, some more temperate than the rest. Perhaps the light they shine is a marker for friends and foe, he thought, like a name is for us – a sign of who we've become and whom we belong to.

I've done it, he thought. His body sang. I'm leaving.

How can I, he thought, love the inside city and yet want more than it has to give? Now that he had acted upon the hunger to know, to see, he wondered what had made him wait so long. My love for the city and my desire to leave it aren't incompatible, he thought. He jumped down and began to walk. The graveyard was immense and from time to time he stopped to read a name on a gravestone. The moon, a fifth- or fourth-day moon, gave, he felt, a strange warmth to his face, kinder than the sun. It was late by the time he got home.

'All this gallivanting around with Mitoo,' she said when he returned.

'This has nothing to do with Mitoo.'

'Do you think you are in any position to answer me back?' He said nothing. 'Good,' she said. Her face softened when she saw his expression. 'Look *beta*, you've got to understand. I didn't know what had gone wrong. Miss Alvi was here and she—'

He was full of consternation. 'I'm sorry, *ammi*. I completely forgot.'

'It doesn't matter,' she said. 'Miss Alvi brought her home.' She paused, then said, 'Miss Alvi said you might just have blanked out in the exam. She says it happens to the best of students. Is that what happened?'

'Maybe I'm just not clever enough.'

She slapped him. She stepped back. He stood still, with his cheek raised. Every time he'd ever hurt himself, she'd rubbed it better. Neither of them now knew what to do.

'Your father will go to your college tomorrow. You'll sit the exam again in December. It will all be all right. Go on. The food's in the kitchen.'

He went straight to his room instead. He kicked off his shoes then lay on his bed, stomach down. He'd done it. Walked in. Joined the army.

If she'd been angry about the exam, she'd go manic over this. The world of solitude he'd chosen or fallen into was not enough. He wanted something with more bite to it, even, he thought, a little spit.

'Work for the British?' Dar said. 'Has nothing I've ever told you gone into that head of yours? Don't you understand? Do you even have an inkling of what you've let yourself in for?' He swung away from Awais and, as if talking to himself, said, 'I'll talk to Shams. He'll know how to get you out.'

'What do you want him to do?' said Khurshid, 'Sell—'

'Go on,' Dar said, his voice grown quiet.

'It's an opportunity.'

He ignored her and turned back to Awais. 'Know where England's heading towards? Well, do you?'

'There won't be a war,' said Awais.

Dar raised his hands and shook his head.

Khurshid said, 'You don't want to go to Government College?'

Alwais looked confused. Why am I doing this? he thought. I do want to go to Government College. The army's just another of Mitoo's crazy schemes. Neither of us is joining; not really. It was just a joke.

'Awais,' said Khurshid, 'go to your room.' But he remained where he was. He glanced at them, then turned away. He felt cruel, buzzingly alive. She looked as if she would faint.

Dar reached out a hand and supported her back. 'See what you've done?' he shouted. 'Come on, let's go to the kitchen. I'll make you some tea.' She turned to look at him and Dar laughed. 'Okay,' he said, 'I'll get Batool to make you a cup.' She began to turn back to the courtyard where Awais still stood. 'No, *meri jan* – my love,' he said to Khurshid, 'leave him for now.'

His brow furrowed. Dar said to Awais, 'We'll talk about this another time.'

Two weeks later, Awais was summoned to the recruitment office. He asked Mitoo if he'd received a letter as well, but Mitoo said no.

'Close the door,' the sergeant said when he entered. He offered Awais a seat then opened Awais's file and began to read. 'What I want to know,' he said putting the file down on his desk and looking at Awais, 'is why you didn't tell us about your heart?'

Awais looked at the file. He didn't say anything. There was nothing to say. He glanced at the letter the sergeant had read out to him. His mother's handwriting was unmistakeable.

'You nearly failed,' said Shams. 'What happened?'

'I guess,' said Awais, 'I'm just not good at remembering things.'

'Awais,' said Shams slowly, 'the first job of the custodian is to remember.'

'But you're the custodian.'

Shams gave Awais a rabid look. 'When you told me you'd started making maps, I...' Awais remembered that conversation, the hardness that had spread across Shams Sahib's face. 'We're going to use your maps. Come here. Look.' And unearthing a sheet of paper he began to draw. 'It's the oldest memory trick in the world. You build a memory palace, and you tack the things you want to remember to each site.' Awais listened intently as Shams Sahib explained. 'You understand?' said Shams. Awais nodded. 'Soon,' said Shams, 'people will come to you with their stories.' He considered Awais again. 'I think, for the moment, it's better that you meet them here. It's going to be your job, Awais, to remember it all – each and every story. Our history isn't a dead history confined to books.'

Awais didn't know what to say. It had never crossed his mind that there'd come a time when the office of custodian would be his.

21

Mitoo was sent to training camp. After six months he returned home. Soon, the day came for him to leave India.

'Want me to come with you to the station?' Awais asked.

'No,' said Mitoo.

'I'll be there by seven-thirty.' They hadn't spoken of Mitoo's going away or the fact that Awais's posting abroad had been revoked and that he was now to be stationed in the army service in Lahore.

'*Ammi…*' said Mitoo, looking back to the closed kitchen door where his mother had disappeared a few moments ago.

'Don't be stupid. You know I will. Let's go and have some dinner somewhere,' suggested Awais.

Mitoo shook his head.

'Tea?'

'Still have some packing to do.'

'Okay,' said Awais.

'Okay,' said Mitoo.

The next morning, the path to the station was swarming with soldiers who were all – even the usually loud ones – trying to keep their voices in check. Mitoo had insisted his mother stay at home. He knew it would be too much for her.

Awais and Mitoo said a quick goodbye at the gate, then Mitoo was gone. Awais regretted he hadn't insisted they mark the occasion somehow.

He started out for home: first a tonga from the station and then, once inside the city, he began to walk. He'd started his explorations of the city alone. But the day after he'd told Mitoo about the maps, Mitoo had tailed him and then jumped out from an alleyway, feet spread apart, arms wide to block him and cried, 'Tah!' Awais had complained for a while but he'd been glad, really. Mitoo rarely wanted to come along after that, but when he did he was the perfect companion; he knew when Awais wanted to talk and knew when words would only get in the way of the things Awais needed to observe. And now, thought Awais, the bastard was gone. He looked up. There was washing hanging out to dry from the walls of top-floor courtyards. The houses looked grim, grey. Everyone had been somewhere, everyone except him. Even his sisters had been to another city. And here he was – stuck.

It was 4.15 by the time he reached Jalgit's *akhara*, where Mitoo trained.

Jalgit, a tall man with a tapered body, skin shiny with oil, was wrestling with a man Awais knew called Mahfouz who weighed in at a lesser bar but who had greater speed. They grunted and slapped their thighs as they made their moves. Jalgit's five students were watching, taking mental notes. Jalgit told them to watch his opponent, for it was from weakness that they'd learn. They didn't listen. All eyes were on Jalgit.

Jalgit, with his broad face and his small wincing eyes, caught sight of Awais and smiled. His opponent seized the moment of lapsed concentration and rushed at Jalgit. Jalgit fell, head first. His opponent, Mahfouz, lunged again. Bones cracked. The students pressed forward, hissing and cursing. With his good right hand Jalgit held them back.

'Oh, was that your hand, Jalgit?' cooed his opponent, his mouth close to Jalgit's ear, his saliva dribbling hotly down Jalgit's cheek. He gripped Jalgit's neck in the crook of his arm and twisted. He was smiling now, a man whose work was done. He looked around at the grim faces of the students, his eyes glistening. With a massive sweep, Jalgit tried to shrug him off. Mahfouz resisted – easily. But Jalgit stayed firm, gaining greater and greater control. And then he got him. He hammered Mahfouz to the ground. He held him there, to loud cries from his boys, until Mahfouz admitted defeat. Jalgit offered him his hand, which Mahfouz wouldn't take.

Awais picked up Jalgit's turban, which during the last minutes of the fight had flown off. Jalgit shook his head and sadly said, 'A Sikh without hair. What to do? Put it down over there. I'm dripping with sweat.' Awais did what he was told.

'Mitoo not with you?' Jalgit asked, beginning to dry his body with a towel.

'Just dropped him at the station,' said Awais. Jalgit stopped rubbing his legs and looked up at Awais. Awais blinked. Had it really just been this morning? Mitoo had practised hard at wrestling, and could have, said Jalgit, become a national champion if he'd set his mind to it. Jalgit pointed with his head to where the old ones were sitting and watching. Sonu Mahraj, a sixty-year-old spice merchant, got up and walked towards the pit. He rubbed the red earth on his chest and said, 'Who's got the courage to fight me today?' A young man stepped forward.

Awais, caught up in the new match, didn't see Jalgit make a signal to a young boy, about eleven, who began to pump water. The boy filled a steel tumbler and brought it over to Awais.

After a while, Awais said, 'I have to go.'

'Stay a little longer, Awais,' said Jalgit. Awais leaned back; the cement of the wall was cool, and from the peepal and neem trees – to which were tied the canopy that kept the wrestlers in the shade – came two mingled aromas; they took away all the tiredness he felt.

'Stay for dinner?' Jalgit said.

'No, really, I have to go.' He stood up and Jalgit sized him up as he always did.

'Come one day and I'll put you in the pit. Try it once.'

Awais smiled. That was Jalgit's set piece. He set off for home. The closer he got, the darker his mood. He had to stay away from her. She'd see it as betrayal, but so what? He feared so much of her was in him now, he'd never get her out.

He frowned, looking down. His shoe was caught in a red kite lying on the ground. He bent to pick it up and the kite ripped. He dropped it quickly and looked around. Had anyone seen? Some poor kid would appear any second in search of his kite, the colour of a blood orange; the kid would work himself into a fit and then examine the kite and see that the damage was not caused by its descent. Had some other jealous boy massacred his kite? The kid would conjure up a few names and send them to the dock: hanging would be too kind. He'd keep them there till he could think of a fitting revenge, and he'd blacken their names eternally, not realising he might, just might, be wrong.

22

Another letter – this time from her sister, and with it, a fresh invitation.

'Why can't she come and see us?' Dar asked.

'Her husband,' said Khurshid. 'You know what he's like.'

'I'll have to stay here,' he said.

'You're not coming?' she said. She raised a hand and he latched onto it. Aware of the children, she tried to pull it back but he wouldn't let it go. The fingers of his other hand clinked through her glass bangles. He tried to get her to meet his eyes but she wouldn't.

'My first trip outside Lahore,' Awais murmured.

'Who said you could go?' Dar said. Awais looked from his father to his mother.

'He's joking,' Khurshid said.

'The look on his face!' Dar laughed.

The next morning the girls lingered in the kitchen after the breakfast dishes had been cleared. Batool checked the passageway again, then nodded. Tanveer lowered the iron rods over the stove while Batool held Maryam down by the shoulders and said, 'Now Maryam, close your eyes.' When they emerged half an hour later, Maryam had a head of curls. Her hand went to touch her hair in wonder and Tanveer slapped it back. Each of their faces was marked with dabs of red.

'You're coming down with something!' said Khurshid.

'No, *ammi*,' said Tanveer. 'It's rouge.' Awais laughed and Tanveer gave him the evil eye. He'd seen them smudge the red borders from their Nelson Reader books onto their cheeks.

It was a short tonga ride to the bus stop on Bull Road. Awais made his sisters and mother wait away from the crowd while he bought five tickets for the Crown Plaza bus.

'Why doesn't the driver start?' asked Tanveer impatiently. Awais told her the driver would wait till the bus was full before he set off.

They disembarked at the Amritsar bus stop and Awais found a tonga to take them to their aunt's house. When they arrived, Awais jumped down and helped his mother out.

'I'll be back in a moment,' Awais said to his sisters, leading his mother indoors.

Urged on by the driver who wanted to be on his way, Batool and Tanveer gathered their boxes and bags and stepped down. Maryam, aping Awais, jumped down – straight into a deep puddle. Muddy water drenched her new clothes. Crying, she raised a tentative hand to her curls.

'It'll wash clean,' said Batool. Maryam cried louder so she could be heard. Smiling, Batool wrapped Maryam in her arms. Their *khala* Munni Bibi opened the door and led them in, eager to show them her new house. They'd moved from Gujranwala to Amritsar two years ago.

Most of the Butt children were around Maryam's age. The exception was Zubi, who was a few months older than Tanveer. Zubi, like Tanveer and Batool, wore a *chaddor*. But whereas they took theirs off once indoors, Zubi kept hers on.

A look passed from Zubi to her mother. Zubi smiled before lowering her head. Awais had never been more aware of a girl in his life. He watched her whenever he had the chance. Later in the day he saw her sitting with Batool and Tanveer, their heads close together in the secret way of girls. Zubi stroked out the creases from her *kameez* and as her hand moved up and down he noticed the curve of her thighs. He fled the courtyard, ashamed.

Tanveer and Batool had Zubi, Khurshid had her sister Munni Bibi, and Maryam was soon at one with her other cousins. Karamat, their aunt's husband, tried to take Awais under his wing but it was hard for them both and so, by silent consent, they decided to leave each other alone.

On the second day, Awais made his way to the Golden Temple. It couldn't be as beautiful as he'd heard. He walked up the promenade, his breath slowing. Around the temple, a pool of clear water. Voices brought low in homage. On the pavement in front of the temple on sheets, rows and rows of Sikh vendors selling all kinds of artefacts: relics, postcards, prints. He looked at the temple, marvelled at its simplicity. The sun dipped and hit the temple's golden skin as if, with a little trying, it could lick it clean. He asked the vendors if he could sit down. They made room for him, and responding to his questions, began to talk. When they turned away to deal with a potential customer his gaze returned to the temple. *I'll go in. Any minute now.*

Back at the house, no one was aware what the younger ones were up to. They'd dressed up Karamat's father, who was eighty-two years old and had long withdrawn into himself. They'd borrowed Zubi's make-up and done up his face. The blusher fell into the hard cracks of his skin like waste deposits on a river bed. His lips, they'd painted a sloppy red. With a *dupatta* on his head – for respect – they'd wheeled him out in the chair Karamat had had made for him, and taken him out for an airing. It had been the siesta hour; but when, puffing heavily, they wheeled him in again, the rest of the family were in the courtyard having tea.

'What's the meaning of this!' shouted Karamat, rushing forward to release his father. Seeing his father's uncomplaining face, Karamat began to cry. The children all stepped back. Khurshid's sister, Munni Bibi, approached, heavy–footed. She slapped Pehtu, the eldest of her boys. Then she picked up her father-in-law's hand, but it slipped, wouldn't stay in hers. Seeing how his head lolled to the right, tears began to stream down her face. She retreated, weeping, to the kitchen, with Zubi fast on her heels.

Khurshid took charge. 'Awais,' she said, 'take *dadaji* to his room.'

Awais wheeled the old man away and she and Karamat followed. Once she'd laid him on the bed, she rested her head against his heart and listened carefully. She said to Karamat, 'Come sit and talk to him.' Then she led Awais from the room and said, 'Go back to Lahore and fetch Roshanay Begum. She'll ask you why she should go with you. Say it's because your grandfather hasn't yet made his peace with God.'

'But *ammi*—' he began.

'Remember,' she said.

Though it was only the late afternoon, Batool brought Awais his dinner, which he forced himself to eat before setting off. As it was, he had to wait half an hour before the bus was ready to depart.

On the edge of the city, frantic, his neck craning out of the window. Thirty-two miles traversed in a blink. The streets shone with rain. It struck him again, as it did from time to time: he'd seen the river Ravi but never the sea. He'd asked Maryam to tell him what it had looked like, how it moved, if it were ever completely still. But all she'd said when she returned from Karachi was: 'It's big. There's water as far as you can see.'

'And the smell?' he'd asked. He'd read that not only the sea, but the surrounding air, smelled of salt.

'Salt?' she'd asked.

Why do I, he thought, who've never seen it, dream of the sea? And sometimes, in the first moments of dawn, I can hear its waves as they rise and fall.

'The city has secrets,' Shams Sahib had once said. Does Shams Sahib take me for a fool? Awais had thought at the time. To be tempted by such children's stories. But what if, he now wondered, Karachi is a city by the sea and Lahore is a city built on one? Maybe it had been depleted and the Punjab's five rivers were all that remained.

Arriving at Bull Road, he hailed a tonga and jumped on board. When he gave the driver the address, the driver smiled an ugly smile, twisted and knowing. 'Aren't you a bit young for this?' he asked. Awais's cheeks burnt red-hot but he didn't reply.

Heera Mandi, with its clusters of shops and houses and temples and mosques, was like any other area in any other part of the city. In the distance, Badshahi mosque, the world's largest mosque. He hated its enormity, its blandness, as if you had to reveal yourself to man before God would accept you at His door. He wondered if the traders who'd settled here had thought they'd only be here a while – till their situation improved, and then maybe they'd stayed because they'd come to

love this quarter, or maybe, he thought, they liked the irony of religion and sin standing side by side. An ordinary locality with ordinary
ways. But then, he thought, it's not night–time yet.

'Don't suppose you want me to wait?' asked the driver as they
rolled into the backyard of the large house.

'No,' said Awais and paid the man. He now knew Roshanay
Begum's annexe well and went straight in. His mother had seemed
convinced Roshanay Begum would accompany him back to
Amritsar. He was doubtful. In all the years he'd fetched Maryam's
medicine he'd never met her. Roshanay Begum's assistant Kasani
greeted him, puzzled. 'Has Maryam run short?' she asked. When
Awais explained the reason for his visit, Kasani led him from the
crowded waiting room.

'Is that…?' he whispered, staring down at the still form of a woman
seated in a high-backed chair. He couldn't tell whether the woman
could hear them or not; her eyes were closed.

'Yes,' said the girl. He was about to step away when Roshanay
Begum grasped his wrist. Shocked, he pulled back. Though her hand
was shaking, its grip on his wrist tightened. Slowly, she opened her
eyes. She let his wrist go. Kasani signalled for him to crouch beside
her so that they were all three at eye-level. He looked cautiously into
Roshanay Begum's face. No one had ever told him about the pecu-
liar strength of her beauty. Her soft green eyes were the only mellow
feature of her face.

'Kasani,' she said. Both Awais and Kasani waited patiently. 'Now
tell me.'

'Begum Sahiba,' said Kasani. 'This young man's *dadaji* – is that
right?' – and she turned to Awais for confirmation – 'is ill. In Sialkot,
did you say?'

'No, Amritsar.'

'In Amritsar,' she said. 'Tell her in your own words what happened.'

Awais explained. His knees began to hurt from the squatting. He
saw how, almost imperceptibly, Roshanay squeezed Kasani's hands.
Once, twice.

Kasani said to Awais, 'Over there, on the cabinet, on the second shelf, you'll see a green bottle. Bring it to me.' Awais fetched it. 'Now pour some into a glass.' She lifted up Roshanay Begum's head and said, 'When I say, tip the liquid down her throat.'

'I can't!' he cried.

'Ready?' said Kasani. 'One, two...' She prised open Roshanay Begum's mouth, while Awais stared at her blankly. 'Quick. I can't hold her for long,' she said, and Awais quickly poured the liquid down the healer's throat. Kasani gently closed Roshanay Begum's mouth, then let go of her. With a cloth from the nearby table, she wiped away the few drops of liquid which had spilled on to her chin.

Awais was disturbed by the sense that he'd intruded on a private act. But he couldn't turn away, not now, and he watched the slow and agonising movements of Roshanay Begum's throat as the liquid was swallowed down. She squeezed shut her eyes again.

'We'll leave her for five minutes.' And with that, Kasani retreated to one of the seats in the corner of the room. Some minutes passed before Roshanay Begum called out Kasani's name. Kasani rose, a smile on her lips. She knelt before the chair and once more took Roshanay Begum's hands in her own.

'Come here,' said Roshanay Begum. Her voice was deep and the words spoken with precision. Awais approached. 'Yes, so you want me to go with you to Amritsar to see your *dadaji*?'

'Yes, Begum Sahiba,' he said.

'Why should I do this for you?' asked Roshanay Begum.

'Because,' he said remembering what his mother had told him to say, 'he hasn't yet asked for the grace of God.'

Roshanay Begum looked hard into Awais's face. Kasani seemed to understand what the look meant and asked, 'Begum Sahiba, do you think you can make the journey?'

Roshanay Begum said, 'Hand me the white bottle.' She took it, measured out a cupful and sipped. 'Give me fifteen minutes.'

Kasani led Awais outside.

'What was the liquid you gave her?' he asked.

'Mercury,' she said.

'Mercury!' he exclaimed. She smiled. 'Are you sure it's safe?' he said.

'It's what she asked for,' Kasani said.

'But mercury?'

'The quality of mercury,' said Kasani, in the tone of a lesson learnt long ago, 'is that if someone is not in their proper spirits, is either high or low, it reacts in the opposite direction, thereby creating a balance. Roshanay Begum says that her illness is an angry masculine illness and that it is only mercury, with its feminine nature, which knows how to bring the spirits to peace.'

'How long will the effect last?' he asked.

'I don't know,' she replied.

Kasani went out briefly to give the gatekeeper instructions and then they both sat down to wait.

'Baji,' said the gatekeeper, coming forward at the allotted time. 'Begum Sahiba is ready.'

Kasani led Awais to the back courtyard where Roshanay Begum was seated in a tonga, a blanket on her lap. Kasani stepped into the tonga alongside her mistress and Awais climbed into the front with the driver.

A few hours later they arrived at the Butts' house. Awais led Roshanay Begum and Kasani inside and introduced them. Roshanay Begum told the family that only one of them could accompany her into the old man's room. She picked Awais.

She took the old man's pulse. She then gently drew back his closed lids to examine his pupils. 'Kasani, as I thought, the sulphur...' Kasani placed a bottle and a pestle and mortar on the table and awaited further instructions. At Roshanay Begum's signal, Kasani poured a few drops of the yellow liquid into the mortar. Then, following her mistress's instruction, she added a few more squares of powder.

'Enough,' said Roshanay Begum. Kasani passed the bowl to the healer who, bending her head, said a prayer and then blew onto the liquid. 'Now give it to him.' As Kasani raised the old man's head to dispense the medicine, Roshanay said, 'Sulphur as the divine will. A celestial liquid to bring man back to his just place.' And again she recited a prayer.

When the mortar was empty, Kasani gently laid back the old man's head. Kasani turned the lamp down and they waited. Two hours passed before the old man opened his eyes and Awais was sent out to tell the family the news. Karamat entered quietly. He raised his father's head and pressed it to his chest. '*Abba, abba* – you're all right?' he said again and again, the tears blurring his words. He began to rock, taking his father with him.

'Bastard! Are you so tight that you won't even put a light on in your father's room?'

'Quick, light the lamp,' said Karamat. Awais lit it. The old man looked up at the press of people around his bedside and said, 'Who are all these children of Satan?'

'So, *dadaji* hadn't taken his final grace from God?' said Roshanay Begum softly to Awais.

Before he could reply, the door opened again and Khurshid and Munni Bibi entered. They broached the question of payment, but Roshanay Begum directed the conversation to other matters. After she had told them how the patient must be cared for, she said she had to return to Lahore as soon as possible.

'Awais will take you back,' said Khurshid.

Squinting at Khurshid, Roshanay asked, 'Have we met before?' Khurshid smiled at being remembered, even if only dimly, by Roshanay Begum.

'A long time ago,' she said.

In the courtyard, Batool, Tanveer, Maryam and their cousins were sitting cross-legged on a *charpoy*, waiting for news.

Roshanay Begum stopped in her tracks. Maryam, who'd been talking to Tanveer, looked up.

'That one,' said Roshanay Begum, leaning in to Munni Bibi. 'The young one. Yours?'

'My sister's daughter, Maryam.' She nodded towards Khurshid.

'Maryam,' said Roshanay Begum. 'And she lives here in Amritsar?'

'No, Lahore. They've come to visit and thank God they did because it was Awais who went to get you. None of my sons is old enough. It's a blessing they were here.'

Roshanay Begum let her talk as she continued to consider Maryam. When Munni Bibi was done, Roshanay Begum crossed to the *charpoy* and said, 'Come here, *beta*.'

Maryam did as she was told. Roshanay Begum took up her hands and held them in her own.

'You go to school?'

'Yes,' said Maryam, conscious of being watched by the others, and above all by her mother. 'Middle school.'

'Middle school, is it?' said Roshanay Begum. 'And are you clever? No, I don't need to ask that. What's your favourite subject?'

'Maths. My teacher, Miss Alvi...'

Khurshid stepped forward and, laughing nervously, said, 'Maryam, Roshanay Begum...'

Roshanay Begum ignored Khurshid. Still looking at Maryam, she said, 'You'll come and visit me? Soon?'

Maryam looked from Roshanay Begum to Awais, then nodded. Roshanay Begum smiled and stroked Maryam's face, from cheek to chin. She turned to Khurshid then and said, 'Send the girl to me.'

When she was gone, Munni Bibi turned to her sister and said, 'What was all that about?' Khurshid shook her head; she didn't know. But of one thing she was certain, though she didn't know why, and it was this: she never wanted to see Roshanay Begum again.

23

OCTOBER 1939, LAHORE

'A new start,' Khurshid said as Awais ate his breakfast. He bolted down the rest before making his escape. His uniform, made from heavy khaki wool, started to itch, but he was on his bike by then and couldn't stop. Without relief, the itch grew.

He turned back to look. Other cyclists, pedalling as hard. Like a flock of birds, they formed a near-perfect 'V'.

He swerved into Civil Lines where he banged the bike into a stand and quickly locked it, looking down so no one who might be watching would think he were suggesting this place abounded in thieves. Then he couldn't help it; he began to scratch: first one leg, then the other, scaling his skin red. A man, older but similarly kitted out, pushed open a door and stood watching Awais.

'It's as if they put lice in the stitching,' the man said. 'You'll get used to it.' He opened his mouth, as if about to spit, then closed it, remembering there was no *paan* left to chew. 'Or,' he said, 'you won't.' And with these words of wisdom, he returned inside. Awais pulled up his socks, though his skin still stung. He approached the door the man had gone through and pushed it open.

By midday it was decided. They didn't like him. They whispered, some of them, but he heard. Some said he was an abysmal newt of a man. There were confident men, braggers, opinionated men, men in love with their looks, and they'd all been tolerated – with time. But they knew, to a man, that they wouldn't and couldn't tolerate Awais. His intensity was so sharp it made their actions – and by actions they meant work and by work they meant the bare minimum they could do – seem like a muddling along. Among all the Indian staff it was only Ain Khan, a broad-backed, simple man, who befriended Awais. The others noted this and put it down in a register they kept for such things.

'What do you expect of a Pathan?' one man said.

Awais had been in the job for a year. He was a sepoy. He'd learnt the ropes and knew whose power was intransigent and who only had power in name; he'd learnt whose jokes were worth laughing at and how to insult others with silent bewilderment. He hardly thought any more about what his mother had told him the pir had said; what he'd been promised. At home, Khurshid, trying to win him back, prepared all his favourite dishes; he ate them ravenously enough, then returned to his room.

A few days before his birthday in November, Maryam knocked on his door and when he opened it she blurted, '*Bhaia*, is it something we've... I've done?' She looked as if she were on the verge of tears.

'Don't be stupid, Maryam,' he said. 'I've just been very busy.' She began to tilt to one side. He instinctively put out a hand, then withdrew it.

'*Bhaia*,' she said, 'you're sure? I thought...'

'Maryam,' he said, laughing, 'one of these days you're going to have to finish your sentences.' She smiled but only half-heartedly. She stepped back through the door, and he didn't ask her to stay.

He'd stopped listening a long while ago. Across his face, a strange sheen, as if he'd completed a long, long run. 'Pakistan,' he said softly.

'Did you say something,' asked Khurshid. Reluctantly, he turned towards her; in his eyes there seemed no recognition of who she was.

Then Tanveer came hurtling in. '*Ammi*, have you seen—'

The radio's static reverberated across the courtyard.

'Turn that down,' said Khurshid. But as Batool moved forward to carry out her mother's command, her father held her back with a raised, weak hand.

'No, no,' he said. 'Don't touch it.'

'What's got into you?' Khurshid said.

He looked at her with his awful knowledge and said, 'War's just been declared.'

24

'Jinnah says the idea of a unified India is a lie – that it's something the British made up.'

Khurshid tried to listen, she really did.

'If it's a lie,' he said, still thinking as the words took shape, 'then the idea of a separate homeland for Muslims is... I don't know.' She understood how hard the words were for him. He'd been a diehard Congress supporter since long before they met.

Dar paused, then said, 'We should support Muslim shopkeepers from now on.'

She nodded but knew she'd go on as before. What did politics have to do with who she bought her vegetables from? More and more his conversation turned to politics. He told her the movement for home rule was growing ever stronger. *He's doing it deliberately*, she thought, *to drive me crazy*. She was relieved when a few days later he said he had to take another trip.

A week later, Dar entered Delhi Gate, relieved to be nearly home. Ahead of him two mingling political processions, Congress and Muslim League supporters bickering, blocking each other's way, voices raised in anger. A man pushed another man. Dar's heart began to thud; sharp shivers of pain. He put a hand to his chest, pressed down. He just wanted to get home. He took a few steps forward; a man trod on his foot, apologised, and was stunned to see Dar collapse to the ground like a dropped bag. The man stared at the prostrate figure, then pushed his way past people mumbling, 'I didn't do anything, I didn't do anything.' The two processions began to diverge and people moved on.

A few minutes later, as the crowd thinned, someone spotted Dar. The man didn't know what to do and called for help. Someone knelt down and checked Dar's pulse. Someone else called the police.

The policeman seemed to know immediately that Dar was dead. He checked his pockets, his bags, but there was nothing that revealed his address. Then of the many passers-by who'd stopped to see what was going on, one cried, 'That's Awais's father!'

How were they to get the body from Delhi Gate to Bhatti Gate? The policeman grunted that he hadn't been trained for this and went to lean against a wall for a smoke, waiting for someone else to decide what to do. The young friend of Awais's who'd recognised Dar commandeered a shopkeeper's cart, and, with the help of the shopkeeper and three other volunteers, laid the body on the cart. Awais's friend walked alongside and led the cart driver to Awais's house. It wasn't so far, but because the cart driver was being careful it took them a long time.

Once they'd arrived, Awais's young friend told the cart driver to wait out of sight. The driver nodded and parked some distance away from the house. The boy knocked on the door, then knocked again.

Tanveer shouted down, 'What do you want?'

'To see Awais.'

'Not here,' said Tanveer, and closed the window shutter. The boy knocked again, gently.

'There's something I've got to tell Awais. When will he be back?'

She opened the shutter again. 'I don't know.'

'Never mind. I'll wait.'

Tanveer seemed to hesitate as if she were consulting with someone. 'Okay.'

The boy returned to the cart driver's side. The driver began a long rant about the loss to his business. The boy adjusted the shawl covering Dar, and the cart driver, watching him with great intent said, '*Ya Allah.*' After that he was silent.

Whistling, Awais turned the corner into his street. His friend stepped forward and raised his hand, and Awais came towards him, smiling. Before the boy could say anything, the cart driver broke into a coughing fit. Awais turned and saw the body covered with the shawl.

'Awais,' said his friend, 'your *abba*…'

Awais ran over to the cart and pulled back the shawl.

His friend approached and said, 'Do you want me to help you take him up?' Awais didn't reply. 'Awais?' the boy said, and replaced the shawl over Dar's face.

'I have to go and tell *ammi*,' said Awais.

Khurshid was in the kitchen. Looking at his stricken face she said, 'What's happened?'

'*Ama*,' he began.

'Tell me!' she cried.

'*Abba*.'

She leapt up and shook him. 'What kind of joke is this?' she said.

'Batool!' Awais shouted. Batool came running into the kitchen, Tanveer following on her heels.

Awais tried to free himself from his mother's grip but she wouldn't let go. 'Batool,' he said beseechingly and together they prised their mother's hands free. Batool led Khurshid to a stool and helped her sit down.

'I'll go and get him,' said Awais, turning to the kitchen door.

'No,' Khurshid cried. He looked at her, helpless, then left to bring his father back home.

25

DECEMBER 1943, LAHORE

Four years. It didn't seem like four years. It seemed like more. They were four years into a war that he cared, he realised, nothing for. What was he doing? He was twenty-four. He'd read of explorers who'd climbed mountains, discovered old and new worlds – all by his age, and here he was, trying with all the effort he could muster not to think. The city was the one thing keeping him sane. With his father's death both his mother and Shams Sahib had withdrawn into themselves. His mother's stares he was used to; Shams Sahib's he found unsettling. When Shams talked of Awais's father or retold Dar's best stories, he'd apologise all the while: 'I don't have Dar's sense of humour.' Awais listened puzzled, not recognising his father in the tales Shams Sahib told.

Two years ago Shams Sahib had declared he was stepping down. Awais was made the city's custodian. No ceremony, nothing. The two men had embraced, that was all. Shams Sahib had then said, 'You won't forget me, will you?' He'd looked up at Awais with unsure eyes. For a whole month afterwards, Shams had stayed away. Then, as if he couldn't help himself, he began seeking out Awais at odd times of the day, either while Awais was already on his way to work or when he was getting ready to leave. Awais learnt how to look happily surprised. At first, what he found strange was that Shams Sahib didn't ask him about the city. He couldn't have lost interest, just like that, Awais thought. Then he discovered that Shams Sahib's pipeline of information hadn't dried up. The old-timers, diligently dutiful towards Awais, remained faithful to Shams as well. And then one day Shams had said, 'I've been a fool, Awais. I thought it'd be easier to give up than this.'

Each hour here's an hour wasted, Awais now thought. I could be in the city. I could be at Shams Sahib's. If I were to count up all the minutes of these years... Pointless.

He was the man of the house now, though the one thing he couldn't do was follow politics. It was too boring for words.

When the whispers began, he wasn't quite sure. It could have been last week or the week before. They were getting a new collector. The English staff had even opened up a betting pool. But since Awais had hardly spoken two words to the outgoing collector – he corrected himself, been spoken to – he didn't really care. Idiots, he thought, looking around. That's what his father's estimation of most people had been and Awais was coming round to thinking his father hadn't been far wrong. 'Dar, can you...' said a voice. Awais stood up and went to answer the call. His English had improved. He wasn't anywhere near to fluent, but he no longer had to stop, think, then translate in his head from Urdu before he spoke. He still didn't like it though, this prickly language. Thank God, he thought, I don't have to use it much.

Like most people, Harold James, the new collector, felt he followed his heart more than he actually did. His uncle, in whose house he'd grown up, and the schooling he'd received had taught him that he was better than everyone else. He'd resisted, feeling somehow that such ideas weren't right, even as he grew into a habit of easy command. At university, he'd broken free, for a while. He'd toyed with the idea of becoming a history lecturer, maybe one day a professor, and when he'd sounded out his uncle he'd been surprised that, while he'd looked at him strangely for a long time, his uncle hadn't disagreed outright. Three years later he'd understood why. His future was already decided. His uncle sent a man to see him. Evidently, Harold's days of play were over. He joined the civil service and here he now was, without an idea of what he was doing or was supposed to do. Already, he'd put people's backs up. He'd ignored the cards sent to his home to join the Gymkhana and other clubs, and he'd snubbed more than one beauty who'd sailed in as a member of the 'Fishing Fleet', the women who came to India with one single intention: to nab a husband.

He stood in the open office space. The formal introductions made, Harold removed himself to the side, his gaze running over his staff. Not one intelligent face in its midst. God, how am I going to survive this? I'd prefer to be breaking bricks, he thought as he escaped to the back of the compound for a smoke. Perched on a wall, an Indian, his head deep in a book. The Indian looked up, startled when Harold approached. Harold raised his hand in a motion that was meant to say 'at ease'. The Indian looked confused and closed his book. Harold read the title slowly: *Ain-i Akbari – The Constitution of the Emperor Akbar.* Awais jumped down and returned to the office. Harold watched him go.

A few days later, Harold called his personal aide, Williams, and Awais to his office.

'Williams,' he said, 'book two seats on the Lahore–Karachi Express for the day after tomorrow. That is what it's called, isn't it?' Williams nodded. 'What time's the first train out?' said Harold.

'Seven am, I think, sir,' Williams said.

'Check,' said Harold, 'and then let me know.'

Awais noticed how hard the aide was trying to keep his head down.

'That gives you enough time to get ready?' Harold said, turning to Awais.

'Dar, the collector asked you a question,' Williams said.

'Yes,' Awais said, 'that's enough time, sir.'

'Williams, we'll stay overnight in Karachi. I'll need a car; from what I hear of the terrain, some kind of jeep, to take us on.'

'Anything else, sir?' Williams asked.

'No,' said Harold, 'that's it for now. If I think of anything else, I'll let you know.'

'Come on, Dar,' Williams said.

'Thank you, Williams,' Harold said, 'you can go.' When the door had closed behind Williams, Harold said, 'You can come, can't you?'

'Yes, sir,' Awais said.

'Do you have any questions?' Harold asked and then smiled as if what he'd said had reminded him of something else. Awais shook his head and waited to be told he could go. The collector nodded and Awais made to leave. As his hand made contact with the brass door-knob, he found himself thinking: why does metal feel like nothing else in the world? He opened the door.

When he told his family, the girls were excited and his mother was all quiet attention.

'Why you, *bhaia*?' asked Tanveer. Awais blinked. He didn't know.

On the morning of their journey, Awais left early for the train station, not wanting to be late. Luckily, it was as if nobody else had anywhere to go that day. The roads were clear and he arrived at the station by a few minutes past six. Its exterior he knew well enough. Like many things in the city it too was built by the British to resemble a red fort. He went inside.

The station, with its ribcage of black iron and green wooden beams, was bustling. Railway staff in white suits walked around busily, one or two of the younger ones, their eyes blurred from a night of vigil, disappearing from time to time for a smoke. Coolies in red and white uniforms, with red turbans to ease the weight of trunks carried aloft heads, and armband–shield numbers like the plates of the trains they served, were spread out on the concourse like a well–thought-out defence on a playing field. As in the city, here too territory was divided by labour and class. Third-class passengers, saving on the cost of a bed the previous night, had carved out corners for themselves, and with scarves serving as headrests and other scarves as bedding, they lay on the hard cement floor and dozed, deaf to the sounds of morning.

And like the bazaars in the city, there were carts selling everything, from milky, sugary tea served in short glasses to buns with buried deposits of jewelled jellies, cigarettes which could be bought by the packet or individually, and *barfi* which, in its adult guise, was a plain block of cream-sweetmeat but here was transformed into a children's game and appeared as melons, bananas and little badges of merit. In a nearby stall, real fruit was being polished. Awais bought a bun and a glass of tea and stood to one side.

Swinging through the throngs of people were young children with caskets and buckets selling 'hot eggs, eggs hot', 'hot potato kebabs, spicy hot potato kebabs' in craggy voices that went with the job. These they served on squares of newspaper, ever watchful and wary of the railway staff. Other vendors called: 'News-paper, news-paper, red-hot newspaper for one paisa. Today's warm, off-the-press news-paper, news-paper', and 'Have breakfast for one paisa – *puris*, spicy *channay* – for only one paisa'. A man with two large pails hanging from a bullock-like shoulder beam shouted, 'Hindu water, Muslim water', to sell water he'd drawn from one well. Awais walked from one area to the next, returning, at last, to the platform from where the Karachi Express was ready to leave. It was 6.45. It was 6.50 before Harold came running onto the platform, a coolie following fast behind.

'Sorry, sorry,' he said on seeing Awais. 'Have you been waiting long?' Before Awais could reply Harold turned to pay the coolie, who said to Awais, 'Carriage A.' They stepped on board and Awais waited, expecting the collector to tell him where he should go.

'Come on,' Harold said, as if for all the world it was Awais and not he who'd been late. They had a compartment to themselves. Harold closed the door. Having put his own bag on the luggage rack, Awais was about to do the same for the collector. 'Leave it. I'll do it,' Harold said, before adding, 'Well, what are you waiting for? Sit down.'

As the train began to pull out of the station, Awais was almost thrown into his seat. Whenever he had previously imagined this moment – his first trip beyond the environs of his family, his first train journey – he hadn't thought that it'd be in the company of someone he didn't know and that that someone would be the collector.

'So,' Harold said, settling down. 'Do you want me to tell you why we're going to Balochistan?'

Awais nodded and the collector began. By the end, all Awais understood was that their trip concerned some sort of feud between two tribes. After some time he excused himself and went into the corridor. As he lit his *biri* he continued to walk. In third class, the doors had been plucked from their hinges. Passengers who didn't have seats were squeezed together on the floor of the gangway. A large woman with two children in tow tried to pass by. '*Haan, bhai,* we're still alive, okay?' said a man. 'Only just,' said the man at his side. The woman said nothing. She pushed her children on. The first man looked at Awais's *biri*. He handed it over. Better get back, he thought. On his return, Harold looked at him quizzically

Awais sat on the very edge of his seat; one sudden jolt on the tracks and he'd surely fall off. He wanted to look out and see where they were going, even if he didn't know the names of the places. But the collector, with his raised and expectant face, demanded his attention. He opened his briefcase and handed Awais a file.

'Should you want to know more, Awais,' he said. 'It is all right if I call you Awais?' Again, Awais nodded. He skimmed the file and then, when he thought it was safe, handed it back.

Harold asked, 'Do you have any brothers and sisters?' And so Awais told him about his family. 'All I have is an uncle,' Harold said, when Awais was finished.

'Just him?'

'Yes. Just him,' Harold said. 'How old are you?'

'Twenty-four.'

'God. That's twelve years younger than me. I know, I know, I don't look my age.' He grinned. 'I look older.' He rested back and said, 'Do you know who I met yesterday? A young writer. He kept on quoting some Sufi poet. Bull... '

'Bulleh Shah,' said Awais.

'Yes, that's right. Now how did that line go? Something about not knowing...' He put his hands to his temple as if he could push the memory out.

Awais waited politely, then said, '*Bullay, ki jaana mein koun? Bullay,* who knows who I am?'

'Yes!' he said, 'Yes. That's it exactly. Anyhow, the young writer was very excited about this trip. Said it was just what was needed.'

Needed for what? thought Awais.

Harold continued to talk. Awais answered as best as he could. At half past seven, a waiter opened the door and laid out a meal table. A second waiter followed with two breakfast trays.

'Go on, then,' Harold said when the two waiters had left. 'Tuck in.'

After they'd eaten and their trays had been removed, Harold laid back his head and was soon asleep. Awais smiled; Mitoo would have done the same. Awais turned to the window and looked out.

The city was soon left behind and then so too were the small towns built on its periphery, until all the eye could see was acre upon acre of green fields. And then, a mustard field broke the continuity, and soon green gave way to gold. Men and women were working the fields. At the sight of the train, the farmers raised their backs from their labour, the younger children ran or tried to run at the train's side, and doubled up with laughter, their heads tucked between their knees as the train passed by. As the train pulled into its first stop, there, on a wall, sat a black crow.

Awais's thoughts drifted back to yesterday. Yesterday two other crows, kin or no kin of this one, had made *khala* Bilquees cry.

Awais had been telling *khala* Bilquees about his work, the collector and his imminent journey to Balochistan. *Khala* Bilquees hadn't interrupted; neither, though, had her gaze registered she was listening.

All at once, her eyes, which had been half closed, had flashed open; the sudden animation on her face was frightening.

'*Khala jan*, what's wrong?'

Khala Bilquees began to rock and sing:

Crows, take this letter
To my love
And tell him how I pine.

The words, ripped from her body, were slow and repetitive, like a dirge.

Now, as the train moved faster and ever faster, the figures and structures of houses and huts spun by like, like... Where had he had this feeling of the world before – of moving through a landscape while he himself stood still, as if the two were governed by different scales of time? And then the recollection of a voice hit him:

Bara man ke dhoban dekho...
See the twelve-ton washerwoman...

Mehm dekho...
See the English lady...
Mehm ke kuta dekho...
See the English lady's dog...

And with these words came the memory of Maryam's hand pulling him towards a man in a bright red *lunghi*, white *kameez*, a checked scarf tied to his head. The man's skin had been a sickly yellow and as he moved to make space for the throng of children, a glimpse of his thin, weak ankles came into view. Awais had quickly looked up. Grey bristles sprung from the man's chin. As he turned the barrel he shouted:

Bara man ke dhoban dekho...
Bara man ke dhoban...

Maryam had looked at Awais pleadingly. Together, they'd approached the man. Maryam had got in line with the other children and within minutes was crouching on a brick, looking down a kaleidoscope at a moving world. Maryam had stepped down, her legs a little unsteady.

As hand in hand, they'd made ready to leave, the man had turned towards Awais and said, '*Beta,* don't you want to see how the world turns?'

Awais had nodded slowly and, after telling Maryam to stay where she was, he'd paid the man, and sat on his haunches before the barrel, as he'd seen the others do. There, he'd seen a world so unreal to him that he'd had to make himself believe it was true. In the barrel, with its flickering picture postcards, some in better condition than the rest, there was the promised washerwoman and the English lady with her legs exposed. Down the back of her legs, stripes. Awais wasn't, as he later learnt, the only one to think that that's how God had fashioned white women's legs. And he beheld buildings, the like of which he'd never seen before: a round, open building with columns holding up a pale blue sky, a tall building which leaned to the side as if whispering its secret to the air.

One turn of the world and then it stopped.

In Karachi, they took a tonga to the Gymkhana where the collector was to stay the night. Awais then went on to his uncle Jamshed's house, with instructions to return to the Gymkhana by eight o'clock the next morning. The following day they set off for Turbat in Balochistan. It was another day and a half before they arrived.

The further away from the centre they moved the more distinctive the land became. But could one really call such bareness distinctive? thought Awais. Long uninterrupted stretches of desert loomed before them. Awais could see neither tree, nor bird, nor animal. And then, gradually, the landscape began to change. The mountains that they now encountered were man-sized; not, that is, that they were man-made – although once the idea had struck Awais it refused to be totally dispelled – but that they were of a height that didn't dwarf. They were not brown or green but the colours of slate: burnt orange, grey, black and even red. In each of the mountains they passed, all these, as well as other less distinct colours, were melded; there was no gradient of colour and in its place was this unique mismatch, as if a box of chalk crayons had been thrown to the ground and from that ground had arisen these rock faces. The land, which had been an unending passage of yellow, in places too took on the same slate mountain shades. Then a dust cloud descended, and once again everything was encased in a yellow so pale and yet so strong, like the light itself, that it seemed to exist beyond all else as the finite measure of things.

Once they'd driven through the curtain of dust, the sun hit them in the eye. The driver, taking heed of the warning, turned the engine off and waited a few minutes until they'd adjusted to the sudden iridescence of light. Nearby, Awais spied a yellow lizard pursued by a yellow mouse.

The desert had seemed solemn when they were at its border, looking in. But further on, all that changed. Awais considered its immense expanse – as sweeping as the sky, as if there were only desert to the very ends of the earth – and then he knew: vibrancy did not require colour or speed. He'd come to relish these still moments of perception, not as plateaus reached but as moments of rest and thought.

'Can we stay here a while?' Awais asked Harold impulsively.

'Here?' On Awais's face, a shutter fell down. Harold hadn't understood. And now Awais was glad.

'I was only joking…' Awais said, and to the driver, 'Let's go on.'

The driver switched on the engine and once more they were on their way.

'What does the name Turbat mean?' Harold asked.

The driver waited until Awais had translated the question and then, looking at Harold, the words tumbling from his mouth unwillingly, he said, 'It means the land of graves.'

'Why?' asked Harold, laughing.

'Why does the *sahib* laugh?' the driver asked Awais. 'Is it any laughing matter?' Awais shook his head. The driver paused, then said, 'Because everywhere you dig, you find a grave. And that,' he added, his tongue now loosened as he pointed to the remains of what looked like a fortress, 'is where the unfortunate lovers Sassi and Panu lie buried.' He turned to Awais once more. 'He does know the story of Sassi and Panu, doesn't he?' he asked, and pulling at his beard, lost control of the steering wheel and sent the car off the edge of the dirt road. He laughed as he steered the vehicle back on track.

Awais said, 'Go on.' And so the driver continued with his tale.

When the driver had finished, Harold squinted at the driver and said, 'I met a man last week who told me that there are monuments to Sassi and Panu all over the country. Well-travelled, weren't they?' This, Awais didn't translate.

'And that?' Harold said, pointing to an upturned section of ground. 'Is that an ancient site too?'

The driver laughed and said, 'He is a little mad, your *sahib*, no? That's where an Englishman buried his dog.'

As they drove through an impossibly tight gorge, Awais scrunched his eyes shut. He opened them to find that the slate and earth colours had receded and that forests of date palms greened the land. They drove through a small pool of running water. Its smell – and could one really smell water? Awais asked, to which the driver replied, 'Yes, in the desert, water has its own perfume' – was so unfamiliar to him that Awais knew he'd never quite be able to capture the essence of it. The driver pointed to a spot some miles away in the distance and said, 'It comes from there. The *kareez* of spring water runs for twenty miles.' He concentrated on a difficult turn and then added, 'Or more.'

'*Kareez?*' Awais asked.

'*Kareezes* are spread all over the land. They're waterways. Hundreds of years old.'

'Not rivers?' Harold asked.

'No,' said the driver. 'They were built.'

'By whom?'

The driver didn't know. One hand shaping a half–circle, he said, 'They've always been here.'

The sky was split in two. One half was a plain streak of blue, the other, decadent with colour: oranges, greys, mauves and pinks. The two halves merged and within minutes were gone. However hard Awais now strained his eyes, there was nothing to be seen except mile upon mile of uninterrupted blue sky. On his face, a splendid cool breeze.

After another two hours, the driver came to a halt in a village. The land was even greener here and in the distance they could see streaks of pink apple blossom and, further away still, forests of the darkest green. The houses were simple in design, square or oblong-shaped, built of mud and some plastered with cow-pat rounds. They got out of the car, their hair and faces stiff with dust, and their eyes unaccustomed to the bright haze of the air around them. From the back of the car, the driver brought out a jerrycan of water and a towel; he poured some water into Awais's cupped hands and Awais washed his hands and face, then towelled his face dry. Awais then took the jerrycan from the driver and poured it first into Harold's waiting hands and then into the driver's.

The driver pointed to a slight incline ahead of them. The path was uneven and still wet from rain. 'Tread in my footsteps,' the driver said. Harold made a few ill-judged moves, till he understood that the indention of the footsteps made it easier for him to walk up the slope. By now a group of children had begun to follow them, slowing their steps deliberately to match those of the visitors. The girls were in long, pleated frock *shalwar kameezes* while the boys were dressed as other boys everywhere, though they wore mirrored skull caps. They were laughing, one and all. Finally tiring at the lack of speed the men imposed upon them, they excitedly ran around them.

'Is that one a Baloch?' one of the boys asked, pointing to Harold.

'Stupid,' replied his brother, cuffing him on the forehead. 'Can't you see he's beardless?'

'When they've got such long legs, why do they take such short steps?'

'*Abba*'s right. You ask too many questions. And you know what happens to those who ask too many questions?' The younger boy nodded, bowing his head to hide his fear. But his elder brother pulled him forward by the waist, and his arm rested upon the younger boy's thin shoulders. 'What's the one thing a Baloch doesn't do?'

'Fear,' replied the younger brother.

'Wash,' muttered the driver under his breath.

The driver came to a halt and so too did Awais and Harold. A group of men approached from the other side. They had granite-grey faces, sharp features, long, ringleted and oiled hair and beards of varying lengths, textures and colours. As he looked at the men, Awais recalled what Harold had told him earlier about the Baloch: that they had refused to join the king's army, not because of a higher ideal, but because they wouldn't follow regulations that required them to cut their hair and beards.

They were led to the tribal leader's house. Once tea had been served the serious business of politics was broached. 'You know,' said the *sadaar*, 'that the commissioner *sahib* is trying to destroy our *jirga* system?'

'*Jirga?*' Harold said. He turned to Awais, 'I thought there was a feud...'

'The *jirga*,' continued the chief, 'is our traditional way of settling disputes: a community of elders. And your commissioner wants to make us follow the foreign law instead. That's not something we can do.'

On the train back to Karachi they easily settled down. Looking out of the window Harold said, 'I think I'm homesick.'

'What is the idea of your home that makes you sick?'

Harold turned to Awais, his lips twitching. 'Oh my God,' he said, 'is that what passes for a joke in these parts?' Awais stared back at him, deadpan. 'Yes. Very funny. I know when I'm being had.'

'Had?'

'All right, you get sarcasm; let's see how good you are at complaining about the weather.' Harold began to talk about their meeting with the *sadaar* and concluded, 'I've messed things up, I fear.'

Dinner was served. They ate quietly.

'How much older did we establish I am than you?' asked Harold.

'Twelve years,' said Awais.

'I could almost be your father,' he said morosely.

Awais laughed, but seeing how serious Harold had become, faltered.

Harold said, 'I'm planning to write a book about India.'

Awais looked up then. 'Why a book on India? I'm sorry, I didn't mean...' Harold's face, shuttered, cold. 'I meant... Why not something smaller?'

'You mean a history of the Punjab? Hmm...' and he paused. 'You could be on to something. Let me think about it.'

'I meant something even smaller,' Awais said.

'Lahore, then?'

Awais didn't reply.

'What, then?' Harold said.

'What about a history of the inside city?'

'My God! That's an idea. I could... But, no, it's impossible. There are probably no records. And even if I were to compile it as an oral history... No, I just wouldn't know where to begin.'

'I could show you,' Awais said.

'You?'

Awais felt sick. *What was I thinking?* Harold was talking. He didn't register a word.

'Awais,' said Harold. Awais looked up. Harold was waiting. 'Collector?' he said.

'Call me Harold,' Harold said. Awais nodded, knowing he never would.

26

'When do we start?' The fifth time Harold had asked him.

Awais had no more excuses to give, so said, 'Tomorrow.'

The next day after work they went to Anarkali, Lahore's largest bazaar, immense and sprawling. Tall Pathans in stiff *shalwar kameezes* and embroidered waistcoats passed by, some carrying boxes, some carpets on their heads.

'Like it?' asked Awais, watching Harold closely.

'It's crazy!' said Harold, turning back and forth as he tried to take it all in. 'It's real, isn't it?' Awais just smiled. I'm a number two, a duplicitous bastard, he thought. If Mitoo had said anything half as stupid I'd have ripped him to shreds. But because Harold's a *sahib*... That he could have such thoughts soured him.

Two men began walking up and down the bazaar's main street, each in the opposite direction to the other. They began to sing. People stopped to listen, and to laugh. Some joined in. A group of young men in shiny Western clothes stepped back, as if they were trying to sink into the bazaar's very walls.

'What are they singing about?' asked Harold.

'Them,' said Awais, pointing to the dandies.

'How do they know the words?' Harold asked.

Awais looked as if were re-adjusting his estimate of Harold. 'The gramophone. They've got the records.'

'Look over there,' said Harold, 'that tonga outside. A shopkeeper's run over to that veiled woman and she's handed him a slip of paper.' He leaned forward. 'Is it a tryst of some sort?'

Awais laughed. 'It's a tracing of her shoe size. And probably the shoe sizes of her daughters as well.'

'*Purdah?*'

Awais nodded. 'It's how my mother and sisters buy their shoes. All except Maryam; she's got difficult feet.' Harold smiled. He'd already visited Awais's house several times.

'Are all the trades divided by religion and sect, too?' Harold asked.

'Yes. Most of the Hindus won't touch the shoe trade. And most of the cloth merchants are Hindus. There are finer distinctions as well.'

'It's never simple, is it?'

'Want to hear the story of Anarkali, then?' asked Awais.

'Go on, teach me, *ustad*.'

Awais looked at him, then. 'The short version?'

'Please!' said Harold grinning.

'It begins, like all good love stories, with a man falling in love with a woman he shouldn't have been looking at. Prince Salim, Emperor Aurangzeb's son, saw a woman whose beauty nearly struck him down. The problem was she belonged to his father's harem.'

'Oh-oh,' said Harold. 'I know where this is going.'

Awais smiled. 'When he found out, the emperor had this woman – Anarkali – buried alive.'

'And what punishment did the son get – a short, sharp reprimand?'

Awais shook his head and continued, 'When Salim became emperor – he was now called Jehangir – he had a tomb made for his lost love. And that's where we're standing; well, almost. Want to go inside?'

Harold shuddered. Awais said, 'Don't worry, you British have taken over all our monuments. It's a warehouse now. There's even one, Haveli Mian Khan, which you use as a police station.'

Harold, his brow and armpits dripping sweat, considered the milling throng. 'I don't like crowds.' He wiped clean his forehead.

'If you see a woman knitting as she walks, dive. I heard a woman's entrails came out that way.'

Harold laughed. 'You're having me on, aren't you, Awais. Awais?' said Harold.

As they left the bazaar Harold asked, his voice light, 'And the inside city – when do we begin exploring that?'

Why, thought Awais again, couldn't I just keep quiet?

Two days later they began – at Badshahi mosque.

'Shall I tell you why I don't like it?' Awais said.

Harold nodded.

'So you think the pir was wrong?' asked Harold.

Awais was settled in a chair, his long legs spread before him, his head tipped back as if he'd only come here to sleep. He sat up at once at Harold's words.

'Look at me, Harold. What do you think?' Awais said, his shoulders hunched.

'Listen, Awais.'

Awais lost his temper. 'You're not going to tell me we all contain genius, are you?'

Harold's voice was calm. 'No I'm not. 'Has it—'

'It's late,' said Awais, and took his leave.

Harold's head was deep in his notes when the telephone rang.

'Yes?' he said briskly.

The operator told him who the caller was. Harold sat still, waiting to be connected.

The voice on the other end was soft, mellow even. 'Collector Sahib, my name is Robert Kelly, secretary to the Viceroy. 'We hear you've begun to explore the inside city.'

An important man, thought Harold. One who doesn't have to waste time on being polite. He tried to focus on what the secretary was saying.

'And this,' said Kelly, 'is something we're deeply interested in.' Below the polish Harold thought he heard an Irish brogue. 'The inside city remains the only area of India's major cities we haven't mapped. It is unknown to us.' There was the slightest of pauses. 'You were, of course, taught to draw during your training?'

Concentrate, thought Harold. This is important.

'You'll have realised by now that the year of Urdu you did in England is completely useless.' Yes, thought Harold. Everyone spoke Punjabi here. 'Learn Punjabi,' the secretary said. He continued to talk and Harold tried to listen.

'I'm glad we understand one another.' With that, the call came to an end. Harold put the phone down. He'd never had any choices. He realised that now.

Awais knocked and entered. Taking advantage of the open door, Ain Khan slipped in as well. Fixing his eyes on the wall behind Harold, Ain Khan said, 'Sir, I have a most special matter to discuss.'

'Can't it wait, Khan?'

'It is important, sir,' Ain Khan said.

'Oh, go on then,' Harold said.

'Prisoner number 420, alias Chand Baba, son of Laik Baba, resident of…'

'Yes, Khan, I think we can skip all those details.'

'Yes, sir. Chand Baba has requested a leave of four days for his son's marriage.'

'What!' Harold exclaimed. Awais smiled and Harold, catching him out, frowned.

Ain Khan continued, 'Chand Baba was arrested in a case of drunken driving. He crashed his donkey cart into the police-station gate and when the police attempted to arrest him, he said they were fools and should arrest the donkey.'

'Let me get this straight,' Harold said. 'Chand Baba, who is a prisoner in our jail, wants leave to go home for his son's wedding?'

'Yes, sir.'

'But how can we let him go? Do you seriously expect him to return after four days and turn himself in?'

'Yes sir. He's a good man. He goes home every weekend and always comes back on Sunday.'

Harold got up. 'Wait a minute. You mean to tell me he has the weekend off?'

'Yes sir,' Ain Khan replied, not understanding why Harold seemed so amused.

'Oh well, in that case, by all means let him go. Shall we all chip in and buy a present for his son as well?' he asked.

'Oh, sir, that's done. We've already collected the money.'

Harold took out two one-rupee notes from his wallet and placed them on the desk. The notes began to flutter in the strong breeze from the window. Ain Khan trapped them under his large, square hand and from his pocket unearthed a wad of notes held together by an elastic band. He put all the notes together and handed them to Harold.

One of the blinds began to sway, and then another. All of a sudden, the shutters were banging with the force of the wind. 'Help me raise the blinds,' Harold said, and together they rolled up all four blinds. Outside, heavy rain had started to lash down, shot by flashes of lightning. The sky darkened till it was almost pitch black and the rain continued to fall. Ain Khan left. Awais made his way to the door.

'That reminds me,' said Harold, not quite meeting Awais's eye. 'I think I should learn Punjabi. Can you find me a teacher? Awais nodded. After work he went straight to Shams Sahib's house. Shams's tremors had recently grown worse and though his youngest son was always at his side, the fact that he couldn't do anything for himself any more made Shams Sahib malevolent.

'These trips across the inside city – whose idea was it?' asked Shams. Awais was still. He should have known. 'The Englishman's,' added Shams. He weighed Awais, the skin beneath his eyes crinkling as if to a hammer blow, and said, 'It couldn't have been yours.'

Awais hadn't realised until that moment how full-blown Shams's hatred of the British had become. His father, and now Shams Sahib as well. He couldn't just go to Government College and hire a teacher for Harold. The teacher had to be, Harold had said, someone whom they could completely trust. Who could he ask?

Awais had never met her himself but he'd heard that she was a person who could get things done, and importantly in this case, that she was discreet. Awais sent one of his scouts out to trace her. The address the man came back with made his head spin. He asked the scout to double-check. Indignant, the scout said, 'I'd bet on my life I'm right.'

When Awais arrived at Harold's house later that evening, he was told to wait at the gate. When Harold appeared fifteen minutes later and heard how long Awais had been waiting, he was furious. 'They didn't tell me you were here!' he said.

Outside, Awais had a tonga waiting. It wasn't long before they entered the red light district. They let the tonga go. They walked through the gullies and maze of streets until the streets became narrower and narrower; they were then compelled to walk in single file. Ahead of them, a group of women playfully arguing with a bangle seller, praising his bangles and bemoaning their lack of money. Awais grinned; the bangle seller had no chance. Children hurtled past on bicycles, over which they appeared to have little control, colliding occasionally with pedestrians with the hurried apology, 'Sorry *baba ji*', or the more frequent insult, '*Aray* – don't you have eyes?'

Most of the rooftops, flat like his home, were busy with evening conferences; only one or two of the roofs were higher than the others, flaunting the wealth of an added storey. From them, women and young girls looked down, brazen in their open wooden verandahs. 'Oi, *baba ji*, come see what a young girl can do. Mister Babu, here. Why are you being shy? Look up. Look up,' and the tinkling sound of laughter.

In the distance they heard a sitar, and a woman's voice singing a *ghazal*. The music contained in it both sadness and joy, as if joy were not a burst of emotion, a momentary sensation that was here and then gone, but something which ran through all things, through sorrow too, not lessening it, but giving it form. Awais and Harold hesitated for a moment, listening.

Then Awais said, pointing, 'That's where we're going.' They walked on until they stopped before a white-plastered house. From behind the wooden trellis of the top-most balcony Awais caught the briefest glimpse of two women's faces, before they flitted away. The house was similar except in one detail to all the other houses in this tightly packed street. What distinguished this house was its huge wooden door. On either corner, guarding the entrance, were gaudily painted plaster lions with tiger stripes. The house was called

Sher Dil – Lionheart – House. Awais had never entered it from this side before.

He knocked on the great door. It had a smaller door within it, and after a moment this was opened by a dwarf, who grinned and invited them in. He led them into a courtyard, in the middle of which stood a fountain. The dwarf's eyes were glassy, and Awais whispered to Harold, '*Charas* – hashish.'

Oblivious, the dwarf carried on his monologue. 'Tom Thumb, you remember? Son of General Tom Thumb of the Carson Theatre Company? Played with all the big names: Commodore Nutt, the Great Spanish Mushroom. Just between you and me,' he lowered his voice, 'in this city alone there are five Tom Thumbs I know of. Wish I had one quarter of my father's stamina.' Then, with the strict instruction that they weren't to touch anything, Tom Thumb took his leave of them.

'What kind of place is this?' asked Harold, squinting at Awais.

'You said you wanted a teacher who was off the radar. I thought…'

'You thought?'

'You said you didn't want to get into trouble.'

'Brilliant,' said Harold turning around to examine the courtyard. 'This is just perfect then, isn't it? I can't imagine I'll get into trouble for coming here.'

'We can go back if you want,' said Awais, his voice petulant.

Two women entered the courtyard, with brushes and cloths in their hands, their *shalwars* rolled up several inches above their ankles. They began to clean, talking all the while.

'…And when I went home I saw that *haramzadi*, dressed in the green outfit Begum Sahiba had given *me*, her whole face covered in red powder. Looking like a street prostitute.'

'Ssh, Hameeda, what if someone hears?' said her friend, turning around. She saw Awais and Harold and touched her friend on the knee. 'Hold onto your faith in God.'

Hameeda shook her head. 'Which god? The God of the poor is dumb and deaf.'

They resumed their work as Tom Thumb returned and told the two men, 'Begum Sahiba said you can come in.' Awais followed

Tom Thumb down a long hallway, with Harold reluctantly tagging along in the rear. At the end of the corridor, Tom Thumb pushed open a door, led them inside, and left.

Harold just stared. The affluence was obvious: both in the Persian rugs spread across the large expanse of floor and in the silver inlaid boxes placed on the side tables. What struck him most though, was… No, he couldn't define it.

A woman entered the room and although he knew it was rude in this setting – in this country, scandalous even – he couldn't take his eyes off her face. He felt ludicrous as he braced himself to meet her. He'd seen more beautiful women; of course he had. Her features were not in the traditional mould of an Indian temptress, those lovers and queens he'd seen in miniature after miniature: no huge almond eyes, no luscious lips. She wore a cream cotton top and *gharara* which flared and swirled softly as she moved; a tightly twisted *dupatta* was wound around her throat. Her hair was pulled back in a tight bun. The closer she came the more solid her beauty grew. She introduced herself. 'Anuradha.' She looked so young that he'd expected a child's voice, but hers was husky, sure.

She invited them to take a seat. They talked of mundane matters. Harold only replied when she asked him a direct question. Yes, he wanted to learn Punjabi. He felt like a fraud, he laughed softly, but it was the truth. Living here without being able to speak the language beyond a few words. And he wanted to read. All that glorious Punjabi poetry.

'Do you like poetry?' she asked.

'God no!' he replied without thinking, then, *she'll think I'm a fool.* But she smiled. *I want to make her smile, make her laugh. I want.*

He was embarrassed that his body would betray him.

'Yes,' she was saying, 'I think I know just the man. I'll ask him and let you know. Can you come back next Saturday?' She stood up, dismissing them.

Look at me, he thought, greedy for her gaze, grimacing in shame. It wasn't her gaze he wanted. At least not just her gaze. She glanced at him, implacable. His face fell. *She sees nothing.* His heart quickened. She'd almost reached the door and Awais was tugging at his arm, telling him it was time for them to go. The door closed behind her.

Awais and Harold then made their way to the courtyard where Tom Thumb lay in a corner, half asleep. They let themselves out.

27

The next morning, Awais lay on his bed, feet crossed, eyes open. There was a tap on the door, then his mother entered. Reluctantly, he sat up. She was excited, pulling at a corner of her *dupatta*. He still felt tired, not ready for this, whatever this was.

'You're not going to believe this,' she said.

He waited.

'There's been a proposal for one of the girls.' She was watching him as she spoke.

'Batool or Tanveer?' he asked, trying to stifle a yawn.

'Maryam,' she said. He looked up, startled. She smiled, triumphant.

'Who?' he asked.

'Hamid Batla.'

'The shoemaker?' he said, his voice brimming with disdain.

'You can't call him that!' she said. 'He's not some *mochi,* some shoe repairer on a street corner!' She paused then asked, 'Do you know how rich he is?'

'Do you know how old he is? Forty, at least.'

'He's twenty-six.'

'Phh... ' He got off the bed.

'He is. His aunt told me.'

'Maryam's not even seventeen.' He stepped forward and looked hard at her face. 'You're considering it,' he said.

'What do I say to a man so rich?' she asked.

'All you have to do is say no. *Ammi...*'

'He's richer than anyone we know.' She raised her hands and added, 'What does he see in Maryam, anyhow?'

'He's seen her?'

'When you took her to get her shoes,' she said. He mumbled something but she didn't catch his words. 'He sent his aunt,' she continued. 'Not a matchmaker. That's a sign of great respect. I told her Maryam knows nothing about running a household; she can't even cook. She just sat politely and nodded and drank her tea.' She shook her head. 'I don't know how to deal with these people.'

'Did you tell her about the epilepsy?'

She looked as if she'd like to smack him. 'Don't be stupid,' she said. 'Anyhow, there hasn't been an incident...' His eyes slitted to sharp points as she spoke 'Since...'

'Does Maryam know?'

'Ammi!' called Tanveer from the passage. Awais and Khurshid stood stock still, one welcoming the interruption, the other dismayed. *'Ammi!'* cried Tanveer again.

'Don't tell anyone yet,' Khurshid said and reluctantly left the room. 'We'll talk about it further when you get home this evening.'

When his father had died, Awais had accepted that he'd have to be the earning hand but he hadn't expected anything like this. His mother asked his advice on everything, big and small. Inside, though, he still felt like a boy. Why couldn't she just leave him alone?

And Batla of all people. He'd seen him one day in the store in Anarkali where he took Maryam to get her shoes. A thin unremarkable man with receding hair. Awais hadn't had anything against him – till now.

Maryam had gone to the room she shared with her sisters a long time ago. Batool and Tanveer now followed. Khurshid watched them go. *They don't know what's happened. Their beauty should have been enough. They should have been married and had children of their own by now.* The proposals, when they came, always had something disreputable about them, and she'd had no compunction in saying no, but it had been a while now – she wouldn't think how long – since a proposal had come their way. People liked families with fathers and theirs was dead.

'Goodnight, *ammi*,' said Awais as he entered the courtyard. He turned towards his bedroom.

'Did you hear the news?' she said. Her voice frail, her face, indignant. He went to touch her arm. She pulled away. 'He's dead,' she said.

He frowned. 'Who?'

'Bablo.'

'Who?' he repeated.

'The singer, Pankaj Gopal,' she said, and her head bent.

'What! But how?'

'Poisoned. By a rival, they think.'

He led her to a chair. She stood before it as if not understanding what purpose it served. 'Come on, *ammi*,' he said, 'I'll take you to your room.'

The next day Pankaj Gopal had the largest funeral the city could remember. They gathered from all corners of the city to march to his home on Beedan Road. The police tried at first to control the swelter of people, then gave up. Leading the funeral march was a middle-aged woman in white who looked vaguely like Pankaj Gopal, though she had a sloppy mouth. Supporting her was her husband and, at her other side, Pankaj Gopal's childhood friend, Kashif. As Kashif lifted a hand to swat away a fly, Awais saw that his wrists, once heavy with the bangles he made, were bare. Awais joined the procession – as he'd promised his mother he would.

When he eventually got to work, it seemed everyone else was late that day. And all they could talk about was why.

The dead take with them, without consent, a portion of the lives of those who loved them. What Bablo took from Khurshid seemed negligible. But her ability to be touched by his voice was her ability to experience beauty. The next day she had Awais remove the chair Dar had put out for her all those years ago, next to his.

Harold couldn't remember how long he'd been going at it. His progress – if you could call it that – was slow. He'd never felt like such a dullard in his life. In all this time he'd only seen Anuradha twice; a quick *salaam* and then she was gone. One evening, early as always for his class, he waited in the drawing room, his heart pulsing in the fear and hope of seeing her again.

As the far door clicked open, Harold picked up his books and stood up. He turned to greet his teacher, '*Asalaam o'leikum*' – his practised 'Good day' – on his lips. But instead of his *ustad* – his tutor – Anuradha stood before him. He was momentarily taken aback. She explained that his tutor's mother was ill and he was away visiting her in their village.

'When will he be back?' Harold asked.

'I don't know,' she said.

'Can I call in tomorrow?' The probability that his teacher would have returned by tomorrow was, he knew, slim.

Looking him straight in the face, she said, 'Yes.'

Harold returned the next day and the day after that, and the coolness between them slowly melted away. At her prompting, he told her about his childhood and then a few days later, about his and Awais's research on the inside city. Once he began, he was surprised by how much of himself he wanted to reveal. It was only later that he realised that, although she did her fair share of talking, most, if not all of her words, took the form of questions.

On the fifth day, he sat in the drawing room, his gaze fixed on the far door. The door clicked and, smiling, he stood. Heavy–footed, wrists jangling, Anuradha's maid appeared, come to tell him her mistress was ill. Message delivered, she turned to leave. Harold, not thinking, not really, jumped up. She scowled at him, but he followed her through the long passageway. She pushed open a door. Harold stood aside, waiting. After some time the maid returned and led him inside. She then turned to leave.

Anuradha lay on her bed, propped up on several pillows. Her skin glistened; her hair, newly brushed, fell around her face. He rushed to her side and picked up her hand, not thinking how inappropriate the action was, nor how it would change things between them – irrevocably.

Sitting at her dressing table, she watched him in the mirror's reflection. She was putting on her earrings.

'I asked your tutor to stay away,' she said.

'Yes?' he said, watching the movements of her hand.

'You're not listening.'

'No? Come here.' And she did, and he marvelled that her doing what he wanted thrilled him so. But everything about her thrilled him, even her black moods, when she just sat and said nothing.

'My maid doesn't like this,' she said.

'No,' he laughed. He settled her back into bed at his side and kissed the back of her neck. He asked her about her day and, as she told him, he thought again how easily she commanded her world, but here, with him, she was as she was nowhere else.

As she spoke, he waited as he did every day, for her to tell him something about her past. And suddenly he felt impatient and wanted to probe. 'Tell me about when you were young,' he said.

'What brought me here?'

'Yes.'

'Why do you want to know?'

'I don't know,' he said and smoothed the cover down. She raised herself up and kissed him, a quick peck, on his forehead.

'All right,' he said, turning away. 'Don't tell me if you don't want to.'

'My mother,' she said, 'was a courtesan.' He lay on his side, looking up at her, 'and my father…'

Harold didn't have much time for exploring the inside city any more. Awais was relieved. It had felt like a betrayal. Side by side with the relief though, something else; something he didn't want to examine too closely. He'd begun to suspect why Harold was always preoccupied.

Days passed and he tried to push the thought away. When his resistance was at its lowest, he went to see Shams Sahib and asked him what he knew of Anuradha Malik.

'You know, of course, who her mother is?' Shams Sahib first asked.

'That doesn't concern me,' Awais said.

'Have patience, Awais,' Shams Sahib said. He called his son and told him they wanted tea. The boy nodded and left. 'This is a long story. Don't rush me. Anuradha Malik's mother is Roshanay Begum,' he said, watching Awais's face.

On Awais's face, the light of understanding.

Shams Sahib smiled. 'Yes, I thought that would interest you. Who her father was is important too. Patience, Awais. Ah, tea. Drink up and let my story take its own pace.'

Awais sat back and tried to relax as Shams Sahib began his tale.

Anuradha's mother, Roshanay Begum, was as you might imagine, a precocious girl. You've seen her, I assume, so you know also that she is and was beautiful. She was stolen one day and taken to Prince Arun's court. Prince Arun was not a good man or a bad man. He was, though, a man of many excesses. One of his excesses was women. Because Roshanay was of a scholarly bent, he arranged tutors for her to fill in the gaps in her education and soon she had mastered everything her teachers knew. And so Prince Arun found her scholars to whom she could address the questions that vexed her brain.

She loved him. Of this, I have no doubt. When I saw… But no, she loved him; that's all you need to know. They had a child, Anuradha, and everything seemed complete. But you've heard the story of how a leopard can't change its spots however hard it tries? Well, soon after Anuradha's birth – I think she must have been seven or eight months old – Prince Arun sought a new companion. The day a new girl was brought into the court, Prince Arun's head steward went to see Roshanay. As he had done countless times before, he gave her two options: she could take a sackful of money – enough to last a lifetime – or else she could stay and move into the servants' quarters. So far, every one of Prince Arun's companions had chosen to take the money and leave.

But Roshanay chose to stay. Love is, as I've said, a strange business. And makes us bear the inconceivable.

Shams urged Awais to take a few sips before he continued.

Roshanay moved into the cramped servants' quarters, and the other servants welcomed her with jeers. She took her books but left behind the jewels she'd been given. Those who'd heard tales of her wisdom now openly called her a fool.

Time passed, as it always does. Roshanay had only made one friend, a woman whose husband was one of Prince Arun's clerks. Majeeda had often asked Roshanay to accompany her to the tombs of the saints. And one day, Roshanay agreed to go with her.

And there, in the darkened chamber of a tomb, with a dhol drumming in the background like a leaden heartbeat, she found… oh, who am I to say what she found? But she was, from that day, a changed woman. There was now no tomb she didn't know and didn't worship before. On a visit to Data Darbar, she saw a young woman fall down. As Roshanay approached, an old woman came forward, raised the hand of the prostrate woman and checked her pulse. She asked for water and it was brought. She opened her purse and fed the woman some herbs; some other women came forward then and held the woman's head in place and helped her to drink.

'Give her some air,' said the old woman and made sure no one got too close. Within fifteen minutes the young woman was sitting up again. Roshanay, whose gaze had been fixed on the young woman, now looked around: the old woman had disappeared. This was the second of the incidents which changed the course of Roshanay's life. She began to read about healing, found herself a teacher, and soon became renowned – though not as renowned as she now is.

'Some more tea, Awais? You're not eating? What will my wife say!'

To appease him, Awais took a bite of *halwa*.

'Is this enough for today? I'm a little tired.'

Awais agreed and helped Shams Sahib up. He saw that Shams Sahib hadn't touched his tea; it had acquired a thick skin, like wet clay that was hardening fast.

That night, as he walked home, Awais recalled the aridity of the Balochistan desert. He found he could smell the water from the *kareez* not as a memory, but as a living thing. Though their driver hadn't known how to answer his question, Awais had later done some research. The waterpaths in Balochistan had been built by the Persians. When the first locals had seen the endless supply of running water where before there'd only been barren land, they thought they'd died and gone to heaven – and that heaven seemed, contrary to what they'd been taught, strangely familiar.

The next afternoon, Awais arrived at Shams Sahib's house at three o'clock. Shams's youngest son led him to the drawing room and said his father wasn't yet home but that Awais was free to wait. By the time Shams arrived, Awais had finished his tea.

Shams Sahib took a seat and smiling, said, 'Where were we? I forget.'

'Roshanay Begum had become a healer,' Awais prompted.

'Ah, yes,' Shams said, 'that's right.' He thought for a moment, and continued his story.

One day she was in the bazaar, talking to Chacha Yusuf, the best sharbat maker in town. Anuradha was by then ten. Anuradha was drinking her sandalwood sharbat as her mother and Chacha Yusuf chatted.

As usual, Chacha Yusuf was bemoaning the stupidity of his sons, none of whom wanted to learn his craft. Now the rumours – which Roshanay well knew – were that Chacha Yusuf dabbled in mysteries far greater than sharbat making. So Roshanay, who'd heard his complaints before, now said, 'I'll become your student, if you'll take me?'

'A woman?' he said, laughing. 'And from outside the family?' He reached forward to stroke Anuradha's hair.

The next week she returned and, as Anuradha drank from a thick sharbat glass, Roshanay waited for Chacha Yusuf's reply.

'Can you read?' he asked.

'Yes,' she said.

'Come to my house next Sunday at four o'clock,' he said.

'And what will your sons say?' she asked.

'They'll say,' he said, displaying his perfectly even white teeth, 'whatever I tell them to say.'

But here Chacha Yusuf was wrong. Though his sons didn't want to learn their father's trade, the idea that someone else – and an outsider, at that – might be brought in for this purpose felt like a theft of their inheritance. When, therefore, Roshanay knocked on the door of Chacha Yusuf's house, she was met with a line-up of young men and a woman – whom she later learnt was Chacha Yusuf's third wife. They stood there, not saying a word, unanimous in their hostility.

Two weeks later Chacha Yusef invited her to visit him again. The family were nowhere in sight. She was a regular visitor from then on. He'd won.

A full year would pass before he reluctantly showed her the book. Tattered and without a cover, it was clearly incomplete. Chacha Yusuf had picked it up at Anarkali bazaar. He'd been looking for something else and had come across this. While he'd been considering it, a breeze had opened up the pages of the book, which looked like a stitched pamphlet. All he saw was one picture, and knew, or thought he did, what it meant. Much to the contempt of the shopkeeper, he agreed, at once, to the full asking price.

It was this book which he now gently unwrapped from its cloth of red and green and laid before Roshanay. As he turned a page he watched her face. He turned another page. The strangest drawings she'd ever seen. The spheres. She knew she shouldn't touch it but the temptation was too great. She reached out her hand and he snapped the book shut and held it close to his chest.

'You can read?' he asked again.

'Yes,' she again said.

'You'll read it to me,' he said. 'Soon.'

A few more weeks passed before he let her see the book again. 'Read,' he said, settling himself in a chair. 'It doesn't leave my house, though,' he added as she opened the first page. Her head bent, she began to read.

Seeing the anxiety he felt each time he put the book in her hands, she said one day, 'Let me teach you to read.'

'I've tried,' he said slowly. 'I can't make the words make sense.'

They worked happily together for many years. What Roshanay didn't tell Chacha Yusuf, though, was that she was compiling and writing a book of her own.

And then, Prince Arun fell ill. He called for Roshany Begum – by now Roshanay Begum the healer; he'd forgotten this was the name of the girl he'd once loved, there'd been so many – before her and since. She hadn't seen him, except fleetingly, in all those years, but of course, when he asked, she went.

She was shocked by the figure she saw, who was so much more – in flesh – and so much less – in spirit – than the man she remembered. She made up some medicine and told his servants how many times a day they should administer it. But aside from his clerk, who was then away, all his old servants had left, and the new ones had no care for anyone but themselves. They forgot to, or deliberately didn't, give the prince the dosage Roshanay had prescribed. The next day he was dead and gone, too, were many of his jewels and his boxes and plates of silver.

When the clerk returned, he rushed Roshanay and Anuradha away. He well knew what the prince's staff were capable of doing and saying. He couldn't repay Roshanay Begum – she'd saved his son's life. The little he could do, though, he did, and he found her a small house in the vicinity of Chacha Yusuf's.

The very next year, Anuradha, now almost a young woman, was in the bazaar at the siesta hour when she was kidnapped by two men who muffled her mouth and huddled her into an awaiting tonga. They carried her to a house and there shook off the blanket that had covered her.

The woman who stood before them was heavily jewelled and perfumed. Appraising Anuradha, she said, 'She's beautiful. You did well.' She had just begun to open her purse when one of her guards walked up to her and whispered in her ear. The woman froze and spat, 'You fools! Do you know who she is?' The men stood immobile. 'She's Roshanay Begum's daughter. My God, what are we going to do?' Even by then, you see, Roshanay Begum's name was a formidable one.

Again the guard approached and said something. 'That's right,' said the woman, 'Take her back. And don't you idiots think of trying anything on... My God, if anyone finds out...' The men wrapped Anuradha in the blanket again and, gently this time, carried her to the waiting tonga. They returned her to the bazaar.

When Anuradha told her mother what had happened, Roshanay called on her friend, the clerk, and he agreed with her fears.

Anuradha now hardly left her room. But one day a friend invited Anuradha to her house. Roshanay said she could go on the condition that one of the clerk's sons take her there. Anuradha agreed.

The clerk's eldest son sat and waited in the tonga as she climbed up the steps to her friend Anjum's house. Anuradha never entered that building. From the moment she'd stepped into the walkway she'd heard shouting. Her friend Anjum had not told her much of her family life; only that a few years ago her mother had taken a new husband. Anuradha couldn't knock and go in, so she stood outside, hoping the voices would relent. She couldn't believe what she heard.

The husband said, 'We have no choice.'

'Find a job,' the mother said. 'That's a choice.'

'You think I haven't tried? Who'd give me a job? Just tell me.'

'I—'

'It's good money. More money than we'll ever see.'

'She's my daughter,' the mother said. She was crying now. 'What do you know...?'

'What do I know? I'll tell you what I know,' and there was a slap, and crying.

The door opened then and Anjum ran out. Her startled eyes saw but didn't recognise Anuradha. She ran to the end of the walkway. Anuradha watched her leap and fly through the open window – and thought how beautiful Anjum looked. And then she realised what she'd just seen. She ran down the stairs to the road. The clerk's son hadn't seen a thing; he was talking with the driver when he saw Anuradha running past the tonga. He jumped down and raced after her. Crouched on the ground, almost as if she were preparing to dig into it, down and down, that's how he found her. Softly, he called her name. She looked up, her face immobile. It was a full ten minutes before she could tell him what had happened. Grimly, he led her back to the tonga and then went to see for himself. He returned to the tonga and spoke to the driver. The driver handed him his shawl. The clerk's son returned to the fallen girl and draped the shawl over her dead body. Back in the tonga, he said, 'Let's go. The police station.'

Anuradha wouldn't speak of the incident to anyone. Even the police had to be satisfied with the second-hand report from the clerk's son.

Roshanay turned once more to her friend the clerk. 'I want her safe. Where's the safest place we can go?'

The clerk bent his head and thought. Roshanay, used to his ways, waited. Finally, he said, 'You'll think it a joke.' And then he told her.

If these words had come from any other man she would have slapped his face but she knew how concerned her friend was for both Anuradha and herself. 'What about Anu's marriage?' she asked. 'No decent man will marry her if we live there.'

The clerk bent his head and she flushed. She knew what he was thinking: which decent man would marry the daughter of a courtesan, anyway? 'She's still young,' the clerk said. 'You don't have to stay there for ever.'

They moved into a house in Heera Mandi, the dancers' and prostitutes' bazaar, the following week.

Despite Roshanay's fears, the move was good for everyone. It was good for her business and good too for Anu. Anu's habit of cultivating strays grew and soon their house was a passageway for women who, burnt by the world, needed a halfway home.

After a month, the clerk rushed in to see Roshanay. 'Baji,' he said, 'people are saying…' He ran with the words, as if scared of what would happen if he slowed down, 'They're saying your house is a brothel.'

Roshanay smiled and said, 'Let them say what they want. My wanting them to think a particular way won't change them.'

'But,' said the clerk, 'what you said about Anu…' He trailed off. Her eyes had become glazed. She told him she'd gone to see Chacha Yusuf and that he'd called her a thief.

As Awais walked home that night, he wondered: how do you know this, Shams Sahib? Is there nothing you don't know?

28

Harold had received another call from the Viceroy's secretary. He called Awais into his office and said, 'Let's start with the bazaars.' They were meeting at Anuradha's house. Harold kept his head lowered as he made his way to Lionheart House.

An hour later, on the same route, Awais turned swiftly to look back. The usual throng of people; nothing exceptional there. He carried on. He came to an alleyway, its walls pale in the early afternoon light, and once more he had the strong sense that he was being watched. He'd told Harold he'd be there by five o'clock, and it was already – he looked down at his watch – yes, it was ten minutes past five. He reached Lionheart House and stood in the alcove around the entrance without knocking. The danger was still there. He was sure it was. Who could be following him and why?

Awais looked again towards the door. Harold was no doubt inside, getting angrier by the minute. Tardiness made him see red. 'My Protestant upbringing,' he'd admitted apologetically. Awais tried to silence his thoughts, the better to hear. Beyond the usual city sounds, nothing. A hand reached out to the alcove wall. It was small. Relief made him stronger. He pulled the figure in. A young boy, wearing a Pathan cap and wrapped in a thick black shawl, stood before him, his head lowered.

'Look up,' commanded Awais, and the interloper obeyed. 'Maryam!' cried Awais. 'What are you doing here? Don't you know how dangerous it is – wandering in the city alone? Where did you get those clothes?' Maryam started to tremble; he folded her in his

arms. 'It's okay,' he said, trying to reassure her. When she'd calmed
down, he looked at his watch again. He didn't have time to take her
home. There was nothing else for it. He knocked on the door. As
they waited, Awais, his voice stern, said, 'Nothing. You say nothing. Understand?' He paused. 'If someone asks you your name you
can answer, but beyond that... Do you know how much danger you
could have been in? What were you thinking?'

'I just wanted to know where you and Harold *bhai* go,' she said.

Before he could reply, Tom Thumb had pulled open the door.
Maryam, wide-eyed, grabbed hold of Awais's hand and he ushered
her towards Anuradha's drawing room. There, they found Harold
and Anuradha standing at opposite ends of the room, as if they were
near strangers who'd already discovered they didn't like each other
very much.

Harold laughed on seeing Maryam and said, 'Hello, scamp. What
are you doing here?'

'She was following me,' replied Awais.

Anuradha softened on seeing Maryam and, approaching, asked,
'And what's your name?'

Maryam looked up at her brother and he nodded. 'Maryam,' she
said.

'Want some *sharbat*? No one makes *sharbat* like my mother.'
Maryam nodded and followed Anuradha to a bureau at the back of
the room.

'You're late,' said Harold.

Awais was still looking at Maryam. He shivered. 'Anything could
have happened.'

The door opened and Roshanay Begum entered. 'Anu,' she said,
then stopped. Awais went forward to say his *salaam*, but Roshanay
Begum didn't take her eyes off Maryam.

'The epilepsy,' she said, turning to Awais, 'it's for her you come?'

'Yes,' he replied.

'Epilepsy?' interjected Harold.

Roshanay Begum's gaze moved to Harold. She stopped, then smiling, she turned back to Maryam.

'Maryam,' she said. Maryam grinned. 'You're good at maths, aren't you?'

'I'm studying the celestial numbers,' Maryam said. She looked as if she expected Roshanay Begum to be awed. But instead, Roshanay Begum stood very still; she watched Maryam intently, then made to leave.

'I have to take her home,' Awais said to Harold. He called to Maryam and said it was time to go. She was reluctant; he could see that. This house and its inhabitants were too fascinating for her to easily let go. Awais held out his hand and Maryam left Anuradha's side and walked towards him.

'*Salaam khala, salaam* Harold *bhai*,' Maryam said.

Awais and Maryam walked towards the door.

'See,' said Harold. 'That's a girl with sense. She calls me her brother and you her aunt.'

Awais didn't hear the reply because the door had closed, but he thought he heard giggling.

Once outside he said, 'You mustn't tell *ammi* – tell anyone – where we've been.'

She laughed. 'Me and you have got a lot of secrets, don't we, Awais *bhai*?'

Awais smiled.

'Oh, no,' she cried, her head bent to the ground.

'What is it?' he asked. 'Are you all right?'

'My shoe!' she said pointing to where the strap had broken. She bent to tuck in the strap of her Batla shoes. Awais frowned, and thought of the one secret she didn't yet know.

That night, Kasani was away. Roshanay Begum, her eyesight having grown faint, self-administered her medication. She overdosed.

As soon as Awais heard the news, he went to tell Harold. Together, they left to pay their respects, but even this soon, the queue of mourners stretched down two streets. They hadn't expected to be able to see Anuradha, but someone must have told her they were there for one of her servants came towards them and led them to the drawing room.

She stood before them dressed in white. As the door closed behind them, she looked up and stared at Harold's face. Her eyes were dry. Harold took her hand, which lay unresponsive in his. As he pressed down on her hand, a thick silver bangle emerged from inside his cuff. Awais heard him mutter, 'I'll come by later.'

As they were about to leave, Anuradha said to Awais, 'Will you wait a minute?' She left by the far door. Awais looked at Harold. Harold shook his head. He didn't know either. He saw Awais's gaze flit to his bangle; he began to tuck it back in, then abruptly stopped. It lay heavy on his wrist.

Anuradha returned. She handed Awais a brass ball and a book bound in green leather.

'These are for Maryam,' she said.

'For Maryam?' he asked.

'It was my mother's wish.'

29

OCTOBER 1944, LAHORE

Maryam's wedding was set for a week after her seventeenth birthday. The Butts arrived from Karachi, the Jehangirs from Amritsar and Dar's sisters travelled from their homes in Uttar Pradesh. The Dars' house was turned upside down.

Two days before the wedding, a few minutes before dawn, Awais heard a soft knock on his bedroom door.

'Who is it?' he said, raising his head.

No answer. He turned with a grateful sigh, burying his face in the pillow. Knocking, again.

'All right!' he said and pulled himself out of bed. He coughed fiercely, his body brittle from the lack of sleep. He opened the door.

Maryam rushed into his arms. Another coughing fit wracked his body. He pushed her away. When she made to leave, he gestured for her to come in, sit down. Still coughing, he made his way to his bed-side table and took a drink. Exhausted, he sat down on the bed, and motioned for her to pull her chair forward.

'Tell me,' he finally said, 'what's wrong.'

She paused, guilt colouring her face as she tried to find the right words.

'The ball,' he asked, 'what is it?'

'They're called astrolabes. They mark the spheres and the move-ment of the sun and moon. I showed it to Miss Alvi. She thinks it was made in Persia. There's a date on it: 1121. Miss Alvi says that's the Islamic calendar. The year would have been 1710.'

'And the book?' he said. 'Can you understand it?'

'No,' she said sounding mournful.

'And Miss Alvi – what does she say?'

'I didn't tell her,' she said.

He knew that it had been a long time since Miss Alvi had had any-thing to teach Maryam. She kept up the routine of lessons for her teacher's sake. He reached now for her right hand. There was a small indentation on the side of her forefinger from the pressure of her pen and, below it, in the dip between forefinger and thumb, a bruise of some sort. It was the size of a small coin and had the shade of dull copper.

'Rest a while,' he said. 'Close your eyes.' She smiled and did what she was told. He could see the effort it took for her to relax and then, after a while, her breathing slowed. Suddenly she shivered awake, her eyes blazing.

'Does he know?' she asked.

He knew what she meant straight away. '*Ammi* told me she told his aunt,' he said. 'Don't worry. Look, it's been ages since you had an attack.'

He took off his shawl and draped it over her, tucking her in. 'Everything will be fine,' he said. She nodded. And within minutes her head drooped and she was asleep.

Awais looked at his sister. *How could I ever have thought…? I've killed it. The evil that was my mother's, not mine.* Maryam smiled in her sleep. *I've killed it.* Or, had she?

The next day, Awais went to see Hamid Batla. It was their first meeting outside the formality of family visits. He was led up the back stairs of the house to the roof, where Hamid and his staff worked. Hamid was giving out orders to an elderly man when Awais entered. He saw Awais, smiled and raised his hand, asking him to wait. In another minute he was done.

Awais watched Hamid approach. He'd learnt that Hamid had led a hard life. His mother had died from tuberculosis when he was five. After a year or two of struggling to look after the child by himself, Hamid's father had called in his wife's maiden sister. He'd promised marriage in return for her caring for the boy as if he were her own.

She'd agreed and preparations for the wedding had begun. But then Hamid's father too had died, in a startling road accident. And, despite what everyone said – she was young; she'd find a husband – Hamid's aunt had decided to stay on.

Money was tight in those years and so Hamid had gone to work for the first neighbour who had offered him a job. Rana the shoe-maker had thought he was doing his old friend's son a favour by tak-ing him on. But he soon realised that Hamid had a feel for leather which he, with thirty years in the craft behind him, had failed to acquire. When Hamid was seventeen, Rana died. He left Hamid a small annuity in his will and, with this, Hamid hired the best of Rana's old team to work for him. At first, his Batla shoes were sold at other shops but within just a few short years there was first one, then two Batla stores in Lahore. As well as a feel for leather, Hamid clearly had a head for business.

'I'm glad you came,' Hamid said. 'Come, let's go downstairs and have some tea.' He led Awais down again and they entered the draw-ing room. Hamid answered all of Awais's questions with ease.

Awais returned home more content than he'd been in many days. He went to look for his mother. He found her with Batool, folding Maryam's new clothes for her trousseau and sewing loose stitches into their corners so that they wouldn't fall out of shape once placed in the suitcase that lay open before them on the floor.

'*Ammi*,' Awais said, 'I have to speak to you.'

Without a word, Batool got up and left. At the door, she said, 'Awais *bhai*, hurry, there's still lots to do.'

'Give us fifteen minutes.'

Awais thought he had never seen his mother look so beautiful. It was as if she'd stored up her beauty for a moment such as this and now it radiated from her skin, her eyes, her mouth. Maryam's impending marriage had brought out in her what nothing else had. The two – Maryam and Khurshid – would never be close but Khur-shid's hostility had ceased. And recently, she'd shown Maryam a leniency she'd not shown before. Maryam didn't, he'd realised, know how to respond.

Conscious of Batool waiting on the other side of the door, Awais quickly told his mother of his visit to Hamid's and how, where he'd once thought her decision wrong, he now thought she'd been right. As he spoke the joy drained from her face. He frowned, not understanding. Then his heart grew cold. She'd agreed to this marriage not because she thought Hamid the best match for Maryam she could find, but the worst.

Shams Sahib's son arrived one day and said, 'My father's dying and is calling for you.'

Awais was granted three days' leave. He intended to spend those days and the nights at Shams Sahib's side, waiting for the old man's final revelations, for him to tell him what to do. Fear came, a fear like none he'd ever known. I can't do this on my own, he thought. On the evening of the second day, Shams Sahib opened his eyes and motioned for Awais to come closer. Awais pulled his chair forward.

'Awais,' said Shams, as Awais leaned in. 'Never believe what the politicians say. It won't happen. They won't partition this country of ours.' Awais's body stiffened. More politics! Why wouldn't they leave him alone? What has politics got to do with anything? He got up and left.

The next day Shams's son told him his father had died just before midnight. I did him wrong, he thought. Another idea banged against the first. Panicked, he wondered, if I'd stayed, what else would he have said?

In the subsequent days, boxes and boxes of files arrived from Shams's house. Awais had already been custodian for three years. But he'd never really felt it till now.

On the eve of the wedding, they all went to bed late, even the young ones. And next morning, though it was still early – which meant Awais had slept only a few hours – he got up and stepped carefully across the pairs of feet which had escaped the comfort of their sheets. The house was overspilling with people and yet in this moment there was no human sound except that of deep and shallow breathing. His bed had been disassembled and placed in the store where it leaned against a wall. And each night for a week now – since the arrival of his Karachi family and, later, his Amritsar and UP cousins – thin mattresses had been rolled out onto the floor.

He went to find her.

She was in the courtyard, in a corner by herself. He put his arm around her. She'd lost weight. He could feel her shoulder blades.

Together they watched the day rise; the sunlight settled on and tinted everything – sky, buildings, streets – with pale gold. The air was cold. Awais sucked in his breath and then blew it out in a perfect 'o'. She laughed and they began, as they had all those years ago when they'd invented the game, to break each other's rings.

'You're spitting!' he said.

'I'm not,' she cried and he got one through.

She turned to him crossly and said, 'That's cheating! I was talking and…' He laughed. He'd done it again.

'Breakfast!' Zubi shouted, coming into the courtyard. They hadn't heard her enter; her bare feet were light. On seeing Awais, she readjusted her *dupatta*. Maryam stepped forward and Awais's arm fell free from her shoulder.

'Zubi,' said Munni Bibi, approaching, 'did you… Maryam! What are you doing over there? Do you want to catch a cold on your wedding day?'

Maryam shook her head.

'Zubi,' Munni Bibi said, 'tell all the girls that breakfast is ready. Awais, wake up the boys.'

Maryam and Munni Bibi turned to leave, leaving Zubi and Awais alone together. He didn't have the courage to look at her, not properly.

'Come on, Zubi,' called Munni Bibi from the corridor, 'what are you waiting for?' Zubi ran after her mother.

Awais knew that people made distinctions; naming 'love' that which is pure and that which is not, lust. But the body was not, he thought, separate from the mind; one can't lust for that which isn't desired. And to desire a thing is to know what it is, or at least, to wish to know.

Soon, more people arrived. On the street, the cooks set up their huge cast-iron pots – big enough to swallow a child of ten or so – and began to cook. The aroma of meat and rice swept over the house. Tanveer and Batool got Maryam ready and then the guests arrived. Within minutes of everyone settling down, the bridegroom's family announced their presence with a twenty-strong band. The children ran to the windows and the alcoves, and looked down on the street at the red-suited musicians who, despite Hamid's best entreaties, wouldn't stop playing. Only when he opened his wallet and paid the band leader an extra sum, beyond what had been agreed, did they turn and leave.

There was silence as Hamid took his first steps towards the house. Awais met him at the entrance and led him inside.

Within a short span of time, Maryam was a married woman.

Barred from entering his own room, Hamid felt stupid.

The wedding day itself, the freight of people whose journeys and resting places he'd had to arrange, the curling bills that his aunt had presented to him with not a few blushes, and the hushed quiet in which they'd agreed to what the *maulvi* had asked of them; this was as far as his imagination had gone, and now he was beyond that point.

He looked in through the open doorway and saw, hanging neatly on a chair's back, a plain new *shalwar kameez*. Beside it, on another chair, was a woman's *shalwar kameez*, smaller, in wilting cream silk. Frightened, he entered. She sat, her hands clasped around her knees, her head bent so he couldn't see her face. The heavy curtains, put up last week, gave the room a new darkness.

He should have asked someone, he thought. What are you supposed to say, to do? The longing he'd felt when he'd first seen her and which had drawn him to this moment was gone. As he looked at her still and huddled form, shielded by her wedding drapery, he felt a sense of self-loathing so strong he stepped back. He collided with the unfamiliar dressing table her people had sent over. She didn't even look up, didn't even ask if he was all right.

He saw the tray on a nearby table with its empty plates. His aunt had fed her but hadn't bothered to ask him if he'd eaten. He'd let the food which had been laid out for him at the reception go cold. He hadn't been able to eat then. Couldn't even look at the food. He now approached the tray, and with his back to her, scraped up with his hands the little heap of rice she'd left. But these few mouthfuls filled him with an even greater hunger. The door closed loudly behind him.

Maryam's head jerked up, her eyes slit-cut with fear.

After a while, the door opened again. She snuck behind her *dupatta*, as she'd been told she must. He took his plate to the table and, head bent forward, began to eat. Halfway through his meal, he said, 'Are you hungry? Do you want something?'

'No,' she said.

The sound of her childlike voice in his room shocked him more than her bodily presence did. He put down his spoon and looked towards the bed and the chains of flowers trailing from the ceiling. He was tempted to go towards her then but his hunger was still not satiated. He finished his meal. Hands washed, he stood darkly before her. He wanted to say something, but what could he say to this girl whom everyone had been at pains to tell him was so bright? He was just a shoemaker and though he had his virtues, they were small virtues; he wondered if they'd be enough. He looked at the empty side of the bed. She was sitting on his side.

'Are you tired?' he asked. She shook her head. He pulled up a chair and sat by her, not too close.

Her wan hand, unadorned, fell from its safe position on her knee. Before she could retrieve it he reached out and tentatively took it in his own. He felt the tug of resistance and the tug to let that resistance go. He stroked its back and felt her tremble.

'I'm going to protect you,' he said. She giggled. He smiled and said, 'Move over. You're on my side of the bed.' She inched over to the other side as he took his place next to her. He lifted her *dupatta* so her face was revealed. 'You're too young for me,' he said.

'Am I?' she said. Onto her wrist he eased a gold bangle.

'You think perhaps...' His words trailed off. He let go of her hand. She frowned. 'Awais tells me you like the stars.'

'Yes,' she said 'and numbers.'

'He told me that too,' he said. He turned the light off and picked up her hand again. 'Look up,' he said.

On the ceiling, a constellation of stars. They didn't twinkle but they shone silvery bright. She squeezed his hand and his grip on hers tightened.

30

NOVEMBER 1944, LAHORE

'Let's go visit Maryam,' said Tanveer.

'Leave her alone for a while,' said Batool.

'But *apa*...'

On his way back from work Awais heard the beat of a *dhol*. Just like the one he'd heard when he'd found Loha. What was the *dhol* calling him to? A stone hit his head. He looked up, thinking it had fallen from a shop awning. And then he saw a boy run off. Safely in the distance, the boy embraced his friends. They laughed. And as Awais stared, bewildered, they shouted at him, 'English toady, *hai, hai!*'

Around him, heads sank as if the other passers–by didn't want to know what had just occurred or what it meant. Is the tide changing, he thought, and is it changing so fast?

The next evening Awais was in his room, reading, when Tanveer rushed in and said, 'Awais *bhai*, there's someone here to see you.' A messenger had arrived from Bilquees's house. He said he was here to get Awais. Awais said he didn't want to be got but his mother said it must be important and urged him to go.

Khala Bilquees stood waiting at the open door. Across the street, a huddle of men were staring at her; she pulled the *dupatta* closer, bent her head. It was only when Awais got nearer that he saw what they'd seen. Her face, ravaged with fear. He stepped forward and said, '*Khala*, what's wrong?'

'Awais, you've come.'

'*Khala*,' he said, 'what's wrong? Tell me – I'll call a doctor.'

'No. It's just…'

'Just what? Tell me.'

'It's…'

'It's me,' said a voice. Mitoo stood in the open doorway, grinning. 'Come in, Awais, or do you want to provide a drama for all these bastards?' he shouted. He glanced over at the men and laughed. Awais took Bilquees's arm and they entered the house. Awais closed the door behind them.

Mitoo helped his mother to a chair and settled her down, before taking a seat beside her. His head was shorn and this made it look smaller. Awais stared at Mitoo's protruding ears and at the mole on his neck below his hair line, both of which he'd never noticed before. Mitoo looked heavier too; not fatter, just heavier. On his fingernails, nicotine, spreading like a dye. He saw Awais looking at him.

'Seen enough?' he said.

'Mitoo!' protested Bilquees.

'I'm only joking. Awais knows that. Don't you, Awais? *Ammi*, you're tired. I'll take you in.'

'No,' she said to her son, 'I'm fine. I'll get…' and she tried to rise.

'I'll do it,' he said.

'It's all laid out…'

'I know, *ammi*. You told me.'

Mitoo left for the kitchen and Bilquees, making sure he was out of earshot, motioned to Awais. He leaned forward.

'Do you see?' she said. 'See what he's become?'

'*Khala*, there's nothing…' he began. But then he couldn't go on. What solace was there in platitudes?

'You must have seen that…' And she looked to the floor as if that's where she'd find her missing words.

'When did he get back?'

'Two days ago.'

'And you… Why didn't you tell me?'

'Today,' she said, lowering her voice further still, 'was the first day he left the house and…'

'Talking about me?' Mitoo said, returning. He put the tray down

216

then slithered back into his seat. Bilquees reached for the tray. 'No, *ammi*,' he said, 'I'll make it.'

'See, Awais,' she said, tilting her head to one side, like a young woman wanting to please. 'He won't let me do a thing.'

Handing Awais his tea, Mitoo said, 'So Awais, what brings you here?'

Awais looked from Mitoo to *khala* Bilquees. She raised a thumb to her mouth and stroked her dry lips.

'I was just on my way…'

'*Ammi*, you didn't ask Awais to come, did you? "Come and see my mad son, your friend?"'

'You're not mad,' she said.

'No,' he said, staring into space, as if seeing neither his mother nor Awais. 'I'm not.'

She said, 'I'll let you both catch up.' She shuffled off to her room.

'So,' said Mitoo, 'does he let you lick his shoes?' Awais was about to laugh. It was a joke, wasn't it? Then he saw Mitoo's face, serious like a new teacher before his first class. Awais stiffened. Mitoo had never been cruel. Or had he always been cruel and he – Awais – had never noticed till now?

'The Englishman – your friend?' said Mitoo.

So, he's back, thought Awais. And I'm what I was always meant to be – an extra, one of a multitude, who weaves in and out of a film at a director's beck and call, doing all kinds of humiliating acts, and yet – was it a curse or a consolation? – never having the camera reveal his identity, the wealth of emotions he could exhibit, if only given the chance.

'Trapped you, has he?' Mitoo continued, his voice full of danger.

Awais made an effort to listen, though his mind was wandering again. There was so much to do. The temple he'd just heard of, the favour he owed Jalgit – he'd visit the *akhara* on his way home. Maybe Mitoo would like to come along? Had he told Jalgit he was back?

Khala Bilquees returned. In his rush to get up Awais bumped into a chair leg. Mitoo's eyes, watching him, the mockery slipping out.

'Don't be such a stranger to this house,' she said as he got ready to leave. He bent his head and shoulders to her blessing, and with a perfunctory hug of Mitoo – they barely touched – he left. Once out of sight, he inhaled deeply and held his breath tight like a hoarder who thinks, this will come in useful one day. The breath was pulled from him. There was no reason to run. He looked back. No. No reason at all.

'My friend,' Awais said to Harold, 'my best friend is back.' They were in Harold's office.

Harold got up and stood at the corner of his desk, tracing the edge with his forefinger. 'What's he like – your friend?'

'You mean to look at?'

'That and...'

'Well, he's a head shorter than me. Not fat, not thin. And the fastest man I ever saw!'

'Did he run?' Harold asked.

Awais frowned. What was Harold getting at? He put the file of notes on the nearest chair. 'You mean in competitions?' Awais said. 'No. Funny but I never... The teachers asked him...'

'Maybe he's not the social type?' Harold said.

'Mitoo?' Awais laughed.

'How did you two meet?'

'We were at the same school.' Awais smiled. 'And there was something else.'

'What?'

'He had a question he wanted to ask me.'

Harold picked up a small piece of marble that he used as a paper-weight. It was the size of a duck's egg and had a pale green tinge to it.

'And the answer – he found it?'

Awais laughed again. 'Anyone else would have asked me what the question was.'

'We'll be leaving soon.'

'We?'

'The English.'

'And you? You'll go too?'

'I don't know. I just... Oh God, I never thought...'

Awais said hurriedly, 'I've found a new place that does the best *faluda*.' Harold looked at him blankly. 'It's a milky dessert.'

'God, no. My teeth. They won't survive.'

'I'll send your body on behind.'

'A true friend.'

'True,' Awais said. 'Yes.'

'You'll introduce me?'

'If you want.' Awais looked across at Harold's hands, which were still holding the paperweight, and once again, he wished that he could draw the way Mitoo could draw. Buildings, yes. Just about. But he'd never have Mitoo's finesse. I'd draw hands, he thought, and use them as a test to see if people could tell who was who. I don't think hands can deceive. As if conscious of his gaze, Harold clasped his hands behind his back, and straightened up.

'When can we go?' Harold said.

'To the *faluda* stall or Mitoo's?' Awais said. Harold tipped up his head. 'I'll ask *khala* Bilquees if it's okay to bring a guest.'

'You have to ask?'

'Well...'

'I see,' Harold said. 'No white men or dogs allowed.' When Awais looked at him, hurt, Harold added, 'It was a joke, Awais, just a joke.'

The introductions made, they sat uncomfortably, as if waiting for someone to make it all easier. Mitoo wore his uniform trousers, ironed to boards, a white vest and nothing else. On his feet were *chappals*.

'You were abroad, Awais tells me?' said Harold.

Mitoo didn't reply.

'Yes,' Awais interposed, 'he was in Egypt, then Belgium and France.'

Mitoo stood up. Harold looked at him startled, then lowered his gaze. Awais turned to see what had caught his attention. As Mitoo walked towards the kitchen, one of his legs dragged slightly behind the other.

'*Ammi!*' Mitoo shouted, nearing the passageway.

'I'm coming,' she said, and entered carrying a tray, her face all held-together smiles.

His leg, wondered Awais. What had happened to his leg? The other day he wasn't limping. Or was he? Maybe he'd twisted it. I'll ask *khala*, he thought, but not today.

Awais kept on thinking Mitoo would explode – not like a thousand fireworks in an elaborate display, but just in one enormous bang. Then it struck him. Mitoo had always been able to work out what made other people tick. *Please don't let him guess what I'm thinking.*

Mitoo's body, which had once seemed so smooth and fluid in movement, was now disjointed: in bits and parts. His leg was lame. Bilquees loudly proclaimed it would heal and Mitoo let her say it. And Awais thought, it's not just for her sake. How can he not want it to be true?

Mitoo walked neither to accentuate his injury nor to disguise it. Already, it had become a part of who he was, like the curvature of his spine, which now, perhaps because of the pressure on his legs, appeared more pronounced. Awais wouldn't have noticed there was anything wrong with Mitoo's back if he hadn't told him about it. Once, when they were very young, he'd ripped off his shirt and said, 'Touch it,' and Awais had, and had thought it wondrous that Mitoo's back was not completely straight, like everyone else's.

'Like an old man's,' he'd said, putting his shirt back on.

'No,' Awais had laughed. 'It's great.'

Mitto had laughed too and Awais had known he was not unhappy. How could a laugh change? Mitoo's had been deep and full of force. You had to laugh when he laughed, or, if you didn't have one single funny bone in your body, you had to at least smile.

His arms were still strong – but what good were arms? It was running that Mitoo had excelled at. And you couldn't run on your hands and arms. It was his face, though, more than anything else, that had changed. Sometimes his head seemed huge and at other times it seemed to have shrunk. Awais tried to see if he could tell what the different sizes meant. Mittoo's face had closed up. Closed up like you close a shop. Why, then, thought Awais, do I think he'll explode?

Through closed eyelids he saw the city ablaze. He'd neglected the city for too long. He set off for Shams's house, which was now his son's house. He still went there to hear the stories people had to tell. The facility to listen and to remember was to hear in an altogether other way. It was the hardest of the lessons Shams Sahib had taught him. *It's time people started coming to me.* His mother came to mind. I don't care, he thought, what she'll say.

31

JANUARY 1945, LAHORE

She had come up to the rooftop workshop, and he was ashamed: of its squalor, after the pristine world he'd built for her downstairs, of his men who were haggard and lewd and, like him, only knew one thing. He was ashamed too, of her. Her married clothes, shiny and stiff, did not suit her, but his aunt insisted she wear them.

At her approach the men, with a pretence of briskness, lowered their heads and set to work again. Radio waves ricocheted. One of the workmen went to retune the radio when Hamid said, 'Turn the volume down.' He shook his head sharply for Maryam to stay where she was, and went over to her. The pen of caged pigeons behind him fluttered softly.

'You look...' he said touching a brocade sleeve. 'Did we get you this?'

'No, my mother... What's that for?' She pointed to several sheets of dull corrugated metal.

'Oh, I keep on meaning to build something,' he said, gesturing vaguely. He was listening to her but he was listening more intently to the silence of his men. They were not a quiet breed; even the shyest of them became, on climbing up these steps, as voluble as a god to whom people must listen. Hamid found he couldn't ask the question he most wanted to ask her: what are you doing here?

He hadn't forbidden her entrance. But who'd have guessed she'd walk up all by herself? He heard a titter and turned round but all heads were lowered together. He knew he was not a hard taskmaster. He grunted; no, not by any measure. If he weren't so good at his work and respected for his craft by men who paid homage to nothing but ability, the situation would have been different. And so consoling himself, he said, 'Come here,' and guided her to behind the water tank.

'What're we hiding for?' she said, giggling.

'We're not,' he said.

'You didn't come down for lunch,' she said.

So that's it, he thought. It's begun. He ought to chastise her, but instead found himself explaining, 'We're busy. We have a large order to meet.'

Someone coughed nearby. Hamid came out from his retreat and faced his chief workman who said, '*Sahib*, we're going now.'

'Is it time already?' Hamid said. He was skittish and his workman gave him a funny look. 'Yes, all right.' He was now half behind the tank and half not. He watched his men pack up then leave. When he turned back, Maryam was sitting on the edge of a wall. He grabbed her and pulled her up and into his arms. 'Don't ever do that again!' he cried.

'Do what?' she said.

Holding her to his side, he showed her how far she might have fallen.

'Oh,' she said and shivered.

'Come on,' he said. 'I'll show you my pigeons.'

'They're not fighting birds?'

'No, they're tame,' he said. And as they reached the large grilled wooden cage he pursed his lips. Tongue to teeth, he called them to him, 'Te, te, te te...' He didn't see how adult Maryam's smile had become.

The Quit India movement had been going since 1942. Now suddenly, the words 'Quit India' appeared wherever you looked: on posters, on walls that the night before had been blank, on the back of donkey carts. The demand for a partition of the states along communal lines was also growing stronger.

Awais had never been so busy. More and more inhabitants of the inside city turned up at his door. There was an urgency in their stories now, though if asked, few of them would have been able to say why. Khurshid asked him just once what it was all about. He said it was work and she didn't ask him again.

Five months after Maryam's wedding, he married Zubi.

He entered his room with trepidation, the room the women had taken her to, and sat with her on the bed. He pushed at her dress, art-fully spread out, to make room for himself. Her clothes were heavy, encrusted with *tilla* work.

As she sat there, her head bent under the weight of her *dupatta*, he tried to remember how much he'd wanted just to touch her. And now he could touch whatever he wanted. With a jittery hand, he pushed back the *dupatta* an inch. Her head was still bent. He felt for her and for himself. She was all woman; it followed then that he must be all man. He said, 'There's nothing to be scared of.'

She looked up. His eyes widened in shock. Her make-up was gar-ish. She looked nothing like the young girl he'd been eager to be bound to. She expected him to know what to do and he didn't. He fumbled through it, feeling not an inkling of desire, just responsibil-ity.

That first night she was pliant. After that, her demands became voracious. She claimed him again and again with open looks and, at first, still curious, he readily obliged. He began to feel worn down, like an old track, by her demands. And then her jibes began. It was a strange way to try and win someone, he thought, as he closed the door on her sleeping form.

She was prone to sharp fits of anger, and each time they occurred they seemed to last a little longer than before. And still he wanted her, part of him despising himself for his need.

Was it joy for her? Or was it something else? But what? Something more sustained? He had no way of knowing, no way of measuring one thing against the other, because the other thing didn't exist for him. And though he watched her face – saw the expression of some-thing he himself didn't feel – he began to suspect that what she expe-rienced wasn't joy. Perhaps, though, he thought, it wasn't joy she was

'No,' he said, 'in two years' time. Of course, today.'

Awais smiled. Mitoo had never asked him to do a single thing. He'd always told him.

'I have to tell Zubi...' he said, getting up.

She was, as always, lying on the bed.

'You're growing fat,' he said.

She turned to her side so that one voluptuous thigh rested on the other. 'Yes. But it suits me.' Awais couldn't dispute this; it did. Her hair was more luxurious; her skin smoother and her body... She touched a hand to her thigh, a stroke that skimmed, dipped and then was still.

It's animal desire, he thought, feeling sick. She hadn't seemed surprised at the force of her body's demands – she'd even laughed, but she couldn't possibly have known. A more quiet thought intruded. A ring of terror. Alive. There was no doubt about it: she was alive to something he had no access to.

She laughed as she registered his inability to turn away. And then suddenly, leaving was the easiest thing to do.

'This is it,' said Mitoo, pointing to a slash of lit windows on Fane Road.

'This is what?' Awais asked. Mitoo knocked and the door opened. The room was full to bursting. The men sat in groups of four or five: one person was reading while the others listened.

Mitoo led Awais through to a second room where a heated discussion on the merits and demerits of the Congress's last tactical move was in full swing. Awais frowned. All the men were dressed in khaki *shalwar kameezes*. 'Are they communists?' Awais asked. Mitoo threw back his head in disgust. He took a seat and motioned for Awais to do the same. Several people nodded in Mitoo's direction.

'And it is against slavery under the British that we have to fight. Not until they have relinquished our land can we call ourselves free.' The speaker was a giant man with feverish eyes. He paused, looking for approval in the direction of a robust, bearded man who sat to his right. The man nodded. The speaker seemed pleased, and continued.

The bearded man wrote something on the pad in front of him, then scribbled over it. The speaker finished; polite clapping.

The bearded man, Allama Mashriqi, got up to wild applause. 'My brothers... what I ask from you is—'

'Our life we give to the cause,' shouted a man.

The *allama* smiled and said, 'What I ask of you is more than your life. I ask you to think; to think as the rational creatures God made you.' They stared back at him, entranced. He continued. 'The two evils we face today are communism and capitalism: one which ignores the human spirit and the other which talks only of human need. The West, my brothers, talks about the survival of the fittest – to vindicate what they see as the supremacy of their race.'

'Shame! Shame!' cried a young man.

'Ah, but are we any better? There are some of us who believe in a renaissance of the east, based on what we regard as our superiority of spirit. This too, is a lie; by looking only at the past we'll miss the opportunity of the future. Those scientists who say God is dead are wrong; those religious leaders who say religion requires no science are wrong. I stand before you as a man of science who believes that there can be a meeting of both worlds... '

When he came to the end of his speech, clapping resounded through the two rooms. Mitoo waited until the crowd had thinned; then he rose. Awais unfolded his legs and followed Mitoo as he made his way over to the *allama*.

Mitoo inclined his head respectfully and, taking the *allama*'s outstretched hand in both of his own, said, 'Allama Sahib, *Aslam-o-alkum.*'

'*Walekum-Asalam,*' the *allama* answered. As he had a hundred times this evening, the *allama* replied to a polite enquiry about his health. They talked for a while until someone else approached, also seeking the *allama*'s attention. Mitoo and Awais walked back into the first room.

'The meaning of revolution,' one of the group leaders was saying, 'is both spiritual and action oriented. A man must believe before he can act. But before he believes he must...'

Awais looked around at the eager faces, not quite understanding what was going on. By the time they left it was getting late. A man was lighting the gas lamps, another was walking through the streets, shouting, 'It's ten o'clock, ten o'clock,' tapping the ground with his stick.

'What was that about?' Awais asked.

'That man I introduced you to, Allama Mashriqi, is the leader of the Khaksar movement.'

Awais looked back blankly. 'Never heard of him.'

'You will,' replied Mitoo.

Awais considered this, then asked, 'Are you a member?'

'No,' Mitoo said.

'What do they do?'

'They oppose the British.'

'But isn't that what the Congress and the Muslim League do?'

'The Khaksars are different.'

'How, different?'

'The Congress is only for the Hindus. The Muslim League's tooth-less. This is the only real movement in the Punjab.'

'Mitoo, I don't—'

'Let me tell you about Allama Mashriqi,' cut in Mitoo. He looked round. 'Let's find somewhere to sit, have a cup of tea. Jalgit Singh's place – let's go there.' They set off.

Above the restaurant, a cut-out poster: Jalgit Singh, with a dog, passive, at his heels. It was a reminder of when Jalgit had fought the mighty Sandoz and had then survived an attack from Sandoz's equally famous 160-pound dog, Sultan. Since Jalgit had opened this restaurant, his younger brother had taken over the running of the *akhara*, though it remained under Jalgit's supervision.

Inside, it was packed. They were about to leave when Jalgit saw them from behind the counter. He collared a young boy and said, 'Make a place for my friends.'

'Oi, you,' said the boy. 'Find somewhere else.' The men he spoke to got up at once, their plates in their hands.

'We'd have been all right at any table,' Awais said, embarrassed.

'But this is the best table,' said the boy, scratching his head.

'But they were sitting here.'

'Just look at them: they're scum.' He turned his gaze on the three men, who were now huddled at another table, from which the remains of earlier dinners had not been yet been cleared. 'Those kind,' he said sharply, 'need to be shown their place.' He wiped the table and Awais and Mitto sat down.

'*Garam dal*, *kebab*, mutton, chicken *karahi*, *roti*, *naan*,' said the boy in one unbroken line.

'Two cups of hot, hot tea,' said Mitoo and the boy looked disappointed.

He made a last attempt. 'The *haleem*'s the best in the bazaar,' he said.

'No. Just two teas.'

'Any shorties?'

'You, Awais?' Awais said no.

'I'll have a bun with butter.' The boy smiled, glad he'd won Jalgit Singh's guests over to some food.

Awais looked out at the bazaar and noticed how their position made them almost invisible to passers–by. 'See these men, Mitoo. Their wives and mothers must feed them. You just have to look at the size of them to know that. And yet each day – between those meals – they come here with their friends, to eat. Anyhow, you were going to tell me about Allama Mashriqi.' Mitoo poured them some water from the jug. He drank.

'Two teas. One bun with butter,' said the boy, returning with a plate balanced on his bent arm, a glass of tea in each hand. When someone shouted, 'Oi, boy!' he turned angrily.

'Someone's died, have they?' he shouted back and moved on. Behind the counter, Jalgit Singh smiled proudly.

'Allama Mashriqi,' said Mitoo, blowing on the tea, then picking off the skin and swallowing it whole, 'is a great leader.' He took a few sips. 'He studied at Cambridge. He comes from an influential family. But he gave it all up to fight the English. The Khaksars wear khaki *shalwar kameezes* – Allama Sahib is very impressed by Hitler's management – and a coffin hood round their heads. Should a man die for the cause he can be buried on the spot. Their sign is the spade.'

'So, they're gardeners or grave–diggers, then.' Awais asked.

'Everyone says that!' said Mitoo.

'Mitoo, I don't understand a word you've just told me.'

Mitoo sighed and began again, tracing out in great detail Allama Mashriqi's life and how this mathematician, a man who was born for the world of ideas, had put it all aside for the political arena. 'When he started out in politics,' said Mitoo, 'his family, friends and colleagues thought him mad. They said, "It's just another challenge he's set himself." They waited for him to tire of his new endeavour and return to reality. But the *allama* says it is here, amongst these people who've never been called on to discipline themselves, that he's found reality, that he's found that existence exists.'

'How long have you been going to their meetings?'

'Two weeks now. Allama Sahib believes very strongly in education for all. The first room we went into – that was the reading group. Though most of the workers are educated men, some have no education. Allama Sahib has designed it so that those who can read, read to those who can't. Awais, Allama Sahib is truly a great man.'

'When are you joining them?'

'Who said I was?' asked Mitoo.

One early Saturday morning, Awais was alone in the courtyard, reading the paper, when Hamid burst in.

'It's Maryam,' he said.

Awais leapt to his feet and started to run downstairs before Hamid caught up with him. Although Awais struggled to be let free, Hamid held onto him long enough to say, 'Awais, she's okay.'

'When?'

'An hour ago.'

'And you left her?'

'My *khala*'s with her. She's sleeping.'

Awais nodded. Hamid's face grew frightened again. 'There was foam every...' Awais stroked his fingers over his eyes. 'You knew?' said Hamid.

'My mother never told you?'

'Told me what? Awais, what didn't she tell me?'

'About the epilepsy.'

'The what?'

Anger rose inside Awais. But calmly he said, 'Listen.'

When he'd finished, he stood braced against all possibilities. Hamid had every right to tear him, them apart. He raised his head. Across Hamid's face, not anger but understanding. Awais's body relaxed. He knew he'd been right about Hamid. 'The dream then...' said Hamid, thinking aloud.

Awais stared at him. 'What dream?' he asked.

'She saw a crowd of men. And shots being fired. And—'

'And?'

'Mitoo was in the crowd.'

Awais hurried downstairs, Hamid not far behind him. In the waiting tonga, they said nothing to one another.

'*Khala!*' Awais shouted when they reached Mitoo's house. '*Khala!*'

'Awais, what's wrong?' Bilquees said, coming into the courtyard with a bowl in her hand. She looked up at Hamid curiously. She put the bowl down on a table and draped her *dupatta* over her head.

'*Khala,*' Awais said, 'where's Mitoo?'

'Awais,' she asked, 'shouldn't you be at work? And who's this?'

'Maryam's husband.' Hamid bent his head to receive Bilquees's blessing. Awais continued, 'I have to see Mitoo.'

'Now?' she said. 'This minute?'

'Yes, *khala.*'

'What's wrong?'

'Nothing's wrong,' he said and tried to smile.

'Then why the rush?'

'It's me, *khala,*' said Hamid stepping forward. 'I have to ask Mitoo something and this is the only time I had free. It's my busiest season.'

'Yes,' she said, nodding. 'I like your shoes.'

'Thank you. Tell me your size and I'll have a pair sent over.'

'No, *beta,*' she said, 'No, I couldn't...'

'*Khala,*' he said. 'What are family for? Please tell me.' He looked down at her feet. 'I'd say a size three.'

'How did you know?' she said, looking down at her feet as if they'd revealed too much.

'*Khala,* Mitoo...' Awais asked, exasperated.

Bilquees sighed. 'He had a meeting with that group.'

'The Khaksars?'

'That's right,' she said. 'Are you a member too, Awais? What kind of people are they?'

'A meeting – at this time of day?' Awais asked.

'I think he said it was something else.'

Hamid looked to Awais and Awais deliberately turned away. '*Khala*,' Awais said, 'do you know where he went?'

'Chauburji, I think,' she said.

'*Khala*,' Awais said, 'we have to go.'

'But—'

'Really, *khala*,' said Hamid smiling, 'I have to speak to Mitoo today.'

'You want his advice on something?' she asked.

'Yes,' he said, 'that's it.'

'Wait a minute,' she said and left. Awais kept his back to Hamid. Coming back, Bilquees put two rupees in Hamid's hand and when he resisted, she closed his fist upon it.

'No, *khala*, I—'

'The first time you've come to my house,' she said.

'I'll come again,' he said.

Back in the tonga, Hamid told the driver to take them to Chauburji. Awais kneaded his left shoulder; it ached.

They were nearly there when the driver reined in his horse.

'What's wrong?' asked Hamid.

'Something's happened,' the driver said.

'How can you tell?' asked Hamid. Awais and Hamid both looked around. To them, the street looked normal enough.

'The horse knows,' said the driver. 'And there are too many people here for this time of day.' Awais and Hamid saw the driver was right.

'Do you know another way?' Awais said.

'*Aray baba*,' said the driver, grinning. 'You chose the right tonga today.'

He turned the tonga around with short sharp clicks and took them down a back street. Ten minutes later, they'd arrived. Ahead of them, yet more people.

'I can't go further than this,' said the driver, and Hamid and Awais stepped down. Hamid asked the driver to wait. They walked through the crowd, approaching the park on which the Chauburji monument, a small white fort, was built.

Awais tried to block out the sound of voices and what they were saying. They somehow arrived at the front of the crowd. The park had been cordoned off and a row of policemen were guarding the entrance in a tight ring. There were flags and ripped pieces of cloth on the ground. And blood.

'Hurry up,' said an English soldier to a gardener who'd appeared with his water sack tied to his middle. 'What took you so long?' The gardener ignored him and leaning forward, sprinkled the ground with water. A boy appeared behind him and began to sweep away the trail of blood.

'What happened?' Awais asked one of the policemen.

'What's it to you?' the policeman said.

'My friend is—'

The policeman laughed and said, 'Your friend *was...*'

Awais would have leapt at the man but Hamid put a strong hand on his arm, warning him. He linked his arm through Awais's and they walked past a second policeman and approached a third. From his pocket, he took out the money Bilquees had given him and put it in the man's hand. The man's eyes glinted, although he continued to look ahead. He pocketed the notes stealthily.

'We're looking for our friend,' said Hamid softly. 'What happened?'

'The English,' the policeman said, looking around, 'they fired.'

Hamid still had a grip on Awais's arm and pressed down.

'The ones who survived,' Hamid said, 'where are they?'

'Some are in the hospital, some in jail,'

Hamid nodded his thanks. Somehow Hamid and Awais managed to get back through the crowds and into their waiting tonga. At the hospital, Hamid wouldn't let Awais go in. Instead, Awais stayed in the tonga, watching while wailing people entered and others came out. After some time, Hamid returned, shaking his head. He climbed back on board the tonga and Awais moved up to make room for him.

'The jail,' Hamid said to the driver.

'No,' Awais said. 'The collector's office. I need to speak to Harold.'

This time Hamid stayed in the tonga while Awais got down. He learnt that Harold was in a meeting. Should I go out and tell Hamid? he thought. No. He decided to wait. His friendship with Harold gave him the special privilege of being left alone, unquestioned. He didn't have to wait long.

'Awais, what's the matter?' said Harold, seeing how anxious he looked. He steered Awais into his office. 'Sit down. Here, drink this,' he said, pushing a glass of water towards him. 'Now tell me.' He listened to what Awais had to say.

'Let's go.' Harold got to his feet. Awais noticed a tension in his friend's body he'd never seen before. Harold was usually a man of reflection. He said it was the highest art to which a man could aspire. But for him now to act? And to act so assuredly? And for him to seem so fitted to the part? The world was indeed growing strange, Awais thought.

When they reached the tonga, Awais reintroduced Hamid to Harold.

'Here,' said Hamid, jumping down, 'take my seat.' But Harold refused and took a seat in the back. The driver drove fast without having to be told. Again, when they stopped at the police station they found themselves in the midst of a throng of people. Once more, there was crying. And screaming.

Harold went inside. Hamid and Awais stepped down, keeping close to the tonga so that the driver wouldn't race off if offered a better fare. Between them, they smoked the last of Awais's *biris*. It was a dirty afternoon, thick with smog. Some of the old men in the crowd began to cough. Eventually Harold came out of the police station and walked quickly down its white steps. Pleading hands tugged at him and faces peered into his. *Is Najm safe?... Is Rehman?* Harold pulled himself free and made his way to Awais and Hamid. Hamid looked to Awais. When he didn't say anything Hamid asked, 'Is Mitoo...?'

'Yes,' Harold said, 'he's alive.'

Hamid stamped out the *biri* and said, 'We should go and tell *khala*

Bilquees.' He and Awais boarded the tonga, but Harold remained standing. He looked up at them, his expression cold.

'Go on,' he said, 'I have to go back to the office.'

When they were nearly at the police compound's front gate, Awais looked back. Harold was leaning against a tree, his head bent forward.

'Stop!' Awais said, and the driver reined in his horse.

'Awais,' said Hamid, 'what is it? We have to go and tell *khala* Bilquees before someone else does.'

'Yes,' Awais said. 'You're right. Let's go.' The driver, muttering, flicked his reins.

32

All along the road, barricades. People everywhere. A man who'd been crouching and pissing against a wall upon which was written the command 'Pissing here forbidden!' got up, tied the string of his *shalwar* and made to join the nearest group.

Awais approached him. 'What's going on?'

'Don't you know? Peace has been declared.'

'Who won?'

'We did,' said the man and rushed off.

Awais moved to the side of the street to avoid the crowds. Soon, aside from the shopkeepers and passers–by, other, more ordered groups appeared. He recognised the flags of the Congress party, the Muslim League and the communists.

'*Inkilab zindabad!* Long live freedom!' and '*Inkilab le key rayngay!* We'll bring freedom whatever the cost!' they shouted. Some men grimaced to find that their chants and those of the other groups were the same; others laughed. After the first furore of chanting was over, flags were rested on shoulders and the men went to mingle: a communist went to talk to his cousin in the Congress party; brother and brother crossed the floor from the side of the Muslim League and that of another group.

Awais walked on. The war, the ensuing peace, the fight for freedom – it all meant nothing. It was like a big game; some people seemed to enjoy it. When he reached the office he found that the old divisions had been erected: the English were jubilant while others hadn't yet worked out what positions to take. Awais knocked on Harold's door and entered.

'It's a great day, isn't it, Harold?' he said dutifully.

'Yes,' said Harold, looking up from the letter he'd been reading. 'A great day.'

'Any news about Mitoo?'

Harold looked grim. 'He'll be a free man soon enough.'

'That's what they say?' said Awais, pointing to the pile of papers on Harold's desk.

'Want to read them?' Harold asked

'No,' Awais said.

'We need to start exploring the city again,' said Harold.

Awais tried to smile.

'There's somewhere I want to take you,' said Harold.

Awais was going to make a quip then saw the look on Harold's face.

'Lawrence Garden. Tomorrow. 8am?'

It wasn't a question. Awais nodded.

The next morning, as he got ready to leave, his mother collared him, furious he'd forgotten it was Eid. 'I'll be back soon,' he said.

Harold was at the gate of the garden. They walked in. Wherever they looked, throngs and throngs of people.

In their best party clothes, the village men and women walked around the garden, respect slowing their steps. Awais knew they'd never seen such largesse, such scale. Women in their *burqahs* clutched at their children, who made constant bids to escape. One child broke free. A cheer cracked the sky, like lightning. Pickpockets joined the jamboree: novices, watching the procession of women and the gold which hung so temptingly from arms and ears, while old hands studied the movement of a face. Sellers – of ice hammered into mountain shapes, *kulfi*, combs, *channay* nuts in newspaper cones – emerged from the city's invisible folds and began their songs of sale. And on and on progressed the sandals, the pointed *khusas* with their gold and silver embroidery, and the leather shoes – some on feet, others in the crooks of arms, where they would be kept safe and new.

All the while, Harold looking as if he were on the far edge of a precipice.

'Was there something you wanted to say?' said Awais.

Across Harold's face, a shower of fast-moving emotions, before he gained control.

'I've got to see the head gardener,' he said. 'Back in a tick.' Awais smiled. He'd never have heard these idiosyncrasies of language if it hadn't been for Harold. He turned his attention back to the crowds.

As if on a pilgrimage, a line of people, or a line and a half, circling the palatial ice-white Lawrence and Montgomery halls. In the evening, Awais had heard, they'd brim with English men and women, and one could hear the sound of laughter and, sometimes, music. He walked past the cricket ground to his favourite spot, a small enclave behind a hill: a mess of flowers and plants. Lawrence Garden, and to a lesser extent, the other English gardens, were so different to the mathematically arranged gardens the Mughals had built. It's as if, thought Awais, it's only in their gardens they can go wild; in everything else, there must be order. He'd read what Kipling and the others had said about the inside city. It only struck him now. They're scared of chaos. He remembered what Harold had asked him. How am I going to say no to him now? Harold returned smiling; in his hands, a small bouquet of flowers. Awais didn't ask whom they were for.

As Harold entered his ugly house, with its still-strong imprint of its former resident, he felt how right his uncle had been to send him here. He'd never been so happy. Never before had he felt how great life's possibilities were. He had a good friend, he had a job which he didn't thoroughly detest, he was working on a project that inspired him and made him see how far short his education had fallen in preparing him for this: the greatest task of his life. And... Anuradha... she'd shaken every certainty he thought he had.

He took off his jacket and sat down at his desk. He slit open the first of the letters his bearer had left for him on a silver tray. An invitation to dine with his only two English friends, Dewey and Wickes, the editors of *The Civil and Military Gazette*. Thinking of the expressions on their faces if he were to take Anu with him, he smiled sardonically. Ever courteous, they'd probably never let her know how put out they were and, if not that, how embarrassed. He remembered conversations in which they'd vigorously sided with the government's clampdown on interracial relationships. Harold penned a reply and placed the sealed letter on another silver tray. There were three other letters, probably of the same ilk; he knew that the local social circle had not quite given up on him, though he'd often wished they would.

'Sorry sir,' said the bearer, seeing Harold start. He was dressed in an all-white uniform, his feet bare. Ghulam Azeez was a solemn man whom no one had ever seen laugh. 'I thought you heard me enter. Will you be dining in tonight, sir?'

'I've already eaten.'

'Sir,' said Ghulam Azeez. 'You remember we're – that is, the staff – are all going to the *mela* – the fair, tonight?'

'Ah,' said Harold, 'that's why you look so dapper.'

Ghulam Azeez looked embarrassed and took a minute to compose himself before saying, 'Will that be all, then, sir?'

Harold nodded. When Ghulam Azeez had gone, Harold stretched in his chair. A soft wind rattled the window blinds. Thank God, he thought. He opened the second letter and then the third. As he'd suspected: two invitations and one flyer from the Salvation Army asking for donations. He threw them in the rubbish bin, half read.

He was surprised at the weight of the fourth letter. He slit it open. The bonded paper was of the most expensive sort. He read the signature first then returned to the top. He stared at the words as if they were a firing squad. *I don't have to tell them a single bloody thing!* The words blurred. *Anu.* He smoothed the letter down, picked up a pen and, with a flourish, wrote two words on the left-hand corner. He opened the bottom drawer of his desk. It only contained one thing. He polished the gun on his thigh. When he raised it and couldn't see his reflection in the steel – a cut of sharp disappointment.

Anuradha was glad, Awais could tell, that he'd come. Aside from his maid, he was the only one who knew what Harold had meant to her. They sat in silence for an interminable time.

She handed him a file. At her signal he sat down, opened it and began to read. Sheaves and sheaves of notes in Harold's hand. All on the inside city. His heart pulsing, he continued to turn over page after page of notes. The realisation, unwanted, was slow to fully emerge. Shams Sahib had been right. He looked up blankly. And though his face held, he was sure, no question, she said, 'One of my men worked at his house. He got me the papers, before the English could.' *Did everyone understand this then, but me?*

Awais's head bent again. The detail of the notes astounded him. It shouldn't have, he realised. Harold had told him again and again about his training. At the first maps, his stomach tightened. *We owe the dead no reverence. They're just as bad as everyone else and bind you and hold you and pull you where you don't want to go.*

He read the next page before he fully understood what he was reading. The letter wasn't meant for him. It was a letter from the secretary to the Viceroy telling Harold to break relations with Anuradha, or the consequences they'd both have to face would be dire. On the left hand corner of this letter in Harold's hand, the words: 'Marry me?'

Closing the file Awais stood up and handed her the letter. He'd never pitied anyone more in his life.

33

NOVEMBER 1945, LAHORE

Khurshid sat near the radio; nowadays she could barely be torn away. Daily, she expected some story to oust news of the war victory, but nothing did and she wondered, though never out loud, if she hadn't developed a taste for calamity.

She turned up the volume and listened to the debate about India and the plethora of comments about the natives not knowing what was good for them and not being able to rule for themselves. She listened, perplexed. Dar would have told her which position was right.

Awais entered. He said his *salaam*, not seeing her, not really, and walked on.

For many months now she'd left him alone. With their father's death, thought Awais, she'd begun to change; with the singer Bablo's, the change had become complete. Their father had, Awais realised, been her reminder of the kindness she owed the world. In the beginning, he saw her try to rein herself in. She had caught her son looking at her once when she was in the midst of her struggle. She'd looked pleadingly, as if to say 'Hold me!' But how could a child hold a mother? Not until she were frail. No, no, he thought; it has to be the other way round.

This evening, he'd come straight from seeing Mitoo in jail and was tired. He pushed open the door of his room. Zubi lay there, as always, waiting. Her voice soft, and, safe behind closed doors, her words lacerating.

His mother had studied the future, he thought, made it her art. Even though his father had thought himself the rational one, it was she who could join cause and effect, and mellowly draw out too the consequences of actions. Himself – he'd abjured the future, turning his back on it as he had on so much of what was categorically hers. But the future had broken through. He glimpsed it in parts. And nowhere in that future could he see Zubi, the woman – and he glanced again at the bed – who was now his wife and whom he was bonded to for life. The only satisfaction he got from his marriage was seeing how much it hurt his mother.

See? See what you've done?

First, there was desire. Her – Zubi's – kind of desire he could roll up in a carpet and push through a window. He knew that if he were to tell any man he knew, Mitoo included, they'd mock him till he turned to stone and crumbled. They wouldn't understand. Desire without emotion is a trap. Not to be dead but the calmness of death; that's what he wanted. And for his heart that was ravaged and shattered to begin to mend.

Zubi stretched out her supine body. Looking at her, he silently laughed.

'No?' she said softly and for a minute or two temptation edged closer to the surface.

'No,' he finally said and walked towards the door.

'I won't bear such insurrections,' she said. He looked at her then, curious. Such words fell heavily from her lips. Whom had she been talking to?

He was too late. He'd intended to be back in his room by early morning but didn't wake up in time. So his mother found him on a *charpoy* in the courtyard. She didn't say anything, but he could see she was confused. When she'd gone, he picked up his bedding and returned to his room, where Zubi lay on her back, fast asleep. This room and this bed had become her island and she seemed ever more reluctant to leave it. His mother and sisters didn't complain that Zubi didn't attend to even the minutest of household tasks, but he felt it strongly. But, by not having said anything at the start, when he'd still exerted a degree of power over her, now that it had waned he could say nothing, rectify nothing. Close upon her now, he listened to her powerful breathing; its rise and fall uneven, as if trying to play catch. I'll tell her today, he said aloud. She has to change.

In the kitchen he sat down to breakfast with his mother. She watched over him as he ate and he thought how countless were the times they'd sat together like this.

'You're going to see Mitoo today?' she asked. Head bent, he kept eating. She knew he went every day. 'I'll come with you,' she said.

He didn't know how to reply, then said, 'I'll have to ask *khala* Bilquees.' She nodded in agreement, then spooned some more *dhal* onto his plate.

He stood up. 'At least,' he said, 'we have one good piece of news – Maryam and the baby.'

She began picking up the dishes.

In his room, his back to the bed, he stared at his locked trunk, which now held Harold's papers as well as his maps.

'Harold the bastard,' he said.

'What did you say?' Zubi asked, laughing.

'Oh,' he said. 'You're awake, are you?' The tone of the day was set, etched out like all the others that had come before.

When he reached home his mother was waiting for him. She said, 'You forgot?' He denied it but he realised he had indeed forgotten to pick Zubi up from her parents' house. That evening, he set out for Amritsar. Arriving there too late to travel back the same night, he decided to stay.

The next morning, he was ready to go. He looked around for Zubi but her mother said she'd gone to the bazaar. 'When she gets back,' he said, 'tell her I've gone out.'

He crossed the footbridge and walked along the streets which he now knew well. Past the National Bank, the chapel and on towards Queen Victoria's statue.

He walked on, up and past the Alliance Bank. I'll stop soon for some tea, he thought, a sudden exhaustion upon him; but still, he walked on. He shook his head, trying to rid himself of this torpor. And then he came to a halt. He'd never been here before, but he knew what it was; it had been described to him many times. On the right, the wall was pitted, as if some force – rain or wind – had defaced it. On the other side, the wall was intact. He looked through the passageway at the empty greenness that lay beyond. It looked like a place where fantasies might be sown as easily as wheat. He walked on, through the small passageway towards the light at the far end. It led to a dead end. He heard laughter; the sound was little and mean.

He turned around so that he faced the wall. He closed his eyes. It was here in Jallianwala Bagh, in the year he was born, that all those people, men and boys, had been gunned down in cold blood – most of them here in Amritsar to celebrate the Sikh Baisakhi festival. At least 379 dead – maybe more; this was the number the British were prepared to admit to; around 1,500 injured. He'd never felt it so directly before, but he felt it strongly now. The English had done that – and Harold…

A crow swooped down. He watched its swift descent. The crow went straight for the wall, as if he always flew to this spot. He began pecking as if he'd break his way through to the other side. Spotting Awais he rested his artful eyes on him. Awais began walking back along the passage. This is not my place, he thought; it's his.

Harold became a hero. His name was brandished about as if it could set things on fire. And for a while, it could. The Khaksars, but the other political groups too, won more and more people to their side because an Englishman had given up (or so they said) his life for their cause.

Mitoo remained strong. And he wouldn't stop talking. He had an opinion on everything. The weaker his opinion, the stronger his defence. The guards had a hard time of it; that much Awais could tell, but it was a few days before he understood why. Those in jail seemed to rule those who kept them there – as if their incarceration were something they'd chosen.

With Bilquees's permission, he took his mother to see Mitoo. Bilquees was there too. There was no hesitation. They moved towards each other laughing and crying. Khurshid marvelled at Bilquees's still jet-black hair. Her own had turned grey a long time ago.

One day Awais arrived early for his visit. Mitoo lay asleep. Watching him, Awais thought: what brought him here? What if chance didn't exist and we were instead, all of us, prey only to the directions and pulls of other people? Each of us pulling and being pulled? Here strangulating possibilities, there opening doors through which others had never thought to step. He held tight to the cold metal bars of the prison cell and watched as one of Mitoo's cellmates began the long process of waking up. The man stared at Awais, puzzled. Awais looked into the man's bloodshot eyes: hell and heaven just an instant apart.

The Khaksars walked into jail as heroes; they walked out free but defeated men. Allama Mashriqi had given up. Awais thought he'd held the adulation he was given cheaply and didn't understand the obligation it put him under. On the day Awais went to fetch Mitoo, there was a strange quietness in the jail, a homely quietness. Even the guards seemed to sense that something was wrong.

Mitoo was clean shaven, yet wore a crumpled pair of trousers and shirt, though Bilquees had sent him a freshly washed and pressed set the day before. When he stepped outside, he blinked and looked around, taking deep breaths, like a fish that finds itself – by some navigational fault – in strange waters. Mitoo and Awais walked to the waiting tonga without saying a word; then Awais deposited Mitoo at home before hurrying off as fast as he could.

Two days later Maryam was rushed to hospital. She was in the fourth month of her pregnancy.

Hamid gripped Khurshid's shoulders, staring hopelessly into her face. She led him to a chair. The doctor looked from Hamid to Awais, then pulled Awais aside.

'What did he say, Awais *bhai*?' Batool asked when the doctor had left.

'He said we have to look after Maryam.' Batool grasped his hand, relieved. He looked down at it and thought: I can't tell them what the doctor said – that Maryam will never give birth to another child. The nurse came up to Hamid and led him to Maryam's ward. Later, Awais thought. I'll tell them later.

Mitoo stood before Khurshid.

'*Ammi* died last night,' said Mitoo.

'Bilquees?' said Khurshid, shock clutching her body. 'But... she wasn't ill—'

'The funeral's today. After Asr. I'll leave after that. I can't live with him any more.'

'But how will your father...' she began. He shrugged.

'Tell me what I can do?' said Awais.

'Nothing.'

'The food?' said Awais.

'There'll be no food.'

Khurshid looked at him, askance. She was on the verge of saying something but held herself back. Mitoo moved towards the stairs.

'Mitoo *beta*,' Khurshid said. He turned towards her, waiting. 'You shouldn't have left her alone.'

He closed the door softly and left.

'What are you waiting for?' said Khurshid. 'Go.' Awais stared at her, deliberating, she knew, whether she'd be all right. 'Go,' she said again. He left.

Khurshid went about her work but something deep inside her was still. Bilquees was dead. Her best friend was dead. She'd never made another friend in all the years after Bilquees, never dared attempt it. She changed into a white *shalwar kameez*, the first Kalima repeatedly on her lips. Bilquees. She hadn't asked, but she knew Bilquees had no one else. The job would be hers. This would be the first dead body she washed. She'd fix Bilquees's hair, which through everything, had remained as luscious as when they were young women and both newly come to the inside city. When Bilquees had befriended her – she remembered the day to the smallest detail – she hadn't known how new Bilquees herself was to this place.

Khurshid put on her *burqah*. She felt old; old and broken. She'd touched her father's dead hand, and Dar's. But it wouldn't just be Bilquees's hand she'd touch. She'd never seen another grown woman's naked body. The thought of someone touching her own body made her cringe in shame. But Bilquees, if she could see them, hesitant and respectful, bent over her flesh, would probably fall into a giggling fit. This thought, finally, made Khurshid smile.

34

MARCH 1946, LAHORE

Harold dead. And Maryam and Mitoo broken. Life had overwhelmed them, he thought. Idiots. So much his father's word. He was tired. The resonance of life that he'd once felt, the quest to hear the sound of the *dhol*, it was all losing its hold. He stared at his face in the mirror. Does everything, every experience that others have of joy and pain, have to come back to me, to be felt as something that is mine too? I want to feel the way everyone else does: my own emotions and nothing else. The massacre at Jallianwala Bagh. He couldn't get the thought of it out of his head. But instead of Dyer, he saw Harold leading the troops. It was stupid; he knew it was. The next day he resigned from the army.

Hamid asked him to join his shoemaking business, but Awais said no, knowing Hamid was only being kind. In the end, Shams Sahib's son found him a job as a railway clerk.

Hamid had told Maryam what the doctors had said. Two weeks had passed since then, and she hadn't said a word.

Mitoo, meanwhile, was still full of talk. He flitted from one idea to the next before the first was resolved. Since he'd come back from the war, many people – including those who'd been his loyal shadows and whose eyes welled up with tears every time they mentioned his name – had offered him jobs. But he'd refused them all. However, when Jalgit Singh offered Mitoo the job of head man at his restaurant, Mitoo accepted.

'I don't know what to do, Awais,' said Hamid as they sat on his roof. The workers had left for the day and their stools were neatly lined up along a wall. A month had gone by, and still Maryam maintained her silence. Awais let Hamid talk.

He returned home to be told the news. A proposal had come for the girls: two brothers. Batool and Tanveer were overjoyed. They could now go on living together for ever. The brothers owned a china factory and had a huge order to meet, so the marriage was scheduled for two weeks' time. Miss Alvi joined the wedding party on their journey to Poona and tried to talk maths to Maryam, who said not a word. Miss Alvi, unrelenting, persevered. After the wedding, as the girls were seeing their family off, Tanveer said, 'Maryam, if I have twins, I'll give one child to you.'

'Tanveer!' said Batool.

'What?' said Tanveer. 'Now what did I say?'

Hamid put his arm protectively around Maryam and led her away.

A month later, Awais dropped by Maryam's house in the afternoon. The door of her room was open. Maryam sat in a chair, wearing an outfit Hamid's aunt had probably dressed her in this morning. It looked uncreased, as if she hadn't moved, not even a hand to swat away a mosquito or a fly.

'Maryam, I've brought you some *firni*,' he said, and placed the twin clay bowls on the table. For some reason, he glanced up. But the stars Hamid had had painted onto the ceiling wouldn't shine till it was dark, and in that they were, he thought, like regular stars: showy and shy at the same time. And then they both heard his voice on the radio. Pankaj Gopal. Some film song. It shouldn't have suited his voice but it did.

'What hope there is in his voice,' he said.

He, who knew her so well, could hear her thoughts. *And yet, he's dead.*

It struck him that while the music played he still had a chance.

'Maryam,' he said.

He'd heard them tell her the same thing: with God's will everything would be all right. The way she held her body, coiled and tight, he knew that's what she expected him to say.

'I need your help,' he said. She looked up. 'Can you help me work out some configuration of longitude and latitude?'

'What do you need it for?' she asked.

Trying to temper his grin, he said, 'For some maps…'

He just wanted to be alone. The joy he felt was too strong to bear company. Maryam was talking again. The next day at work was manic, and he didn't mind, was glad, really, except when he remembered that he wanted to see her. Hamid sent a message: 'All's fine.'

When he arrived home, he was buzzing, beyond being tired. He was surprised, as it was so late, to see his mother sitting in the courtyard like a beacon who could transmit to no one.

'She's gone,' she said. He looked at her, not understanding. 'Zubi,' she added.

'Gone to her mother's? By herself? And you let her?'

Khurshid picked up one of Zubi's *dupattas*, newly ironed and folded, which lay on a chair.

'No, not to her mother's,' she said.

'*Ammi*,' he said, 'I don't understand.' Head lowered, she told him. In crude and graphic detail, she told him everything. How, a while ago, Bilquees had seen Zubi in the street with a man. How she'd seen them again, talking with their heads close together. How she'd asked Mitoo to find out, and from that, how they'd discovered that everybody knew. That Zubi and the man… Bilquees had confronted her, but Zubi had merely laughed in her face. It was at this point that Bilquees had finally told Khurshid.

'I watched her all the time, Awais,' Khurshid said. 'I don't know how she…'

'How she what, *ammi*?' he asked.

'How she escaped.'

She waited. He said nothing. The first thing he felt was relief.

Khurshid's view of heaven collapsed. Not like something that has been pulled up by its roots, but like something beset by gnawing rats. She still prayed, still read the Qur'an, but now her actions had a quality to them that was new. She sought in these things something else, a validation, perhaps, that the time she'd given to faith had not been wasted, that it was all being marked up; that her prayers would count for something.

Watching her Awais thought: fear hangs over us all. I fear. Someone else fears, and fears the things they think control others as well. He'd avoided her before; now he stood where she stood, sat where she sat. Let her see it, he thought, let her see me, and know.

'Awais,' she said, 'maybe... maybe you should get married again... Munni Bibi said...' She stopped.

'You're still talking to her?'

'She wrote me a letter.'

'And you read it?' He got up.

'Where are you going?' she said.

'Out.'

He raced down the steps and stood in the street to collect himself for a moment. Then he walked past the shops, which were just opening up for the second part of the day, and watched as the *jalebi* maker poured liquid into a vat, dipped in a ladle and spooned his *jalebis* out, all shiny and orange-hot. The *jalebi* maker's brother sat weighing the *jalebis*; without a word to his customers, he put the crispy confections in bags made from cut-up newspapers. Awais moved on. Everywhere he went, people either raised their hands in greeting or shouted out a few words to him.

A shopkeeper shook out a purple, yellow and red silk bedspread. Awais had never seen a thing he'd desired to touch and hold so much. Without intending to he walked over to the man's shop. Seeing him approach, the man spread his hand over the bedsheet and let it slide down, as if telling him how it would feel, and that it could be his. He looked up slyly and grinned, revealing a red-stained mouth; then he leaned towards Awais and whispered, 'For your bride to be.' Awais jumped back and the man laughed at the look on his face. The man caught himself then; he'd behaved not like a shopkeeper courting a customer but like anybody else. As Awais turned to walk away, the man crooned 'He's a shy one, that one', his plump hand still stroking the bedspread.

Awais carried on down the street and looked up. It was as if there were a net between the sky and the roofs of the buildings overhead, for the light, which in the sky was strong, didn't reach the world around him. He frowned. The buildings looked brown and old, as if a breeze with little more strength than a kiss could blow them all down. And when they were gone, no one would know how to build them again and so people would stay in their shop-hole, house-hole spaces, living their lives, oblivious – because that was the art that they'd learnt and perfected in the face of change.

And if love can pluck you from the place in which you stand and make something else of you, can the other state, too? Not hatred but the opposite of love: non-love? He hadn't realised how far he'd walked until he stood in an alleyway that would lead him to Delhi Gate if he went on. And then, as if it had come from nowhere, but just required the shifting of his gaze, he saw a huge red flame. He heard a scream – short and sharp – and ran towards the fire.

'Quick, help me!' said a man, emptying a bucket of water onto the flame. Awais did as he was bid. It took them over fifteen minutes to fully douse it. When they were done they were both covered in grime. The man grinned and Awais grinned back.

'How...?' said Awais. The man took out a packet of cigarettes and offered one to Awais. Awais took it and lit it, still smiling to himself.

'I'm a Hindu,' the man said, 'and this is a Muslim neighbourhood.'

'But...' said Awais.

The man raised his other hand and Awais saw it was a stub. Awais looked around. All the doors and shutters of the houses were closed. The man laughed, threw down the cigarette and walked back into what was left of his home.

No one knew where Zubi was. 'She'll be back,' they said, and in the very same breath, 'but who wants a woman like that?'

Those who'd forgotten the ill fortune associated with Loha remembered it now. And those who'd never heard the gate's name thought it bad enough to lose your wife, not by her falling under a train or some other act of God, but by her packing her things and walking out. Awais didn't go to work for a couple of days after the news spread. It wasn't fear or shame, it was sheer hollowness.

Early one morning, Mitoo called. It must have been six in the morning or earlier. The sky was undecided; what kind of day would it be? Mitoo smelt of mustard oil and, although Awais had got used to his limp, it was Mitoo's posture now that took him by surprise; he stood as if a thread ran through the middle of his spine. That smell of oil and this new way of standing: had he been to the *akhara*? Was he wrestling again?

Mitoo grinned and said, 'Thought I'd walk you to work.'

'I'm not…'

'Spoke to Shams Sahib's son yesterday,' Mitoo said. He whistled sharply through his teeth.

'And?'

'He said…'

'He got me this job, you know,' Awais said, getting up. He straightened the bed sheet as Mitoo watched.

It struck him then how much he disliked the curtains Zubi had put up. They were dark blue with symmetrical lines of small gold flowers.

35

On 5 March, Khurshid received a letter from Batool. Tanveer was getting close to her due date and wanted her mother there at the birth. By rights, Tanveer should have returned home three months ago, but her husband, Nawaz, wouldn't let her go, so she had stayed in Poona.

'It's okay, *ammi*, I'll take you.'

'What about work?'

'It'll be fine. Let me see the letter.'

'I told you what she said.'

'But still...'

Reluctantly, she handed Awais the letter. He read it then looked at her. 'Batool says to bring Maryam.'

Khurshid silently put out her hand and he gave her back the letter. He went to see Maryam later that same day.

'Tanveer wants you there for the birth,' he said.

'But, *bhaia*,' she said. Her head fell to one side as it did when she was thinking and the thoughts were not happy.

Hamid was worried that it would be unsafe. He'd heard the stories that were proliferating everywhere about attacks on the railways.

'We'll be all right,' said Awais. 'If there were any problem, I'd know.'

Three days later, they all – Maryam, Awais, their mother and Hamid – travelled to Poona.

When the rest of the family was asleep, Awais went in search of Batool.

'It was you who wanted Maryam to come. Why?'

'It was Tanveer, *bhaia*,' she replied, busying herself by arranging the tea things on a tray.

'Batool, I think—'

There was a gasp, and then a cry, *'Apa!'*

They both ran to Tanveer's room. Batool rushed inside and Awais, tense as a coil, waited outside. Then he remembered, and rushed to find Nawaz, who called the midwife.

Nearly four hours later, the *dai* opened the door.

'She's...?' asked Nawaz.

'Be a man,' the midwife said disgustedly, and let him enter. He laughed; a laugh that Tanveer returned. Khurshid, Maryam, Hamid and Awais gave them some time alone, then went in to join them. Tanveer lay raised on the bed, a baby in her arms. Her husband stood beside her, looking at her admiringly, tears streaming down his face. On the chair to Tanveer's left sat Batool, holding another baby. Maryam stood very still. Batool stood up and, smiling at Tanveer, came forward. She placed the baby in Maryam's unsteady arms.

'Don't you want to hold your daughter?' she said.

'Maryam,' Hamid said, 'we'll call her Maryam.'

'But Hamid...' she said and laughed. Awais knocked and pushed open the door. She turned, the baby still in her arms, and said, *'Bhaia,* listen to this. He wants to call the baby Maryam.'

'It's a beautiful name,' Hamid said, looking fierce.

Awais opened his arms and she let him take the baby. He looked down at the child. 'Manu,' he said.

'But that's just a shortened version of Maryam!' she replied.

'Manu,' said Hamid. 'I like it.' She shook her head. 'Awais,' Hamid continued, 'come with me to the bazaar? I have to get some sweet-meats.'

Awais kissed the baby's forehead and handed her back to Maryam, who sat down and began rocking her.

Hamid bought enough sweatmeats to keep the shopkeeper happy for a week, telling everyone, 'My wife's just had a girl.'

They stayed two months. Even when she had to put the baby down she couldn't stop looking at her. I'll watch you always, she thought, fascinated by the flit of emotions on Manu's face and her own steady joy in attending so closely to another person's life. As she watched Tanveer feed her baby she felt a pang that her breasts had no milk to give. But that was her only regret. Everything else was perfect.

Tanveer and Batool pleaded with them all to stay – just a little longer – but Hamid said he'd already left his business for far too long. Tanveer and Batool's husbands nodded. They were business-men themselves and explained to their wives as best they could that business couldn't wait. The Lahore family then went to their rooms to pack.

Awais closed his suitcase. He had time for a walk. As he neared the door, someone pushed at it from the other side. His mother entered.

'You knew,' she said.

'*Ammi*,' he said and laughed. Her gaze was steady. 'How could I...? I was going out for a walk.'

'It's her,' she said. 'The pir said... It has to be her.' He was silent. 'What if...?' she began.

'What if what, *ammi*? Just for a minute, just for one minute, think...' He turned away from her, then.

'Why has nothing worked out?' she persisted. Stepping closer, she said, 'Why's your life, my life, gone like this? Why, Awais? You've never thought...?'

'That Maryam took my gift?'

She jerked her head around, as if startled. 'What was that?' she asked.

'What?' he asked.

'I heard something.'

'Where?'

'Outside the door.'

'It's been a long day, *ammi*,' he said, wearily.

'No,' she said. 'There was a—' Frightened, she continued to stare at the door.

He opened it. 'See, see, there's nothing there.'

A shiver ran through her and her shoulders hunched. He frowned. It was time to end this, once and for all.

'If it had been mine, Maryam couldn't have taken it.'

'The pir said...' she began.

'*Ammi*, for God's sake!' he said. She stared at him as if she were seeing both him and something else. He walked out, leaving her alone.

Three quarters of the journey had passed. Khurshid was asleep, leaning against the train's window. Hamid and Awais, whose friendship this journey had cemented, hardly spoke a word. Their gaze was drawn again and again to Maryam and the baby. She glanced at Hamid. Awais smiled, thinking, it's made her shy.

Having settled the baby down, Maryam fell asleep. Hamid too leaned back.

Awais turned to look out of the window. The smells, the feel of metal and of earth that change as the seasons change. Nothing was ever static in the world. Even stillness, he thought, was a charade, pretending to be what it never was. He frowned. Another village, another field. This one looked as if it had never been cultivated. Maybe the soil was acidic and unsuited to growth. But where were the people? Someone had to live here. It was inhospitable – true – but time could change anything. All that was required was a skilled pair of hands. But no. The hands had to know what to do. How long could you survive on luck and the mistakes it yields? He saw two crows fly down and then swoop almost immediately up. They knew what he hadn't wanted to acknowledge: the land was dead.

Fragments, harsh, cruel, but when brought together, and seen as a composite whole, beautiful. Not because pain has been transcended; no, there is no golden gate through which we pass into a never–ending circle of light. Why trust the light, when we've trusted the dark and believed the shadows we

have seen could, if only we could get close enough, be touched? Pain isn't to
be transcended, not till the very end, if even then. It's to be borne.

He'd taught her she was beautiful but now the old ideas bubbled
up. Maybe her sharp lines were just that – sharp lines. Maybe her aunt
had been right.

Khurshid jolted awake from her sleep. The piercing ringing of a
bell cut the air, panicking the children who began to bawl and cry.
She looked over at Manu, who was lying miraculously asleep in the
comfort of Maryam's arms. Maryam's head was thrown back; she
too was asleep and Khurshid found her anger rising again. The train
screeched to a halt but the bell went pulsing on.

'What's wrong?' said Khurshid.

'It's all right, *ammi*,' Awais said. 'They've just stopped the train,
that's all.'

She shook her head. 'Why?'

No one knew.

Awais frowned. Here in this wilderness, which appeared to be
without beginning or end, did someone want to get off or come
aboard?

Soon, the complaints began. 'What are we doing, stopping here?'
'I have to get back. I'm going to be late.' 'My son's getting married
tomorrow. He can't get married without me.' 'Probably some official
wanting to see his aunt.' 'Someone wanting to pee…'

'Look, Awais,' said Hamid, pointing out of the window. Awais
looked. People were descending from the train in throngs.

'Maybe there's a problem with the engine?' Awais said.

'Look over there,' said Hamid quietly. But before Awais could see
what Hamid was pointing at, a young man, a gun gripped tightly
in his hands, strode into their carriage. He was scruffily dressed but
his shoes, though old, were immaculately polished. He was hardly
twenty, thought Awais. He leaned against the barred and pane-less
window frame and shouted, 'Idiot! Turn it off!' Within moments the
bell was switched off. He turned back to the passengers, smiling, then
shouted, 'Get off the train.' When no one moved he cried, 'Now!'
There was a scramble for baggage. 'Leave it,' he said. The passengers
began to make for the doors. He laughed. Awais nudged Maryam.

She woke, Khurshid noticed, with a smile. More young men boarded their carriage. Like the first, they were all dressed in black *shalwar kameezes*. And they were all wielding guns. One, clearly the leader, a man who looked to be no more than twenty-two or three, was the only one whose clothes were neatly pressed. He had a clean–shaven face and a sensualist's lips.

'You can't make us get down; you can't,' said a passenger with a perfectly round face and small disappearing eyes. One of the brigands came up to the man, looked at him for a moment, then spat in his face. The man sank down in his seat, bawling.

'Here,' said a passenger urgently. He handed Awais his scarf, which was worn, but thick. 'Put it on your sister's head.' Maryam looked startled when Awais pulled her *dupatta* off. But she didn't say a word as he tied the man's scarf around her head. He thought, she can pass – just about – for a boy. Khurshid's face was panic stricken. '*Ama*,' said the passenger who'd given Awais his scarf, 'you'll be all right.' Awais took the baby from Maryam's reluctant arms. 'Good,' he thought as it gurgled in its slumber, 'stay asleep.' They climbed out of the train together.

Outside, the heat was searing although the sun was beginning to sink in the sky. The passengers from the various carriages had, by some instinct, come together. Huddled as if under a tent, they waited. The smartly dressed young man who'd cleared the train now stood on its uppermost steps. Before he said a word, all eyes turned to him in fear. He planted his legs squarely and stroked his gun.

'You know what this is,' he said. Some of the passengers bent their heads in submission. Like them, Awais had heard about these sorts of attacks, which were becoming daily more frequent. What government there was seemed lame in the face of them. But even if the government had had a better grip on security, what could it have done? The attacks were not coordinated, or run by one mastermind. They were random, copycat acts, and therefore, said the police, impossible to control; though the word on the street was that the police, as always, accepted their share of the booty. Awais couldn't look at Hamid. He'd thought the stories overblown, that he, as a railway man, would know if the railways weren't safe. Hamid's instincts had been right.

'Empty your pockets, your bags,' shouted the leader. Some of the male passengers sighed with relief and urged their women to hand over their jewellery to two young men who were now passing through the crowd with sacks. That's all this was: a robbery. When the money and gold were collected, the leader smiled and said, 'Men this side. Women that.' Khurshid stared at the commander and saw he was really just a boy. Someone's son. Someone who... She put an end to that line of thought.

When no one moved, the bandits pushed through the crowd, pointing their weapons at heads, at hearts. Some of the women broke into wild sobs and clutched at their men. One of the brigands shouted, 'Didn't you hear what he said?'

The crowd began to separate into two groups. Maryam stepped forward to join the women but Awais pulled her back to his side. Khurshid went to join Awais but a man dragged her towards the other group. 'No!' cried Awais, trying to pull her back. The man laughed, and Kurshid was led away. Awais watched the shadows play on the baby's face. Manu was now wide awake, her eyes fixed on his face. It was getting dark. He'd counted on that. Two of the brigands began passing through the unsteady lines the passengers had made. The men got closer. At their approach, Manu began to wail. Before he could stop her, Maryam grabbed the baby from him; within seconds she had lulled her back to sleep and smiled up at Awais. One of the boys laughed. With an easy, careless gesture, he pulled the scarf from Maryam's head. Then he wrenched the baby from her, thrust Manu into Awais's arms again and dragged Maryam away.

'This is where you belong,' he said, shoving her into the line of women.

'No!' said Hamid, leaping forward. The boy held him easily back.

Maryam, terrified, looked from her husband to her brother.

The men were enclosed by a circle of guards with guns, while five of the brigands led the women away. The men turned their backs; some cried like women, others were sick, others stared at the bare earth. When the brigands returned, shirts hanging out of their trousers, some of their faces marked by scratches, they nodded to their companions and switched roles.

The women came back in dribs and drabs from the darkness of trees and even when a hand lightly held onto the hand of another woman or pulled her along, each looked as if she was walking alone.

The men and boys who followed jeered them on towards their families and the shame that would now stand present in their lives forever. Heads lowered, the women walked on, their eyes only flicking up to check their steps and then flicking quickly away. They returned and were grasped with relief, with fear. The women accepted everything: warmth, coldness, loathing. They realised their bodies had never been their own.

'*Ammi!*' Awais said, rushing forward. 'You're...'

'They didn't...' Khurshid said and began to cry.

'Where's Maryam?' said Hamid, looking around. Other men were calling out for their mothers, sisters, wives.

Awais, Hamid and Khurshid's gaze ran across the pool of women and then back to the darkness of the trees from which they'd emerged.

'There!' said Hamid. Awais looked up in the direction Hamid was pointing at. Hamid lunged forward, ready to run towards her. Somebody grasped Hamid's hand.

'Dog!' said the boy and twisted Hamid's hand till it burnt and his knees bent under the pressure. The boy looked down at him in disgust. 'What good is she to you now?' said the boy. He spat on Hamid's face and walked off. Hamid sat there, spit dribbling down his cheek. Awais handed Manu to his mother, bent down and angrily wiped the spit away.

'Hamid,' Awais said, 'come on, for God's sake.'

Hamid allowed himself to be helped to his feet. Once up, he pulled free from Awais. Awais caught him again and held him firm.

'Look over there,' said Hamid softly. Awais looked. A woman was coming towards them. Awais's grip softened; he felt Hamid squirm and tightened his hold on Hamid again. The woman stepped forward into the light. It wasn't Maryam. She was just a girl, hardly fifteen. She looked around in fear. No one came to claim her. The bandits, huddled together, at the front of the train, laughed to see her walk straight towards them.

'Come with us,' one of them sang. She shivered and an old woman stepped forward. The old woman wrapped her shawl around the girl and led her away.

'Everyone aboard!' shouted the driver. The passengers seemed startled by this reminder of ordinary life and shuffled towards the train.

'Maryam!' shouted Hamid, his eyes raging with despair. This time, Awais let him go.

The boy who'd brought Hamid to his knees returned – with a thick branch clasped in one hand. He was clearly edging for a fight. His frame was slight, yet his arms were muscled and strong. When the boy turned to Hamid, smiling, Awais stepped forward, blocking his path.

Sullen, but weighing the cost of tackling two men, the boy said, 'Didn't you hear what the driver said?' He raised his stick.

'My wife…' said Hamid.

Awais grasped Hamid's hand, signalling him to be quiet, but Hamid wasn't listening.

'She hasn't come back,' Hamid said.

The boy laughed and stepped forward. Awais didn't move. Hamid was still behind him, still safe.

'She—' began the boy.

Another man suddenly appeared in their midst. 'What're you doing?'

'This one doesn't want to go,' said the boy, pointing at Hamid. The man looked at the boy in disgust. He grabbed the boy's branch and struck Hamid hard on the shoulder twice, knocking him to ground.

'Get him on the train,' the man ordered Awais, before dropping the branch and leaving them to it.

Awais began to lift Hamid to his feet; the boy offered his hand. Awais raised his head to stare incredulously at the young man, who lowered his drowsy face in reply. He stood back and watched as Awais picked Hamid up, lugged him onto his shoulder, nearly keeling over with the weight, before righting himself.

The baby began to whimper. Awais looked at his mother. She covered the baby in her shawl. 'Go on,' he said. Awais followed her on board.

'Put something on his wound,' Khurshid said as the train began to pull out. Awais ignored her. He sat down and stared out of the window. How will I recognise this place again? There's nothing to mark it out from the countless other villages we've passed. And anyhow, it was now even darker. Ten minutes later, they arrived at a station. He read its name and said it aloud to himself five times.

Maryam's *dupatta* still lay on the seat where he'd dropped it. Awais picked it up and pressed it to the cut on Hamid's shoulder.

As night settled, the train sped back to Lahore as if, he thought, there was something stupendous waiting for them there. When they arrived, Awais led his family off the train. Khurshid held the baby. Awais propped up Hamid who'd only just woken. Everywhere, people. He looked up. A fire, so huge it seemed to be sucking up the sky. 'Awais!' cried Khurshid.

'Shahalmi bazaar is burning!' said a man rushing from group to group, his face contorted with crazy joy.

I feel nothing, he thought.

Among the passengers waiting to board the onward service, a woman he thought he recognised. She swerved easily through the crowds till she stopped before another woman whose head was bent low to her chest. 'I've got them!' the first woman said, two tickets gripped in her hand. The other woman readjusted her *dupatta*. In her arms, half hidden, lay a baby. Anuradha smiled and the three of them moved towards the train. Awais pushed his family on, homewards.

The next day, everyone had their own reports. Nothing, not one single story touched Awais till he heard of a girl who'd survived the fire. Pulling herself free from the rubble she'd watched her legs snap off as if they were the hunks of trees that had been felled. There was a follow–up story a week later but he wouldn't read it. Living was now about the avoidance of news, he thought. Except they were still searching for news of Maryam.

Hamid had set in motion the search and then crumpled, as if all the living he'd had to do was done. It was now left to Awais to find Maryam.

Was she dead? No, Awais thought. If something had happened to her, I'd know.

Khurshid and Awais stayed with Hamid to help look after him and Manu. Hamid's aunt had become increasingly demented over the past year and recognised no one. Growing ever frailer, she spent her days brushing her hair again and again and singing the songs she'd learnt as a child. Hamid closed himself off in his quarters and wouldn't come out, even when he heard Manu cry. A servant brought him food and forced him to eat a few mouthfuls; the same man changed Hamid's bedding and his clothes. A young cousin of Hamid's, Fatima, was called in to take charge of Manu.

I know, thought Awais, what women know: that pain exists side by side with living. Just this task. That's all. What was the point of thinking about the next moment? It will all change, anyhow.

As he'd been with Maryam, he was helpless before the baby. He put a finger before her face. Manu did nothing, gurgling to herself. Awais's breath grew shallow. Then all at once she grabbed his finger and enclosed it. She was laughing. He looked down into her face that was almost Maryam's and the deep longing that had stretched him thin began to crack. Since that day Shams Sahib had begun to teach him, he'd begun to hone his memory. It had never failed him. He remembered everything. And now he wanted to fail. Wanted to cut the past, that day, up into infinitesimally small pieces and scatter them underground. Through the pain, a deep desire to laugh. There was neither complexity nor simplicity. Everything was a farce. Manu gurgled. She was Maryam again. He picked her up and held her close. I didn't realise it till then. In every moment there's the possibility of danger. How am I going to keep her safe? In his head he was already building walls.

It was initially only supposed to be for a few days, but soon their temporary stay became more permanent, and Awais and Khurshid moved in with more than a couple of bags of clothes. Then the workmen started asking Awais what to do. He told the foreman, Haroon, what had happened to Hamid; Haroon nodded and said, 'But the men need to be given orders.'

'I don't know anything about shoes!'

'I'll teach you,' Haroon said, 'if you won't mind?'

Awais agreed and Haroon began to teach him what he knew. It nevertheless took Awais a long time before he felt he wasn't a fraud, deceiving both the workmen and himself.

'Why is she crying?' said Hamid, one day coming out of his room. They'd hardly seen him these six months.

'Near to teething,' said Khurshid simply.

He picked up Manu, opened her mouth and said, 'No, that's not it. Where's my aunt? She'll know what it is.' He handed Manu back to Khurshid.

Khurshid looked over at Awais, then told Hamid, 'She died two weeks ago.'

Hamid turned his back on them. 'I want to start the search again,' he said.

'I never called it off,' Awais replied.

With a last look at Manu, Hamid returned to his room.

'She's dead,' said Khurshid.

Awais took Manu from her arms, began humming.

'She has to be dead,' she said.

The song he used to sing to Maryam. How did it go? He was still singing as he took Manu upstairs to the workshop. She fell quiet.

Haroon said, 'She's got a good head for heights.'

'And I thought it was my voice,' Awais said, smiling.

Hamid was back. But he was a different man, a man who measured everything he said and did. Each week, on Friday morning before Hamid left for the mosque, Awais shared the latest reports with him. The news was always the same: nothing found. And then one day, eight months after she'd disappeared, one of the two boys Hamid and Awais had used as scouts arrived at their door, accompanied by his father. Both Hamid and Awais hurried to welcome them, yet the man couldn't look Hamid in the eye. The extent of the shoemaker's wealth astounded him. Cautiously, he eyed the house and everything it contained.

From his cloth bag he took out a gold bangle. Hamid prised the item from the man's rough hands. It was the one he'd given Maryam on their first night together in exchange for her unveiling her face. The man then took out the scarf Awais had wound around her head on the day of her abduction. Someone had washed it and ironed it; it must have been stained with mud, maybe other things.

At that moment, Haroon descended from the workshop, a whistle on his lips. 'Awais *bhai*,' he said, 'you'll never...' He stopped in his tracks. In an instant he understood everything; he ushered the boy and the man to another room.

When they were gone, Hamid fell into a squat on the floor and rocked. Harder and harder. 'Dead,' he said. 'Dead.' Awais shouted at Hamid to stop until Khurshid came in and pulled him away.

It was only when Awais held Manu in his arms that he felt at peace. How do you face death? And what they call its reality? And why is its reality different to the reality of everything else?

Khurshid called in a doctor for Hamid. The doctor came in coughing, with a pocketbook full of fatuous statements about the healing power of time. But the problem was time: the future Hamid had glimpsed. It had Maryam in it at every turn. The past might loosen its grip, so he'd forget what her favourite food was; or that, he might remember, but then forget the last or the first words she'd ever said to him alone. Who, thought Awais, looking at Hamid, knows what we recall? The consequential or that which has no meaning at all? We give the insignificant meaning but it remains insignificant for all that. Hamid was, he saw, locked, irretrievably, in time.

They buried her scarf and the bangle the boy had found. They felt they were burying her. Khurshid insisted, saying it had to be done. Hamid was too weak these days to decide anything. And Awais? He didn't know what to say. He knew what he thought – that it was all an elaborate joke, a way for them to perpetuate the illusion of respect. But they weren't respectable, not any more. And all that was left was this, this ritual that his mother demanded and got.

Awais never went to the grave, though he was the one who'd had the tombstone made, in heavy black marble with words carved in gold leaf: 'Maryam Batla: 1926–date of death unknown.' When Hamid had seen it he'd been as angry as hell, but it was done and paid for by then.

'It's disrespectful,' Hamid said.

'Disrespectful to whom?' Awais said. 'She's not there, Hamid. It's a scarf and bangle we've buried under that expensive slab of marble.' Hamid walked away in the middle of Awais's words. He was always doing that now, shuffling away with his old man's gait which Awais so hated.

'She's not dead,' Awais had said. 'I'd know.' And Hamid had believed him. It was the truth. Awais had thought it was the deeper truth – if not the truth as he rationally understood it – till that boy had come along with his father, demanding a reward.

A reward for a declaration of death?

That night, as Awais lay flat on his back in bed, heavy as stone, Harold appeared in the darkness. He didn't say anything, just stood over him, watching with some purpose of his own.

'Speak, you bastard! Speak!' Awais shouted.

No one rushed to his room to save him. And the bastard, he simply smiled.

36

JUNE 1947, LAHORE

On a blisteringly hot June evening in 1947, Lahore and all of India's cities buzzed with electricity. Radios played in homes and were linked up to loudspeakers in the streets as well. At 7pm on All India Radio, four men came up to the mic to speak: the British Viceroy Mountbatten, Congress party leader Nehru, the Muslim League leader Jinnah and Baldev Singh, the representative of the Sikhs. Despite the fact that this was what two of the men had campaigned for for many years, they, as well as Mountbatten and Singh, spoke listlessly. They told the world the British Empire of India would be partitioned.

Awais, walking home later that evening, remembered what his father had told him once about the power of the radio to transform lives. He tried but couldn't remember a single thing any man had said during the broadcast. All he could recall was the date that had been set for partition: June 1948.

He could hear laughter and music coming from the workshop. He strode upstairs and pushed open the red tin door. The men looked up; Rafiq, one of the younger boys, apprenticed to Haroon, was doubled over with laughter. Haroon went up to the boy and laid a hand on his shoulder. The boy straightened up, then glanced at Awais with frightened eyes before looking down at his feet.

Haroon approached and said, 'Boss,' – for two weeks now he'd been calling Awais boss – 'is everything all right?'

'Yes,' Awais said, then heard a sound he recognised. The swish of kites.

Following the direction of his gaze, Haroon said, 'Turn that radio down.' Someone turned it off.

There were five kites in the sky, kites that weren't fighting kites; the wind was being tested, as was the skill of hands that had made nothing fly all summer long.

The music, yes. He understood the men had to have music while they worked. The laughter – that too; the boy was young and what he'd just heard was probably very funny and would have made him laugh as well. But music and laughter, together? Awais closed his eyes. Harold was fading and Maryam was fading.

Later that week, he went to find Mitoo and asked him to draw them both from memory, which Mitoo did. In his drawings, Maryam looked alive; he'd captured the way her mouth curled and something of her eyes. But Harold. Harold looked cruel and stupid at the same time. Still, they were like enough. He had the pictures framed and put them up in his room.

Khurshid shook her head when she saw them and muttered something about not being Hindus.

Awais spent a few minutes each morning trying to imprint their faces on his mind, though Harold, as Mitoo had drawn him, was resistant to being taken up. But what choice did he have? He could, he suppose, get Ain Khan or one of his other former colleagues to track down a photo of Harold in the files. But he knew what kind of photo it would be. Harold had shown him one once and they'd laughed. In such photos, Harold and all the other Englishmen had been snapped at some parade or other, surrounded by bunting and crowds. Harold was in ceremonial dress, at his hip a sword, which he didn't know, he told Awais, how to use; on his head, a hard white sun hat.

Why can't I see them at will, he thought, even if they no longer stand before me? The city: I can see that all the time; eyes open and eyes closed. Then why not them?

They sped it up. As if they couldn't wait to be shot of it now, that jewel. Instead of June 1948, August 1947. Deep in the country, in the villages and in the remoter plains, people didn't hear about the fighting, or about the lure of freedom and the vandalism that such ideas allowed men to perpetrate. In the cities one couldn't escape the news; escape the knowing. Pilfering, arson, rape. Reports of trains arriving, then leaving with sackloads of dead passengers. Those Hindus and Sikhs who'd stayed behind now began the desperate business of packing their things and storing what they couldn't carry with friends, to be picked up later 'when things have settled down, when this madness has ended'.

Partition. Of course no one was ready.

And so the division was made. India for the Hindus, Pakistan for the Muslims, with all the others – Sikhs, Christians – left to decide or not decide – where they wanted to go. A ridiculous distance of 2,208 kilometres from West to East Pakistan. When the Punjab was divided – Lahore to Pakistan and last–minute changes giving Amritsar and Jalander to India – there was bewilderment. Divide one nation into two – yes. But divide the Punjab?

The trust, the open-heartedness. *My house is your house. Welcome. Whatever's mine is yours.* Smiles. Relationships so nuanced they couldn't survive: on one side, obligation, on the other, virtue; sometimes true and honest, sometimes so layered and layered it was hard to ever know what was really there. A people, that's what they were. Joined by something. What was it? They'd forget. Not that it mattered, did it?

There was surveillance, too, just beginning. Come on, said some, how long do you think trust will last? To their questions, replies, laughter. That long?

The administration of the city, of the whole country, collapsed.

Awais walked home from their shop in Anarkali.

The streets, roads, wherever there was a path, however small, all swarming with people. A cast of a multitude, all bent, with hunger for the future to begin and with despair for the so–recent past, and the older despair too, thrown in as well – for it all to be sucked down a drain and never reappear. Wiped clean. A life with no memory of evil, of the crazy torture a human mind could, and did, conceive of: what was to stop that hurtling out into the world, as if it were zooming heedlessly into glass, splintering everything on its way? And then for the wondering to begin, because we must wonder; it's lodged like shrapnel in the human breast.

What, he thought, angrily, do these people believe? That by moving a mile, five hundred, they've shifted lane? The mothers without children, their eyes snapping at women who were still complete. 'Fools,' whispered the now childless mothers under their breaths. Decaying in their old musty clothes, proud of their power to repel. Awais moved closer. The women's voices growing louder as if their audience or they themselves were deaf. 'So they didn't take your child away? There's plenty of time yet. That child will pierce your heart somehow, will never be capable of loving you back, never love you enough. For children are born innocent, then they are cruel.' And then there were the old people who said they'd have preferred to die but were feeding their bodies ravenously whenever they could as if they still had time and the citadel could yet be built.

A new start. That's what the politicians continued to promise. That's what the newspapers were full of too.

Even when he tried not to look, they forced themselves upon his vision. Bodies, dragging or being dragged, skin slackening on bone as if yielding to a greater pull of gravity. All these bodies had one story – a story of collective fear. The whispering in his ear, the desire to die, to not have to weigh, contemplate anything ever again. To just let go. Manu smiling. Having a tantrum he didn't know how to placate. That's how, he thought, they get us in the end and we step back into place, our will for independent flight, even if that flight is to death, chopped at the bottom, chopped at the top and put into the pot.

A young man stepped before Awais, laughing, apologising. *How did he spring free from the band of history?* Longing to hold him, Awais watched him go. I'll appropriate you, he thought. He shrugged, as if slithering off skin. And for a whole half hour the feeling lasted. By the time he got home, he was tired again.

A dry heat. They'd all gone to bed but he couldn't sleep. No thoughts raging in his brain. Just a perpetual blankness.

A knock at the door. Who the hell is disturbing us at this time of night, he thought as he angrily opened the door. On the threshold, Mitoo and Jalgit. Mitoo still carried his Khaksar spade. Once, when Awais had asked him why, Mitoo had replied, 'I like it.' Hanging back, Jalgit, looking shamefaced. Awais invited them inside.

'Jalgit Singh needs your—' Mitoo said.

'Mitoo thinks you can—' Jalgit said.

'Help!' they both finished together.

'You do the telling, Mitoo,' said Jalgit.

And so Mitoo explained how Jalgit and those of the Sikh community who remained – they, who'd never contemplated leaving Lahore – were becoming increasingly nervous. Most of their family and friends had left and though they themselves had laughed away the idea, they'd now begun to think they had no other choice. They felt they'd made a grave mistake, felt they'd been naive. If they left now perhaps they'd survive, perhaps they wouldn't. But what if they survived and their families were killed? They couldn't take the risk. They had been frozen into immobility by the daunting enormity of it all. But now they'd decided. Jalgit had gone to Mitoo and Mitoo, remembering how Awais had once made a few maps of the inside city, had brought Jalgit to Awais.

Awais asked them to wait and hurried to his room. He returned with seven large rolls of paper in his arms. He asked Mitoo and Jalgit to clear the desk, which they did, and he unfurled the first roll to reveal a map.

Jalgit and Mitoo looked at each other. Mitoo laughed.

'So you think you can do it, Awais?' Mitoo asked.

'Yes,' Awais said; only afterwards did he recall the gentle mockery in Mitoo's voice. An hour later, the plan was complete.

The next day Jalgit and Mitoo returned at ten in the evening, when they were sure everyone else would be in bed. Jalgit had with him a cousin, and over the next few days the cousin brought with him more friends. Each night, with his maps unfolded, Awais would show Jalgit's friends places in the city that would be safe. With Mitoo's help and with the help of others they could trust, they acquired food, lamps and bedding. Awais then got busy on new maps. As he drew them up, he felt a gnawing sickness grow: he was making maps of escape. He'd herd them out, with his hidden buildings being their resting ground and safety net.

As the nightly visits continued, Khurshid began to look at Awais with suspicion. Still, she didn't ask him anything.

It all began to fit together – the maps, Shams Sahib's tales, even Loha – from the very beginning, a pattern. In the street outside, he could hear the sound of horses' hooves, but no tonga wheels. His instinct was to get up and look, but at that moment he happened to glance down at one of his maps and saw something he hadn't seen before. He'd marked the warehouse basement as derelict and unsafe. But it was big. Big enough to house fifty people at least. *My God, why haven't I...? As long as there are no children, and people are careful...* He picked up his pen and scribbled a note. In a few hours' time, a boy whom he didn't know – they never spoke – would come to collect what he'd written. The boy would then leave. One day, when it is all over, thought Awais, I'll invite him to tea. The thought made him smile.

It was almost morning. His favourite part of the day. And though his body was aching from lack of sleep, he stayed up to watch the dawn. The birds too had been flying away. He didn't usually like the racket they made. But today he wanted to hear their voices, to hear them sing.

37

SEPTEMBER 1947, LAHORE

Time began again. Politicians spoke of a new dawn, and people, willing to believe, felt its coming. The shape of the inside city was once more changing. Boards that had been hammered onto homes and shops by owners who had no faith in the permanency of Independence – and who thought that one day they, and with them their families, would return – were ripped off buildings and burnt by people who, though not thieves, were used to cooking on gas and not dung and who could no longer wait for the government to find the engineers to fix the faults in the pipelines. The dark spaces left by the wrenched-free boards resembled nothing so much as mouths, gaping, gum-diseased mouths.

The newcomers, confident of their citizen status and not knowing or caring for the old ways, cut their own paths.

Everywhere, watchers. Not the police, who were nowhere to be found, but those whose claim was one of priority. 'We were here first,' they said. Their sense of moral worth was strong, their sense of self-preservation acutely felt.

One rainy night in mid-September, Awais sat at his desk, his head bent over his maps. With the clandestine movement of food and other resources one of the most challenging things he had to manage, he'd been thinking how he could side-step the watchers. He picked up a biscuit and put it whole into his mouth. No one made biscuits like Rahim. There was a soft tap on the door. He looked at his watch: 1am.

'Who is it?' he said, going to the door without opening it.

'Awais, it's me,' said the voice on the other side.

He opened the door. Jalgit Singh stood there, trying to mop dry his face with a big white handkerchief.

'Only an idiot or a Sikh would come out in this weather, Jalgit Singh,' Awais said, grinning.

Jalgit Singh laughed, a deep warm laugh that crackled as it hit the air. He stepped inside. Jalgit made way for Awais to lock the door and then stood, dripping, waiting to be told what to do. Awais pointed to one of the room's two chairs, then began opening the doors of one cupboard after another.

'Found it,' he said, and threw Jalgit a towel. Jalgit unwound his turban and began to dry his bald head. When he was done he sank further back into his chair. Awais could tell he wanted to talk. He brought his own chair forward and sat down.

'You know, Awais,' Jalgit said, 'there's something strange happening in the world and I don't quite know what it is. And I don't just mean this current madness. That will pass – maybe as quickly as it came. But there's something else. Have you noticed it? You have, haven't you? I can smell it. It has a rank, dirty smell, like shit, only not healthy animal shit but shit gone bad; shit that's been pissed on. And the ones who smell the worst are the young people. Me, I know what I'm scared of: I'm scared of the future. It will never be like the past, it won't even be able to measure up to this moment here and now. But as for the young ones, I can't understand what they fear.'

'Perhaps they fear nothing?' Awais said.

'But there has to be fear, Awais,' said Jalgit.

'Why?'

'I don't know,' he said, his hand going to his temple to rub away the last remnants of rain. 'But there has to be fear. Doesn't there?' He paused. 'You know, Awais, when the others left I called them cowards, bastards, to their faces. You know what I'm like. I never did understand what my mother meant when she said – when she found out, as she always did, what a mess I was in, and it was true, I was always in some kind of mess or the other – she said that the fruit of patience is sweet. I could never wait for anything. This is the longest I've waited in my life. But it's not going to change. I mean, it's not going to change back. So now I'm one of the bastard cowards too. It's God's little joke: I criticise someone for something and then end up doing the same thing myself. He doesn't even give me the chance to be right once in a while.' He laughed sadly then continued, 'So, I'm going and that's why I'm here – to thank you.' The clock struck the half hour.

'You insult me,' said Awais, getting up, the anger showing readily on his face. 'You don't thank your own.'

'No, no, Awais,' said Jalgit, turning and moving towards him. 'I didn't mean… What you did for me and my family and for all…'

'Just leave it,' said Awais.

'All right, Awais,' said Jalgit. 'If there's ever anything I can do…' He took Awais's hands in both of his and held them tightly. Then he let go, squeezing shut one of Awais's hands.

'What are these?' Awais said, opening his fist.

'Keys,' said Jalgit. 'To my home and restaurant. For Mitoo. He'd never take them from me.'

'Neither can I.' Awais made to give the keys back but Jalgit wouldn't accept them. 'All right, he'll keep them for when you come back.'

'Yes, Awais,' said Jalgit, smiling.

Awais put the keys away in his desk drawer. 'Now go,' he said. 'Or you'll be late.'

'May God be with you, Awais,' said Jalgit.

'And with you.'

Jalgit hugged his hard wrestler's body to Awais's. Awais then opened the door.

'It's still raining,' Awais said. 'Maybe He needs a bribe?'

'Maybe He does. If I have anything left, I'll…'

A flash of lightning cut through the air.

'I don't think He likes your sense of humour,' Awais said.

'He, and my wife,' said Jalgit. He shrugged and began to run through the rain.

Awais closed the door. His head fell forward onto the table but he felt too tired to attempt to raise it.

With Jalgit Singh gone, he thought, I'll have to find someone else to help, someone I can trust implicitly. There were just a few families left. There was little money now to buy food and the other supplies they needed. As he sat there, an ant climbed onto his hand and stood on it as if it had reached a plateau. He watched it for a while, then blew it away; the ant began its search for another ascent. Awais raised his head and, opening the drawer, brought out Jalgit's heavy keys. He considered them for a moment. Tomorrow, if Mitoo agreed, he'd start looking for a buyer, not for the house – there were no property laws any more – but maybe some money was to be had for the furniture. He put the keys back and locked the drawer. He then smoothed out the maps he'd creased, picked up his pencil and began to write.

38

MARCH 1947, A VILLAGE IN INDIA

When she finally awoke they told her she'd been unconscious for ten days. They'd had to hold her mouth open and feed her with a spoon. She assumed the people before her, their faces gentled in care, were her family. When she began to eat and then was able to take her first steps, uncertain, because her muscles had grown slack, they told her how they'd found her. They didn't say they'd found her in a ditch, her clothes smeared with dirt and blood. They didn't tell her what they thought had happened. They'd had a girl, only sixteen, who'd disappeared. All around them, similar stories.

Slowly, under her new family's care, Maryam – whom they called Hema – grew stronger. She knew nothing about her life before she'd been found. Always busy, she looked happy enough, but when she stopped you thought she'd never be able to drag herself up again.

One day, as she was finishing her chores, she accidentally knocked over a pile of the children's books. She sat down on the floor to right them, flicking through a few pages here and there. She knew what, deep in her heart, she wanted, but when she saw that she couldn't even remember the letters that made up the words, her fear grew monstrous. The words looked like so many scrawls. She piled the books neatly together, her hands deliberately sure. A book fell open. She stared; her fingers then raced through its pages. This, she understood.

When Maryam told the woman she now called *massi*, the woman smiled and said, 'Maybe it's coming back.' Maryam nodded, her eyes alight. She didn't notice the stricken look that passed over *massi*'s face.

From that day on, Maryam began teaching the family's children maths. Soon, other parents knocked at the door, begging her to take on their children as well.

Two years passed. As Maryam looked out at the bent heads of her students, she smiled. With the income she earned, she'd been able to repay, in part, her new family's kindness. She had learned to write again. She raised her arm to write on the board, and her glass bangles clinked. Six months ago she'd married the family's eldest son. She turned back to the class. A flurry of hands. Maryam hoped she'd soon have a child of her own.

But there were no children. Her husband said he didn't mind. However, his parents, who'd once loved Maryam so much, urged him to take another wife. He was thinking angrily of his mother's words as he fixed an electricity cable. My wife's right, he thought. I'm good at this. I'll do an electrician's course.

When they found his dead body, his face was set in remorse. Soon after that, Maryam left for Delhi, hurt that no one tried to stop her, not even once. She joined a college and raced through one maths course, and then another. One of her friends sent some of Maryam's work to a professor in Cambridge in England. He was startled by the ingenuity of her thinking and thus began a correspondence, and then a collaboration.

Returning to her hostel after another department meeting that had gone on too long, Maryam felt drops of rain fall on her shoulders and head. She looked up, grinning. *Thank God for the monsoon.* She rushed to a bus shelter just in time – before the few drops transformed into a downpour. For the first time, she looked, really looked at the city in which she lived. Her heart raced. There had been another city she'd once called home. The second thing she remembered was a name: Awais Dar. She began to cry, then brutally wiped the tears away. As the rain continued to fall she pulled out a notebook from her bag and began to write – so rapidly that when she was finished and looked at what she'd written, she felt the words were all jumbled, out of place. *It'll have to do.* The rain stopped as suddenly as it had begun. The bus ride home felt as if it would never ever end. Once inside her room, she hunted for an envelope, and on its front, wrote: Awais Dar, The Inside City, Lahore, Pakistan.

Why can't I remember the address? He'll never get it.

But he did. Everyone knew the custodian of the inside city.

She wanted to come home. He wanted to bring her home. But he didn't know how to do it. All her letters were now filled with questions about Manu and Hamid. They had to wait.

The figures were just coming in. The movement of people during Partition – at ten million – was the greatest the world had ever seen. It was estimated that anywhere from half a million to a million people had been killed. Maryam grew anxious, then angry. 'You don't want me home,' she wrote.

'Wait, Maryam,' he wrote, 'just wait.' He thought things were changing. Any day now it would be possible. But then Gandhi was assassinated, and in September the same year, Jinnah died. Finally, he found a way to get her over. He couldn't believe how stupid he'd been.

Jalgit wrote, 'Why didn't you ask me before? No problem.'

Maryam gave in her notice. The principal didn't ask for an explanation. She'd always expected this, she realised. In the next few days Maryam bought presents, small enough to fit into the one bag Awais had told her to bring. Each afternoon when she came back from work she sat on the borrowed chair in her bare room and waited for another day to end. Two weeks later she went to the bus depot to meet a man who told her he owed her brother his life.

At the moment that Maryam boarded the bus with Jalgit's cousin, Awais was sorting through his desk and deliberating again on whether he should tell the family that Maryam was coming home.

She's late, he thought as he waited. He sat with Manu in the café they'd designated as their meeting ground. When Manu began, an hour later, to get grouchy, he knew it was time to return home. She'll come to the house, he thought and felt more at ease. But she didn't come after lunch. And then it was evening and he still hadn't heard anything.

He got a message to Jalgit who wrote back: 'She left for Lahore yesterday as planned. My cousin took her to Delhi Gate.'

Trying to keep calm, Awais put the word out to his scouts, whom he'd inherited from Shams Sahib when he became what Shams Sahib had been: the person people came to for news. At first, they could discover nothing, no news of her through either the official or unofficial lines. Disappeared again? No, he thought. It didn't make sense. She'd been ready to come back to her family. He knew that for sure. He returned home, feeling a sense of vertigo, as if any minute he'd tip over, face flat on the ground.

He overheard his mother castigating Manu and Manu giving as good as she got. He would never have had the courage to do that. He slipped out of the house, unnoticed. He had someone to meet, one last trail to follow.

The scout was wrong but one of his friends was right. They found her on the second day. As the scout lifted the sheet that covered her Awais's body stiffened.

'An epileptic fit,' the doctor said. 'Was she prone to them?'

'Yes,' Awais replied.

'Why didn't she ask for help? Isn't she from here?'

'Yes,' he said, 'she was from here.' He, who'd mapped a city, had lost a sister who didn't know her way around its walls.

Later that same night he had Maryam buried under the tombstone that bore her name. The next Friday, when Hamid got ready, as usual, to leave for the cemetery, Awais said he'd join him. Hamid stared at him in surprise; Awais had never visited the cemetery beyond that first time. At Awais's suggestion, they took Manu with them as well.

'*Mamun*,' said Manu to him with wonder, 'your face is all wet.'

When they returned home Manu asked to see her mother's book. She opened its pages then looked up at Awais.

'What does it mean?'

He shook his head and said, 'I don't know.'

'She was clever?' she asked.

'Yes,' he said pinching her cheek. 'Just like you.'

She laughed. Manu had shown no aptitude for study, lacking the stillness it required.

'I'll put it away?' he asked and she nodded and watched as he put it at the back of a shelf of books.

'It's our secret?' she said.

'Yes,' he said. 'And one day, you'll get another.'

'Another book?' she asked. She looked disappointed but tried to look cheerful for his sake.

'Wait and see. The fruit of patience is sweet.' He winced, remembering Jalgit.

She wrinkled her nose at him.

39

On her eighth birthday he gave her a torn corner of a map.

'What's that?' she said, looking at it eagerly.

'Just wait till you get back from school.'

'But people don't go to school on their birthdays,' she said.

'Who told you that?'

'One of the girls…'

'Well, this one does,' he said. 'Now get moving or we'll be late.'

Later that day, he taught her to read the map by taking her to the places marked on it. He told her the histories of the mosque and the temple they visited. And she listened without once interrupting. She held his hand all the way home.

'You like it, then?' he said and she threw him an angry look. It was clearly a stupid question. She was amazed that a drawing could convey you to where you wanted to go.

And when they stood at the door of their house she turned back and looked at the city with his eyes and said, 'When can we do it again?'

Manu was forever getting into trouble. She was running, skipping, climbing dynamite. 'She'll break her neck, see if she doesn't,' Khurshid said, and Awais was frightened that she might be right. He began keeping a closer eye on Manu. When one day Manu fell from a wall and he rushed over to her, he saw his mother watching them both, with a curious look on her face he couldn't decipher.

'You're a devil,' he said, carrying Manu.

'But a brave one?' she said, looking impishly into his face.

'All animals have courage,' Khurshid said, and walked away.

One day, Khurshid and Awais were in the courtyard when he spied Manu on the highest branch of the tallest tree.

'Monkey, get down,' he said. Manu waved to him. 'How did she get up there?' he asked Khurshid. That tree, they both knew, had no footholds near the ground, which was why they'd thought it safe. He'd had all the other trees felled a long time ago. The courtyard had become a monument to Manu's childhood and the trouble she'd got into. Each tree had been cut lower and lower every year till all that was left were their stumps, which they now used as stools.

'How does she do it?' Khurshid asked, the words reluctantly drawn from her. They both considered Manu, sat on her high perch, biting into an apple and staring into space.

Suddenly Awais shouted angrily, 'Manu, get down!' And she did, immediately. Khurshid and Awais both watched the swiftness of her descent, and Khurshid's body softened in defeat.

'What are you, a monkey's child?' he said as she came forward, grinning.

'But *mamun*, I was only... '

'I'll *only* you!' he said and began chasing her round the courtyard. As she turned a corner, she burst into peals of laughter; so did he. Khurshid came into view. He'd seen that look on her face before. In his heart, the first formation of ice.

A few days later he entered Khurshid's room. She was sitting in the middle of the bed, one knee raised, her other leg tucked behind her, working on the household accounts.

'*Ammi*,' he said. She looked up and smiled, thrilled he'd come of his own accord. He remained unmoved and she withdrew her smile for another time.

'What's happened?' she said.

'Nothing,' he said and sat down. She took a last look at the slips of paper, as if to fix them in her memory till she could return to them, then shifted to the edge of the bed. He looked at her feet, which were flat and thin. I have her feet, he thought.

'*Ammi*,' he said, quickly, 'I've received a letter from Batool. She's having a baby in a few months' time and wants you to…'

'Again? After what the doctor said?'

'She says the doctor told her this one will survive if she takes good care of herself…' he said. Khurshid lowered her gaze. 'And she wants you there to help,' he said.

'Oh,' she said. 'But the border?'

'I have friends,' he said, smiling.

She sighed. 'When does she want us to go?'

'Not *us*, *ammi*,' he said, 'you.' He'd meant to be kinder, meant to say he couldn't leave the business, but something in her very being made him, as always, revolt.

When she'd gone, the house felt brighter at once. He smiled at Manu as she raced downstairs. She wouldn't understand the nature of his victory. They settled down into what was to become their daily routine. No one spoke about the recent past but Awais began telling Manu more about Maryam. Hamid listened too and smiled.

Five months later, after Batool had given birth to a boy, the letters began to arrive: 'Batool and the baby are both healthy. Tanveer looks after them both very well. There's nothing more here for me to do.' And then as more months passed, a note of panic began to creep into her letters. Awais replied to what she said and not what he knew she meant. Then travelling between Pakistan and India became increasingly difficult and the letters stopped.

Manu's safe, he thought. That's enough.

40

She closed her eyes and found herself not at the beginning of a story, but in the middle. Dead ahead of her stood a wall. She'd been running and now had a decision to make. Right or left? Before the question was fully formed, she turned left. There, as she knew it would be, was a shop whose shadow stretched out into the street. She went in. The shopkeeper smiled and she returned a rueful grin and went to crouch in her usual place and wait. She had strategic spots throughout the city; this was only one of them.

The shopkeeper's radio, tuned into request hour, was turned down as a customer entered the shop. Outside, the sound of pounding feet, of arguing.

'*Kambakht!* We always lose her,' said one of the four girls – it sounded like Jamila – who now stood not two feet away from the shop.

'Maybe Huma and Nachi have found her?' replied one of the others, forced hope in her voice. She frowned. She was new. They'd told her this was a game. That they were all friends. But it seemed rougher than any game she'd ever played.

'*Mai munda, Manu, hai, hai!*' the youngest of the girls started shouting. The chant was taken up by the other three; it was not a victory cry but the sound of those who needed to pretend victory was theirs. Manu, in her hideaway, the cold beginning to creep into her bones and her feet starting to ache now that she had stopped running, muttered, 'Idiots.' And anyhow, she didn't mind being called a boy.

She looked around, spotted a couple of sacks of rice, got up and went to sit down on them. She knew this game. And the waiting was the hardest part. The smell of dried spices was strong; it spread over her as she leaned back against the whitewashed wall. Her face relaxed and, with her eyes closed, she resembled, she knew, the kind of well–behaved girl her grandmother used to tell her she ought to be.

Manu, mai munda, mai munda. She'd never minded the taunt, though once, when her grandmother had heard it, it had driven her into a state of inexplicable rage. Before Manu could reach the balcony, and pop her head out of the open wooden shutters, her grandmother had opened the door. The look on her face had been enough to scare the girls away.

A piece of wall crumbled onto her shoulder. She brushed it off and tried to listen once more, but it was no good. She couldn't tell whether the girls were still waiting outside or not. A few minutes later, the shopkeeper came in; at home in the darkness, he spotted Manu with ease. 'They've gone,' he said, extending his hand. She took it and got up. But then he held on a little too long. Manu shook herself free. In her throat, a clamminess. She left without turning back.

It was the girls who'd told her about the circus. Only one of them had actually been, but they all spoke knowledgeably about elephants and lions, and the curious things that went on inside the big tent. She'd seen pictures in the streets of strange people and animals, carried aloft as cardboard cut-outs on the backs of donkey carts, and displayed as posters on the coal-black sides of shops that flanked alleyways. Beyond something to laugh at, it had meant nothing to her. If it hadn't been for Jamila, whose idea it was, she wouldn't have gone.

The hardest thing was finding the money for the tickets. They all knew, from experience, that asking never worked. So they decided they'd each pocket as much as they could, meet near Rahim's biscuit cart at eleven (when, as Jamila had discovered, the circus put on a morning performance), split the money and watch the show.

'And if anyone sees us?' asked one of the younger girls, who'd confessed she wanted to see the elephant more than anything on this earth, but feared her mother's wrath. They discussed the possibility of their families finding out, but in the end, still decided to go.

The next day Manu and her six friends escaped from school and met beside Rahim's cart as planned. Each of them handed over their money to Jamila, who counted it and then re-counted it.

'We've got one rupee extra,' said Jamila.

'Let's get some biscuits,' said the youngest.

'*Haan, bhai* – yes,' said Arif, Rahim's eldest son, smiling his shop-seller smile. 'Newly baked plain biscuits, *zeera* biscuits.' If he sold them one rupee's worth, he could go home and back to sleep. With a finger, he prised out a piece of meat stuck at the back of his teeth, inspected it and wiped his hand on his *kameez*.

Anis, the girl who had already been to the circus, said quietly. 'Jamila, there's much better food over there.'

'And where would there be, *haan bhai*?' said Arif scornfully. 'If your friends want biscuits, nice plain biscuits, *zeera* biscuits, who are you to say no?'

'Let's go,' said Jamila, pocketing the money.

'Daughters of owls. Biscuit thieves!' shouted Arif to their backs.

Manu, who'd broken into a fit of giggles at Arif's words, couldn't stop.

'Oi, *munda*, what's got into you?' Jamila asked.

They arrived at an enclosure at the edge of the city's gates, where a huge tent had been erected in a space where one week ago there had barely been anything. Even in broad daylight, the girls were mesmerised by the sight of the rouged and white faces of the performers. Three things stood out for Manu that day: the trapeze act, the human pyramid and the man on the high wire.

Without telling the others, she pocketed a few more coins and escaped to the circus the next day, too. On the fourth day, as she was about to make her escape, Jamila cornered her and blocked her. Gripping Manu by the arm, she said, '*Munda*, you've gone mad, have you?'

Manu laughed, then tears suddenly filled her eyes. Jamila was shocked into silence; she'd never seen Manu cry.

'It's nothing, Jamila. Let me go.'

Jamila stepped aside and Manu disappeared.

Once the performance was over, Manu lingered in the emptying tent. A girl a few years older than herself, dressed from head to toe in red, approached and said, 'My name's Dina.'

Manu looked at her, puzzled, trying to figure out which act she belonged to. Dina raised her arms and did a pirouette; she was the girl on top of the horse.

'Is this your second time here?' asked Dina.

'Fourth.'

'What do you like the best?' asked Dina.

'The man on the high wire,' Manu replied automatically. Realising what she'd just said, she added, 'But you're very good too.'

'The wire *wallah*'s my father,' Dina said, smiling. 'Would you like to meet him?' Manu didn't know what to say. Someone called over and Dina gave a small wave. 'You'll come again tomorrow?' she asked. Manu nodded and Dina went to answer the call.

'I might not be able to come any more,' Manu told Dina the next day, explaining how each day she'd had to steal the entrance fee, and how she increasingly feared being found out.

Dina smiled and linked her arm through Manu's. She led her to one of the pristine makeshift tents that surrounded the big top, and shouted, 'Bona *bhai*!'

A green tent flap was raised and Bona, the dwarf clown, poked out his stubbly, round coin face.

'What is it?' he shouted.

'Bona *bhai*,' Dina said. 'This is my friend, Manu. Can you let her in each night?'

'Everyone wants something for free!' he muttered.

'But you'll let her in?'

Bona grunted and went back inside.

'That's settled then,' Dina said.

'But he didn't say anything,' Manu said. Dina laughed and pulled her new friend along to see the rest of the showground.

Each afternoon, Manu watched the circus and then stayed while Dina told her circus stories. Seeing how his daughter had warmed to the stranger, the high-wire artist Shafu gradually told Manu more about his act. One day, at his daughter's behest, he let Manu have a go on the practice wire. She walked a few steps and then he led her back.

'*Bhai*, it's in your blood! You have no fear,' he said, laughing.

'That's what my *nani* always says,' said Manu. She frowned. The way Dina's father had said it made it sound different somehow.

That night, lying on her bed, her index finger drew a line in the air, backwards and forwards.

When Manu first spoke of her idea, Shafu was against it, Dina for it and the others in the troupe equally divided.

'We can't do it,' Shafu said to his wife, all the while shaking his head. 'Do you know what people will say? They'll say we put a spell on her and stole her away from her family. And what if she were our daughter – how would we feel about it then?'

Three weeks later, when the circus began to be dismantled in preparation for moving on, Manu was ready.

41

SEPTEMBER 1959, KHANEWAL
A SMALL TOWN, PAKISTAN

Awais stood in the queue, his tall frame curving into his coat. This was the third circus he'd come to in a month. It was the furthest one he'd been to from Lahore; he was tired of the travelling. He just wanted to be home.

For ten minutes now there'd been no movement. He could hear the sound of raised voices: fighters and eggers-on. Could this be the one? He wanted to race inside and grab them all by the throats and yell: 'My niece – have you seen her?'

The man ahead of him shuffled forward and Awais stepped into his place.

Inside, where the open guts of the structure lay bare in beams and ropes, necks that were craned backwards straightened, and eyes stared at the half-moon of empty space in front of them. The audience took their seats. They waited, some even dozed, the initial excitement of being somewhere special already beginning to wear thin; they were inured to the inevitability of things either not happening on time or not working at all. Only order, they felt, had the capacity to surprise.

The fragrance of damp hay, sweet and light, was soon lost to a concoction of animal smells.

Suddenly, a shower of rain exploded over their heads, blue and green and white – white like they'd never seen. This vision of beauty was seen through a rip in the worn canopy roof. Those standing outside, not rich enough to pay the entrance fee, too raised their heads and saw the firework display in full. They hovered outside the huge tent with its arabesque of red, green and blue, built like a handkerchief house for the amusement of children; afterwards the older men, their eyes still raised to the now blank sky, talked of the cold in their bones. They were already waiting for the wind which they knew would come to blow the tent and all its inhabitants into another field, another town. A pack of boys, who for the past week had watched the lions and the monkeys and the women in half–dress, squatted bravely near the tent's opened flaps, waiting for things they could only imagine, and listened. A cigarette was pulled on, then passed from one hand to the next.

And into the centre of the circle strode the ringmaster. He introduced the band. The musicians were dressed in a motley selection of clothes – the tall ones, the short ones, the ones with eyes that had seen the world and those who had not yet seen their first dog fight – a band of men who looked as if they could have been born of one mother. They began to play an old British regimental tune.

'*Bhai*, the English have gone, don't you know? Maybe they left you here as punishment!' shouted a man in the crowd. The crowd laughed; the heckler swelled under the adulation.

'It's 1959, not 1939,' belted out a young boy. But no one laughed this time.

The first heckler smiled and shouted for them all: 'Play a tune of Madam's!'

Cries of 'Play!', 'Play!' dotted across the tent in a pattern the eye couldn't see.

To the nod of the ringmaster, the band played Madam Noor Jehan's taunting love song about a boy from Sialkot: '*Tere mukhre da kala kal til ve*' – 'On your face there's a black, black beauty spot.' The crowd, quiet now. A uniformed monkey led on a dancing bear. Surprised laughter. The monkey let the bear go and stepped towards the crowd. From his pail, he showered them in red rose petals.

To the crack of the *doog-doogi* drum, the main programme began.

Her gaze fixed straight ahead, Manu unclasped her cloak of blue. The cold air hit her bare back and she heard the collective gasp of the audience as the glittering cape swirled once, twice, thrice and then dropped, like a dead object, into the safety net far below. She stepped out onto the wire. Slowly, she dropped into a toe hang, then swung to the other side before righting herself. As the music built to a crescendo, she swung out into a star. The audience, awed, fell silent, then broke into riotous applause. Manu waited for the clapping to die down. She breathed deeply to steady her pulse and got ready for her return.

The flaming torch on the other side that should have lit her way back fizzed and died.

'Now what?' she said, though no one could possibly hear her words. Slowly, she took a step, another.

Shafu grabbed her waist from behind. Manu turned around, grinning into his solemn face, then slid down the rope he held out for her. He followed her down. The main lights went back on.

Next to Awais, a thin man, his belt pulling his trousers up to just below his chest, jumped from his seat. He turned to Awais. 'What d'you think of that!' Awais said nothing.

Manu stood very still. Any moment now she knew it would hit her and the crowd would break into ecstatic applause – as they had done every night since she'd first been thought competent enough to master the high wire and been given an act of her own. Shafu slid down from the rope and together they bowed. He walked off, not turning to see whether Manu followed.

Manu, with her hair tied back and her taut body held in rigorous control, though just twelve, looked like the woman she would be at seventeen. Small regular features, neatly composed. The mischief that often flashed across her face like a streak of morning sun was barely held in check. Her hands, which could never be still when she talked, were locked behind her back.

Never had she felt so happy – the realisation was strangely complete, and though she tried to stem the joy, to ward off the evil eye, the music began playing in her head. She let it swim over her, as she always did.

Machli di hadi – Bone of a fish.

Machli di hadi – Bone of a fish.

Khel mein kabadi – I'll wrestle.

Rona na pawan – I won't cry.
Shadi karawan – I'll marry.
Khel mein kabadi – I'll wrestle.
...*Khel!* – Let's play!

Where the words came from, she didn't know; but she knew they always came over her when she felt the lightest.

By now, the ringmaster was making frantic signals for her to leave. She couldn't move. She was pinned by the white glow of the spotlight, gazing out at the smiling faces of the crowd, although Shafu had warned her, 'No, don't do it. It's bad luck.' The ringmaster now sent on the next act, two jugglers. They were working around her, setting up their bags and boxes as if she didn't exist.

'*Besharam* – shameless!' shouted her grandmother, disembodied, and frightening.

The ringmaster, in a fading red and black suit, copied by his wife from a picture she'd seen in a magazine, and no shirt to cover the nakedness of his chest, pulled the crowd in, clapping energetically as he thanked Miss Manu, the Lucky Rani Circus's newest star, and paved the way for her exit. Manu found her feet and returned to the shelter of darkness.

Awais looked around, lost. A sharp intake of breath. The show should have ended. All circuses end with the high wire, he thought. But instead, there was more music and a flurry of activity in the wings. The man sitting next to Awais tried to engage him in conversation again, then, exhausted, gave up and turned to his other neighbour.

Running into the wings, Manu bumped into Bona the clown; she scarpered off. A broad painted smile on his face, Bona stood leering at the crowds, a spittle-soaked cigarette burning limply from a corner of his mouth. Each night he played the buffoon; recently he'd been upgraded. 'Works like the government,' said the elephant trainer. 'The longer you've been here, the higher you get.' Now, instead of riding a very large dog with horse-like ears attached to its head, he'd been given a bicycle. 'The bastards could at least have asked me what colour I wanted,' he'd said.

'It's what the audience want,' the ringmaster had repeated, to Bona's pleas that the act be changed.

'What – a dwarf who farts and gets water thrown on his face?'

Bona turned to watch the next act.

The ringmaster introduced the Lucky Rani Circus's oldest and brightest star – an elephant festooned with paint and flowers, locked into a moment of perpetual bride-hood. The elephant danced with one leg bent in the air to the sound of the *doog-doogi* drum. The audience broke into spontaneous rapture.

'I worked the trapeze for ten minutes – ten minutes,' said a thin man in white tights, 'without a net; and look at this.'

But the crowd was largely poor and, sitting on the edge of hard plank seats, was willing to be entertained.

'English woman's beehive!' shouted a man in an immaculate white *shalwar kameez* as he walked through the aisles with his duck– and boat-shaped yellow and pink candyfloss. A woman frowned at him as her children pulled at her *kameez*. 'What can I do, *sisterji* – I have to earn money,' he said, his smile a thin line of embarrassment, and added, 'I have children to feed too.'

'Couldn't you find any honest work to do?' she said as he handed her two mounds of yellow candyfloss.

From the cover of darkness at the edge of the ring, the ringmaster watched the candyfloss man manoeuvre his way through the rows of people. The candyfloss man was also the circus's best knife thrower. The ringmaster, watching the crowd, bent one leg forward and stretched back the other, and threw an imaginary knife. He squinted to see it hit its imaginary target. He was leaning back for another shot when he saw Manu approach. He stopped.

The ringmaster was called the man of dates, because of the magical calendar he possessed which could chart the movement of the days and months. He was also, until Manu came along, the only one in the troupe who could read. And it was for this reason that he acted as the intermediary between the circus people and its faceless owner. Recently, a number of the troupe had also begun to ask Manu to calculate how much debt still had to be cleared from their wages, and since that day the ringmaster had begun to watch her more closely than he watched the rest.

The new snake charmer, who was bolder than most, now approached the ringmaster. 'I know the time's not right, but I never get the chance to talk to you. I've got so much training to do, and then there's the new wife, the old one, too. Who says children are God's gift? I swear, they're not mine, they're Satan's. They told me the new one couldn't have children. Why do people lie? It's not good for the soul and it makes you lose your hair. Did I tell you about Nafees Mian's latest?' he said, patting the snake around his neck. 'Just an hour before we're supposed to go on and what does he do?'

'Not dead?' asked the ringmaster, staring at the snake.

'No, no,' said the snake charmer. 'It's like this…' he said, stroking his Adam's apple till it turned pink. 'I was wondering… Is it possible, if you don't mind, to get a copy of my accounts?'

'So you can do what – wrap your shoes in them?' the ringmaster said, and the snake charmer walked away, defeated and tired.

His outsize shoes flapping like wet duck feet, one of the younger clowns waddled up to the ringmaster, almost knocking him down. 'One of the…' and his voice broke. 'One of the…' The ringmaster gripped both the clown's shoulders. The clown rapidly blinked. 'One of the camels is…' he said.

The ringmaster waited.

The clown said, 'Rafiq put it on the roof of a house.'

'The roof?' said the ringmaster.

'A bet. For a bottle of whisky. And now he can't get the camel down.'

'You're killing me,' said the ringmaster. The heel of his hand against his forehead, he knocked, waiting for an answer.

The elephant trainer walked past. 'We all have to die some time.'

The ringmaster frowned at him and let go of the clown, who began to bob backwards and forwards before righting himself with an outstretched hand on the shoulder of the bearded lady who, at that moment, was making her way to the stage. She smiled coyly and waited. The clown walked off. The ringmaster stepped forward and introduced 'the fattest bearded lady in the world'. The act was a weak one and therefore his calloused voice was encouraging. He returned to the wings and nodded to the horse trainer, who was standing nearby, giving a final brush to his horse.

'*Mooch nahin thay kuch nahin!* Who doesn't have a moustache isn't a man,' shouted a voice from the crowd. The ringmaster shook his head and said to the horse trainer, 'Fifteen years and always the same joke.' He cupped his own well-developed parts and said, 'Who says it's only a moustache that makes a man?'

They talked about how, with each passing year, the audience's taste for the grotesque increased, and how there'd been a time when bearded ladies were quite a crowd-puller, but now they were thought too tame, and a time when a performer could raise applause by lying on a bed of nails, but now audiences were satisfied with no less than seeing a woman sawn in half and put together again.

'If they want to see freaks, why don't they go and look at the beggars?' said the ringmaster.

Later that night, in the darkness of the empty circus tent, Manu walked an imaginary tightrope. She bowed to the right, to the left and then deeply to the centre. She still had on her blue outfit, spangled with sequinned curls and waves of moonshine. She walked out of the arena without turning back, the circus lore of superstition now a maggot in her head. At the gate she saw Bona still wearing his luminous smile, and nodded. Bona had been one of the last of the troupe to accept her. The change had come about without any warning when, one day, as if they'd always been in the habit of speaking on a level of intimacy, he'd told her how he'd first come to the circus. His parents and his eight brothers and two sisters were all average-sized. At the age of eight, when the novelty of being *bona* – short – had begun to lose its shine and when the demands of feeding a large family had begun to be increasingly felt, his father had sold him for the price of ten packs of cigarettes – he'd witnessed the transaction – to a man who knew a man in the circus. His mother had cried (he'd heard that too): 'Cigarettes are more important than food, *haanji?*'

At first Manu had been thrown by Bona's constant watchfulness.

It had irked her. Now she felt as if he watched over her and always would.

She walked on, thinking of her grandmother. What did that momentary vision of her mean? The fear that her family would find her, once strong, had become weak with time. She turned to look back to the big tent.

'You think your family will look for you here?' Shafu had asked, pointing to the crates and wires, and despite his words, he'd looked carefully all around, like a villager caught in the city traffic of bullock and donkey carts, tongas and school buses.

And for the first time in a long time, that night, Manu – huddled in the bed that she shared, with one of Shafu's daughters to her right, and another to her left – remembered that she had been part of another world before this one had made her its own.

As he lay on the hard *charpoy* in the town's only hotel, he thought back over the last six months. Six months of living between hope and fear.

What am I doing here? Why didn't I take Manu home at once?

As he'd watched Manu on the high wire, he'd felt fear but knew it wasn't wholly for her. Something he'd long ago thought closed had begun to open again.

The hotel room was empty save for the *charpoy*, a chair, and a mirror, framed in shiny lime-green plastic, that hung from one wall. The room's only light was a bare bulb, around which fireflies and moths gathered for their nightly sharing of news. Unable to sleep, he jumped off the bed. His jacket was slung across the back of the chair; he searched the pockets for his cigarettes and, as he raised his head, caught his reflection in the mirror. His skin was turning a brown-grey. He moved to the mirror and turned it to the wall. He then went to the window and, lighting a cigarette, looked out at the still night. He didn't want to think of what they might have done to compel her to stay.

After a while, he stubbed out the cigarette. Reaching into his pocket he took out the letter. He held it, his thumb going back and forth over the jagged tear in the envelope. A letter from Jalgit Singh.

Again, thanking Awais for all he'd done. Awais had had a long time now to think about the events of twelve years ago. Jalgit and the others thought he'd acted from courage when all he'd acted from was a practical facility. Nothing else.

Jalgit Singh. Once he'd filled a page and a half with his thanks and his blessings, he talked, as he always did, of coming home. And Awais, when he wrote, would, as he always did, talk of the party he'd throw in Jalgit's honour when that day arrived. This was the least of the lies they told each other, for time and circumstances had transformed them from two friends into two separate individuals who had once shared a past. He put the letter away, changed out of his clothes and, leaving the light on, lay down for the night.

The next afternoon he stood, once again, in the queue, waiting to be admitted to the big tent. He found his seat at the back, far away from the bright lights.

Long after the show had finished, he hung about in an unlit patch of ground, a short distance from the young boys who also loitered outside the circus's closed gates. Finally, he knocked on the gate. When there was no answer he knocked louder, the fierceness of his actions surprising him.

'I want to see the ringmaster!' he shouted.

'You'll get no money off him today!' replied a voice from the other side. The man laughed. The boys were listening and watching Awais now.

'I've come to get my niece,' Awais said, 'Manu.'

The gate opened.

A drop of sweat slid down his face, licked at his collarbone, then disappeared into his open shirt. He didn't dare brush it away; he didn't want to give offence. But the smell and sight of so many people in such a small space was oppressive.

Manu nodded at a gesture Shafu made. He led his family out of the tent. Awais crumpled. He'd imagined everything but this. She looks happy, he thought. Was that enough, though – for her and for them? It wasn't happiness, he realised, that you wanted for those you loved; it was their happiness tied to yours. Before he knew what he was doing he'd wiped his brow with his sleeve. He laughed – and like an animal caught in wire meshing, the sound choked, died. 'It's so hot suddenly. Don't you feel it?' he said. 'How much you've grown! A whole two inches I'd say, though Hamid…'

She looked up, then. The acute precision with which she'd held her body on the high wire still lingered in her movements; only her shoulders seemed to arch unnaturally and her right foot was pointed outwards, as if ready, at any moment, to lead an escape. She blinked fiercely and then closed her eyes, as if to make a wish. When she opened them, tears were streaming down her face. He opened his arms and she ran into them. He stroked her bent head and tucked her into his chest.

'Ssh, *beta*,' he said, kissing her forehead.

Less than half an hour later, Shafu, his family and the ringmaster said their goodbyes and let her go. Manu looked around for Bona, but he'd kept away.

42

Hamid was waiting for them at the station. At his side was Khurshid. Out of the corner of his eye, Awais saw Manu look up at him; she squeezed his hand.

Hamid ran forward and took Manu in his arms, leaving Khurshid and Awais to face one another. He saw on her face that she knew, knew that he could have brought her back, but hadn't. Now Hamid had fetched her and she was here for good. Slowly, he approached, and she embraced him as Hamid had embraced Manu: a parent returned to a child, a child to a parent.

Hamid, who had been quiet for so long, talked all the way home. Some of his mannerisms were new: clearing his throat to speak, slamming his hand against his thigh when he made a point or tried to make a joke. When they reached home and Manu had been packed off to sleep, the three sat down to discuss what to do next. Hamid insisted they leave the city. 'Until the gossip dies down,' he said. Awais tried to reason with him but nothing he said could make Hamid budge. Awais stared at his friend, confused. Hamid was one of the most amenable men he knew. He heard his mother make a sound; a whistle? Impossible, he thought. Her head was dipped, looking at the ground.

Over the coming weeks, it became apparent that Hamid had found a new ally in Khurshid and, together, they found somewhere on the outskirts of the city for the four of them to live.

Two weeks before the family was scheduled to move, Awais shocked them by bringing home a new wife. The proposal had come from Shams Sahib's brother several months ago, but at the time he'd been busy searching for Manu. Yet he hadn't dismissed it as he'd dismissed others that had come his way. Awais told Shams Sahib's brother to explain about his divorce; the family were okay, even with that. Noor was a simple woman, soft, who laughed a lot, and Awais thought himself lucky. Manu clearly liked her too.

'Hold me,' he'd said and smiling, she had. *Against the torrent of the wind. Against the blight of other people's words and the greater blight of my fiercest thoughts.* I don't want sublimity, he thought. Just a surface life that doesn't ask too much. She'd hugged him harder and he'd thought, her body understands my body. That's enough – for now.

'I can't go,' he said not looking at his mother or Hamid but at Manu.

After three years, Awais was the father of two children of his own. The boys called Manu *apa*. She pretended to be strict with them but they only laughed at her face.

One afternoon, as the children lay resting in bed, the men lounged, as usual, on *charpoys* in the courtyard, a brass hookah passing from man to man. Noor's youngest brother was holding up a plastic mirror to his eldest brother's face. The elder man trimmed his luscious black moustache with the precision of a butcher/surgeon. Awais read from the paper: 'A dead dog was found on the main road.'

'And this is what they call news?' interjected Noor's uncle, his eyes following the movement of the hookah.

'No, listen,' Awais said. 'It had been seen on the Grand Trunk Road for one hour. The doctor said—'

'Doctors to look at dogs and animal doctors to look at men!' said the youngest brother.

'The doctor said,' Awais said loudly, 'that the dog had died from exhaustion. Eye witnesses say they saw a boy riding the dog.' They laughed and he read on: '*Said one man, "The boy was smoking a ciga-rette. Do parents teach their children nothing these days?" Another witness said the boy's face was painted white and he had a huge red banana-shaped smile on his face, and that he'd cut off the dog's ears and attached them to his own.'*

'Not donkey's ears?' said Noor's youngest brother, who now had the scissors and was mindlessly snipping at the air.

'It's these newspaper *wallahs* who make us into donkeys with their lies,' said Noor's uncle. His hand curled around the hookah; he inhaled.

'And what of the boy?' asked Noor's father but no one had an answer for that.

43

His mother began to take Manu in hand. Manu revolted at first, giv-ing as good as she got. He smiled. It was just like old times. But Khurshid was relentless and Manu saw that her father wanted her to behave in the way her grandmother thought she should; and so, she changed, bending her strong will till she was the girl her father deserved. Awais, who visited as much as he could and who had Hamid's business to run and inside city matters to attend to as well, could do nothing.

He looked at the docile, impeccably neat creature that his mother had created and thought: I've failed Maryam; I've failed again. He rubbed at his eyes. His sight was getting worse. Soon he'd have to start wearing the glasses he'd been prescribed four months ago.

He stood now in the courtyard, watching the two women, and realised that Khurshid had just to raise her hand – no, not even that – merely give her granddaughter a look and Manu would run to do her bidding. How on earth had she managed to achieve that, he won-dered. He waited till his mother had disappeared, then called Manu to his side. She came running.

'You're growing so big!' he said, surprised again at how tall she seemed to have grown overnight. She smiled and sat down.

'Do you still remember it?' Awais asked.

'Yes,' she said. Aside from her friends, it was the smells she told him she remembered the most: the hay, and the musty clothes with holes covered by sequins which dazzled when the lights shone on them, and the dung of the elephants and horses; and though she'd searched, she'd never been able to discern the monkey shit, as if, public in everything else, in deification they were a private breed. And the patchwork tent with its lights on and its lights off and the spectrum of colour she had helped build.

When Manu turned fourteen, Awais thought it was time to give her her mother's astrolabe. But he couldn't find it, wherever he looked. He grew frantic and went to Hamid's room, his head already bowed in defeat.

'Did you leave it behind when you moved from the city?' he asked.

'No,' Hamid said. But they both knew that the possibility existed.

Khurshid was growing old and tired. It started with her eyes, which weakened and then developed the black pearl disease – cataract. Manu effectively became the housekeeper in her stead. She kept immaculate household accounts, with slips from the grocers, the tailors and other shopkeepers all in separate cloth bundles.

More and more, Khurshid kept to her room and her bed. Awais had been watching over her broken sleep one evening when she awakened and said, 'Awais.' He leaned in towards her. 'It was always…'

'*Ammi*, rest.'

'Did I dream it?' she said, looking at him with frightened eyes. 'The pir…' Her breathing become shallow. She closed her eyes.

I could have told her, he thought, about Jalgit and the others. That I'm custodian of the city. If his life had had meaning – and meaning that shone brightly for everyone to see – she would have thought she'd done her duty by him, and, he knew, because he'd felt it too, she would have pushed past the void, triumphant. But he'd made a promise of silence to Shams Sahib. He couldn't have told her – even to ease her pain. And then he thought of all the others he had told: Mitoo, Harold, Jalgit and the hundreds of others whom he'd helped to escape.

She coughed. It sounded like no cough he'd ever heard. Her eyes open now, blistering.

'Hamid!' Awais shouted. He would have gone to find him if her grip on his arm weren't so tight. How could a woman so frail have so much strength? She smiled weakly. *Does she even know I'm here?* he thought.

'Awais,' she said.

On the way back from the cemetery he thought, *it's not over. It'll never be over. I failed her.* Tanveer and Batool had been refused visas so it was left to Manu and Noor to arrange everything. The words of ritual aside, Awais said nothing. The family understood, even his young sons, that Awais had to be left alone. A week passed.

I should have told her. It would have made her life easier, her leaving of it, too.

Noor, who'd been sorting out Khurshid's things, came to him and asked, 'What do you want me to do with these?'

He looked down at the envelopes in her hand. *I know that writing! How did she get my letters?* A throbbing in his head. She'd taken his... Noor handed him the envelopes. The letters though, were not letters addressed to him, but to his mother. When Noor left, he opened the first of the letters and began to read. When he'd finished, he started another. Letters to Khurshid from Jalgit, thanking her for everything Awais had done for him and his community.

It took Awais just a few minutes to convince Hamid that he and Manu should return to the inside city.

Three days later, helping Hamid unpack, Awais heard a loud knock at the door. He ran down the steps to see who it was. Twin boys stood outside, pots of food in their hands.

'From Mitoo *bhai*,' they said. Awais grinned and led the way upstairs.

Once the boys had left, Awais went to Manu's room. She wasn't there and so he laid it on her pillow: a section of a map, with the word 'Tomorrow?' written underneath. It was time to start again.

44

MAY 1964, LAHORE

Both Hamid and Awais stood at the gate of their house, waiting to receive Manu's *barat*, the bridegroom's family. In the last year, Hamid had come some way to becoming closer to Manu. He had fleshed out a little too and looked happier than he'd looked in a long while. Awais fingered the key in his pocket, the key to the locked room from which they'd just come and which contained Manu's dowry.

A gift had arrived without a name, but Awais knew immediately who it was from. A pamphlet of *sharbat* recipes and, wound around it, a Jairpuri necklace. He shouldn't have been surprised. She'd had as many spies as he now had. Anuradha Malik hadn't forgotten them. The last gift had arrived only the night before. They'd rolled out the carpet and looked in wonder at its intricate design of flowers and insects. The note attached to the carpet said that eighty-five different colours had been used in it. Rashid and Nawaz's new carpet business was doing well. They and Batool and Tanveer had hoped till the very last minute that they would make it to the wedding, but the visas had proved impossible to get. Looking closer, Awais spotted, in one corner, a minuscule tea cup. Rashid and Nawaz hadn't completely forgotten their porcelain business, then, he thought. He smiled.

Hamid and Awais welcomed the *barat* and waited with the others for the appearance of the bride. As she came forward, her head weighed down by her heavily brocaded *dupatta*, Hamid and Awais went to greet her. They were all smiles.

One year later, she came home to tell them the news.

'He says he's taking another wife.'

Hamid got to his feet. 'I'll…'

'And I'm…' She looked down. Hamid didn't understand. Awais whispered in his ear.

'A child?' Hamid said, and picked up her hand and kissed it. Not looking at her, he left the room, saying he had people to meet.

'What are we going to do?' Awais asked. She didn't know. 'When?' he asked next.

'A few months, I think.'

'As if you're just some village wife!' he exclaimed.

'I think his new wife is very modern and well-connected. At least, that's what the servants say.' She knew she'd hurt him and said, 'I have to go.'

He got up and asked her to wait. When he returned, he found her standing at the window, staring out. 'You should keep it now,' he said, handing her the book that Roshanay Begum had given Maryam. He gave her another package, wrapped in brown paper. 'And this.'

'What is it?' she asked.

'Look,' he said.

She pulled back the paper and stared at the cover: *The Inside City* by Harold James and Awais Dar. She opened it to the first page and the dedication: 'To Maryam and Manu.' She looked up at him, her eyes melting. She read the opening lines: 'A city of mortar and wood and glass and living flesh. The inside city, within what is now called Old Lahore, has twelve gates.' She smiled because he'd told her how he'd found the thirteenth.

'I didn't know you were writing this!'

'Remember when you and I began our trips again? That's when I started. I went back over the old notes. I hadn't read them since… well… I began reading and something Harold had written really irritated me. He'd got something seriously wrong. So, I began… I had to wait, of course. But now that the English are gone…'

She looked at him indulgently and he felt old. She pulled out a loose paper from amongst the pages of his book and asked, 'What's this?'

'Look at it later,' he said. She nodded and hugged both books to her and, after a while, she left for home.

After the wedding ceremony, the other women clustered noisily around Azeem's new bride, Shereen, and led her to her bedroom in the new wing. Manu had wanted to follow them, to see the new room festooned with flowers; to see, hear everything, but she knew she couldn't.

Back in her own quarters, she noticed how nothing had changed; the very orderliness of the room made her start. She looked down at her child asleep in his cot. Then she went to the bookshelf and pulled out two volumes. One was the book of her mother's that had once belonged to Roshanay Begum, and which her mother had filled. The other was her uncle Awais's book. She sat down on the floor, her back to the cold wall.

She opened her mother's book and, as she'd frequently done before, flicked through its pages of text, diagrams and numbers. She found again the picture of the strangely drawn dragon sitting upon a tree, the roots of which were sucking at the earth, the whole surrounded by seven stars. The image had fascinated her as a child and fascinated her still, though she didn't understand its meaning. When she was done she closed the book and rested a heavy hand on it. She closed her eyes.

She smiled and, still with her eyes closed, opened the book again at random. She stared down at the page. All the pages had ample margins. However, where the margin on the right-hand side of this page had been left blank, the margin on the left had been filled with notes. Awais had told her this was her mother's handwriting and she had often stared long and hard at the swirl and curve of letters, interspersed with figures; not trying to understand what meaning lay hidden within the notes, but rather what kind of person her mother had been. She now began to read:

From the Book of Seven Chapters: 'I have opened unto you what was hid. The work is with you and amongst you; in that it is to be found within you and is enduring: you will always have it present, wherever you are, on land or on sea.'

She closed the book and turned next to her uncle's book. She pulled out the loose page and saw it was a bookmark for something he'd underlined. Here, she read:

The inside city was built as a fortress: to protect those who sought to be protected. A fortress, though, is foremost – before it is bricks and mortar – a concept in the mind's eye.

For close to an hour she continued to sit, looking at nothing, seeing nothing. She wanted to laugh. It was as simple as that. She now understood what she had to do. She got up, hid both books under her bed and then fell into an easy sleep.

The next morning, she washed, fed the baby and then fetched a pot from the kitchen. Back in her room, she opened the buttons of her *kameez* and cupping one full breast, she bent and squeezed her milk into the pot. She stared down at the milk for a moment and then carefully buttoned up her *kameez* again. She draped a *dupatta* over her shoulders and carried the pot into the kitchen.

The cook looked at her in surprise.

'It's all right, Praveen,' Manu said. 'I'll make *sahib*'s breakfast. You go and look after the baby.' Praveen looked at Manu questioningly but nevertheless did as she was bidden.

Manu put the water on to boil and waited. She then emptied the pot of milk into another saucepan and warmed it. Praveen had already laid out the breakfast things on a tray. Manu added the tea pot and the milk and carried the tray slowly to her husband's new wing.

She found Azeem and Shereen seated on two separate chairs. From the surly look on Shereen's face, Manu realised they'd had an argument. *Already?*

Azeem almost jumped at her entrance. 'What are you doing here?' he asked.

'Praveen came to see the baby,' Manu replied, 'and so I told her I'd make the tea.'

'There are other servants,' he said, and Shereen looked at him with open loathing.

Manu poured the tea, added the milk and handed one cup to Shereen and the other to Azeem. Manu watched them take two then three sips of tea.

'What are you smiling at?' he asked.

'You've drunk of my milk, and so are now brother and sister!' she said.

Shereen spat out the tea and wiped her mouth with her sleeve. She looked wildly at Azeem. He moved towards her.

'Don't touch me!' she cried.

'Don't be ridiculous!' shouted Azeem.

'It's true,' said Shereen. 'I know it is!'

Good, thought Manu, and left.

The phone hadn't stopped ringing. It had rung while she was here but since she'd left, it hadn't stopped. He's got a heavy hand, I'll say that for him, Awais thought. He reckons someone will break and pick it up but there's no one here save me. I could pull out the wire but I like the idea of him knowing it's ringing and wondering why no one's picking it up. Tricks like that can ruin the best of minds. And Azeem's mind is, well…

They'd left after wishing him happy birthday and handing him the presents he didn't want. There they lay on the table, still wrapped.

'Ring, you bastard. Till your finger drops off.'

Forty-five years old. Such a definite age.

Again, his gaze turned to the window. Stuck? Was he stuck?

I could rip that thread on which he hangs or blow him down, so small he is. Why do spiders make me think of caves – and caves of revelation? What did I tell her? Where did I begin? With Maryam's birth? With mine? I guess it doesn't matter now.

The ringing finally stopped. That meant he was on his way. He'd be here in fifteen minutes. Maybe less. *What will I say? Whatever it is, I won't face him as if I'm holed up in this room too frightened to leave. I'm here to watch the spider.*

He reached up to open the door and the pain seared through his arm like an electric shock. His knees buckled. *How can I keep on forgetting how much it hurts? I'm getting old.* And then he heard it; faint at first, then louder. He had to get to the window, but he couldn't move. Each time it took longer. And then, then, the pain crumbled. Slowly, it disappeared.

With his left arm, he unlatched the window bolt and inhaled the cold winter breeze: there must be snow in the mountains, he thought. He knew what the sound was before he looked. Dressed all in white, the *dhol* player played a steady beat, yellow tassels hanging from his drum.

When the *dhol* beats fast, it signals ecstasy. Or madness. A *dhol* is a herald. But this one – of what?

The last of the rains had fallen over a month ago. And while the wind had rustled through the streets since then, with whispered premonitions of change, the sky had remained dry – till early this morning. And now the air was fresher than before. He saw people breathing in its freshness, as if to keep hold of it for a dry season. The streets had broken up under the load of this one day of rain and he knew he'd hear people lament, as they always did: though we have God, the West has efficient drainage.

All around he looked and the mud seeped everywhere. And children emerged from their homes, brought out by the smell of the rain and the desire to touch it as you might touch skin that's smooth and yours to hold. As the *dhol* beat on, more and more children ran into the streets, where they stood as if waiting to be herded into nationhood.

And then the first mud-ball flew. And everyone took a side. There were no screams, though, because that, the children knew, would call the wrath of their mothers down upon them – and an end to this, the shortest and best of days.

The *dhol* player continued to play. And though this wasn't music, Awais was enraptured still. It was just sound. He said the words out loud so that they too could live a brief moment. Just sound. But the sound was a memory, not a memory that belonged to him but a memory of something that had been passed on to him for safe-keeping.

The *dhol* player turned a corner and disappeared.

Awais left the window open; not too far. His shoulder and arm might stiffen in the cold. He remembered and looked down.

The spider had gone. He'd watched for an hour, and nothing. He'd turned away for ten minutes and there it was: his web. One tribe, one web? Like birds or... It looked like all the others he'd seen. But maybe there was ingenuity in what the spider had made and he couldn't tell.

Awais heard a car swerve into the road. A moment later, Azeem raced into the house, shouting, *'Mamun! Mamun!'* He had the audacity to call him 'uncle' still. Awais inched back, his arm blazing. He heard Azeem stride up the stairs then stop. He'd never been up to this part of the house before, so didn't know where to go. Awais pulled himself forward. The chair was just a few steps away now. He smiled, then his wounded arm hit the chair's side. Arrows of pain seared across his face. The door pushed open an inch. He heard Azeem hesitate.

Awais had learnt to interpret the different forms silence could take; on a scale of one to a hundred, he was ninety per cent certain what this particular pause meant. Azeem's silence meant he was unsure and was weighing up the options he could take. Finally, he knocked on the door and when Awais didn't answer he called again, *'Mamun?'* then stepped inside.

Awais was back in his chair. He held his body straight. The pain began to loosen its hold. Though this had been one of the hardest days of his life, he was now glad Noor had forced him to dress in his birthday clothes: the trousers and shirt crackled with newness.

The images flew before him as he saw what Manu had told him. And what she'd left unsaid. He thought it had died – this facility to hate; that he'd cut it out from his spleen like a disease that had spread, been caught and overcome. I'll breathe slowly, he said, like I was taught, once, long ago.

Why didn't she...? He'd taught her resilience. Hadn't he? She'd said it now. It was done.

He still hadn't spoken and he hadn't stood up. He watched Azeem blink rapidly; even he'd understand that something was wrong. What he couldn't know was what and why.

'Mamun,' he said again.

Awais looked up then. Azeem was neither tall nor short. He had thick-set shoulders and a belly he tried to keep in shape by short periods of abstinence. Awais had seen his naked ankles once, or was it twice? His legs were thin and bare, with a burn mark on the left. Perched on top of his square shoulders, with hardly a neck in view, was his small head. Behind his glasses, large childlike eyes, as if he were constantly surprised. It was not the surprise of curiosity, though. The world held no wonder for him. This, Awais had always known, even if he'd held the thought in check.

Now, Azeem was looking at Awais helplessly. Even with one good arm, thought Awais, I could wring his neck. One click and… I could kill him and feel nothing.

'Manu,' Azeem began again, licking his lips as if they were lined with sugar, 'she didn't say anything?'

'About?' asked Awais.

A bird fluttered against the window shutter as if wanting to break in and know what indoor living was like. Azeem shivered, startled, then stiffened. He looked at Awais as if to ascertain whether his moment of weakness had been spotted or not. His eyes dropped. Despite the pain in his arm, which had again flared up, Awais smiled.

'About going somewhere?' Azeem said.

'No,' said Awais, 'at least, I don't think—'

But before Awais could finish his sentence, Azeem jumped in. 'Did she stay a while?'

'The same as always.'

Azeem took this in, then said, 'But she usually comes to see you on Saturdays. And today's Wednesday.'

Awais hadn't thought of this. His eyelids felt heavy and tired. Then he heard the sound of quiet laughter, like that of a child trying to be good. He turned to look. On the table, his presents. 'Today's my birthday,' Awais said. He should close the window; it was getting cold.

'Oh,' said Azeem. 'Happy birthday.' He stared at the presents as if they offered another clue he couldn't solve. Awais saw a question shade his face. And from somewhere deep inside came Awais's old man's voice; his new find, which had already saved him so much strife.

'Why so many questions, Azeem?'

Again, Awais saw, Azeem's politician's mind was weighing things. Awais had never thought him clever but now, as if struck by a revelation, he saw where Azeem's cleverness lay. *That's it! My God, that's it! He doesn't weigh ideas or words. He weighs people.*

Awais saw Azeem hesitate. He's wondering, thought Awais, whether he should speak or wait. I'd advocate waiting but then – he smiled – that's something in my line. Azeem had no one to ask. And so, for once, perhaps the first time in his adult life, he had to decide for himself. Looking tired, he said, 'She's gone.'

But Awais wasn't tired. And he'd had time to think. He said, 'Who?'

'Manu,' said Azeem. 'She's left.' His fingers reached inside his pocket. *A lucky stone or some blessed words of God?* He was still standing. Awais hadn't asked him to sit.

'What do you mean "gone"?' Awais asked.

'Our son…?'

'Yes,' Awais said, 'she had Nasir with her.' He lowered his head so Azeem couldn't see his eyes.

'She's all right?' he asked.

'Yes, yes, she's fine. At least… She hasn't come back yet.'

Azeem looked at an empty chair and then at Awais's feet. Awais was wearing shoes, not slippers. Azeem asked, surprised, 'You were going out?'

'No,' said Awais. He hadn't wanted to meet Azeem half-dressed. I can smell my lies, he thought. Can he?

'Manu,' Azeem said, 'she—'

'But she left here,' Awais began and saw the widening of Azeem's eyes. Information was gold. 'She left a long time ago,' he added.

'How long ago, *mamun*? Do you remember?'

Awais saw Azeem watching him. He relaxed his shoulders and smoothed back his hair. 'How long? An hour. Maybe two. I fell asleep.'

Azeem nodded his understanding.

'But, she said…' Awais began.

'Yes?'

'No. Nothing.'

'*Mamun*, please, think.'

Although Azeem's was not a face he knew well, it was one that was easy to read. It was just beginning to dawn on Azeem what Manu's leaving might mean. Azeem was seeing what so few men are given to see: the consequences of their actions. And in that minute, that one brief minute, Awais pitied him.

'Did she say where she was going?' Azeem asked. 'To a friend's, perhaps?'

'No,' Awais says. 'No. Kar—'

Azeem pounced on the word. 'Karachi! She's gone to Karachi? To your uncle's?'

'No,' Awais said quickly. 'She didn't say.'

And suddenly Azeem's face closed in upon itself. And Awais could see nothing more in it. Was the revelation, then, part of his art, a way to lure him in? He looked again but again drew a blank. He's playing with me, Awais thought. A game of some sort – but what?

'I have to go,' Azeem said.

'You're sure?' Awais said, the words of courtesy sticking in his throat.

'Yes.' Azeem came forward, smelling of the cloying perfume he wore. He straightened and smiled. Awais had always hated his smile; it was a shambles, like an old man trying to get into a suit.

Azeem went to leave. When he was at the door, Awais called across, 'Leave it open. I like the breeze.' Azeem turned around sharply. What did he hear in my voice? thought Awais.

'She's safe, you think?' Azeem asked.

'Yes…' Awais replied. He couldn't look at him now. He leaned back and Azeem closed the door firmly behind him.

Bastard.

Can that gada – ass – *feel nothing? No desire for truth? No desire to hide his face?*

But he was gone now. I've done it, he said to himself. It's as if I've taken a hammer to his head and split it open. And everywhere there's blood. It's thin but it runs, how it runs. If he starts out for Karachi, he'll… And if he doesn't find her now, he'll never find her. Where did I learn that from? It felt so easy but… Oh God. My arm. When will it stop?

Slowly, he eased his head and shoulders back. He dozed off. She was in a box. He could hear her scream. Azeem held the key and was smiling that smile again.

He woke with a start and knew he wouldn't sleep any more that night.

The light from outside was too bright. That street lamp never usually worked. But tonight. *God. Why won't someone turn it off?*

·Did I say something he'd understand? he wondered. That would lead him to her? No. At least… No.

It was three in the morning. All at once, getting up was easy. His throat was parched dry. And the skin on his face felt as if it might flake off to reveal something deeper, newer, but what? He remembered his shoulder for once, and was careful not to twist and turn. He couldn't take any more pain.

Downstairs he switched on all the lights. The rooms seemed hollow in their glare. With a glass of water in his hand, he was just about to go back upstairs to try to sleep when he saw a strip of white paper pushed under the front door. As he got closer he realised it was an envelope. He ripped it open and read: 'I'm fine, we're fine.' He read on. Of course he recognised the hand; he'd been the one who'd taught her to write. He opened the door and looked out into the street. In a corner, he saw Manu's most trusted servant. He called her over, and slowly, she approached. The woman entered and told him all she knew.

His thirst had gone. Back in bed, he tucked the letter under his pillow and lifted the sheet till all that was visible was the top of his head. He smiled as he recalled what Manu had written, and what her servant had told him.

After the incident with the milk, Azeem had tried to calm Shereen down but had done the wrong thing: he'd laughed at her superstition. For modern as Shereen was, she'd been brought up on beliefs such as this, and refused to be calmed or touched by him. Furious, Azeem had gone in search of Manu. But she wasn't in her room and neither was the baby.

He went to the store room where she kept her bundles of receipts, but she wasn't there either. He'd mocked her way of filing – or, as he called it, hoarding – paperwork. Now he ripped the cord off one of the bundles and kicked it, scattering it across the room. A breeze through the small vent window that Manu insisted always be left ajar sent the receipts flying. Azeem bent to gather them up. He frowned. Face down, the receipts should have been blank, but they weren't; upon some were colour pictures of elephants and monkeys, and upon others, pictures of a high wire. The floor was covered in posters that had been cut into tiny receipt-sized slips. They dated back years.

'Let her tidy that up when she comes back!' Azeem shouted as he stormed out, nearly colliding with Praveen, the cook.

After leaving Shereen and Azeem, Manu had returned to her room, picked up the baby and her two books. Outside, waiting for her under the shade of the ashoka tree – as she knew he would be – was Bona, the dwarf clown. In one hand he held her mother's astrolabe.

Awais woke late. His first clear thought: she's escaped. Soon, his family would be back. He got up. On the bedside, his book. Patterns; he'd been obsessed by patterns all his life. Shams Sahib had been right. In that, he was like the English. But he only saw it when he finished the book. One thousand and one stories, recording the singularity of each and every life.

Glossary

abba – father, dad(dy)

abu – father, dad(dy)

aiy – 'oh'

akhara – wrestling ground

allama – honorary title carried by scholars of Islamic jurisprudence and philosophy

ama – mother, mum(my)

ammi – mother, mum(my)

apa – elder sister

aray/ay baba – interjection used to express mild surprise or annoyance

Asr – afternoon prayer, the third of the five daily prayers

azaan – call to prayer

barfi – dense, milk-based sweet

Basant festival – springtime kite-flying festival

beta – son

betel – the *areca nutis* commonly referred to as betel nut. Usually for chewing, a few slices of the areca nut are wrapped in a betel leaf

bhai – brother

bhaia – elder brother

chador – large piece of cloth, wrapped around the head and upper body leaving only the face exposed

channay – chickpeas

chappals – leather sandals

charpoy – bed consisting of a frame strung with tapes or light rope

chaudhry – ancient Sanskrit term for the head of a community or caste. The title gained prominence during the Mughal and British periods

chowkidar – gatekeeper

dadaji – paternal grandfather

dai – midwife

dandasa – dried bark of walnut trees, cut up into strips and used to whiten teeth

dhol – double-headed drum widely used, with regional variations, throughout the Indian subcontinent

doog-doogi – simple drum-like instrument similar to a miniature *dhol*

dupatta – shawl-like scarf

faluda – dessert made with milk, vermicelli, rose syrup and sweet basil seeds *firni* – dessert made with milk, powdered rice, almonds, saffron and cardamom

gada – donkey/ass

gharara – a pair of wide-legged pants ruched so that they flare out at the knee, worn with a *kurti* (a tunic) and *dupatta*

ghazal – lyric poem in Islamic literature, composed of a minimum of five couplets – and typically no more than fifteen – that are structurally, thematically, and emotionally autonomous

gurdwara – place of worship for Sikhs

haleem – stew of wheat or barley with lentils or meat

halwa – dense, sweet confection, made with semolina, or tahini or other nut butters

hammam – public bathing place where bathing involves a hot steam bath and massage

haramzadi – female child born of unmarried parents; an obnoxious or despicable female

jalebi – sweet made of deep-fried batter that is then soaked in syrup

kareez – below- and above-ground channel system used to bring water to a settlement or fields from a natural source

khala – aunt

khusas – handcrafted shoes made of one piece of leather or textile embroidered and embellished with brass nails, shells, mirrors, bells and ceramic beads

kulchay – small round bread, typically stuffed with meat or vegetables

kulfi – kind of ice cream

lassi – yogurt-based drink

lunghi – type of sarong worn around the waist

Maghrib – prayer at sunset, the fourth of the five daily prayers

mamun – uncle

mandir – Hindu temple

massi – aunt

maulvi – doctor or teacher of Islamic law

mela – fair or festival

munda – boy

nani – maternal grandmother

nimbu pani – lemon drink

paan – a combination of betel leaves and Areca nut widely consumed in Southeast Asia

panditji – Hindu scholar

paratha – type of flatbread

pir – Sufi master

piri – low stool

purdah – practice of screening women from men or strangers

roti – type of flatbread

sahib – master/mister/sir

salaam – respectful ceremonial greeting

sepoy – infantryman in the British East India Company, later in the British Indian Army

shalwar kameez – long shirt and loose trousers worn by men and women

sharbat – sweet drink prepared from fruits or flower petals

sisterji – sister, as a respectful term of address

taweez – talisman or charm

tilla – embroidery in silver or gold thread

tonga – light carriage drawn by one horse

ustad – expert or highly skilled person

wallah – person responsible for a particular kind of work

Zuhr – prayer at midday, the third of the five daily prayers

Acknowledgements

A huge thank you to everyone who has supported this book, either with pledges or blessings or both, and to the wonderful Unbound Facebook Social Group without whom I'd have sunk. Thank you to the Arts Council England for a small grant when I needed it the most.

A special thank you to my friend Alexandra Murrell, for reading the whole manuscript and her spot-on suggestions. And great thanks to my editor Mary Chesshyre for her oh-so-fine eye.

Books read and relished include: *Plain Tales from the Raj* by Charles Allen (Abacus); *Mapping an Empire* by Matthew H. Edney (University of Chicago Press); *The Sole Spokesman: Jinnah, the Muslim League and the Demand for Pakistan* by Ayesha Jalal (Cambridge University Press); *The Making of the Raj* by Lawrence James (Abacus); *Lahore: Its History, Architectural Remains and Antiquities* by Khan Bahadur Syad Muhammad Latif (Sang-e-Meel Publications); *Lahore: A Sentimental Journey* by Pran Neville (Penguin India). And throughout it all, *Manto ke Afsanay – Manto's Short Stories* (Dua Publications), playing in my head, reminding me how short I've fallen.

The biggest thanks, though, go to my rocks: my immediate family aside, Asad Ali, Naila Hussain Aayesha Ikram, Efthalia Kalegoropolou, Nicola Migliorino, Rabia Nudrat and Aasima Yawar.

To J. – for tearing the manuscript apart and helping me stitch it back together again – what can I say?

Patrons

Aayla Aftab
Zufie Ahmad
Sarah Alford-Smith
Karen Attwood
James Aylett
Suchada Bhirombhakdi
Dorothy Blane
Anna Blurtsyan
Andrew Budden
Dorris Burgess
A Butt
Maryam Chaudhry
Saleh Chaudhry
Suleman Chaudhry
Nadir Cheema
Lauren Cooney
Duard Dard
Sue Dunderdale
Adil Farooq
Jamie Gambell
Humdah Hassan
Maximilian Hawker
Amir Ifthikhar
Saqlain Imam
Mian Hassan Javaid

Elena Kaufman
Mark Kelly
Abda Khan
Ghiasuddin Khan
Rae Knowler
Laura Louise Creighton
Ayesha Malik
Eva Martín
Pravin Mayor
Marlene McCormick
Ejaz Mehmood
Nicola Migliorino
Judy Munday
Bilal Nabiel
Stu Nathan
Carlo Navato
Tim Niblock
Margaret Page
Stef Pixner
Fauzia Qureshi
Abdul Rehman
Mark Renshaw
Lewis Rice
Barbara Riley
Tauseef Saeed
Nafisa Shah
Zainab Shahid
Tamim Shaikhali
Abbi Shaw
Susan Snoxall
Scott Steinkerchner
Rebecca Storer
Nawaira Tariq
Sarah Vernon
Traci Whitehead

Derek Wilson
Miho Zlazli